ON, OFF

Colleen McCullough

McArthur & Company
Toronto

First published in Canada in 2006 by
McArthur & Company
322 King St. West, Suite 402
Toronto, Ontario
M5V 1J2
www.mcarthur-co.com

Library and Archives Canada Cataloguing in Publication

McCullough, Colleen, 1937-
On, off : a novel / Colleen McCullough.

ISBN 1-55278-571-8

I. Title.

PR9619.3.M32O5 2006   823'.914   C2006-902230-5

Cover design by Honi Werner
Printed in Canada by Webcom

10 9 8 7 6 5 4 3 2 1

For Helen Sanders Brittain
with fond memories of the old days,
and much love.

ON, OFF

PART ONE

October & November
1965

CHAPTER 1

Wednesday, October 6th, 1965

Jimmy woke up gradually, conscious at first of only one thing: the perishing cold. His teeth were chattering, his flesh ached, his fingers and toes were numb. And why couldn't he see? *Why couldn't he see?* All around him was pitch darkness, a blackness so dense he had never known anything like it. As he grew wider awake he realized too that he was imprisoned in something close, smelly, alien. *Wrapped up!* Panic set in and he began to scream, to claw frantically at whatever was confining him. It ripped and tore, but when the stygian coldness persisted after he managed to free himself, his terror drove him mad. There were other things all around him, the same smelly kind of restraints, but no matter how he shrieked, ripped, tore, he couldn't find a way out, couldn't see a particle of light or feel a puff of warmth. So he shrieked, ripped, tore, his heart roaring in his ears and the only noises his own.

Otis Green and Cecil Potter came into work together, having hooked up on Eleventh Street with a broad grin for each other. Dead on 7 A.M., but wasn't it great not to have to punch a time clock? Their place of work was civilized, man, no arguments there. They put their lunch pails in the small stainless steel cupboard they had reserved for their own use—no need for locks, there were no thieves here. Then they started the business of their day.

Cecil could hear his babies calling for him; he went straight to their door and opened it, speaking to them in a tender voice.

"Hi, guys! How ya doin' huh? Everybody sleep well?"

The door was still hissing shut behind Cecil when Otis saw to the least palatable job of his day, emptying the refrigerator. His wheeled plastic bin smelled clean and fresh; he put a new liner in it and pushed it over to the refrigerator door, a heavy steel one with a snap-lock handle. What happened next was a blur: something streaking past him as he opened the door, screaming like a banshee.

"Cecil, get out here!" he yelled. "Jimmy's still alive, we gotta catch him!"

The big monkey was in a state of gibbering frenzy, but after Cecil talked to him a little while and then held out his arms, Jimmy bolted into them, shivering, his shrieks dying to whimpers.

"Jesus, Otis," Cecil said, cradling the beast like a father his child, "how did Dr. Chandra miss that? The poor little guy's been locked in the fridge all night. There there, Jimmy, there there! Daddy's here, little man, you're okay now!"

Both men were shocked and Otis's heart had a jelly roll beat to it, but no real harm was done. Dr. Chandra would be pleased as punch that Jimmy hadn't died after all, thought Otis, returning to the refrigerator. Jimmy was worth a hundred big ones.

Even a cleanliness fanatic like Otis couldn't banish the smell of death from the refrigerator, scrub it with disinfectant and deodorant though he did. The stench, not of decay but of something subtler, surrounded Otis as he flipped the light switch to reveal the chamber's stainless steel interior. Oh, man, Jimmy had made a regular mess of it! Torn paper bags were strewn everywhere, headless rat carcasses, stiff white hair, obscenely naked tails. And, behind the dozen rat bags, a couple of much bigger bags, torn up too. Sighing, Otis went to fetch more bags from a cupboard and began to make order out of Jimmy's chaos. The dead rats properly bagged again, he reached into the chilly chamber and pulled the first of the two big bags forward. It had been rent from top to bottom, most of its contents on full display.

Otis opened his mouth and screamed as shrilly as Jimmy, was still screaming when Cecil erupted out of the monkey room. Then, not seeming to notice Cecil, he turned and ran out of animal care, down the halls, into the foyer, out the entrance, legs opening and closing in a punishing run down Eleventh Street to his home on the second floor of a shabby three-family house.

Celeste Green was having coffee with her nephew when Otis burst into the kitchen; they leaped to their feet, Wesley's passionate diatribe about Whitey's crimes forgotten. Celeste went for the smelling salts while Wesley put Otis on a chair. Back with the bottle, she pushed Wesley roughly out of her way.

"You know your trouble, Wes? You always in the way! You didn't get in Otis's way all the time, he wouldn't call you a good for nothin' kid! Otis! Otis, honey, wake up!"

Otis's skin had faded from a warm deep brown to a pasty grey that didn't improve when the ammoniac vapors were jammed under his nose, but he came around, jerked his head away.

"What is it? What's the matter?" Wesley was asking.

"A piece of woman," Otis whispered.

"A what?" sharply from Celeste.

"A piece of woman. In the fridge at work with the dead rats. A pussy and a belly." He began to shake.

Wesley asked the only question that mattered to him. "Was she a white woman or a black woman?"

"Don't bother him with that, Wes!" Celeste cried.

"Not black," Otis said, hands going to his chest. "But not white neither. Colored," he added, slipped forward off the chair and fell to the floor.

"Call an ambulance! Go on, Wes, *call an ambulance!*"

Which came very quickly, due to two fortunate facts: one, that the Holloman Hospital was just around the corner, and the other, that business was slack this hour of morning. Still very much alive, Otis Green was put into the ambulance with his wife crouched beside him; the apartment was left to Wesley le Clerc.

He didn't linger there, not with news like this. Mohammed el Nesr lived at 18 Fifteenth Street, and he had to be told. A piece of woman! Not black, but not white either. Colored. That meant black to Wesley, as it did to all the members of Mohammed's Black Brigade. Time that Whitey was called to account for two hundred years and more of oppression, of treating black people as second-rate citizens, even as beasts without immortal souls.

When he'd gotten out of prison in Louisiana he'd decided to come north to Tante Celeste in Connecticut. He yearned to make a reputation as a black man who mattered, and that was easier to do in a part of the nation less prone than Louisiana to throw blacks in jail if they looked sideways. Connecticut was where Mohammed el Nesr and his Black Brigade hung out. Mohammed was educated, had a doctorate in law—he *knew* his rights! But for reasons that Wesley saw every day when he looked in a mirror, Mohammed el Nesr had dismissed Wesley as worthless. A plantation black, a nobody nothing. Which hadn't dampened Wesley's ardor; he intended to prove himself in Holloman, Connecticut! So much so that one day Mohammed would look up to *him,* Wesley le Clerc, plantation black.

Cecil Potter had soon discovered what sent Otis screeching out of animal care, but he wasn't a panicky man. He did not touch the contents of the refrigerator. Nor did he call the cops. He picked up the phone and dialed the Prof's extension, knowing full well that the Prof would be in his office, even at this hour. His only peace happened early in the mornings, he always said. But not, thought Cecil, this morning.

✦

"It's a sad case," said Lieutenant Carmine Delmonico to his uni-formed colleague and nominal superior, Captain Danny Marciano. "With no other relatives we can find, the kids will have to go into the system."

"You're sure he did it?"

"Positive. The poor guy tried to make it look like some stranger busted in, but there's his wife and her lover in the bed and her lover's cut up some but she's mincemeat—he did it. My bet is that he'll confess later today voluntarily."

Marciano rose to his feet. "Then let's get some breakfast."

His phone rang; Marciano wriggled his brows at Carmine and picked up. Within three seconds the police captain had stiffened, lost all contentment. He mouthed "Silvestri!" at Carmine and com-menced a series of nods. "Sure, John. I'll start Carmine now and get Patsy there as soon as I can."

"Trouble?"

"Big trouble. Silvestri's just had a call from the head of the Hug—Professor Robert Smith. They've found part of a female body in their dead animal refrigerator."

"Christ!"

Sergeants Corey Marshall and Abe Goldberg were breakfasting at Malvolio's, the diner the cops used because it was next door to head-quarters in the County Services building on Cedar Street. Carmine didn't bother walking in; he rapped his knuckles on the glass in front of the booth where Abe and Corey were washing down hotcakes and maple syrup with big mugs of coffee. Lucky stiffs, he thought. They get to eat, I get to give my report to Danny, now I don't get to eat. Seniority's a pain in the ass.

The car Carmine regarded as his own (it was really a Holloman Police Department unmarked) was a Ford Fairlane with a souped-up V-8 engine and cop springs and shocks. If the three of them were in it, Abe always drove, Corey rode shotgun, and Carmine spread him-self and his papers in the back. Telling Corey and Abe took half a minute, the trip from Cedar Street to the Hug less than five.

*   *   *

Holloman lay about halfway up the Connecticut coast, its spacious harbor looking across the Sound to Long Island. Founded by dissenting Puritans in 1632, it had always prospered, and not only because of the numerous factories that lay on its outskirts as well as up the Pequot River. A good proportion of its 150,000 people were connected in some way to Chubb University, an Ivy League institution that admitted itself inferior to none, even Harvard and Princeton. Town and Gown were inextricably intertwined.

Chubb's main campus lay around three sides of the big Green, its early colonial Georgian and nineteenth-century gothic buildings joined by some startlingly modern edifices tolerated only because of the august architectural names associated with each; but there was also Science Hill to the east, where the science campus was located in square towers of dark brick and plate glass, and, way across town to the west, the Chubb Medical School.

Because medical schools grew up alongside hospitals, by 1965 they tended to be situated in the worst part of any city; in this respect Holloman was no different. The Chubb Medical School and the Holloman Hospital straggled down Oak Street on the southern border of the larger of Holloman's two black ghettoes, called the Hollow because it lay in a hollow that had once been a swamp. To compound the health care woes, in 1960 the oil reservoirs of East Holloman were relocated at the end of Oak Street on waste ground between I-95 and the harbor.

The Hughlings Jackson Center for Neurological Research sat on Oak Street right opposite the Shane-Driver medical student apartments, 100 for 100 students. Next to the Shane-Driver was the Parkinson Pavilion for medical research. It faced the Hug's neighbor, the Holloman Hospital, a twelve-storey pile that had been rebuilt in 1950, the same year that saw the Hug go up.

"Why do they call it the Hug?" Corey asked as the Ford swung into the temporary road that bisected a gigantic parking lot.

"First three letters of Hughlings, I guess," said Carmine.

"*Hug?* It's got no dignity. Why not the first four letters? Then it'd be the Hugh."

"Ask Professor Smith," said Carmine, eyeing their destination.

The Hug was a shorter, smaller twin of the Burke Biology Tower and the Susskind Science Tower cross-campus on Science Hill; a baldly square, squat pile of dark brick with plenty of big plate-glass windows. It sat in three acres of what had used to be slum dwellings, demolished to make way for this monument perpetuating the name of a mystery man who had had absolutely nothing to do with its genesis. Who on earth was this Hughlings Jackson? A question all of Holloman asked. By rights the Hug should have been named after its donor, the enormously wealthy, late Mr. William Parson.

Having no gate key to the parking lot, Abe put the Ford on Oak Street right outside the building. Which had no entrance onto Oak Street; the three men tramped down a gravel path along the north side to a single glass door, where a very tall woman was waiting for them.

It's like a child's building block in the middle of a huge room, Carmine thought; three acres is a lot of land for something only a hundred feet per side. And shit, she's holding a clipboard. Office, not medical. His mind automatically registered the physical details of every person who swam into his piece of the human sea, so it was busy as she drew closer: six-three in bare feet, early thirties, navy pant suit on the baggy side, flat lace-up shoes, mouse-brown hair, a face with a biggish nose and a prominent chin. She'd never have made Miss Holloman ten years ago, let alone Miss Connecticut. Once he halted in front of her, however, he noted that she had very fine, interesting eyes the color of thick ice, which he had always found beautiful.

"Sergeants Marshall and Goldberg. I'm Lieutenant Carmine Delmonico," he said curtly.

"Desdemona Dupre, the business manager," she said as she took them into a tiny foyer, apparently only there to accommodate two elevators. But instead of pressing the UP button, she opened a door in the opposite wall and led them into a wide corridor.

9

"This is our first floor, which contains the animal care facilities and the workshops," she said, her accent placing her as someone from the other side of the Atlantic. Turning a corner put them in another hall. She pointed to a pair of doors farther down. "There you are, animal care."

"Thanks," said Carmine. "We'll take it from here. Please wait for me back at the elevators."

Her brows rose, but she turned on her heel and disappeared without comment.

Carmine found himself inside a very large room lined with cupboards and bins. Tall racks of clean cages big enough to take a cat or dog stood in neat rows in an area fronting a service elevator many times the size of the two in the foyer. Other racks held plastic boxes topped with wire grids. The room smelled good, pungent like a pine forest, with only the faintest hint of something less pleasant below it.

Cecil Potter was a fine-looking man, tall, slender, very well kept in his pressed white boiler suit and canvas bootees. His eyes, Carmine fancied, smiled a lot, though they were not smiling now.

One of Carmine's most important policies in this year of busing turmoil was that the black people he met in the course of his job or social life be treated courteously; he held out his hand, shook Cecil's firmly, performed the introductions without barking them or looking rushed. Corey and Abe were his men through thick and thin, they followed suit with the same courtesy.

"It's here," said Cecil, moving to a closed stainless steel door with a snap-lock handle. "I didn't touch a thing, just shut the door." He hesitated, decided to risk it. "Uh, Lieutenant, do you mind if I get back to my babies?"

"Babies?"

"The monkeys. Macaques. Rhesus mean anything to you? Well, that's them. They in there, an' very upset. Jimmy won't lay off telling them where he been, an' they very upset."

"Jimmy?"

"The monkey Dr. Chandra thought was dead, an' put in a bag in

10

the fridge last night. Jimmy really found her—tore the place apart when he woke up in the dark freezing his buns off. When Otis—he my assistant as well as the handyman—went to empty the fridge, Jimmy came outta there screeching and yelling. Then Otis found *her*, an' he was outta here screeching worse than Jimmy. I looked, an' called the Prof. I guess the Prof called you."

"Where's Otis now?" Carmine asked.

"Knowing Otis, he run home to Celeste. She his mama as well as his wife."

They were gloved now; Abe wheeled the bin away from the door and Carmine opened it as Cecil, already crooning and clucking, went into the monkey room.

Of the two big bags, one still lay at the back of the chamber. The other, rent from where the top folded over clear to the bottom, had exposed the lower half of a female torso. When Carmine noted its size and its lack of pubic hair his heart sank—a prepubescent child? Oh, please, not that! He made no movement to touch a thing, just leaned his shoulders against the wall.

"We wait for Patrick," he said.

"I never smelled a smell like it—dead, but not decomposing," said Abe, dying for a cigarette.

"Abe, go find Mrs. Dupre and tell her she can go upstairs as soon as the uniforms arrive," Carmine said, knowing that expression well. "Post them on all the entrances and emergency exits." Then, alone with Corey, he rolled his eyes. "Why in there?" he asked.

Patrick O'Donnell enlightened him.

Sporting the very modern title of Medical Examiner in a city that had always had a coroner without forensic skills in earlier days, Patrick had espoused pathology because he didn't like patients who talked back, and the life of a public pathologist because it meant plenty of criminal cases as well as all the other kinds of sudden or mysterious death. Thanks to Patrick's ruthless campaign to bring Holloman into the latter half of the twentieth century, he had managed to shed most of a coroner's court duties on to a deputy coroner and build a little empire that encompassed far more than mere autopsies. He believed in the new science of forensics, and played an active part in any case that interested him, even if no body was involved.

He looked as Irish as his name from the reddish hair to the bright blue eyes, but in actual fact he and Carmine were first cousins, the sons of two sisters of Italian extraction. One married a Delmonico, the other an O'Donnell. Ten years older than Carmine and a happily married man with six children, Patrick let neither of these impediments spoil their deep friendship.

"I don't know much, but here's what I do know," said Carmine, and filled him in. "Why in there?" he repeated at the end of it.

"Because if Jimmy the monkey hadn't woken up undead and flown into a panic, these two brown bags, unmarked and intact, would have been dumped into some kind of receptacle and taken to the animal care incinerator," Patrick said, grimacing. "This is the perfect way to get rid of human remains. Poof! Up in smoke."

Abe came back in time to hear this, and went pale. "Jeez!" he breathed, horrified.

Photographs taken, Patrick lifted the first bag onto a gurney and tucked it inside an open body bag. Then he examined what he could see without disturbing the torn brown paper.

"No pubic hair," said Carmine. "Patsy, if you love me, tell me this isn't a child."

"The hair's been—not shaved—no, plucked—so she's postpubescent. Small girl, though. As if what our killer really yearned for was a child, but wasn't game to follow through on all his disgusting desires." He lifted out the second bag, not as mangled, and placed it beside the first. "I'll get back to the morgue—you'll want my report a.s.a.p." His chief technician, Paul, was already preparing to vacuum the chamber's interior; after that he would dust for fingerprints. "Lend me Abe and Corey as well, Carmine, and we can let Cecil get on with his work. Except for the monkeys, they must keep their experimental animals elsewhere—these are the day's clean cages ready to go."

"Leave no stone unturned, guys," said Carmine, following his cousin and the gurney's grisly contents out.

Desdemona Dupre—what a strange name!—was in the foyer waiting, flicking through the contents of a thick sheaf of papers on her clipboard.

"Mrs. Dupre, this is Dr. Patrick O'Donnell," said Carmine.

Whereupon the woman bristled! "I am not a missus, I am a miss!" she said with a snap, that odd accent pronounced. "Are you coming upstairs with me, Lieutenant, or may I go? I have work to do."

"Catch you later, Patsy," said Carmine, following *Miss* Dupre into an elevator.

"You're from, uh, England?" he asked as they ascended.

"Correct."

"How long have you been at the Hug?"

"Five years."

They left the elevator on the fourth floor, which was the top floor, though the last button said ROOF. Here the Hug's interior decor was better displayed. It was little different from the first floor: walls painted institution cream, dark oak woodwork, banks of fluorescent ceiling lights under plastic diffusers. Back down a twin of that first-floor corridor to a door opposite its far end, where it met another hall at right angles.

Miss Dupre knocked, was bidden enter, and pushed Carmine into Professor Smith's private domain without entering herself.

He found himself staring at one of the most strikingly handsome men he had ever seen. Robert Mordent Smith, William Parson Chair Professor at the Hughlings Jackson Center for Neurological Research, was over six feet tall, on the thin side, and possessed an unforgettable face: wonderful bone structure, black brows and lashes, vivid blue eyes, and a mop of wavy, streaky white hair. On someone still young enough not to have lines or wrinkles, the hair set him off to perfection. His smile revealed even white teeth,

13

though the smile wasn't reaching those marvelous eyes this morning. No surprise.

"Coffee?" he asked, gesturing Carmine to the big, costly chair on the opposite side of his big, costly desk.

"Thanks, yes. No cream, no sugar."

While the Prof ordered two of the same via his intercom, his guest inspected the room, a generous 20 x 25 feet, with those huge glass windows on two walls. The Prof's office occupied the northeast corner of the floor, so the view was of the Hollow, the Shane-Driver dormitory, and the parking lot. The decor was expensive, the furniture walnut, the fabric chintz, the rug Aubusson. An imposing assemblage of degrees, diplomas and honors sat on a green-striped wall, and what looked to be an excellent copy of a Watteau landscape hung behind the Prof's desk.

"It's not a copy," said the Prof, following Carmine's gaze. "I have it on loan from the William Parson Collection, the largest and best collection of European art in America."

"Wow," said Carmine, thinking of the cheap print of van Gogh's irises behind his own desk.

A woman in her middle thirties entered bearing a silver tray on which stood a vacuum flask, two delicate cups and saucers, two crystal glasses and a crystal carafe of iced water. They sure do themselves proud at the Hug!

A severely tailored looker, thought Carmine, examining her: black hair piled up in a beehive, a broad, smooth, rather flat face with hazel eyes, and a terrific figure. Her suit was coat and skirt, snugly cut, and her shoes were Ferragamo flatties. That Carmine knew such things could be laid at the door of a long career in a profession that required intimate knowledge of all aspects of human beings and their behavior. This woman was what Mom called a man-eater, though she didn't seem to have an atom of appetite for the Prof.

"Miss Tamara Vilich, my secretary," said the Prof.

No atom of appetite for Carmine Delmonico either! She smiled, nodded and departed without lingering.

"Two mature misses on your staff," said Carmine.

"They are just wonderful if you can find them," said the Prof, who seemed anxious to postpone the reason for this interview. "A married woman has family responsibilities that sometimes tend to eat into her working day. Whereas single women give their all to the job—don't mind working late without notice, for example."

"More juice to pump into it, I can see that," said Carmine. He sipped his coffee, which was terrible. Not that he had expected it to be good. The Prof, he observed, drank water from the lovely carafe, though he poured Carmine's coffee himself.

"Professor, have you been down to the animal care room to see what's been found?"

The Prof blanched, shook his head emphatically. "No, no, of course not! Cecil called me to tell me what Otis found, and I called Commissioner Silvestri at once. I did remember to tell Cecil not to let anyone into animal care until the police came."

"And have you found Otis—Otis who?"

"Green. Otis Green. It seems he has sustained a mild heart attack. At the moment he's in the hospital. However, his cardiologist says it's not a severe ictus, so he should be discharged in two or three days."

Carmine put down his coffee cup and leaned back in his chintz chair, hands folded in his lap. "Tell me about the dead animal refrigerator, Professor."

Smith looked a little confused, clearly had to summon up inner reserves of courage; maybe, thought Carmine, his brand of courage doesn't run to coping with a murder crisis, just grant committees and awkward researchers. How many Chubb receptions have I stood through listening to those?

"Well, every research institute has one. Or, if it isn't a big unit, shares one with other laboratories nearby. We are researchers, and, given that ethically we cannot use human beings as experimental animals, we use animals lower on the evolutionary scale than ourselves. The kind of animal depends on the kind of research—guinea

pigs for skin, rabbits for lungs, and so on. As we are interested in
epilepsy and mental retardation and they are situated in the brain,
our research animals go rat, cat and primate—here at the Hug,
macaques. At the end of an experimental project, the creatures are
sacrificed—with extreme care and kindness, I hasten to add. The
carcasses are put into special bags and taken to the refrigerator, where
they remain until about seven each weekday morning. At that hour
Otis empties the contents of the refrigerator into a bin and wheels
the bin through the tunnel to the Parkinson Pavilion, where the
medical school's main animal care facility is located. The incinerator
that disposes of all animal carcasses is a part of P.P.'s animal care, but
it also is available to the hospital, which sends amputated limbs and
the like to it."

His speech patterns are so formal, thought Carmine, that he talks
as if he's dictating an important letter. "Did Cecil tell you how the
human remains were discovered?" he asked.

"Yes." The Prof's face was beginning to look pinched.

"Who has access to the refrigerator?"

"Anyone here in the Hug, though I doubt anyone from outside
could use it. Our entrances are few, and barred."

"Why's that?"

"My dear Lieutenant, we are on the very end of the Oak Street
medical school–hospital line! Beyond us is Eleventh Street and the
Hollow. An unsavory neighborhood, as I'm sure you know."

"I notice that you call it the Hug too, Professor. Why?"

The slightly tragic mouth twisted. "I blame Frank Watson," he
said through his teeth.

"Who's he?"

"Professor of Neurology in the medical school. When the Hug
was opened in 1950 he wanted to head it, but our benefactor, the late
William Parson, was adamant that his Chair should go to a man
experienced in epilepsy and mental retardation. As Watson's field is
demyelinating diseases, naturally he wasn't suitable. I told Mr. Parson that he ought to have chosen an easier name than Hughlings

Jackson, but he was determined. Oh, a very determined man, always! Of course one expects to see the name abbreviated, but I had thought it would be the Hughlings, or the Hugh. However, Frank Watson had a small revenge. He thought it terribly clever to call it the Hug, and the name stuck. *Stuck!*"

"Exactly who was or is Hughlings Jackson, sir?"

"A pioneer British neurologist, Lieutenant. His wife had a slow-growing tumor on the motor strip—the gyrus anterior to the fissure of Rolando that represents the cortical end of the body's voluntary motor function—muscles, that is."

I do not understand a single word of this, Carmine thought as the level voice continued, but does he care? No.

"Mrs. Jackson's epileptic seizures were of a very curious kind," the Prof went on. "They were limited to one side of her body, started on one side of her face, marched down to the arm and hand on that same side, and finally involved the leg. They are still known as Jacksonian marches. From them Jackson put together the first hypotheses about motor function, that each part of the body had its own invariable place in the cerebral cortex. However, what fascinated people was the indefatigable way that he sat beside his dying wife's bed hour after hour, taking notes on her seizures with the most minute attention to detail. The researcher par excellence."

"Pretty heartless, if you ask me," said Carmine.

"I prefer to call it dedication," Smith said icily.

Carmine rose. "No one can leave this building unless *I* give them permission. That means you too, sir. There are police on the entrances, including the tunnel. I suggest you say nothing about what's happened to anyone."

"But we have no cafeteria!" said the Prof blankly. "What can the staff do about lunch if they don't bring it from home?"

"One of the policemen can take orders and bring food back." He paused in the doorway to look back. "I'm afraid we'll have to take fingerprints from everyone here. An inconvenience worse than lunch, but I'm sure you understand."

*   *   *

The Holloman County Medical Examiner's offices, laboratories and morgue were also located in the County Services building.

When Carmine entered the morgue he found two pieces of a female torso fitted together and laid out on a steel autopsy table.

"Well nourished, a part-colored female about sixteen years of age," Patrick said. "He plucked the mons Veneris before introducing the first of several implements—might be dildoes, might be penis sheaths—hard to tell. She's been raped many times by increasingly larger objects, but I doubt she died of that. There's so little blood in what we have of the body that I suspect she was bled out the way you would an animal for slaughter on a farm. No arms or hands, no legs or feet, and no head. These two pieces have been scrupulously washed. Thus far I've found no traces of semen, but there's so much contusion and swelling up there—she's been anally raped too—that I'll need a microscope. My personal bet is that there will be no semen. He's gloved and probably uses his sheaths as condoms. If he comes at all."

The girl's skin was that lovely color called café au lait, despite its bleached bloodlessness. Her hips swelled, her waist was small, her breasts beautiful. As far as Carmine could see, she bore no insults outside the pubic area—no bruises, slashes, cuts, bites, burns. But without the arms and legs, there was no way to tell if or how she had been tied down.

"She looks like a child to me," he said. "Not a big girl."

"I'd say about five-one, tops. The second most interesting thing," Patrick went on, "is that the dismemberment has been done by a real professional. One sweep with something like a fileting knife or a postmortem scalpel, and look at the thigh and shoulder joints— disarticulation without force or trauma." He pulled the two sections of torso apart. "The transverse section was done just below the diaphragm. The cardia of the stomach has been ligated to prevent leakage of the contents, and the esophagus has been ligated too. Disarticulation of the spinal column is just as professional as the joints. No blood in the aorta or the vena cava. However," he said, pointing to the neck, "her throat was cut some hours before he removed her head. Jugulars incised, but not carotids. She would have bled out slowly, no spurting. Hung upside down, of course. When he took her head, he separated it at the C-4 to C-5 junction of the spine, which gave him a small amount of neck as well as the entire skull."

"I wish we had the arms and legs at least, Patsy."

"So do I, but I suspect they went into the fridge yesterday, together with the head."

Carmine spoke so positively that Patrick jumped. "Oh, no! He's still got her head. He won't part with that."

"Carmine! That kind of thing doesn't happen! Or if it does, it's some maniac west of the Rockies. This is Connecticut!"

"He's still got the head, no matter where he comes from."

"I'd say he works at the Hug, or if not at the Hug, then at some other part of the medical school," Patrick said.

"A butcher? A slaughterman?"

"Possible."

"You said, the second most important thing, Patsy. What's the first?"

"Here." Patrick turned the lower torso over and pointed to the right buttock, where a heart-shaped scab about an inch long showed dark and crusted against the flawless skin. "At first I thought he had cut it there on purpose—heart, love, that kind of thing. But he made no template incision around the edge. It's simply one neat transverse slice, the way I've seen a knife man slice off a woman's nipple. So I wondered if she'd had a nevus there, a birthmark raised well above the surface of the skin."

"Something that offended him, destroyed her perfection," said Carmine thoughtfully. "Who knows? Maybe he didn't know she had it until he got her to wherever he did his nasty things to her. Depends if he picked her up or knew her previously. Any idea about her racial background?"

"No idea, other than that she's more Caucasian than anything else. Some Negroid or Mongoloid blood, or both."

"Are you picking that she's a prostitute?"

"Without arms to look for needle tracks, Carmine, difficult, but this girl is—I don't know, *healthy* looking. I'd search the Missing Persons files."

"Oh, I intend to," said Carmine, and went back to the Hug.

Where to begin, given that Otis Green couldn't be questioned until tomorrow at the earliest? Cecil Potter, then.

"This is a real good job," Cecil said, sitting on a steel chair with Jimmy on his knee, and apparently indifferent to the fact that the macaque was busy grooming Cecil's hair, picking with delicate fingers through its dense closeness in a kind of intent ecstasy. Jimmy, he had explained, was still very upset over his ordeal. Carmine would have found the entire bizarre sight easier to cope with if the big monkey hadn't been wearing half a tennis ball on top of his head; this, said Cecil, was to protect the electrode assembly implanted in his brain and the bright green female connector embedded in pink dental cement on his skull. Not that the half a tennis ball seemed to worry Jimmy; he ignored it.

"What makes the job so good?" Carmine asked, aware that his belly was rumbling. Everyone at the Hug had been fed, but thus far Carmine had missed out on breakfast *and* lunch.

"I'm the boss," Cecil said. "When I worked over in P.P. I was just one more shit shoveler. At the Hug, animal care is mine. I like it, specially 'cos we got the monkeys. Dr. Chandra—they his, really—knows I am the best monkey man on the east coast, so he leaves them to me. I even get to put them in the chair for their sessions. They crazy about their sessions."

"Don't they like Dr. Chandra?" Carmine asked.

"Oh, sure, they like him fine. But me, they love."

"Do you ever empty the refrigerator, Cecil?"

"Sometimes, not much. If Otis goes on vacation, we hire a man off of P.P.'s plant physical reserves. Otis don't work this floor with me much—he the upstairs man. Gets to change the lightbulbs an' dispose of the hazardous waste too. I can mostly manage this floor's animal care on my own, 'cept for bringing the cages up an' down from the other floors. Our animals get clean cages Mondays through Fridays."

"They must hate the weekends," said Carmine solemnly. "If Otis doesn't work with you much, how do you clean the cages?"

"See that door there, Lieutenant? Goes to our cage washer. Automated like a fancy car wash, but better. The Hug got everything, man, everything."

"Getting back to the refrigerator. When you do empty it, Cecil, what size are the bags? Is it strange to see bags as big as the—er—?"

Cecil thought, his fine head to one side, the monkey seizing the chance to look behind his ear. "Ain't *strange,* Lieutenant, sir, but you best ask Otis, he the expert."

"Did you notice anyone yesterday putting bags in the fridge who doesn't usually do that?"

"Nope. The researchers mostly bring their bags down theirselves after Otis an' me are gone for the day. Technicians bring bags down too, but small. Rat bags. Only technician brings down big bags is Mrs. Liebman from the O.R., but not yesterday."

"Thanks, Cecil, you've been a great help." Carmine extended his hand to the monkey. "So long, Jimmy."

Jimmy held out his hand and shook Carmine's gravely, his big round amber eyes so full of awareness that Carmine felt his skin prickle. They looked so human.

"Just as well you a man," Cecil said, laughing, escorting Carmine to the door with Jimmy on his hip.

"Why's that?"

"All six of my babies are male, an' man, they hate women! Can't stand a woman in the same room."

✦

Don Hunter and Billy Ho were working together on some sort of Rube Goldberg apparatus they were assembling out of electronic components, Plexiglass extrusions and a pump designed to take a small glass syringe. Two mugs of coffee stood nearby, looking cold and scummy.

That they had both been trained in the armed services was plain the moment Carmine uttered the word "Lieutenant." They sprang away from the gadget and stiffened to attention. Billy was of Chinese ancestry; he had become an electronics engineer in the U.S. Air Force. Don was an Englishman from what he called "the north" and had served in the Royal Armoured Corps.

"What's that gizmo?" Carmine asked.

"A pump we're fitting to some circuitry so it only delivers one-tenth of one em-el every thirty minutes," said Billy.

Carmine picked up the mugs. "I'll bring you some fresh from that urn I saw in the hall if you'll let me have a mug of it and shovel in plenty of sugar."

"Gee, thanks, Lieutenant. Take the whole sugar jar."

If he didn't get some sugar into his system, Carmine knew, his attention would start to flag. He detested very sweet coffee, but it stopped his belly growling. And over it, he could settle to a friendly chat. They were loquacious men, eager to explain their jobs and very keen to assure Carmine that the Hug was great. Billy was the electronics engineer, Don the machinist. Between the two of them they painted Carmine a fascinating picture of a life largely spent designing and building things no sane person could envisage. Because researchers, Carmine learned, were not sane persons. They were mostly pain-in-the-ass maniacs.

"A researcher can fuck up a carload of steel balls," Billy said. "They might have brains the size of Madison Square Garden and win Nobel Prizes all over the shop, but man, can they be dumb! Know what their main problem is?"

"It'll be a help," said Carmine.

"Common sense. They got fuck-all common sense."

"Yoong Billy is raht abaht thaht," said Don. Or at least it sounded as if that was what he had said.

When he departed Carmine was convinced neither Billy Ho nor

22

Don Hunter had left two pieces of woman in the dead animal refrigerator. Though whoever had was not lacking in common sense.

Neurophysiology lived on the next floor up, the second. It was headed by Dr. Addison Forbes, who had two colleagues, Dr. Nur Chandra and Dr. Maurice Finch. Each man had a spacious laboratory and a roomy office; beyond Chandra's suite was the operating room and its anteroom.

The animal room was large and held cages containing two dozen big male cats as well as cages for several hundred rats. He started there. Each cat, he noted, lived in a spotlessly clean cage, dined on canned food as well as kibble, and did its business in a deep tray filled with aromatic cedar shavings. They were friendly beasts, neither spooked nor depressed, and seemed quite oblivious to the presence of half a tennis ball on their heads. The rats lived in deep plastic bins filled with finer shavings through which they dived like dolphins through the sea. In, out, around and about, curling their little hand-like paws around the steel gratings covering their bins with a great deal more joy than human prisoners grabbed the bars of their cells. The rats, Carmine saw, were happy.

His tour guide was Dr. Addison Forbes, who was not happy.

"The cats belong to Dr. Finch and Dr. Chandra. The rats are Dr. Finch's. I don't have any animals, I'm a clinician," he said. "Our appointments are excellent," he droned on as he conducted his guest down the hall between the animal room and the elevators. "Each floor has a male and a female rest room"—he pointed—"and a coffee urn that our glass washer, Allodice, takes care of. The cylindered gases live in this closet, but oxygen is piped in, as are coal gas and compressed air. The fourth line of pipe is for vacuum suction. Particular attention was paid to grounding and copper shielding—we work in millionths of one volt, and that means amplification factors that make interference a nightmare. The building is air-conditioned and the air is filtered minutely, hence the no smoking regulation."

Forbes ceased the drone to look surprised. "The thermostats

actually work." He opened a door. "Our reading and conference room. Which completes the floor. Shall we go to my office?"

Addison Forbes, Carmine had decided within a very few moments, was a complete neurotic. He sported a sinewy, gaunt leanness that suggested an exercise freak with vegetarian tendencies, was about forty-five years of age—the same age as the Prof—and not much to look at if you were a movie director searching for a new star. Facial tics and abrupt, meaningless gestures with his hands larded his conversation. "I had a most severe coronary exactly three years ago," he said, "and it's a miracle that I survived." Clearly it obsessed him, not unusual in medical doctors, who, Patrick had told him, never thought that *they* could die, and became atrocious patients when mortality thrust itself upon them. "Now I jog the five miles between the Hug and my home every evening. My wife drives me here in the morning and picks up yesterday's suit. We don't need two cars anymore, a welcome economy. I eat vegetables, fruit, nuts and an occasional piece of steamed fish if my wife can find some that's genuinely fresh. And I must say that I feel wonderful." He patted his belly, so flat that it caved in. "Good for another fifty years, ha ha!"

Jeez! thought Carmine. I think I'd rather be dead than give up the greasies at Malvolio's. Still, it takes all kinds. "How often do you or your technician take dead animals down to the first-floor refrigerator?" he asked.

Forbes blinked, looked blank. "Lieutenant, I have already told you that I am a clinician! My research is *clinical,* I don't use experimental animals." His brows tried to go in opposite directions. "Even if I have to say so myself, I have a genius for giving each individual patient exactly the right anticonvulsant medication. It is a widely abused field—can you imagine the gall of a fool general practitioner taking it upon himself to prescribe anticonvulsants? He diagnoses some poor patient as idiopathic and stuffs the poor patient full of Dilantin and phenobarb, when all the time the poor patient has a temporal lobe spike you could impale yourself on! *Tch!* I run the epilepsy clinics at the Holloman Hospital, several other hospitals, and I'm in charge of the Holloman Hospital EEG unit attached to the epilepsy clinic. I don't concern myself with *ordinary* EEGs, you understand. There is another unit for Frank Watson and his neurological and neurosurgical minions. What I'm interested in are spikes, not delta waves."

"Uh-huh," said Carmine, whose eyes had begun to glaze halfway through this semi-diatribe. "So you definitely don't ever dispose of dead animals?"

"Never!"

Forbes's technician, a nice girl named Betty, confirmed this. "His work here concerns the level of anticonvulsant medications in the bloodstream," she explained in words Carmine had a hope of understanding. "Most doctors overmedicate because they don't keep track of drug levels in the bloodstream in long-term disorders like epilepsy. He's also the one the pharmaceutical companies ask to try new drugs out. And he has an uncanny instinct for what a particular patient needs." Betty smiled. "He's weird, really. Art, not science."

And how, Carmine wondered as he went in search of Dr. Maurice Finch, do I get out of being buried under medical gobbledygook?

But Dr. Finch wasn't the man to bury anyone under medical gobbledygook. His research, he said briefly, concerned movement of things called sodium and potassium ions through the wall of the nerve cell during an epileptic seizure.

"I work with cats," he said, "on a long-term basis. Once their electrodes and perfusion cannulae are implanted in their brains—under general anesthesia—they suffer no trauma at all. In fact, they look forward to their experimental sessions."

A gentle soul, was Carmine's verdict. That did not put Finch out of the murder stakes, of course; some brutal killers seemed the gentlest of souls when you met them. At fifty-one he was older than most of the researchers, so the Prof had said; research was a young man's game, apparently. A devout Jew, he and his wife, Catherine, lived on a chicken farm; Catherine bred for the kosher table. Her chickens kept her busy, Finch explained, as they had never managed to have any children.

"Then you don't live in Holloman?" he asked.

"Just within the county line, Lieutenant. We have twenty acres. Not all chickens! I'm an ardent cultivator of vegetables and flowers. I have an apple orchard and several glasshouses too."

"Do you bring your dead animals downstairs, Dr. Finch, or does your technician—Patricia?—do that?"

"Sometimes I do it, sometimes Patty does," Finch said, his wide grey eyes looking at Carmine without guilt or unease. "Mind you, my kind of work means I don't do a lot of sacrificing. When I finish with a pussycat, I take the electrodes and cannulae out, castrate him, and try to give him to someone as a pet. I don't *harm* him, you see. However, a cat may develop a brain infection and die, or simply die of natural causes. Then they go downstairs to the refrigerator. Mostly I take them—they're heavy."

"How often does a dead cat happen, Doctor?"

"It's hard to say. Once a month, maybe only every six months."

"I see you take good care of them."

"One cat," said Dr. Finch patiently, "represents an investment of at least twenty thousand dollars. He has to come with papers that satisfy the various authorities, including the A.S.P.C.A. and the Humane Society. Then there is the cost of his upkeep, which has to be first-class or he doesn't survive. I need healthy cats. Therefore a death is unwelcome, not to say exasperating."

Carmine moved on to the third researcher, Dr. Nur Chandra.

Who took his breath away. Chandra's features were cast in a patrician mold, his lashes were so long and thick that they seemed false, his brows were finely arched and his skin the color of old ivory. His wavy black hair was cut short, in keeping with his European clothes; except that a master cut the hair, and the clothes were cashmere, vicuña, silk. A buried memory unearthed itself: this man and his wife were known as the handsomest couple in all of Chubb. Ah, he had Chandra now! The son of some maharajah, rolling in riches, married to the daughter of another Indian potentate. They lived on ten acres just inside the Holloman County line, together with an army of servants and several children who were tutored at home. Apparently the swanky Dormer Day School was not swanky enough. Or might give the kids too many American ideas? They enjoyed diplomatic immunity, quite how, Carmine didn't know. That meant kid gloves, and *pray* he wasn't the one!

"My poor Jimmy," said Dr. Chandra, voice sympathetic but not oozing the tenderness Cecil's did when speaking of Jimmy.

"Give me Jimmy's story, please, Doctor," Carmine said, gaze riveted on another monkey, its legs crossed nonchalantly, seated in a complicated Plexiglass chair inside an enormous box with its door open. The beast was minus its tennis ball hat, revealing a pink mass of dental cement in which was embedded a bright green female connector. A bright green male plug had been inserted into it, and a thick, twisted cable of wires in many colors ran to a panel on the box wall. Presumably the panel connected the monkey to a lot of electronic equipment in nineteen-inch racks around the box.

"Cecil called me yesterday to tell me he'd found Jimmy dead when he went in to see the monkeys after lunch," the researcher said in the most pear-shaped English accent Carmine had ever heard. Nothing in common with Miss Dupre's or Don Hunter's accents, different though they were from each other. Amazing that such a tiny country had so many accents. "I went downstairs to see for myself, and I swear to you, Lieutenant [another *left*enant], that I deemed Jimmy dead. No pulse, no respiration, no heart sounds, no reflexes, both pupils dilated. Cecil asked me if I wished Dr. Schiller to perform an autopsy, but I declined. Jimmy hasn't had his electrodes implanted for long enough to have been of any experimental value to me. But I told Cecil to leave him be, that I'd check again at five, and if he hadn't changed, I'd pop him in the refrigerator myself. Which is what I did."

"What about this guy?" Carmine asked, pointing at the monkey, which bore the same expression as Abe when dying for a cigarette.

"Eustace? Oh, he's of immense value! Aren't you, Eustace?"

The monkey transferred its gaze from Carmine to Dr. Chandra, then grinned ghoulishly. You are one arrogant bastard, Eustace, thought Carmine.

Chandra's technician was a young man named Hank, who took Carmine to the O.R.

Sonia Liebman greeted him in the anteroom, describing herself as the O.R. technician. The anteroom was given over to shelves of stores to do with surgery; it also contained two autoclaves and a formidable-looking safe.

"For my restricted drugs," Mrs. Liebman said, indicating the safe. "Opiates, Pentothal, potassium cyanide, a bunch of nasties." She handed Carmine a pair of canvas bootees.

"Who knows the combination?" he asked, putting them on.

"I do, and it is not written down *anywhere*," she said firmly. "If they have to carry me out feet first, they'll have to bring in a safecracker. Share a secret, and it's no secret."

The O.R. itself looked like any other operating room.

"I don't operate under fully sterile conditions," she said, leaning her rump on the operating table, which was an expanse of clean linen savers and had a curious apparatus mounted at one end, all aluminum sticks, frames, knobs geared down to Vernier scale. She herself was clad in a clean boilersuit—ironed—and canvas bootees. An attractive woman of about forty, he decided, slim and businesslike. Her dark hair was drawn back in a no-nonsense bun, her eyes were dark and intelligent, and her lovely hands were marred by nails cut very short.

"I thought an O.R. had to be sterile," he said.

"Scrupulous cleanliness is far more important, Lieutenant. I've known O.R.s more sterile than a zapped fruit fly, but no one ever really *cleaned* them."

"So you're a neurosurgeon?"

"No, I'm a technician with a master's. Neurosurgery is a man's field, and they give women neurosurgeons hell. But at the Hug I can do what I love to do without that kind of trauma. Due to the size of my patients, it's very high-powered neurosurgery. See that? My

Zeiss operating microscope. They don't have one in the Chubb neurosurgery O.R.s, not one," said the lady with great satisfaction.

"You operate on what?"

"Monkeys for Dr. Chandra. Cats for him and Dr. Finch. Rats for the neurochemists upstairs, and cats for them too."

"Do they die on the table often?"

Sonia Liebman looked outraged. "What do you think I am, ham-fisted? No! I *sacrifice* animals for the neurochemists, who don't often work on live brains. Neurophysiologists work on live brains. That's the main difference between the two disciplines to me."

"Uh, what do you sacrifice, Mrs. Liebman?" Tread carefully, Carmine, tread carefully!

"Rats in the main, but I do Sherringtonian decerebrations on cats too."

"What's that?" he asked, writing in his notebook, but not really wanting to know—more abstruse details coming up!

"Removal of a brain from the tentorium up under ether anesthesia. The moment I shell the brain out, I inject Pentothal into the heart and wham! the animal's dead. Instantaneous."

"So you put fairly large animals into bags and take them to the refrigerator for disposal?"

"Yes, on decerebration days."

"How often do these decerebration days happen?"

"It depends. If Dr. Ponsonby or Dr. Polonowski asks for cat forebrains, about every two weeks for a couple of months, at the rate of three to four cats on any one day. Dr. Satsuma doesn't ask nearly as often—maybe once a year, six cats."

"How big are these decerebrated cats?"

"Monsters. Males about twelve to fifteen pounds."

Right, two floors down and two to go. Utilities, workshops and neurophysiology done. Now it's up to see the office staff on the fourth floor, then down to the third and neurochemistry.

There were three medical typists, all with science degrees, and a filing clerk who had nothing more imposing than a high school diploma—how lonely she must feel! Vonnie, Dora and Margaret used big IBM golfball typewriters, and could type "electroencephalography" faster than a cop could type "DUI." Nothing there; he left them to it, Denise the filing clerk sniffling and mopping her eyes as she peered into open drawers, the typewriters clattering like machine guns.

Dr. Charles Ponsonby was waiting for him at the elevator. He was, he said to Carmine as he escorted the visitor to his office, the same age as the Prof, forty-five, and filled in for the Prof when he was away. They'd gone to the Dormer Day School together, did their premed at Chubb together, then their medical degrees at Chubb. Both, Ponsonby explained gravely, were Connecticut Yankees back to the beginning. But after medical school their paths had diverged. Ponsonby had preferred to stay at Chubb to do his neurological residency, while Smith had gone to Johns Hopkins. Not that the separation had been a long one: Bob Smith came back to head up the Hug, and invited Ponsonby to join him there. That had been in 1950, when both were thirty years old.

Now why did you stay home? Carmine wondered, studying the chief of neurochemistry. A medium-sized man of medium height, Charles Ponsonby had brown hair streaked with grey, watery blue eyes above a pair of half glasses perched on a long, narrow nose, and the air of an absentminded professor. His clothes were shabby and tweedy, his hair wisped about, and his socks, Carmine saw, were mismatched: navy on the right foot, grey on the left. All this might confirm that Ponsonby was an unadventurous man who saw no virtue in going farther afield than Holloman, yet something in those rheumy eyes said he might have ended a different kind of man had he too gone elsewhere after finishing his medical degree. An hypothesis based on gut instinct; *something* had kept Ponsonby at home, something concrete and compelling. Not a wife, because he had said, quite indifferently, that he was a lifelong bachelor.

Interesting too to discover the contrasts between their various offices. Forbes's had been awesomely neat with no room for plush furniture or wall hangings; books and papers everywhere, even the floor. Finch went in for potted plants and actually had a stunning orchid in bloom; his walls cascaded ferns. Chandra preferred the leather Chesterfield look, with leaded glass-paned book cabinets and a few exquisite Indian artworks. And Dr. Charles Ponsonby lived tidily among gruesome artifacts like shrunken heads and death masks of people like Beethoven and Wagner; he also had four reproductions of famous paintings on his walls—Goya's Cronus eating a child, two sections of Bosch's Hell, and Munch's screaming face.

"Do you like surrealist art?" Ponsonby asked with animation.

"I'm into Oriental art myself, Doctor."

"I've often thought, Lieutenant, that I mischose my calling. Psychiatry fascinates me, particularly psychopathia. Look at that shrunken head—what beliefs can provoke that? Or what visions my paintings?"

Carmine grinned. "No use asking me. I'm just a cop." And you, he ended in a silent comment, are not my man. Too obvious.

Up here, he saw as Ponsonby conducted him through the labs, the equipment was more familiar: an atomic absorption unit, a mass spectrometer, a gas chromatograph, centrifuges large and small—the kind of apparatus Patrick had in his forensic lab, just newer and grander. Patrick had to scrape; here, they spent and spent.

From Ponsonby he learned more about the cat brains that were made into what Ponsonby called "brain soup" so naturally that it had no element of jocularity about it. They used rat brain soup too. And Dr. Polonowski was conducting some experiments on the giant axon of a lobster leg—not the big claws, the little legs. Those axons were huge! Polonowski's technician, Marian, often had to call into the fish shop on her way to work to buy the four biggest lobsters in the tank.

"What happens to the lobsters afterward?"

"They are rostered between those who like lobster," Ponsonby said, as if the question had no merit whatsoever when the answer was so patently clear. "Dr. Polonowski doesn't do anything to the rest of the beast. It is very kind of him to rotate them, actually. They *are* his experimental animals, he could eat them all himself. But he takes his turn with the rest of us. Except for Dr. Forbes, who has gone vegetarian, and Dr. Finch, who is too orthodox to eat crustacea."

"Tell me, Dr. Ponsonby, do people *notice* bags of dead animals? If you saw a big dead animal bag stuffed full and you did notice it, what would you think about it?"

Ponsonby's face registered mild surprise. "I doubt I would think about it, Lieutenant, because I doubt I would notice it."

Miraculously, Ponsonby wasn't agog to go into detail about his work, which he simply said had to do with the chemistry of a brain cell involved in the epileptic process.

"So far everybody seems to be into epilepsy. Is anyone into mental retardation? I thought the Hug was for both."

"Unfortunately we lost our geneticist several years ago, and Professor Smith hasn't found a suitable man to replace him. The DNA business is attracting them, you see. More exciting." He giggled. *"Their* soup is made out of E. coli."

And thus to Dr. Walter Polonowski, who had a big chip on his shoulder having nothing to do with his Polish ancestry: that, like Ponsonby's art, would have been too simple.

"It isn't fair," he said to Carmine.

"What isn't fair, Doctor?"

"The division of labor here. If you have a medical degree, like me, Ponsonby, Finch and Forbes, you have to see patients at the Holloman Hospital, and seeing patients eats into research time. Whereas Ph.D.s like Chandra and Satsuma do research all the time. Is it any wonder that they're way ahead of the rest of us? When I agreed to come here, the understanding was that I'd see idiopathic retards as patients. And what happens? I inherit the patients with malabsorption syndromes!" Polonowski said angrily.

Oh, Jesus, here we go again! "Aren't they retarded, Doctor?"

"Yes, of course they are, but secondary to their malabsorption! They are *not* idiopathic!"

"What does idiopathic mean, sir?"

"A disorder of unknown etiology—no known cause."

"Uh-huh."

Walt Polonowski was a very presentable man, tall, well built, his dark gold hair and eyes blending into a dark gold skin. The kind of man, Carmine judged, who wasn't really griping about his patient load because that was what bothered him; what bothered him were core emotions like love and hate. The guy was miserable all the time, it was there in the set of his face.

But, like all the others, he never noticed anything as mundane as a dead animal bag, let alone noticed how big a dead animal bag was. And why am I fixated on dead animal bags anyway? Carmine asked himself. Because someone very clever took advantage of the dead animal refrigerator knowing that the Hug personnel never ever noticed dead animal bags. That's why, yet—by the pricking of my thumbs, something wicked this way comes. It isn't over. Yeah, I know it, I know it!

Polonowski's technician, Marian, was a pretty girl who told Carmine that she took Dr. Polonowski's bags downstairs herself. Her manner was wary and defensive, but not about dead animal bags was his guess. This was an unhappy girl, and unhappy girls were usually unhappy over personal problems, not their workplace. Jobs were easy to find for these young people, all science graduates, some with little projects on the side that would count toward a master's or a Ph.D. Marian, Carmine was willing to bet, sometimes came into the Hug wearing dark glasses to hide the fact that she'd been crying half the night.

After the others, Dr. Hideki Satsuma was great. His English was perfect and American; his father, he explained, had been at the Japanese Embassy in Washington, D.C., from the time diplomatic relations had been reopened after the war. Satsuma's schooling had finished in America, and his degrees came from Georgetown.

"I'm working on the neurochemistry of the rhinencephalon," he said, caught the blank look on Carmine's face, and laughed. "What is sometimes called the 'smell brain'—the most primitive of human grey matter. It's very involved in the epileptic process."

Satsuma was another looker; the Hug sure had its share of them among the men! His features were patrician too, and he had undergone surgery to retract the epicanthal folds of his upper eyelids, thus liberating a pair of twinkling black eyes. Quite tall for a Japanese. He moved with the grace of Rudolf Nureyev, had that same slightly Tartar look. Carmine summed him up as an unerring kind of person who would never fumble a catch or drop a beaker. Likeable too, which troubled Carmine, who had spent his war years in the Pacific, and had no love for the Japs.

"You must understand, Lieutenant," Satsuma said earnestly, "that we who work in a place like the Hug are not the noticing kind unless it involves our actual work, when we become endowed with X-ray vision better than Superman's. A brown paper dead animal bag might intrude as an offense, but otherwise would not intrude at all. As the Hug technicians are very good, dead animal bags do not lie around intruding. I never carry them downstairs. My technician does that."

"He's Japanese too, I see."

"Yes. Eido is my assistant in every way. He and his wife live on the tenth floor of the Nutmeg Insurance building, where I have the penthouse. As you well know, since you live in the Nutmeg building yourself."

"Actually I didn't know. The penthouse has a private elevator. Eido and his wife I've seen. Are you married, Doctor?"

"Not I! There are too many beautiful fish in the sea for me to have singled just one out. I am a bachelor."

"Do you have a girlfriend here at the Hug?"

The black eyes flashed—amusement, not anger. "Oh, dear me, no! As my father told me many years ago, only a foolish bachelor mixes business with pleasure."

"A good rule of life."

"Would you like me to introduce you to Dr. Schiller?" Satsuma asked, sensing that the interview was over.

"Thanks, I'd appreciate it."

Well, well, another Hug looker! A Viking. Kurt Schiller was the Hug's pathologist. His English had a very slight Germanic inflection, which no doubt accounted for the look of savage dislike Dr. Maurice Finch had produced when he mentioned Schiller's name. No love lost there. Schiller was tall, a trifle on the willowy side, with flaxen-blond hair and pale blue eyes. Something about him irritated Carmine, though it had nothing to do with his nationality; the sensitive cop nose smelled homosexuality. If Schiller isn't one, there's something wrong with my cop nose, and there isn't, Carmine thought.

The pathology lab occupied the same site as the O.R. did on the floor below, save that it was somewhat larger thanks to an animal room without any cats. Schiller worked with two technicians, Hal Jones, who did the Hug's histology, and Tom Skinks, who worked exclusively on Schiller's projects.

"Sometimes I am sent brain samples from the hospital," said the pathologist, "due to my experience in cortical atrophy and cerebral scar tissue. My own work involves searching for scarring of the hippocampus and uncinate gyrus."

And de-de-da-de-da. By this time, Carmine had learned to switch off when the big words started. Though it wasn't the size of the words, it was their abstruseness. Like Billy Ho the electronics engineer talking about a magnetic mu of less than one as if Carmine would automatically know what he meant. We all speak our own kind of specialized lingo, even cops, he thought with a sigh.

By this time it was 6 P.M. and Carmine was ravenous. However, best to finish seeing everyone so they could all go home, then he could eat at leisure. Only four on the fourth floor to go.

He started with Hilda Silverman, the research librarian, who ruled over a huge room packed with steel bookshelves and banks of drawers that held books, cards, papers, abstracts, reprinted papers, articles, significant excerpts of tomes.

"I keep my records on our computer these days," she said, waving her unmanicured hand at a thing the size of a restaurant refrigerator, equipped with two fourteen-inch tape reels, and, on a console in front of it, a typewriter keyboard. "Such a help! No more punch cards! I'm much luckier than the medical school library, you know. *They* still have to do things the old way. At the moment there is a facility being put together in Texas that we'll be able to tap into. Enter key words like 'potassium ions' and 'seizures' and we'll be sent the abstracts of every paper ever written as fast as a teleprinter can produce them. Just one more reason why I quit the main library to come here and have my own domain. Lieutenant, the Hug is *swimming* in money! Though it's hard to be so far from Keith," she ended with a sigh.

"Keith?"

"My husband, Keith Kyneton. He's a postgraduate fellow in neurosurgery, which is right down the other end of Oak Street. We used to eat lunch together, now we can't."

"So Silverman is your maiden name?"

"That's right. I had to keep it—easier, when all the pieces of paper say Silverman."

He guessed her at the middle thirties, but she could have been younger; her expression was a little careworn. She wore a badly tailored coat and skirt that had seen better days, scuffed shoes, and no jewelry other than her wedding band. The wavy auburn hair was badly cut and held back with ugly bobby pins, her rather nice brown eyes were diminished by a pair of Coke-bottle-bottom glasses, and her face was free of makeup, neutrally pleasant.

I wonder, asked Carmine of himself, what makes librarians look like librarians? Paper mites? Dust bunnies? Printer's ink?

"I wish I could help you more," she said a little later, "but I really can't ever remember seeing one of those bags. Nor have I ever visited the first floor, except for the elevator foyer."

"Who are your friends?" he asked.

"Sonia Liebman in the O.R. No one else, really."

"Not Miss Dupre or Miss Vilich on your own floor?"

"That pair?" she asked scornfully. "They're too busy feuding to notice my existence."

Well, well, a useful item of information at last!

Who next? Dupre, he decided, and knocked on her door. She had the southeast corner room, which meant windows on two sides, one looking over the city, the other looking south across the misty harbor. Now why hadn't the Prof grabbed it? Or didn't he trust himself not to waste time looking at a gorgeous view? Miss Dupre, who was definitely not gorgeous, also had enough steel, he judged, to resist what lay outside her windows.

She rose from her desk to tower over him, something she clearly enjoyed doing. A dangerous hobby, madam. You too can be cut down to size. But you're very clever, and very efficient, and very observant; they're all there in your beautiful eyes.

"What brought you to the Hug?" he asked, sitting down.

"A green card. I used to be a deputy administrator in one of England's regional health care areas. I had responsibility for all the research facilities in the area's various hospitals and red-brick universities."

"Uh—red-brick universities?"

"The ones they send the working-class students to—my sort. We don't get into Oxford or Cambridge, which are *not* red brick, even when their new buildings are."

"What don't you know about this place?" he asked.

"Very little."

"How about brown paper dead animal bags?"

"Your inexplicable fixation upon dead animal bags has been noticed by many more than me, but none of us have any idea what their significance may be, though I can guess. Why not tell me all the truth, Lieutenant?"

"Just answer my questions, Miss Dupre."

"Then ask me one."

"Do you ever see the dead animal bags?"

"Of course. As the business manager, I see everything. The consignment before the last one consisted of an inferior product, which led me to go into the matter exhaustively," said Miss Dupre. "However, as a usual event I don't see them at all, especially when occupied by a corpse."

"At what hour do Cecil Potter and Otis Green finish work?"

"Three in the afternoon."

"Does everybody know that?"

"Naturally. From time to time it leads to complaints from a researcher—they sometimes assume that the whole world exists to service their needs." Her pale brows flew up. "My answer to them is to say that Mr. Potter and Mr. Green work animal care hours. The circadian rhythms of animals like attention within three or four hours after sunrise. Evenings matter less, provided they have been well serviced with food and clean premises."

"What other jobs does Otis do apart from animal care?"

"Mr. Green's day is largely taken up by his duties in the upstairs animal rooms; his other duties are not terribly demanding. He does the heavy lifting, maintenance of light fixtures, and the disposal of hazardous wastes. It might surprise you to know that female technicians ask Mr. Green to fetch them cylinders of gas. We used to let the girls move their own until a full cylinder was accidentally knocked over and the pressurized contents escaped. No harm was done, but if the gas had not been an inert one—" She looked rueful. "There are also times when one of the researchers works with substances giving off gamma radiation. That requires the erection of barriers consisting of lead bricks—*very* heavy."

"I'm surprised that in this Hilton of a place everything is not piped in or laid on."

She rose to her feet to tower. "Have you anything more to ask me, sir?"

"No. Thanks for your time."

How do I get on the right side of her? he wondered as he walked up the hall to Tamara Vilich's office. She's a fount of information that I need badly.

The Prof's secretary's office had a door that directly communicated with his own office, Carmine noted as he entered.

"Do you realize," Tamara Vilich said with a touch of acid in her voice, "that leaving us until last has created considerable inconvenience? I am late for an appointment."

"The penalties of power," Carmine said, not sitting. "You know, I've heard more stilted language and technical jargon today than I usually hear in months? I'm inconvenienced too, Miss Vilich. No breakfast, no lunch, and so far no dinner."

"Then get on with it! I have to go!"

Desperation in her voice? Interesting. "Do you ever see the dead animal bags, ma'am?"

"No, I don't." She looked fretfully at her watch. "Damn!"

"Ever?"

"No, never!"

"Then you can keep your appointment, Miss Vilich. Thanks."

"I'm too late!" she cried in despair. "Too late!"

But she was gone, running, before Carmine could knock on the communicating door.

The Prof was looking more worried than he had that morning, maybe, thought Carmine, because nothing's happened since then to soothe his anxieties or satisfy his curiosity.

"I will have to inform the Board of Governors," Smith said before Carmine had a chance to speak.

"Board of Governors?"

"This is a privately endowed institution, Lieutenant, that is supervised from on high by a board. You might say that we all have to sing for our suppers. The generosity of the Board of Governors is in direct proportion to the amount of genuinely original and significant work the Hug produces. Our reputation is second to none, the Hug has indeed made a difference. Now this—this—this *singularity* happens! A random event that has the power to affect the quality of our work drastically."

"A random event, Professor? I don't call murder random. But let's leave that aside for a moment. Who's on this board?"

"William Parson himself died in 1952. He left two nephews,

39

Roger Junior and Henry Parson, in control of his empire. Roger Junior is Governor-in-Chief of the Board. Henry is his deputy. Their sons Roger III and Henry Junior are also Board members. The fifth Parson member is Richard Spaight, director of the Parson Bank and the son of William Parson's sister. President Mawson MacIntosh of Chubb is a Governor, as is the Dean of Medicine, Dr. Wilbur Dowling. I, as Chair Professor, am the last," said Smith.

"That gives the Parson contingent a strong majority. They must crack the whip hard."

Smith looked astonished. "No, indeed! Anything but! As long as we produce the kind of brilliant work we have done for fifteen years, we have a virtual carte blanche. William Parson's will was very specific. 'Pay peanuts and you get monkeys' was one of his favorite maxims. Therefore we do not pay peanuts at the Hug, and our researchers are infinitely brighter than the macaques downstairs. Hence my concern over this singularity, Lieutenant. Half of me insists it is a dream."

"Professor, the body is real and the situation is real. But I want to digress for a moment." Carmine's face assumed a look that most who saw it found disarming. "What's going on between Miss Dupre and Miss Vilich?"

Smith's long face puckered. "Is it that obvious?"

"To me, yes." No need to mention Hilda Silverman.

"For the first nine years of the Hug's existence, Tamara was both my secretary *and* the business manager. Then she married. I assure you that I know absolutely nothing about the husband, except that after a few months he left her. During the time they were together, her work suffered terribly. With the result that the Board of Governors decided that we needed a qualified person to head our business affairs."

"Was Miss Vilich's husband a Hug-ite?"

"The term is 'Hugger,' Lieutenant," Smith said as if he were chewing wool. "Frank Watson's barb went deep. If there are Chubbers, he said, then there ought to be Huggers as well. And no, the husband was not a Hugger *or* a Chubber." He drew a deep breath.

"To be perfectly candid, he led the poor girl into an embezzlement. We worked it out and took no further action."

"I'm surprised the Board didn't insist you fire her."

"I couldn't have done *that*, Lieutenant! She came to me from the Kirk Secretarial College here in Holloman, and has never had another job." A huge sigh. "However, it was inevitable that when Miss Dupre arrived, Tamara took against her. A pity. Miss Dupre is excellent at her job—much better than Tamara was, in all honesty! Degrees in medical administration *and* accountancy."

"A tough lady. Maybe they'd have gotten on better together if Miss Dupre was more of a glamour girl, huh?"

That bait was ignored; the Prof chose to say, "Miss Dupre is very well liked in all other quarters."

Carmine glanced at his watch. "Time I let you go home, sir. Thanks for being so cooperative."

"You don't really think that the body has anything to do with the Hug and my people?" the Prof asked as he walked with Carmine down the hall.

"I think that the body has everything to do with the Hug and your people. And, Professor, postpone your board meeting until next Monday, please. You're at liberty to explain the situation to Mr. Roger Parson Junior and President MacIntosh as of now, but the information chain cuts off right there. No exceptions, from wives to colleagues."

Being next door to the Holloman County Services building meant that Malvolio's found it profitable to stay open twenty-four hours a day. Perhaps because so many of its patrons wore navy-blue, the decor was after the manner of a powder-blue Wedgwood plate, with white molded plaster maidens, garlands and curliques to break up the blueness. Corey and Abe had long gone home when Carmine parked the Ford outside it and went in to order meat loaf with gravy and mashed potatoes, a side salad with Green Goddess dressing, and two wedges of apple pie à la mode.

Stomach full at last, he walked home to take a long shower, then fell naked into bed and didn't remember his head hitting the pillow.

◆

Hilda Silverman, home to find that Ruth had already made the dinner: a casserole of pork chops she hadn't bothered to de-fat, Smash powdered mashed potatoes, a salad of iceberg lettuce limp and transparent from Italian dressing applied far too early, and a Sara Lee frozen chocolate cake for dessert. At least I have no trouble keeping my figure, Hilda thought; the miracle is how Keith manages to keep his, because he *loves* his mom's cooking. That is about the only evidence of his poor white trash origins left in his character. No, Hilda, be fair! He loves his mom just as much as he loves her cooking.

Not that he was present. His plate was sitting, covered in foil, atop a pot of water that Ruth kept on the simmer until her son came in, even if that meant two or three in the morning.

Hilda disliked her mother-in-law because she was so defiantly poor white trash to this day, but they were joined at the hip—a hip named Keith—and jealousy did not enter the picture. Keith was all, that simple. If Keith preferred people not to know of his background, that was fine by his mom, who would have died for him as cheerfully as Hilda would have.

Ruth made a great deal of difference to Keith's and Hilda's comfort in that her presence enabled Hilda to continue in her very well-paid job. Even better, Ruth actually liked living in an awful house in an awful neighborhood; it reminded her (and a shrinking Keith) of her old house in Dayton, Ohio. Another place where people filled their backyards with dead washing machines and rusted car bodies. As damp, as depressing, as cold as Griswold Lane in Holloman, Connecticut.

Keith and Hilda lived in the worst house on Griswold Lane because its rent was a pittance, enabling them to save most of their combined salaries (hers was twice his). Now that Keith was out of his residency and marking time as a postdoctoral fellow, he was planning to buy into a lucrative neurosurgical practice, preferably located in New York City. Not for Keith Kyneton the low-paid drag of academic medicine! Mother and wife struggled heroically to help him achieve his ambition. Ruth was a natural cheapskate who deemed J.C. Penney's outrageously expensive and bought the day before yesterday's produce at the supermarket; Hilda scrimped over something as trivial as a haircut, wouldn't buy a nice pair of barettes, and suffered her Coke-bottle-bottom glasses. Whereas Keith's clothing and car had to be the best, and his work made the huge expense of contact lenses mandatory. What Keith wanted, Keith must have.

At which moment, just as Ruth and Hilda were sitting down, in breezed Keith, and with him the sun, the moon, the stars and all the angels in heaven. Hilda leaped to throw her arms around him, nuzzle her head under his chin—oh, he was so tall, so—so fantastic!

"Hi, honey," he said, one arm about her, and leaning across the top of her head to peck his mother on the cheek. "Hi, Mom, what's for dinner? Is that your pork chops I smell?"

"Sure is, son. Sit down while I get your plate."

So they sat around three sides of the small square table in the kitchen, Keith and Ruth devouring the greasy, rather ersatz meal with gusto, Hilda picking at it.

"We had a murder today," Hilda said, sawing at a chop.

Keith looked up, too busy to comment; Ruth put down her fork and stared.

"Criminy!" she said. "An honest-to-God murder?"

"Well, a body, at any rate. That's why I was so late home. The police were all over the place and wouldn't let any of us leave, even for lunch. For some reason they left the fourth floor until last, though how would anybody on the fourth floor know anything about a body in animal care on the first floor?" Hilda huffed indignantly and succeeded in de-fatting her chop.

43

"It's all around the hospital and medical school," Keith said, pausing to help himself to two more chops. "I've been in the O.R. all day, but even in there the anesthetist and the instrument nurse were full of it. As if a bifurcated aneurysm on the middle cerebral artery weren't enough! Then the radiologist came in with the news that there's another aneurysm on the basilar artery, so all our work will probably go for nothing."

"Surely the angiogram showed that before you started?"

"Basilar didn't fill properly and Missingham didn't see the films until we were almost done—he'd been in Boston. His deputy couldn't find his ass with both hands inside his shorts, let alone an aneurysm on a poorly filled basilar artery! Sorry, Mom, but it was a frustrating day. Nothing went right."

Eyes soft, Hilda gazed at him adoringly. How had she ever managed to capture Keith Kyneton's attention? A mystery, but one she was permanently grateful for. He was all her dreams rolled in one, from his height to his curly fair hair, his beautiful grey eyes, his chiseled facial bones, his muscular body. And he was so charming, so well spoken, so eminently likeable! Not to mention a highly able neurosurgeon who'd chosen a good speciality, cerebral aneurysms. Until recently they had been inoperable death sentences, but now that neurosurgery had body-freezing techniques and the heart could be stopped for a few precious minutes while an aneurysm was clipped off, Keith's future was assured.

"Go on, give us the details," said Ruth, eyes glistening.

"I can't, Ruth, because I don't have any. The police were very closemouthed about it, and the lieutenant who talked to me could have given lessons in discretion to a Catholic priest. Sonia told me he impressed her as a very intelligent and quite well-educated man, and I saw what she meant."

"What was his name?"

"Something Italian."

"Aren't they all?" Keith asked, and laughed.

*　　*　　*

Professor Bob Smith, home with his wife, Eliza, after dinner was finished and the boys sent to do homework.

"It's going to make life difficult."

"The Board, you mean?" she asked, pouring him more coffee.

"Yes, the Board, but more the work, dear. You know just how temperamental they can be! The only one who doesn't bug me is Addison. He's grateful to be alive, his ideas on anticonvulsants are as pleasing to him as they are to me, and provided none of his equipment breaks down, he's content. Though how anybody can jog five miles a day and be content, I don't know. Lazarus complex." He grinned, which did wonders for his already striking face. "Oh, how upset he was when I told him jogging to work in the mornings was not going to happen! But he managed to sit on his rage."

She giggled, an attractive sound. "You'd think it would occur to the jogger that having to smell his B.O. after he jogs doesn't make him an ideal work companion." She sobered. "It's his poor wife I feel sorriest for."

"Robin? That nonentity? Why?"

"Because Addison Forbes treats her like a servant, Bob. Yes, he does! The lengths she has to go to to find food he'll eat! And washing smelly clothes—she has no kind of life."

"That sounds rather petty to me, dear."

"Yes, I suppose it does, but she's—well, not the world's brightest person, and Addison makes her feel it. Sometimes I've caught him looking sideways at her and had the heebie-jeebies—I swear he hates her, really hates her!"

"It can happen when a medical student has to marry a nurse to get through," Smith said rather dryly. "There's no intellectual equality, and after he makes his mark, she's an embarrassment."

"You're such a snob."

"No, a pragmatist. I'm right."

"So okay, maybe you do have a point, but it's a pitiless attitude just the same," Eliza said valiantly. "I mean, even in their own home he locks her out! There they have this gorgeous turret with a widow's walk overlooking the harbor, and he won't let her up there! What is it, Bluebeard's chamber?"

"Evidence of her untidiness, and his obsession with order. I lock you out of the basement, don't forget."

"You'll get no complaints from me about that, but I do think you're too hard on the boys. They're way past the destructive age now. Why not let them go down?"

His jaws clamped, hardening his face. "The boys are barred from the basement permanently, Eliza."

"Then it isn't fair, because you spend every free second you have down there. You ought to spend more time with the boys, so let them share your folly."

"I wish you wouldn't refer to it as a folly!"

She changed the subject; he had that obdurate look now, he wasn't about to listen. "Is this murder really such a problem, Bob? I mean, it can't possibly have anything to do with the Hug."

"I agree, dear, but the police think otherwise," said Smith mournfully. "Would you believe that we've been fingerprinted? Lucky we're a research lab. The ink came off in xylene."

Walt Polonowski, to his wife, his tone ungracious.

"Have you seen my red-checkered jacket?"

She paused in her rounds of the kitchen, Mikey straddling her hip, Esther clinging to her skirt, and looked at him in mingled scorn and exasperation. "Christ almighty, Walt, it can't be the hunting season yet!" she snapped.

"Just around the corner. I'm going up to the cabin this weekend to get it ready—and that means I need my jacket—and I can't find it because it isn't where it ought to be."

"Nor are you." She put Mikey in his highchair and Esther on a chair with a fat cushion, then hollered for Stanley and Bella. "Dinner's ready!"

A boy and a girl galloped into the room, whooping that they were starving. Mom was a great cook who never made them eat things they didn't like—no spinach, no carrots, no cabbage unless she'd made it into coleslaw.

Walter sat at one end of the long table, Paola at its other end where she could spoon slop into Mikey's mouth, open like a bird's, and correct Esther's table manners, still far from perfect. "The other thing I can't stand," she said as soon as everyone was eating, "is your selfishness. It would be great to have somewhere to take the kids on a weekend, but no! It's *your* cabin, and we can whistle—Stanley, that is not permission to whistle!"

"You're right when you say the cabin is mine," he said coldly, cutting his very good lasagna with a fork. "My grandfather left me the cabin, Paola—to me, and me alone. It's the one place where I can get away from all this mayhem!"

"Your wife and four children, you mean."

"Yes, I do."

"If you didn't want four children, Walt, why didn't you tie a knot in the goddamn thing? It takes two to tango."

"Tango? What's that?" asked Stanley.

"A sexy dance," said his mother curtly.

An answer that for some reason inexplicable to Stanley caused Dad to roar with laughter.

"Shut up!" Paola growled. "Shut up, Walt!"

He wiped his eyes, put another piece of lasagna on Stanley's empty plate and then replenished his own plate. "I am going up to the cabin on Friday night, Paola, and I won't be home until dawn on Monday. I have a mountain of reading to do, and as God is my witness, I cannot read in this house!"

"If you'd only give up this stupid research and go into a good private practice, Walt, we could live in a house big enough for *twelve* kids without destroying your peace!" Her big brown eyes sparkled with angry tears. "You've gotten this fantastic reputation for dealing with all those weird and wonderful diseases that have people's names—Wilson, Huntington, don't ask me to remember all of them!—and I know you get offers to go into private practice in much better places than Holloman—Atlanta, Miami, Houston—*warm* places. Places where house help is cheap. The children could have music lessons, I could go back to college—"

His hand came down on the table violently; the children went still, shivered. "Just how do you know I've had offers, Paola?" he asked dangerously.

Her face paled, but she defied him. "You leave the letters lying around, I find them everywhere."

"And read them. Yet you wonder why I have to get away? My mail is private, do you hear me? *Private!*"

Walt threw his fork down, shoved his chair away from the table and stalked from the kitchen. His wife and children stared after him, then Paola wiped Mikey's slimed face and rose to get the ice cream and Jell-O.

There was an old mirror on the wall to one side of the fridge; Paola caught a glimpse of herself in it and felt the tears overflow. Eight years had been enough to turn the vivacious and very pretty young woman with the great body into a thin, downright plain woman who looked years older than she was.

Oh, the joy of meeting Walt, of captivating Walt, of *catching* Walt! A fully qualified medical doctor who was so brilliant that they would soon be rich. What she hadn't counted on was that Walt had no intention of leaving academic medicine—plumbers earned more! And the children just kept coming, coming. The only way she could prevent a fifth child was to sin—Paola was taking the Pill.

The quarrels, she understood, were totally destructive. They upset the children, they upset her, and they were driving Walt to seek his cabin more and more often. His cabin—she'd never even *seen* it! Nor would she. Walt refused to tell her where it was.

"Oh, wow, fudge ripple!" cried Stanley.

"Fudge ripple doesn't go with grape Jell-O," said Bella, who was the fussy one.

According to her own lights Paola was a good mother. "Would you prefer your Jell-O and your ice cream in separate bowls, honey?"

*   *   *

Dr. Hideki Satsuma, letting himself into his penthouse apartment atop Holloman's tallest building, and feeling the day's stresses slide from his shoulders.

Eido had come home earlier than he, set everything out as his master liked, then gone ten floors down to the far less elegant apartment where he lived with his wife.

The decor was deceptively simple: walls of beaten copper sheeting; checkered doors of black wood and frail paper; one very old three-leafed screen of expressionless slit-eyed women with pompadour hairstyles and ribby parasols; a plain polished black stone pedestal that held one perfect flower in a twisted Steuben vase; glossy black wooden floors.

A cold sushi supper was laid out on the black lacquer table sunk into a well, and when he went through to his bedroom he found his kimono spread out, his Jacuzzi giving off lazy tendrils of steam, his futon down.

Bathed, fed, relaxed, he went then to the glass wall that framed his courtyard and stood absorbing its perfection. To have it built had put him to a great deal of expense, but money wasn't a commodity Hideki needed to worry about. So beautiful, living as it did inside the apartment where once had been an open area of roof garden. On the courtyard side its walls were mirrored, but from the room that surrounded it the walls were transparent. Its contents were sparse to the point of austerity. A few bonsaied conifers, a tall Hollywood cypress growing in a double helix, an incredibly old bonsaied Japanese maple, perhaps two dozen rocks of assorted sizes and shapes, and varicolored marble pebbles laid down in a complex pattern not meant to be walked upon. Here the forces of his private universe came together in the way most felicitous to his own well-being.

But tonight, his fingertips still reeking faintly of xylene to his exquisitely sensitive nose, Hideki Satsuma stared at his courtyard in the sure knowledge that his private universe had shifted on its foundations; that he had to rearrange the pots, the rocks, the pebbles, to neutralize this profoundly disturbing development. A development beyond his control, he who was driven to control everything. There . . . There, where that pink rivulet meandered through the glowing jade pebbles . . . And there, where the sharp grey rock leaped like a sword blade in front of the tender vulvar roundness of the cloven red rock . . . And there, where the double helix of the Hollywood cypress tapered up to the sky . . . They were suddenly wrong, he would have to start again.

His mind went wistfully to his beach house up on the elbow of Cape Cod, but what had happened there recently required a period of recovery. Besides, the drive was too long, even in his maroon Ferrari through the night marches. No, that house had a different purpose, and while it was connected to the shifting of his universe, the epicenter of the disturbance lay in his Holloman courtyard.

Could it wait until the weekend? No, it could not. Hideki Satsuma pressed the buzzer that would summon Eido upstairs.

Desdemona, erupting into her apartment on the third floor of a three-family house on Sycamore Street just beyond the Hollow. Her first stop was the bathroom, where she ran a warm bath and removed the lingering traces of her two-mile walk home. Then it was into the kitchen to open a can of Irish stew and another of creamed rice pudding; Desdemona was no cook. The eyes that Carmine had been surprised to find beautiful took no notice of the pitted linoleum or the wallpaper lifting around the edges; Desdemona did not live for creature comforts.

Finally, clad in a checkered flannel man's dressing gown, she went to the living room, where her cherished work lay in a big wicker basket atop a tall cane stand beside her favorite chair, whose herniating springs she didn't notice. Frowning, she dug in the basket to find the long piece of silk on which she was embroidering a sideboard panel for Charles Ponsonby—surely it had been right on top? Yes, it had, she was positive of the fact! No chaos for Desdemona Dupre; everything had its place, and lived in it. But the embroidery wasn't there. Instead, she found a small clump of tightly curling, short black hairs, picked them out and studied them. At which moment she saw the panel, its rich blood reds muddled on the floor behind the chair.

Down went the hairs; she scooped up the embroidery and spread it out to see if it had sustained an injury, but, though a little creased, it was fine. How odd!

Then, the answer occurring to her, her lips tightened. That Nosey Parker of a landlord of hers who lived in the apartment below had been snooping. Only what could one do about it? His wife was so nice; so too was he in his way. And where else would she get a fully furnished apartment for seventy a month in a safe neighborhood? The hairs went into her trash bin in the kitchen, and she settled, feet under her, in the big old chair to continue with what she privately considered the best piece of embroidery she'd ever done. A complicated, curving pattern of several reds from pinkish to blackish on a background of pale pink silk.

But bugger her landlord! He deserved a booby trap.

Tamara, tired of the painting, her imagination incapable for once of envisioning a face ugly enough, terrifying enough. It would come, but not tonight. Not so soon after today's disaster. That insolent cop Delmonico, his bullish walk, the shoulders so broad that he looked much shorter than he was, the neck so huge that on anyone else the head would have been dwarfed—but not his head. Massive. Yet try though she would, eyes shut, teeth clenched, she couldn't make his face assume a piggish cast. And after he made her miss her appointment, she wanted badly to paint him as the ugliest pig in creation.

She couldn't sleep, and what else was there to do? Read one of her whodunits for the millionth time? She flopped into a big magenta leather chair and reached for the phone.

"Darling?" she asked when a drowsy voice answered.

"I've told you, never call me here!"

Click. The line went back to its dial tone.

*   *   *

Cecil, lying in bed with his cheek on Albertia's beautiful breast, trying to forget Jimmy's terror.

Otis, listening to the rhythmic beep-beep-beep of his own heart, the tears rolling down his seamed face. No more lead bricks to move, no more cylinders of gas to wriggle onto a dolly, no more cages to shove into the elevator. How much would his pension be?

Wesley, too happy and excited to sleep. How Mohammed had straightened up at his news! Suddenly the hick postulant from Louisiana loomed important; he, Wesley le Clerc, had been given the job of keeping Mohammed el Nesr informed about the murder of a black woman at the Hug. He was on his way.

Nur Chandra, exiled to his cottage in the grounds where only he and his whipping boy, Misrarthur, ever came. He sat, legs crossed and braided, hands on his knees with palms upraised, each finger precisely positioned. Not asleep, but not awake either. A different place, a different plane. There were monsters to be banished, terrible monsters.

Maurice and Catherine Finch, sitting in the kitchen poring over the accounts.

"Mushrooms, schmushrooms!" said Catherine. "They'll cost you more than you can make, Maurie, and my chickens won't eat them."

"But it's something different to do, sweetheart! You said yourself that digging out the tunnel was good exercise, and now it's dug, what have I got to lose by trying? Exotic varieties for a few exclusive shops in New York City."

"It'll cost a lot of money," she said stubbornly.

"Cathy, we're not short of a dime! No kids of our own—for why do we need to worry about money? What are your nieces and my nephews going to do about this place, huh? Sell it, Cathy, sell it! So let's get all the fun we can out of it first."

"Okay, okay, grow your mushrooms! Only don't say I didn't warn you!"

He smiled, reached over to squeeze her roughened hand. "I promise I won't gripe if it fails, but I just don't think it is going to fail."

CHAPTER 2

Carmine's day began in Commissioner John Silvestri's office, where he sat in the middle of a semicircle around the desk. On his left were Captain Danny Marciano and Sergeant Abe Goldberg, on his right Dr. Patrick O'Donnell and Sergeant Corey Marshall.

Not for the first time by any means, Carmine thanked his lucky stars for the two men senior to himself in the hierarchy.

Dark and handsome, John Silvestri was a desk cop, had always been a desk cop, and confidently expected that when he retired in five years' time, he would be able to say that he had never drawn his side arm in a fracas, let alone fired a rifle or a shotgun. Which was odd, since he had joined the U.S. Army in 1941 as a lieutenant and emerged in 1945 bedaubed with decorations, including the Congressional Medal of Honor. His most irritating habit concerned cigars, which he sucked rather than smoked, leaving slimy butts in his wake to impart an odor to the air Carmine fancied might resemble the odor given off by a spittoon in an 1890s Dodge City saloon.

Fully aware that Danny Marciano hated the cigar butts most, Silvestri loved to push his ashtray under Marciano's snub nose; north Italian blood had given Marciano a fair and freckled complexion and blue eyes, and sitting at a desk had given him a few extra pounds. A good second man who lacked the cunning patience to wind up the Commissioner.

They left Carmine and his two fellow lieutenants to get on with the real police work, ignored political pressures from Town, Gown and Hartford, and could be relied upon to go to bat for their men. That Carmine was their favorite everybody knew; hardly any resentment stemmed from that fact because what it really meant was that Carmine inherited the ticklish cases requiring diplomacy or liaison with other law enforcement agencies. He was also the department's top murder man.

He had just finished his freshman year at Chubb when Pearl Harbor was attacked, so he postponed his education and enlisted. By sheer chance he was seconded to the military police, and once he got past guard duty and arresting drunken soldiers he found that he loved the work; there were as many violent or crafty crimes in the teeming wartime army as on the streets of any city. When the war and an occupation stint in Japan were over, he was a major, eligible to complete his degree at Chubb under an accelerated program. Then, a sheepskin in his hand that would have let him teach English literature or mathematics, he decided that he liked police work best. In 1949 he joined the Holloman Police. Silvestri, a deskbound lieutenant at the time, soon spotted his potential and put him in Detectives, where he was now the senior lieutenant. Holloman was not big enough to have a homicide squad or any of the subdivisions larger city police forces had, so Carmine might find himself working all kinds of crime. However, murder was his speciality and he had a formidable solve rate: just about a hundred percent—not all convicted, of course.

He sat looking eager yet relaxed; this would be *juicy*.

"You go first, Patsy," said Silvestri, who disliked the Hug case already because it was certain to become high profile. Only a small paragraph in the *Holloman Post* this morning, but as soon as the details leaked, it would be front-page news.

"I can tell you," said Patrick, "that whoever dumped the torso in the Hug's dead animal refrigerator left no fingerprints, fibers or any other trace of himself. The victim is in her middle teens, and has some colored blood. She's small in size, and she looks well cared for." He leaned forward in his chair, eyes glistening. "On her right buttock she has a heart-shaped scab. A nevus, removed around ten days ago. However, it wasn't a pigmented birthmark, it was a hemangioma— a tumor made up of blood vessels. The killer used a pair of diathermy forceps to nip off every feeder to the growth, coagulate it. Must have taken him hours. Then he packed it with gelfoam to assist clotting, and after that he let the wound crust over, get nice and dry. I found traces of what I thought was an oil-based ointment, but it wasn't." He drew a deep breath. "It was greasepaint exactly the same color as her skin."

Carmine's own skin began to creep; he shivered. "She still didn't look perfect after he removed the birthmark, so he covered it with greasepaint to *make* her perfect. Oh, Patsy, this is one weird dude!"

"Yeah," said Patrick.

"So he's a surgeon?" asked Marciano, pushing Silvestri's ashtray and its contents away from his nose.

"Not necessarily" from Carmine. "Yesterday I talked to a lady who does *micro*surgery on the Hug's animals. She doesn't have a medical degree. There are probably dozens of technicians in any big center for research like the Chubb Medical School who can operate as well as any surgeon. For that matter, until Patsy just told us how the guy coagulated the bleeding nevus, I was considering butchers and slaughtermen. Now I think I can safely rule them out."

"But you do think that the Hug's involved," said Silvestri, picking up the disgusting cigar and sucking on it.

"I do."

"What's next?"

Carmine got up, nodding to Corey and Abe. "Missing Persons. Probably statewide. Holloman doesn't have one on the files unless the killer held her for much longer than it took him to do what he did. Because we don't know what she looked like, we'll concentrate on the birthmark."

Patrick walked out with him. "You won't break this one in a hurry," he said. "The bastard's left you nothing to go on."

"Don't I know it. If that monkey hadn't woken up in an icehouse, we wouldn't even know a crime had been committed."

Holloman's Missing Persons having yielded nothing, Carmine began to phone around the other police departments in the state. The State cops had found the body of a ten-year-old girl in the woods just off the Appalachian Trail—a big, part-colored child reported missing by camping parents. But she had died of a cardiac arrest, and there were no suspicious circumstances.

The Norwalk police came up with a missing sixteen-year-old girl of Dominican extraction named Mercedes Alvarez, who had disappeared ten days ago.

"Five feet tall, curly but not kinky dark hair, dark brown eyes—a real pretty face—mature figure," said someone who had announced himself as Lieutenant Joe Brown. "Oh, and a large heart-shaped birthmark on her right buttock."

"Don't go away, Joe, I'll be there in half an hour."

He put the flashing light on the Ford's roof and gunned the car down I-95, siren screaming; the forty miles took him slightly more than twenty minutes.

Lieutenant Joe Brown was around his own age, early forties, and more excited than Carmine had expected him to be. Brown was on edge, so were the other cops in the vicinity. Carmine studied the color photo in the file, looked for the reference to the birthmark, which some untutored hand had attempted to sketch.

"She's our girl, all right," he said. "Man, she's pretty! Fill me in, Joe."

"She's a sophomore at St. Martha's High School—good grades, no trouble, no boyfriends. It's a Dominican family been here in Norwalk for twenty years—the father's a toll collector on the Turnpike, the mother's a housewife. Six kids—two boys, four girls. Mercedes is—was—the eldest. Youngest is three, a boy. They live in a quiet old neighborhood, mind their own business."

"Did anyone see Mercedes abducted?" Carmine asked.

"No one. We busted our asses to find her because"—he paused, looked worried—"she was the second girl of that type to go missing within two months. Both sophomores at St. Martha's, in the same class, friends but not bosom buddies, if you get me. Mercedes had piano practice after school finished, was due home at four-thirty. When she didn't turn up by six and the nuns said she had definitely left when she was supposed to, Mr. Alvarez called us. They were already upset over Verina."

"Verina was the first girl?"

"Yeah. Verina Gascon. A Creole family from Guadeloupe, been here a long time too. She disappeared on her way to school. Both families live within walking distance of St. Martha's, just a block away in either direction. We ransacked Norwalk looking for Verina, but she'd gone without a trace. And now this one, the same."

"Any possibility either girl took off with a secret boyfriend?"

"Nope," Brown said emphatically. "Maybe you should see both families, then you'd understand better. They're old-fashioned Latin Catholics, bring their kids up strict but with lots of love."

"I'll see them, but not yet," said Carmine, shrinking inside. "Can you organize Mr. Alvarez to identify Mercedes on the basis of the birthmark? We can't show him more than a tiny patch of skin, but he'll have to know beforehand that—"

"Yeah, yeah, *I* get the job of telling the poor bastard that someone chopped his beautiful little daughter into pieces," said Brown. "Oh, Jesus! Sometimes this is a shit job."

"Would their priest be willing to go with him?"

"I'll make sure. And maybe a nun or two for extra support."

Someone came in with coffee and jelly doughnuts; both men wolfed down a couple, drank thirstily. While he waited for copies of the files of both girls, Carmine called Holloman.

Corey, said Abe, was already at the Hug, and he himself was about to see Dean Wilbur Dowling to find out how many dead animal refrigerators existed within the medical school.

"Did we get any other missing persons who might have fitted our girl's description?" Carmine asked, feeling better for the food.

"Yeah, three. One from Bridgeport, one from New Britain, and one from Hartford. But when none of them had the birthmark, we didn't follow up. They all happened months ago," said Abe.

"Things have taken a turn, Abe. Call Bridgeport, Hartford and New Britain back, and tell them to send us copies of those files as fast as a siren can travel."

When Carmine walked in, Abe and Corey got up from their desks and followed him into his office, where three files lay waiting. Down went the two files Carmine carried; he unclipped the five photographs, all in color, and laid them out in a row. Like sisters.

Nina Gomez was a sixteen-year-old Guatemalan girl from Hartford, and had disappeared four months ago. Rachel Simpson was a sixteen-year-old light-skinned black girl from Bridgeport, disappeared six months ago. Vanessa Olivaro was a sixteen-year-old girl from New Britain of mixed Chinese, black and white blood whose parents hailed from Jamaica; she had disappeared eight months ago.

"Our killer likes curly but not kinky hair, faces that are fantastically pretty in a certain way—full but well-delineated lips, wide set and wide open dark eyes, a dimpled smile—a height of no more than five feet, a mature figure, and light but not white skin," Carmine said, flicking the photos.

"You really think the same guy snatched them all?" Abe asked, not wanting to believe it.

"Oh, sure. Look at their backgrounds. God-fearing, respectable families, all Catholic except for Rachel Simpson, whose father is an

Episcopalian minister. Simpson and Olivaro went to their local high schools, the other three went to Catholic high schools, two at the same one, St. Martha's in Norwalk. Then there's the time span. One every two months. Corey, go back to the phone and ask for all missing persons who fit this description from as far back as—say, ten years. The background is as important as the physical criteria, so I'd be willing to bet that all these girls were famous for—well, if chasteness is too old-fashioned a word, at least *goodness*. They probably volunteered for things like Meals on Wheels or were candy stripers in some hospital. Never missed on church, did their homework, kept their hems at knee level, maybe wore a touch of lipstick, but never full makeup."

"The girls you're describing are thin on the ground, Carmine," Corey said, his dark and beaky face serious. "If he's snatched one every two months, he must waste a lot of time finding her. Look at how far afield he's gone. Norwalk, Bridgeport, Hartford, New Britain—why no girls from Holloman? Mercedes at least was dumped in Holloman."

"They're all dumped in Holloman. We've only got five girls so far, Corey. We won't know his pattern until we've traced him back as far as he goes. In Connecticut, at any rate."

Abe swallowed audibly, his fair, broken-nosed countenance pale and sick looking. "But we're not going to find any of the bodies prior to Mercedes, are we? He cut them up and put the pieces in at least one dead animal refrigerator, and from there they went to the medical school incinerator."

"I'm sure you're right, Abe," said Carmine, who to his loyal and most constant companions looked unusually cast down. No matter what the case, Carmine sailed through it and over it with the ponderous grace and power of a battle wagon. He felt—he bled—he pitied—he understood—but until this case he had let nothing burrow in as far as his central core.

"What else does all this tell you, Carmine?" Corey asked.

"That he's gotten a picture of perfection in his mind's eye that these girls resemble, but that there's always something wrong with each of them. Like the birthmark on Mercedes. Maybe one of them told him to go fuck himself—he'd hate language like that coming from virginal lips. But what he gets off on is their suffering, like any rapist. That's why I don't honestly know if we should be cataloging him as a killer or a rapist. Oh, he's both, but how does his mind work? What's the real purpose of what he does to *him?*"

Carmine grimaced. "We know what kind of victim he likes and that they're relatively rare, but ghosts are more visible than he is. In Norwalk, with two abductions on their plate, the cops have busted their asses looking for prowlers, peeping Toms, strangers on the street around the school, strangers contacting the school or the families. They've looked at everybody from United Way collectors to garbage collectors to postmen to encyclopedia salesmen to people purporting to be Mormons, Jehovah's Witnesses or any other proselytizing religious group. Meter readers, council workers, tree surgeons, power and phone linesmen. They actually formed a think tank and tried to work out how he might have gotten close enough to abduct the girls, but so far they've come up with zilch. No one remembers anything that might help."

Corey got to his feet. "I'll start calling around," he said.

"Okay, Abe, fill me in on the Hug," Carmine said.

Out came Abe's notepad. "There are thirty people on the Hug staff, if you count Professor Smith at one end and Allodice Miller the bottle washer at the other end." He fished two pieces of paper from a file folder under his elbow and handed them to Carmine. "Here's your copy of their names, ages, positions, how long they've worked there, and anything else I thought might be useful. The only one thought to have real surgical expertise is Sonia Liebman in the O.R. The two foreigners aren't even medically qualified, and Dr. Forbes said he passed out watching a circumcision."

He cleared his throat, flipped a page over. "There are any number of people who wander in and out pretty much at will, but their faces are well known—animal care, salesmen, doctors from the medical school. Mitey Brite Scientific Cleaners have the contract to clean the Hug, which they do between midnight and 3 A.M. Mondays to Fridays, but they don't handle the hazardous waste. Otis Green does that. Apparently you have to be trained, which adds a few bucks to Otis's pay packet. I doubt that Mitey Brite have anything to do with the crime because Cecil Potter walks back to the Hug at 9 P.M. each evening and locks animal care up better than Fort Knox in case a cleaner pokes around in there. It's his babies—the monkeys. They hear the slightest noise at night, they raise a helluva rumpus."

"Thanks for that, Abe. I hadn't thought of Mitey Brite." Carmine looked at Abe with great affection. "Any impressions of the inmates worth reporting?"

"They make godawful coffee," said Abe, "and some smart-ass in neurochemistry fills a beaker with these delicious-looking candies— pink, yellow, green. But they're not candies, they're polystyrene packing material."

"You got caught."

"I got caught."

"Anything else?"

"Negative information only. You can rule Allodice the bottle washer out—too dumb. I doubt the bags were put in the fridge while Cecil and Otis were on duty. Later in the day, is my bet."

"What about the possible number of dump sites?"

"I finally found seven different dead animal refrigerators, excluding the Hug's. Dean Dowling wasn't amused to have to talk to a cop about something so far underneath his job description, and no one seemed to have a list. No way any of them once I found them would have been as easy as using the Hug's—all more public, busier. Man, they must get through millions of rats! I hate 'em alive, but I hate 'em dead a lot worse after today. I'm putting my money on the Hug."

"So am I, Abe, so am I."

Carmine spent the rest of his day at his desk studying the case files until he could recite them off by heart. Each was fairly thick because of the quality of the victims. Clearly the police of each city had put a great deal more work into their investigations than was usual; the average sixteen-year-old girl who disappeared had a reputation (sometimes a rap sheet) that fitted in with disappearance. But not these girls. The pity of it is, thought Carmine, that we don't liaise with each other enough. If we did, we might have gotten on to this guy earlier. However, no body and there's no physical evidence of murder. No matter how many bodies there have been—and I won't know that for a while yet—I know that they wound up in the medical school incinerator. So much safer than, say, burying them in the woods. Connecticut has plenty of forests, but they're *used,* they're not limitless like Washington State forests.

My gut instinct says that he's keeping their heads as memorabilia. Or else if he disposes of their heads too, he's got the girls on film. Super-8 in color, maybe several cameras to catch every angle of their suffering, his own power. I *know* he's a memorabilia man. This is his private fantasy, he'll be compelled to record it. So he's either filming it or he's keeping the heads in a freezer or in glass jars of formalin. How many cases have I investigated involving memorabilia? Five. But never a multiple killer. That is so rare! And the others left me evidence. This guy doesn't. When he looks at his films or his heads, what does he feel? Exultation? Disappointment? Excitement? Remorse? I wish I knew, but I don't.

When he went into Malvolio's to eat dinner he sat in his usual booth aware that he wasn't hungry, even if he knew he had to eat. Early days; he had to keep his strength up for this one.

The waitress was a new girl, so he had to let her write it down, from the Yankee pot roast to the rice pudding. A beautiful girl, but not his killer's type; the way she eyed Carmine up and down was a blatant invitation that he ignored. Sorry, baby, he said silently, those days are over. Though she did remind him a little of Sandra: a looker marking time for some better job like acting or modeling. New York City was just down the road.

How many things had happened in 1950! He was a brand-new detective; the Hug was built; the Holloman Hospital was built; and Sandra Tolley had come to wait on table at Malvolio's. She had knocked him off his feet at first glance. Tall, stacked like Jane Russell, legs six feet long, a mass of gold hair and wide, myopic eyes in a gorgeous face. Full of herself and the career she knew she was going to have as a model; she'd put her portfolio in to all the New York agencies, but couldn't afford to live there. So she had moved a two-hour train ride into Connecticut, where she could rent for less than thirty dollars a month and eat for free if she was a waitress.

And then all her ambitions went west because the sight of Carmine Delmonico had knocked her off her feet too. Not that he was handsome or more than acceptably tall at five-eleven, but he had the kind of beat-up face that women adored, and a body bulging with natural muscle. They met at New Year's; they were married within the month; and she was pregnant within three. Sophia, their daughter, was born right at the end of 1950. In those days he'd rented a nice house in East Holloman, which was the Italian quarter of town, thinking that if he surrounded Sandra with hordes of his relatives and friends she wouldn't feel so alone when his job kept him working long hours. But she was from Montana ranching stock, and neither understood nor liked the way of life that East Holloman practiced. When Carmine's mother called in to see her, Sandra thought that Mom was checking up on her, and by extension she saw all the kind visits and invitations from his family circle and his friends as evidence that they didn't trust her to behave.

There was never a genuine quarrel, or even much discontent. The baby was the image of her mother, which pleased everyone; no one knows better than the Italians that they paint the angels fair.

As a matter of course Carmine was in line for free tickets whenever a play on tryout for Broadway had its final airing at the Schumann Theater; at the end of 1951, when Sophia was a year old, his turn for free tickets came. The attraction was an important play that had already received rave reviews from tryouts in Boston and

Philadelphia, so everyone from New York City would be there. Sandra was ecstatic, dug out her most glamorous strapless dress, cyclamen satin that fitted like a second skin and then flared at the knees, a white mink stole to keep her warm against what was a cold winter. She pressed Carmine's dinner suit, frilled shirt and cummerbund and bought him a gardenia for his buttonhole. Oh, how excited she had been! Like a kid going to Disneyland.

A case intruded and he couldn't go. Looking back on it, he was glad now that he hadn't seen her face when she found out; he had called her on the phone. Sorry, honey, I have to work tonight. But she went to the play anyway, all on her own in the cyclamen satin strapless dress and the white mink wrap. When she told him later that night, he hadn't minded a bit. But what she didn't tell him was that she had met Myron Mendel Mandelbaum the movie producer in the Schumann's foyer, and that Mandelbaum had usurped Carmine's seat, though his own was in a box much nearer to the stage.

A week later Carmine came home to find Sandra and Sophia gone, a brief note on the mantel to say that Sandra had fallen in love with Myron and was taking the train to Reno; Myron was divorced already and wanted desperately to marry her. Sophia was the icing on the wedding cake, as Myron couldn't have children.

It came like a bolt from the blue to Carmine, who hadn't begun to realize how unhappy his wife was. He didn't do any of the things wronged husbands were supposed to do. He didn't try to kidnap his daughter, beat up Myron Mendel Mandelbaum, take to the bottle, or fail to give of his best to his work. Not for want of encouragement; his outraged family would have done the first two of those things for him gladly, and couldn't understand why he wouldn't let them. Simply, he admitted to himself that his had been a misalliance based on profound physical attraction and nothing else. Sandra wanted glamour, glitz, gallivanting, a life he wouldn't give her. His pay was good but not princely, and he was too in love with his job to lavish attention on his wife. In many ways, he decided, Sandra and Sophia would be better off in California. Oh, but it hurt! A hurt he mentioned to no one, even Patrick (who guessed), just buried deeper than remembrance.

Every August he went to L.A. to see Sophia, for he loved his daughter dearly. But this year's visit had revealed to him a burgeoning facsimile of Sandra, limo'd every day to a fancy school where booze, pot, cocaine and LSD were easier to buy than candy, bored by possessions. Poor Sandra had become a cokehead on the Hollywood party circuit; it was Myron who tried to give the child a life, out of his depth though he was. Luckily Sophia shared some of her father's inquisitiveness, was intellectually bright, and had gained a little wisdom from watching her mother's deterioration. Between them, Carmine and Myron had spent three weeks persuading Sophia that if she stayed off the booze, pot, cocaine and LSD and worked on her education, she wouldn't end like Sandra. Over the years Carmine had come to like Sandra's second husband more and more; this last trip had cemented a strong bond, the cause of which was Sophia.

"You ought to get married again, Carmine," Myron had said, "bring our little girl to some place saner than here. I'd miss her like hell, but I love her enough to know it would be better."

But, never again, Carmine had vowed after Sandra, and was as true to that vow today as ever. For sexual solace he had Antonia, a widowed remote cousin in Lyme; she had offered him this with great candor and no love.

"We can get our rocks off without driving each other crazy," she had said. "You don't need the shenanigans of a Sandra, and I can't ever replace Conway. So when you need it, or I need it, we can call each other."

An admirable arrangement that had lasted now for six years.

Patrick came into Malvolio's just as he was finishing his rice pudding, a creamy, succulent, sweet mush liberally laced with ribbons of nutmeg and cinnamon.

"How'd it go with Mr. Alvarez?" Carmine asked.

A shudder, a twisted grimace. "Terrible. He knew why we couldn't let him see more than the birthmark, but he begged and begged, cried so much that I had to hide my own tears. His priest and the couple of nuns were a blessing. They carried him out in a state of collapse."

"Have a whiskey on me."

"That's what I hoped you'd say."

Carmine ordered two double Irishes from the ogling waitress and said nothing more until Patrick had swallowed a good half of his drink and the color began to return to his fresh face.

"You know as well as I do that our kind of work hardens a man," Patrick said then, turning the glass between his hands, "but at least most of the time the crimes are sordid and the victims, even if pitiable, don't have the power to haunt our dreams. Oh, but this one! A downright preying on the innocent. The death of Mercedes is going to tear that family apart."

"It's worse than you know, Patsy," Carmine said, glanced about swiftly to make sure they couldn't be overheard, and told him of the four other girls.

"He's a *multiple?*"

"I'd stake my life on it."

"So he's cutting a swath through those in our society who least deserve to be preyed on. People who give no one any trouble, or cost governments money, or make nuisances of themselves phoning up about barking dogs, the party two doors down, or rude bastards in the IRS. People my Irish grandfather would have called the salt of the earth," said Patrick, finishing his drink in a gulp.

"I'd agree with you, except on one point. So far they're all part-colored, and there are some would take offense at that, as you well know. Despite long residence in Connecticut, their roots are Caribbean. Even Rachel Simpson from Bridgeport turns out to have been of Barbadian origins. So it begins to look as if there is some kind of racial vendetta involved."

Down went the empty glass with a thump; Patrick slid out of the booth. "I'm going home, Carmine. If I don't, I'll stay here and keep on drinking."

Carmine wasn't far behind his cousin; he paid his check, gave the waitress a two-dollar tip for Sandra's sake, and walked the half block to his apartment eight floors below Dr. Hideki Satsuma's penthouse in the Nutmeg Insurance building.

CHAPTER 3

B y Friday, the *Holloman Post* and other Connecticut papers were full of the murder of
Mercedes Alvarez and the disappearance of
Verina Gascon, also feared dead, but no sharp reporter had yet picked
up on police vibes that they were dealing with a multiple rapist/killer
of carefully reared, sheltered, teenage girls—or that Caribbean origins might play a part.

There was a message on Carmine's desk that Otis Green was out
of the hospital, at his home, and anxious to see him. Another said
Patrick also wanted to see him. Abe was in Bridgeport making
enquiries about Rachel Simpson, and Corey had been given the
double job of Nina Gomez in Hartford and Vanessa Olivaro in New
Britain. As Guatemala had one coast on the Caribbean, the new
emphasis was definitely Caribbean.

Since Patrick was just an elevator ride away, Carmine went to see
him first. He was in his office, his desk littered with brown paper
bags.

"I know you've seen plenty of these already, but you don't know as much about them as I do," Patrick said, waiting while his cousin poured freshly brewed coffee from a percolator.

"So tell me," said Carmine, sitting down.

"As you see, they do indeed come in all shapes and sizes." Patrick held up a specimen 12 x 6 inches. "This holds six hundred-gram rats, this rather larger one holds four two-hundred-fifty-gram rats. A researcher rarely uses rats bigger than two-hundred-fifty grams, but as rats continue to grow for as long as they live, they can get up to the size of a cat or even a small terrier. However, no one at the Hug uses rats that large." He held up a 24 x 18 inch bag. "For reasons that escape me, the Hug cats are all large male animals, just as the rats are all males. And the monkeys. This is a cat bag. I went over to the Hug first thing this morning and managed to have words"—not an unfair summary of the encounter, Carmine was sure—"with Miss Dupre, who deals with all purchasing *and* stock taking. The bags are specially made by a firm in Oregon. They consist of two layers of very stout brown paper separated by a three-millimeter-thick padding of fiber made from sugarcane bagasse. You'll note that there are two plastic discs on the outside of the bag. Fold the top of the bag over twice and the two discs lie in close proximity to each other. The picture wire on the top disc is twisted in a figure-of-eight around the bottom one and the bag can't come open. Same way you'd close an interdepartmental memo envelope, except that its tie is thread. A dead animal will keep inside a bag without body fluids leaking through for up to seventy-two hours, but no carcass is kept half so long in a bag. Any animals that die over the weekend aren't found until Monday unless the researcher is in over the weekend. He'll put the carcass in a bag, but then throws the bag into one of the freezers that dot his floor. His technician then takes it down to animal care on Monday morning, though it won't go to the incinerator until Tuesday morning."

Carmine held a bag up to his nose and sniffed intently. "I see that they're treated with a deodorant."

"Correct, as Miss Dupre would put it. What a snooty bitch!"

✦

"It's just too much!" cried the Prof to Carmine when they met in the Hug foyer. "Did you read what that antivivisectionist idiot wrote in the *Holloman Post?* We medical researchers are pure sadists, indeed! It's your fault, trumpeting about the murder!"

Carmine had a temper, usually well controlled, but this was more than he could stomach. "Considering," he said bitingly, "that I'm only here in the Hug because a number of innocent young girls have suffered as I'm darned sure no animal ever has in the Hug, you would do better to focus your attention on rape and murder than on antivivisectionism, sir! Where the hell are your priorities?"

Smith rocked. *"A number?* You mean more than one?"

Sit on your rage, Carmine, don't let this introverted specimen of splendid isolation get under your skin! "Yes, I mean a number! Yes, I mean more than one—many more! You have to know, Professor, but the information is strictly classified. It's high time you took this seriously, because your singularity is anything but a singularity! It's multiple! Hear me? Multiple!"

"You must be mistaken!"

"I am not," Carmine snarled. "Grow up! Antivivisectionism is the least of your worries, so don't come whining to me!"

There were three-family houses in the Hollow in far worse condition than Otis's. Around Fifteenth Street, where Mohammed el Nesr and his Black Brigade lived, the houses had been gutted, their windows boarded up with plywood, their walls inside lined with mattresses. Here on Eleventh Street was shabbiness, peeling paint, evidence that the absentee landlords didn't bother with maintenance, but when a still simmering Carmine trod up the stairs to the Green's apartment on the second floor he found what he had expected to find: clean premises, nice homemade drapes and dust covers on the upholstery, polished wooden surfaces, rugs on the floor.

Otis lay on the sofa, a man of about fifty-five years, fairly trim but with enough loose skin to suggest that at one time he had carried forty pounds more than he did now. His wife, Celeste, hovered aggressively. She was somewhat younger than Otis and dressed with a certain elegant flashiness that fell into place after he learned she was from Louisiana. Frenchified. A third person cluttered up the room, a young, very black man with the same mannerisms as Celeste, though he utterly lacked her looks or her way with clothes; he was introduced as Wesley le Clerc, Celeste's nephew and the Green's boarder. The look in his eyes told Carmine that he had a very big racial chip on his shoulder.

Neither wife nor her nephew was willing to leave, but Carmine didn't have to exert his authority: Otis exerted his.

"Go away and leave us be," he said curtly.

Both of them left immediately, Celeste with warnings of what would happen to Carmine if he upset her husband.

"You have a loyal family," said Carmine as he perched on a large, clear plastic ottoman filled with red plastic roses.

"I got a loyal *wife*" from Otis, followed by a snort. "That kid's a menace. Wants to make a name for hisself in the Black Brigade, says he's found the prophet Mohammed an' is gonna call hisself Ali somethin' or other. It's the roots thing, like with any people stolen in millions, but far as I know, the le Clercs come from a part of Africa worshipped King Kong, not Allah. I am an old-fashioned man, Lieutenant, don't hold with tryin' to be someone I ain't. I go to the Baptist church an' Celeste goes to the Catholic church. I been a black man in a white man's army, but if the Germans and the Japs had won, I'd a been a helluva lot worse off, is how I see it. I got a little money in the bank, an' when I retire, I am goin' back to Georgia to farm. I had it up to here"—he put his hand to his throat—"with Connecticut winters. Still an' all, that's not why I wanted to see you, sir."

"Why did you want to see me, Mr. Green?"

"Otis. To get it outta the way. How many people know what I found in that fridge?"

"Hardly any, and we're trying to keep it that way."

"It was a little girl, wasn't it?"

"No. Not a child, at any rate. We know she was from a family of Dominicans, and we know she was sixteen years old."

"So she black, not white."

"I'd prefer to say she was neither, Otis. A mixture."

"Lieutenant, this is a terrible sin!"

"Yes, it is."

Carmine paused while Otis muttered under his breath, let him calm down, then broached the subject of bags.

"Is there a usual pattern to the number and size of the bags in the fridge, Otis?"

"I guess so," Otis said after some thought. "I mean, I know when Mrs. Liebman's doin' decerebrations 'cos there's four to six cat bags. Otherwise, it's mostly rat bags. If a macaque dies, the way we thought Jimmy had, then there's a real big bag, but I will always know what's in it 'cos Cecil will be cryin' his heart out."

"So when there are four to six cat bags in the fridge, you know that Mrs. Liebman has been decerebrating."

"'s right, Lieutenant."

"Can you remember any time in the past when there were four to six cat bags in the fridge that Mrs. Liebman couldn't have had anything to do with?"

Otis looked surprised, tried to sit up.

"You want your wife in jail for murdering me, Otis? Lie back down, man!"

"About six months ago. Six cat bags when Mrs. Liebman was away on vacation. I remember wonderin' who was fillin' in for her, but then I was needed, so I just threw them bags into my bin an' wheeled them off to the incinerator."

Carmine rose. "That's a great help. Thanks, Otis."

The visitor hadn't let himself out of the downstairs front door before Celeste and Wesley were back.

"You okay?" Celeste demanded.

"Better than before he came," said Otis sturdily.

"What color's the body?" Wesley demanded. "Did the cop say?"

"Not white, but not black either."

"A mulatto?"

"He didn't say that. That's a Louisiana word, Wes."

"Mulatto's black, not white," said Wesley with satisfaction.

"Don't you go makin' mountains outta molehills!" Otis cried.

"I gotta see Mohammed" was Wesley's rejoinder. He zipped himself into his black imitation leather jacket with the white fist painted on its back.

"You're not seeing Mohammed, boy, you're going to work this minute! You do not qualify for welfare and I am not boarding you for nothing!" Celeste snapped. "Go on, shoo!"

Sighing, Wesley divested himself of his passport to Mohammed el Nesr's headquarters at 18 Fifteenth Street, put on a down jacket instead, and hied himself off in his battered 1953 De Soto to Parson Surgical Instruments. Where, if he had bothered to enquire, which he didn't, he could have discovered that his dexterity at crafting mosquito forceps had more than once made the difference between continued employment and a pink slip.

For Carmine the day was depressing and bitter; the missing persons files that fitted the Mercedes description were beginning to arrive on his desk. Six more, to be exact, one every two months throughout 1964: Waterbury, Holloman, Middletown, Danbury, Meriden and Torrington. The only place where he had repeated himself in nearly two years was Norwalk. Every girl was sixteen years old and of mixed-blood originating in the Caribbean, though never a family of recent immigrants. Puerto Rico, Jamaica, the Bahamas, Trinidad, Martinique, Cuba. Five feet tall, stunningly pretty, of mature figure, extremely carefully reared. All the new arrivals on his desk were Catholic, though not all had gone to Catholic schools. None had had a boyfriend, all were straight-A students and popular with their classmates. More importantly, none had confided in a friend or a member of her family about having a new friend, or a new kind of good deed to practice, or even a new acquaintance.

At 3 P.M. he climbed alone into the Ford and started down I-95 to Norwalk, where Lieutenant Joe Brown had arranged for him to see the Alvarez family in their home. He couldn't be there himself, he was quick to add; Carmine knew why. Joe couldn't face another session with the Alvarezes.

The house was a three-family one that José Alvarez owned; he lived in the bottom-floor apartment with his wife and children, and rented out the middle and top-floor apartments. This was how all working people aspired to live: virtually rent free themselves, the middle apartment paying the mortgage and utilities, and the top one bringing in that little extra against repairs as well as to save for rainy days. Living on the bottom floor, they had the backyard, half of the four-car garage, and the basement for their own use. And a landlord who lived on the premises was able to keep a stern eye on the tenants.

Like all its neighbors, the house was painted a darkish grey, had double windows whose outer sets were replaced in summer by insect screens, a front porch right on the sidewalk, but a big backyard surrounded by a high chain-link fence; the garage sat across its back beyond a driveway down one side of the house. As Carmine stood on the oak-lined street looking, he could hear the baying of a large dog; scant chance of anyone's breaking in via the back porch with a hound on patrol.

The priest opened the front door, which was separate from the door leading to the two upstairs apartments. Carmine gave the cleric a smile and shrugged himself out of his overcoat.

"I'm sorry to have to do this, Father," he said. "My name is Carmine Delmonico. Should I be Lieutenant or Carmine in there?"

After some consideration the priest said, "Lieutenant would be better, I think. I'm Bart Tesoriero."

"Do you need to speak Spanish in your parish?"

Father Tesoriero opened the inner door. "No, though I do have a fair number of Hispanic parishioners. It's an old part of town, they've all been here a long time. No Hell's Kitchen, that's for sure."

The living room, quite a large one in this bottom apartment, was full of people and silence. Himself of Latin origins, Carmine knew that relatives would have come from everywhere to be with the Alvarezes in their time of need. This meant that he knew how to deal with them, but he didn't have to. The priest ushered all save the immediate family into the kitchen, with a woman who looked like the grandmother leading a toddling boy.

That left José Alvarez, his wife, Concita, their eldest son, Luís, and three daughters—Maria, Dolores and Teresa—in the room. Father Tesoriero put Carmine in the best chair, and himself sat between husband and wife.

It was a home of lace doilies, lace curtains under drapes of synthetic velvet, respectably well-worn furniture and floors tiled in terra-cotta beneath busy rugs. The walls bore pictures of the Last Supper, the Sacred Heart of Jesus, Mary holding the Christ Child, and many framed photographs of the family. Vases of flowers were everywhere, each bearing a card; the perfume of freesias and jonquils was so heavy Carmine felt choked. Where did florists get them at this time of year? On the center of the mantelpiece was a silver-framed photograph of Mercedes, in front of it a burning candle in a red glass bowl.

The first thing Carmine did when he entered a house of grief was to imagine how the bereaved must have looked before tragedy struck. Nigh impossible here, but nothing could alter bone structure. Strikingly handsome, all of them, and all with that café au lait skin color. A little Negro, a little Caribbean Indian, a great deal of Spanish. The parents were probably in their late thirties, but looked a decade and more older than that, sitting like two rag dolls in their own ghastly world. Neither of them seemed to see him.

"Luís, is it?" he asked the boy, whose eyes were swollen and reddened from tears.

"Yes."

"How old are you?"

"Fourteen."

"And your sisters? How old are they?"

"Maria is twelve, Dolores is ten, and Teresa is eight."

"Your baby brother?"

"Francisco is three."

By now the boy was weeping again, the dreary, hopeless tears that can only fall after too many have gone before them. His sisters lifted their faces from soaked handkerchiefs for a moment, their little bony knees clenched together under the margins of matching plaid pleated skirts like pairs of ivory skulls. Shaken by great hiccoughs, they sat and writhed from the pain of it, the terrible shock that was now wearing itself down to exhaustion after the days of worry and then the news that Mercedes was dead, cut into pieces. Of course no one had intended that they should find that out, but they had.

"Luís, could you take your sisters into the kitchen, then come back for a minute?"

The father, he saw, had finally focused on his face, viewing it with confused wonder.

"Mr. Alvarez, would you rather we postponed this for a few more days?" Carmine asked softly.

"No," the father whispered, dry-eyed. "We will manage."

Yes, but can I?

Luís returned, tears gone.

"Just the same old questions, Luís. I know you've already been asked them a million times, but memories can bury themselves and then suddenly come back for no reason, which is why I'm asking them again. I understand that you and Mercedes went to different schools, but I've been told that you were great pals. Girls as pretty as Mercedes get noticed, that's natural. Did she ever complain about being noticed? Followed? Watched from a car or by someone on the other side of the street?"

"No, Lieutenant, honestly. Boys would wolf-whistle her, but she ignored them."

"What about when she worked as a candy striper last summer?"

"She never said anything to me that wasn't about the patients and how nice the sisters were to her. They only let her into the maternity hospital. She loved it."

He was beginning to weep again: time to stop. Carmine smiled and nodded toward the kitchen.

"I apologize," he said to Mr. Alvarez when the boy was gone.

"We realize that you must ask and ask, Lieutenant."

"Was Mercedes a confiding child, sir? Did she discuss things with her mother or with you?"

"She confided in both of us all the time. Her life pleased her, she loved to talk about it." A great spasm went through him, he had to cling to the arms of his chair to suppress it. The eyes that stared into Carmine's own were transfixed with pain, while the mother's seemed to stare into the depths of Hell. "Lieutenant, we have been told what was done to her, but it is almost impossible to believe. We have been told that Mercedes is your case, that you know more about what happened to her than the Norwalk police do." His voice went thin with urgency. "Please, I *beg* you, tell me! Did she—did my little girl suffer?"

Carmine swallowed, impaled on those eyes. "Only God really knows the answer, but I don't think God could be so cruel. A murder of this kind needn't be done to watch the victim suffer. The man may well have given Mercedes drugs to make her sleep through it. Of one thing you can be sure: it was not God's purpose to make her suffer. If you believe in God, then believe that she didn't suffer."

And God forgive me for that lie, but how could I tell this devastated father the truth? He sits there, dead in mind, dead in spirit, sixteen years of love, care, worry, joy and minor sorrows gone up like a puff of smoke from a incinerator. Why should I share my opinion of God with him and make his loss worse? He has to pick up the pieces and continue; there are five other children who need him, and a wife whose heart isn't merely broken—it's mashed to pulp.

"Thank you," said Mrs. Alvarez suddenly.

"Thank you for bearing with me," Carmine said.

"You comforted them immeasurably," said Father Tesoriero on the way to the door. "But Mercedes did suffer, didn't she?"

"My guess is, beyond description. It's hard to be in my line of work and believe in God, Father."

Two journalists had appeared on the street, one with a microphone, the other with a notepad. When Carmine emerged they ran toward him, only to be roughly shoved away.

"Fuck off, you vultures!" he snarled, climbed into the Ford and drove away in a hurry.

Several blocks later, sure no reporters were on his tail, he pulled to the side of the road and let his feelings overwhelm him. Did she suffer? Yes, yes, yes, she suffered! She suffered hideously, and he made sure she stayed awake for all of it. Her last glimpse of life must have been her own blood flowing down a drain hole, but her family must never know that. I've gone way beyond disbelief in God. I believe that the world belongs to the Devil. I believe that the Devil is infinitely more powerful than God. And the soldiers of goodness, if not of God, are losing the war.

CHAPTER 4

Monday, October 11th, 1965

As Columbus Day wasn't a public holiday, nothing impeded the gathering of the Hughlings Jackson Center for Neurological Research Board of Governors at 11 A.M. in the fourth-floor boardroom. Well aware that he hadn't been invited, Carmine had every intention of sitting in. So he arrived early, took a thin china mug to the hall coffee urn, helped himself to two jelly doughnuts on a thin china plate, and had the effrontery to sit in the far end chair, which he turned to face the window.

At least "effrontery" was what Miss Desdemona Dupre called it when she strode in to find him curling his tongue sensuously around the Board's goodies.

"You're lucky, you know" was Carmine's reply. "If the Holloman Hospital architects hadn't decided to put the parking lot in front of the building, you'd have no view at all. As it is, you can see all the way to Long Island. Isn't it a beautiful day? The fall is just about at its best, and while I mourn the passing of the elms, you can't beat maples for color. Their leaves have invented new shades at the warm end of the spectrum."

"I didn't realize you had either the words or the science to express yourself!" she snapped, eyes like ice. "You are sitting in the Governor-in-Chief's chair and partaking of refreshments to which you are not entitled! Kindly pick up your traps and go!"

At which moment the Prof walked in, propped at the sight of Lieutenant Delmonico, and sighed deeply. "Oh, dear, I hadn't thought of you," he said to Carmine.

"Whether you like it or not, Professor, I have to be here."

President Mawson MacIntosh of Chubb University arrived before the Prof could answer, beamed at Carmine and shook him warmly by the hand. "Carmine! I might have known that Silvestri would put you on this," said M.M., as he was universally known. "I am tremendously cheered. Here, sit next to me. And don't," he added in a conspiratorial whisper, "waste your tastebuds on the doughnuts. Try the apple Danish."

Miss Desdemona Dupre made a small sound of suppressed fury and marched out of the room, colliding with Dean Dowling and his own neurology professor, Frank Watson. He who authored "the Hug" and its staff of "Huggers."

M.M., whom Carmine knew well from several awkwardly delicate internal Chubb cases, looked far more imposing than that other President, he of the United States of America. M.M. was tall, perfectly dressed, trim in the waist, his handsome face crowned by a head of luxuriant hair whose original auburn had transformed to a wonderful apricot. An American aristocrat to his fingertips. Despite his height, L.B.J. paled to insignificance whenever the two men stood side by side, which they did occasionally. But persons of M.M.'s august lineage would far rather preside over a great university than over an undisciplined bunch of rowdies like Congress.

On the other hand, Dean Wilbur Dowling looked the psychiatrist he was: untidily dressed in a combination of tweed, flannel and a pink bow tie with red polka dots, he wore a bushy brown beard to counterbalance his egg-bald head, and stared at the world through horn-rimmed bifocals.

And on the few times that he had seen Frank Watson, Carmine was always reminded of Boris out of *The Adventures of Rocky and Bull-winkle.* Watson dressed in black and had a long, thin face whose upper lip bore a lounge-lizard's black mustache; sleek black hair and a permanent sneer completed the Boris similarity. Yes, Frank Watson was definitely the kind of person who drank regularly from a cup of vitriol. But surely he wasn't on the Hug's Board of Governors?

No, he wasn't. Watson ended his conversation with the Dean and slithered away with a metaphorical flourish of a black cape he wasn't wearing. Interesting guy, thought Carmine. I will have to see him.

The five Parson Governors trooped in as a group, and knew better than to query Carmine's presence when M.M. made a subtly effusive introduction.

"If anyone can get to the bottom of this unspeakable affair, Carmine Delmonico can," M.M. ended.

"Then I suggest," said Roger Parson Junior, taking the chair at the end of the table, "that we put ourselves at Lieutenant Delmonico's disposal. After, that is, he has told us precisely what has happened and what he intends to do in the future."

The Parson contingent looked so alike that anyone would have picked them as closely related; even the thirty years' difference in age between the three elderly and two youthful members of the clan made little difference. They were a trifle over medium height, thinly stooped, with long necks, beaky noses, prominent cheekbones, downturned mouths and scant heads of lank, indeterminately brown hair. Their eyes, to a man, were grey-blue. Now, M.M. looked like a regal tycoon, whereas the Parsons looked like academic paupers.

Carmine had spent some of his weekend in researching them and the Parson group of companies. William Parson, the founder (and uncle of the present Governor-in-Chief) had started with machine parts and parlayed his holdings until they stretched from motors to turbines, and surgical instruments through typewriters to artillery. The Parson Bank had come into being at exactly the right time to go from strength to strength. William Parson had left it rather late to marry. His wife produced one child, William Junior, who turned out to be mentally retarded and epileptic. The son died in 1945, aged seventeen, and the mother followed in 1946, leaving William Parson alone. His sister, Eugenia, had married and also produced only one child, Richard Spaight, now head of the Parson Bank and a Hug Governor.

William Parson's brother, Roger, was a drunkard from an early age and absconded in 1943 to California with a sizeable slice of the company profits, abandoning his wife and two sons. The affair was hushed up, the loss absorbed, and both Roger's boys had proven loyal, devoted and extremely capable heirs for William; their sons came out of the same mold, with the result that in this year of 1965 Parson Products stock had been blue chip for decades. Depressions? Chicken feed! People still drove cars that needed motors, Parson Turbines made diesel turbines and generators long before jet planes flew, girls went on pounding typewriters, surgical operations kept increasing, and countries were always blazing away at each other with Parson guns, howitzers and mortars, big, medium and small.

In an interesting aside, Carmine had discovered that the family black sheep, Roger, having sobered up in California, had founded the Roger's Ribs chain, married a movie starlet, done very nicely for himself, and died on top of a whore in a seedy motel.

The Hug had come out of William Parson's desire to do something in memory of his dead son, but its birth pangs had not been easy. Naturally Chubb University expected to head it and manage it, but such was not Parson's intention. He wanted affiliation with Chubb, but refused to yield up its governance to Chubb. In the end Chubb had crumbled after being presented with an ultimatum of horrific proportions. His research center, said William Parson, would, if necessary, be attached to some sordid, non-Ivied, tin-pot institution of learning out of the state. When a Chubber like William

Parson said *that,* Chubb knew itself beaten. Not that Chubb hadn't come in for a slice of the pie; 25 percent of the annual budget was paid to the university for affiliation rights.

Carmine also knew that the Board of Governors met every three months. The four Parsons and Cousin Spaight came up from their New York City apartments by limousine and stayed in suites at the Cleveland Hotel opposite the Schumann Theater for the night after the meeting. This was necessary because M.M. always gave them a dinner, hoping that he would be able to coax the Parsons into endowing a building that would one day house the William Parson art collection. This most important collection in American hands had been bequeathed to Chubb in William Parson's will, but its delivery date was left to the discretion of his heirs, who thus far had preferred to hang on to even the tiniest Leonardo cartoon.

When the Prof's hand went out to start the reel-to-reel tape recorder, Carmine held up his own.

"Sorry, Professor, this meeting is absolutely confidential."

"But—but—the minutes! I thought that if Miss Vilich was excluded, she could type up the minutes from tape."

"No minutes," said Carmine firmly. "I intend to be frank and detailed, which means nothing I say goes out of this room."

"Understood," said Roger Parson Junior abruptly. "Proceed, Lieutenant Delmonico."

When he finished, the silence was so complete that a sudden sough of wind outside sounded like a roar; to a man they were ashen, trembling, open-mouthed. In all the times he had met M.M., Carmine had never seen the man thrown off balance, but in the wake of this report even his hair seemed to have lost its luster. Though perhaps only Dean Dowling, a psychiatrist famous for his interest in organic psychoses, fully understood the implications.

"It *can't* be anyone at the Hug," said Roger Parson Junior, dabbing at his lips with a napkin.

"That has yet to be established," Carmine said. "We have no particular suspects, which means that all the members of the Hug are under suspicion. For that matter, we can't rule out any persons in the Medical School."

"Carmine, do you genuinely believe that at least ten of these missing girls have been *incinerated?*" asked M.M.

"Yes, sir, I do."

"But you haven't offered any real evidence of it."

"No, I haven't. It's purely circumstantial, but it fits what we do know—that were it not for the vagaries of chance, Mercedes Alvarez would have been completely incinerated by last Wednesday."

"It's disgusting," whispered Richard Spaight.

"It's Schiller!" cried Roger Parson III. "He's old enough to have been a Nazi." He rounded on the Professor fiercely. "I *told* you not to hire Germans!"

Roger Parson Junior rapped the table sharply. "Young Roger, that is enough! Dr. Schiller is not old enough to have been a Nazi, and it is not the business of this Board to speculate. I insist that Professor Smith be supported, not upbraided." His annoyance at his son's outburst still in his eyes, he looked at Carmine. "Lieutenant Delmonico, I thank you very much for your candor, however unwelcome it may be, and I direct *all* of you to maintain silence on every aspect of this tragedy. Though," he added rather pathetically, "I suppose we must expect that some of it at least will leak to the press?"

"That's inevitable, Mr. Parson, sooner or later. This has become a statewide investigation. Those in the know are on the increase every day."

"The FBI?" Henry Parson Junior asked.

"Not so far, sir. The line between a missing person and a kidnap victim is thin, but none of the families of these girls has ever received a ransom demand, and the matter remains at the moment confined to Connecticut. But rest assured, we will consult any agency that might be able to help," said Carmine.

"Who is heading the investigation?" asked M.M.

"For want of someone better, sir, at present I am, but that could change. There are so many different police departments involved, you see."

"Do you want the job, Carmine?"

"Yes, sir."

"Then I shall call the Governor," said M.M., positive of his power, and why not?

"Would it help if Parson Products offered a large reward?" asked Richard Spaight. "Half a million? A million?"

Carmine blanched. "No, Mr. Spaight, anything but! For one thing, it would focus press attention on the Hug, and for another, massive rewards only make the police's task harder. They bring every cuckoo and zealot out of the woodwork, and while I can't say a reward wouldn't produce a good lead, the chances are so slight that following up thousands and thousands of reports would tax police reserves beyond endurance for the sake of a carload of nothing. If we continue to get nowhere, then maybe twenty-five thousand in reward money could be offered. Take my word for it, that's plenty."

"Then," said Roger Parson Junior, getting up and heading for the coffee, "I suggest we adjourn until Lieutenant Delmonico can give us some new developments. Professor Smith, you and your people must give the Lieutenant complete co-operation." He started to pour into a cup and stopped, aghast. "The coffee's not made! I *need* a coffee!"

While the Prof fluttered about apologizing and explaining that Miss Vilich normally dealt with the coffee toward the end of the meeting, Carmine switched the several percolators on and bit into an apple Danish. M.M. was right. Delicious.

Before Carmine left his office that afternoon, Commissioner John Silvestri barreled through the door to tell him that word had come from Hartford that there was to be a special police task force operating out of Holloman, as Holloman had the best police laboratories in the state. Lieutenant Carmine Delmonico was appointed to head the special task force.

"Budget, unlimited," said Silvestri, looking even more like a large black cat than usual, "and ask for any cops you want from anywhere in the state."

Thank you, M.M., said Carmine to himself. I have a virtual carte blanche, but I'm willing to bet my badge that the press will know everything before I leave this office. Once the public servants get in on the act, tongues are bound to wag. As for the Governor—multiple murders, especially of admirable citizens, add up to political odium.

To Silvestri he said, "I'll visit every police department in the state personally to brief them, but for the moment I'm happy to keep the special task force to me, Patrick, Abe and Corey."

CHAPTER 5

Wednesday, October 20th, 1965

Two weeks had gone by since the discovery of Mercedes Alvarez in the Hug dead animal refrigerator, and the tide of news items in the newspapers and on TV and radio had begun to ebb in an informational vacuum. Not a whisper of incineration had leaked, which amazed the special task force. Apparently pressure from on high by all kinds of influential and political people had suppressed this as too sensitive, too nightmarishly disturbing. Of course the Caribbean factor had been harped on remorselessly. The number of victims had been set at eleven; no case prior to Rosita Esperanza in January of 1964 had come to light, including in any other state of the Union. Of course the killer had been given a nickname by the press: he was the Connecticut Monster.

Hug existence was no longer just a matter of a minor triumph in the behavior of potassium ions through the neuronal cell membrane, or a major triumph when Eustace had a focal temporal lobe seizure upon a tickling electrical stimulation of his ulnar nerve. Now Hug existence was fraught with tensions that exhibited themselves in sideways glances, statements cut off in mid-utterance, uneasy avoidance of the subject never far from any Hugger mind. One small comfort: the cops seemed to have given up visiting, even Lieutenant Delmonico, who for eight days had haunted every floor.

The cracks that were appearing in the Hug's social structure mostly radiated from the figure of Dr. Kurt Schiller.

"Stay away from me, you Nazi cur!" Dr. Maurice Finch shouted at Schiller when he came enquiring about a tissue sample.

"Yes, you are allowed to call me names," Schiller retorted, gasping, "but I dare not retaliate, here among American Jews!"

"If I had my way, you'd be deported!" Finch said, snarling.

"You cannot blame a whole nation for the crimes of a few," Schiller persisted, face white, fists clenched.

"Who says I can't? You were *all* guilty!"

Charles Ponsonby broke it up, took Schiller by the arm and escorted him to his own domain.

"I have done nothing—*nothing!*" Schiller cried. "How do we know—*really* know!—that the body was cut up to be incinerated? It is gossip, wicked gossip! I have done nothing!"

"My dear Kurt, Maurie's reaction is understandable," Charles said. "He had cousins who went to the ovens at Auschwitz, so the very thought of incineration is—well, profoundly disturbing to him. I also understand that it isn't easy to be on the receiving end of his emotions. The best thing you can do is keep out of his way until things die down. They will, they always do. For you're quite correct—it's just gossip. The police haven't told us a thing. Keep your chin up, Kurt—be a *man!*" This last was said with an inflection that caused Schiller to put his head in his hands and weep bitterly.

"Gossip," said Ponsonby to himself as he returned to his lab, "is like garlic. A good servant, a bad master."

Finch wasn't the only one who used Schiller as his butt for frustrations. Sonia Liebman ostentatiously withdrew from his vicinity whenever she encountered him; Hilda Silverman suddenly mislaid his journals and articles; Marvin, Betty and Hank lost his samples and inked swastikas on the rats whose brains would go to pathology.

Finally Schiller went to the Prof to tender his resignation, only to have it refused.

"I can't possibly accept it, Kurt," said Smith, whose hair seemed to grow whiter every day. "We're under police observation, we can't change staff. Besides, if you left now, it would be in a cloud of suspicion. Grit your teeth and get through this, just like the rest of us."

"But I've had it up to here with gritting my teeth," he said to Tamara after the devastated Schiller had gone. "Oh, Tamara, why did it have to happen to us?"

"If I knew that, Bob, I'd try to fix it," she said, settled him in his chair more comfortably and gave him a draft of Dr. Nur Chandra's paper to read, the one that coolly and clinically went into the details of Eustace's incredible seizure.

When she returned to her own office she found Desdemona Dupre there, but not waiting where anyone else would have. That English bitch was unashamedly scanning the contents of Tamara's cluttered desk!

"Have you seen my wages sheet, Vilich?"

The corner of a highly confidential handwritten communication was poking out from under a sheaf of rough-draft dictation she had transcribed from the Prof; Tamara leaped to shove Desdemona away.

"Don't you dare look through my papers, Dupre!"

"I was simply fascinated by the chaos you work in," Desdemona drawled. "No wonder you couldn't administer this place. You couldn't organize a booze-up in a brewery."

"Why don't you go fuck yourself? One thing for sure, you're too ugly to get a man to fuck you!"

Up went Desdemona's rather invisible brows. "There are worse fates than to die wondering," she said, smiling, "but luckily some men like scaling Mount Everest." Her eyes followed Tamara's red-varnished nails as their hands shuffled the papers, tucked the vital sheet out of sight. "A love letter?" she asked.

"Fuck off! Your wages aren't here!"

Desdemona departed, still smiling; through the open door she could hear the distant ringing of her phone.

"Miss Dupre," she said, sitting down.

"Oh, good, glad to know you're in to work," said the voice of her other bête noire.

"I am always in to work, Lieutenant Delmonico," she said very curtly. "To what do I owe this honor?"

"How about having dinner with me one evening?"

The request came as a shock, but Desdemona didn't make the mistake of thinking that he was paying her a compliment. So the Lord High Executioner was desperate, was he?

"That depends," she said warily.

"On what?"

"How many strings are attached, Lieutenant."

"Well, while you're trying to count them, how about you call me Carmine and I call you Desdemona?"

"First names are for friends, and I regard your invitation more in the light of an inquisition."

"Does that mean I can call you Desdemona?"

"May, not can."

"Great! Uh—dinner, Desdemona?"

She leaned back in her chair and closed her eyes, remembering his impressive air of calm authority. "Very well, dinner."

"When?"

"Tonight if you're free, *Carmine.*"

"Great. What kind of food do you like?"

"Ordinary old Shanghai Chinese."

"Fine by me. I'll pick you up at your house at seven."

Of course the bastard knew everybody's home address! "No, thank you. I prefer to meet you at the venue. Which is?"

"The Blue Pheasant on Cedar Street. Know it?"

"Oh, yes. I'll meet you there at seven."

He hung up without further ado, leaving Desdemona to deal with a query from Dr. Charles Ponsonby, standing in her doorway; only once she was rid of him could she plot and plan not a seduction but a fencing match. Oh, yes indeed, a little thrust and parry with the verbal rapier would be welcome! How she missed that aspect of life! Here in Holloman she was in exile, banking her lavish salary as fast as she could to get out of this vast and alien country, return to her homeland, pick up the threads of a stimulating social life. Money wasn't everything, but until you had some, life of any sort was depressing. Desdemona wanted a small flat at Strand-on-the-Green overlooking the Thames, several consultancies at private health clinics, and all of London as her backyard. Admittedly London was as unknown to her as Holloman had been, but Holloman was an exile and London was the hub of the universe. Five years down, five more years to go; then it would be goodbye to the Hug and America. A super reference to get herself those consultancies, a plump bank account. That was all she wanted or needed from America. You can take the English out of England, she thought, but you can't take England out of the English.

She always walked to and from work, a form of exercise that suited her hiking soul. Though this activity appalled some of her colleagues, Desdemona didn't think herself imperiled because her route led right through the Hollow. Her height, her athletic stride, her air of confidence and her lack of a pocketbook rendered her an unlikely victim of any kind. Besides, after five years, she knew every face she encountered, and received none but friendly waves in answer to her own.

The oak leaves were already falling; by the time Desdemona turned on to Twentieth Street to walk the block to Sycamore, she shuffled through piles of them because the council trucks hadn't been this way yet. Ah, there he was! The Siamese who always hung out on top of a post to say hello as she passed; she stopped to pay homage. Behind her, footsteps shuffled for a fraction of a second after hers had ceased. It was that made her turn in surprise, a tiny hackle prickling. Oh, surely not after five years! But there was no one in sight unless he lurked behind a nearby oak. She went on, ears tuned, and stopped again twenty feet farther on. The rustle of dead leaves behind her stopped too, half a second too late. A faint sweat broke out on her brow, but she continued as if she had noticed nothing, turned onto Sycamore, and astonished herself by racing the last block to her three-family house.

Ridiculous, Desdemona Dupre! How silly of you. It was the wind, it was a rat, a bird, some small creature you didn't see.

When she climbed the thirty-two stairs to her third-floor apartment she was breathing harder than either the run or the steps warranted. Involuntarily her eyes went to her work basket, but it was undisturbed. Her embroidery lay exactly where it ought to be.

Eliza Smith had made Bob's favorite dinner, spare ribs with a side salad and hot bread. His state of mind worried her hugely. Ever since the murder he had gone steadily downhill; touchy in temper, critical of things he usually didn't even notice, often somewhere so distant that he neither saw nor heard anything. She had always known that he had this side to his nature, but between a brilliant career and his folly in the basement—as well as a good marriage, she hastened to add—she had been positive that it would never dominate his thinking, his world. After all, he had gotten through Nancy—oh, been a bit rocky for a while, yet rallied—and what could be worse than that?

Though the papers and the TV news programs had ceased to harp on the "Connecticut Monster," Bobby and Sam hadn't taken their hint. Every day that they went to the Dormer Day School they basked in the glory of having a dad closely involved in the murders, and failed to see why they ought not to harp on them some more after they came home. I mean, *cut in pieces!*

"Which one do you think it is, Dad?" Bobby asked again.

"Don't, Bobby," said his mother.

"I reckon it's Schiller," said Sam, gnawing at a spare rib. "I bet he was a Nazi. He looks like a Nazi."

"Hush up, Sam! Leave the subject alone," said Eliza.

"Pay attention to your mother, boys. I've had enough," the Prof said, his plate hardly touched.

Conversation ceased as the boys ate more spare ribs, crunched through crusty bread, and eyed their father speculatively.

"Aw, gee, Dad, please, *please* tell us who you reckon it is," Bobby cajoled.

"Schiller's the killer! Schiller's the killer!" sang Sam. "Achtung! Sieg heil! Ich habe ein tiger in mein tank!"

Robert Mordent Smith put both hands on the table and lifted himself to his feet, then pointed to a vacant space in the big room. Bobby gulped, Sam whimpered, but both children got up and went to where their father had pointed, rolling their pants up to their knees. Smith took a long switch with a shredded end from its traditional position on the sideboard, walked across to the boys, and swung the implement at Bobby's calf. He always hit Bobby first because Sam was so terrified of the switch that having to watch Bobby doubled his own punishment. The first cut raised red welts, but five more followed while Bobby remained still, manfully silent; Sam was bawling already. Six more cuts on Bobby's other calf and it was Sam's turn for six on each calf, laid on as hard and viciously as Bobby's despite the screams. Sam was a coward in his father's opinion. A *girl*.

"Go to bed and think of the pleasures in being alive. Not all of us are that lucky, remember? I'll have no more of this pestering, hear me?"

"Sam maybe," Eliza said when the boys had gone, "he's just twelve. But you shouldn't take a switch to a fourteen-year-old, Bob. He's bigger than you already. One day he'll turn on you."

For answer, Smith went to the basement door, the keys to its police locks in his hand.

"And there's no need for this obsessive locking up!" Eliza called from the dining room as he disappeared. "What if something happened and I needed you in a hurry?"

"Holler!"

"Oh, sure," she muttered, starting to carry the remains of dinner to the kitchen. "You wouldn't hear over the racket. And mark my words, Bob Smith, one day our boys will turn on you."

The strains of a Saint-Saëns piano concerto erupted from a pair of gigantic speakers poised in the doorless aperture that led out of the kitchen. While Claire Ponsonby shelled raw shrimp in the ancient stone sink and picked the veins from them, her brother opened the "slow" oven of the Aga combustion stove, hands inside mittens, and withdrew a terra-cotta casserole dish. Its lid was glued on with a dough of flour-and-water to keep in every last drop of precious juice; depositing the dish on the marble end of the three-hundred-year-old worktable, Charles then began the tedious job of chipping the casserole lid free from its sealing of dough.

"I coined an excellent aphorism today," he said as he toiled. "Gossip is like garlic—a good servant, but a bad master."

"Appropriate considering our menu, but is the gossip at the Hug really that bad, Charles? After all, no one *knows.*"

"I agree that no one *knows* whether the body parts went to the incinerator, but speculation is rife." He tittered. "The main object of gossip is Kurt Schiller, who blubbered all over me—pah! An ornamental Teuton, a furtive fumbler—I had to bite my tongue."

"That smells divine," Claire said, turning to face him with a smile. "We haven't had a beef daube in God knows when."

"But first, shrimps in garlic butter," said Charles. "Have you finished?"

"Last one being deveined now. Perfect music for a perfect meal. Saint-Saëns is so *lush.* Shall I melt the butter, or will you? The garlic's crushed and ready to go. That saucer there."

"I'll do it while you set the table," Charles said, pushing a block of butter into his pan, the shrimps ready for their brief immersion the moment the butter boiled and the garlic was brown. "Lemon! Did you forget the lemon juice?"

"Honestly, Charles, are you blind? Right beside you."

Every time Claire spoke in her husky voice the big dog lying with its chin on its paws in an out-of-the-way corner would lift its head, thump the floor with its tail, its lumpy blond brows rising and falling expressively in its gentle black face like an accompaniment to the music of Claire speaking.

The shrimps in Charles's capable hands, the table set, Claire moved to the battered, stained marble counter and picked up a large bowl of canned dog food. "Here, Biddy my love, dinner for you too," she said, crossing the room to where the dog lay and putting the bowl down just beyond its front paws. On its feet in a trice, Biddy gulped at the food hungrily. "It's the labrador in you makes you greedy," said Claire. "A pity the shepherd can't tone you down. Pleasures," she went on with a purr in her voice, "are infinitely sweeter when taken slowly."

"I couldn't agree more," said Charles. "Let's take an hour at least to get through our meal."

The two Ponsonbys sat down one on either side of the wooden slab end of the table to eat, a leisurely process that was only interrupted when the LP record on the turntable needed replacing. Tonight was Saint-Saëns, but tomorrow might be Mozart or Satie, depending on the dinner menu. To choose the right music was as important as the right wine.

"I presume you're going to the Bosch exhibition, Charles?"

"Wild horses couldn't keep me away. I can't wait to see his actual paintings! No matter how good the color prints in a book are, they can't compare to the originals. So macabre, so full of what I don't know is conscious or unconscious humor. Somehow I can never get inside Bosch's *mind!* Was he schizophrenic? Did he have a source of magic mushrooms? Or was it just the way he'd been brought up to see not only his world, but the next? They thought of life and death, reward and punishment, differently than we do today, of that I'm certain. His demons *ooze* glee while they subject their hapless human victims to torture." He chortled. "I mean, no one in Hell is supposed to be happy. Oh, Claire, Bosch is a genuine genius! His work, his work—!"

"So you keep telling me," she said rather dryly.

Biddy the dog bustled over to put its head in Claire's lap. Her long, thin hands pulled at its ears rhythmically until its eyes closed and it groaned in bliss.

"We'll have a Bosch menu to celebrate when you get back," Claire said with a laugh in her voice. "Guacamole with plenty of chili, tandoori chicken, devil's food cake . . . Shostakovitch and Stravinsky, some Moussorgsky thrown in . . . An old chambertin . . ."

"Speaking of music, the record's stuck in a groove. Fix the daube, will you?" he asked, moving to the never-used dining room.

Claire walked around the kitchen efficiently while Charles, now in his chair, watched her. First she took the tiny potatoes off the Aga hotplate, strained them in the sink, patted a dab of butter over them in their bowl, then carried the bowl to the table. The daube she divided into two pieces which she placed on two old Spode plates and put one between each set of knife and fork. Last to come was a bowl of blanched green beans. Not one container or plate clinked accidentally against another; Claire Ponsonby laid everything on the table exactly. While the dog, knowing itself unneeded in the kitchen, went back to its square of rug and put its chin on its paws again.

"What do you intend to do tomorrow?" Charles asked when the daube had been replaced by treacly black demitasse espresso and both of them were savoring the smell-taste of mild cigars.

"Take Biddy for a long walk in the morning. Then Biddy and I are going to hear that talk on subatomic particles—it's in the Susskind lecture theater. I've booked a taxi there and back."

"It should not be necessary to book a taxi!" Charles snapped, watery eyes gone dry with anger. "Those unfeeling cretins who drive taxis ought to know the difference between a guide dog and any other dog! A guide dog, piss in a taxi? Rubbish!"

She reached out, put her hand on his unerringly; no groping, no slipping. "It's no trouble to book one," she said pacifically.

The dinner menu at the Forbes house was very different.

Robin Forbes had tried to make a nut loaf that didn't crumble ruinously the moment a knife hit it, and drizzled thin cranberry sauce over it to, as she said to Addison,

"Ginger it up a tad, dear."

He tasted the result suspiciously and reared back in horror. "It's sweet!" he squeaked. *"Sweet!"*

"Oh, darling, a tiny bit of sugar won't cause another heart attack!" she cried, striking her hands together in exasperation. "You're the doctor, I'm only a humble R.N. of the old-fashioned, non-degreed kind, but even nurses know that sugar is the ultimate fuel! I mean, everything you eat that isn't built into new tissue is turned into glucose for right now or glycogen for later. You are killing yourself with *un*kindness, Addison! A twenty-year-old football star doesn't train as hard."

"Thanks for the lecture," he said bitingly, ostentatiously scraped the cranberry sauce off his nut loaf, then piled his big plate high with lettuce, tomato, cucumber, celery and capsicum. No dressing, even vinaigrette.

"I had my weekly talk with Roberta and Robina this morning," she said brightly, terrified that he would notice that her loaf was meat loaf from the deli, and that creamy Italian dressing lurked under her own modest salad.

"Did Roberta get accepted into neurosurgery?" he asked, only slightly interested.

Robin's face fell. "No, dear, they rejected her, she says because she's a woman."

"And rightly so. You need a man's stamina for neurosurgery."

No point in going there; Robin changed the subject. "But," she said chirpily, "Robina's husband got a big promotion. They can buy that house they love in Westchester."

"Good for what's his name," he said absently; his work was calling to him from the top of the tower.

"Oh, Addison, he's your son-in-law! Callum Christie is his name." She sighed, tried once more. "This afternoon I saw a rerun of *Quo Vadis*—goodness, didn't they give the poor Christians a hard time? Lions dragging human arms around—brr!"

"I know scads of Christians I'd happily throw to the lions. Rob you blind six days of the week, then go to church on Sunday and fix it up with God. Pah! I'm proud to stand by my sins, no matter how awful they are," he said through his teeth.

She giggled. "Oh, Addison, honestly! You do talk nonsense!"

The salad had gone; Addison Forbes put down his knife and fork and wondered for the millionth time why he had ever married an empty-headed nurse halfway through medical school. Though he knew the answer, just didn't care to admit it; he hadn't had the money to finish, she was crazy about him, and a nurse's income was just enough. Naturally he had planned to get through his residency before contemplating a family, but the fool woman fell pregnant before he graduated. So there he was, battling with an internship and twin daughters she had insisted on naming Roberta and Robina. Despite their homozygousness, Roberta had inherited his medical bent, whereas Robina the airhead had become a successful teenaged model before marrying an up-and-coming stockbroker.

His repugnance for his wife hadn't dissipated with the years; rather, it had grown until he could hardly stand the sight of her, and had private fantasies of killing her an inch at a time.

"You would do better, Robin," he said as he rose from the table, "to enroll in some degree program at West Holloman State College instead of scoffing popcorn in a movie theater. Or you could throw pots, which I'm told is what middle-aged women with no talent do. You couldn't take a refresher course in nursing, you'd never manage the math. Now that our daughters have left the safety of your maternal river for a life in the ocean, your river has turned into a stagnant pond."

The same ending to the same meal; Addison stalked off up the spiral stairs to his padlocked eyrie while Robin shrilled after him.

"I'd sooner be dead than run a vacuum over your stupid eyrie, so leave the door open, for God's sake!"

His voice floated back. "You're nosy, my dear. No, thanks."

Mopping at her eyes with a tissue, Robin mixed the creamy Italian through her salad and flooded her meat loaf with cranberry sauce. Then she jumped up, ran to the refrigerator and unearthed a container of potato salad she'd hidden behind the cans of Tab. It wasn't fair that Addison visited his pitiless regimen on her, but she knew exactly why he did: he was petrified of falling off his wagon if he saw *real* food.

Carmine Delmonico stood leaning his shoulders against the florid blue and gold pheasant painted on the restaurant window, a big brown bag tucked in the crook of one arm. His eyes followed the bright red Corvette idly, then widened when it backed neatly into the curb and Miss Desdemona Dupre extricated her impressive length from it lithely.

"Wow!" he said, straightening. "Not the kind of car I had picked for you."

"It will appreciate, not depreciate, so when I sell it I won't lose money on it," she said. "Shall we go in? I'm starving."

"I thought we'd eat at my place," he said, beginning to walk. "The joint's jumping with undergrad Chubbers, and my face is well known these days thanks to the *Holloman Post*. A pity to make the poor guys go to the john to take a swig from their brown bags."

"The Connecticut liquor laws are archaic," she said, walking with him. "They can be killed in a war, but they can't drink."

"You'll get no argument from me, though I expected you to put up a fight over where we eat."

"My dear Carmine, at thirty-two I'm a trifle old to bridle girlishly at eating in a man's apartment—or is it a house? Do we have a long walk?"

"Nope, just to the corner. I live on the twelfth floor of the Nut-meg Insurance building. Ten floors of offices, ten floors of apart-ments. Dr. Satsuma has the penthouse, but that rich I am not. Just modestly well off."

"Modesty," she said, preceding him into a marble foyer, "is not a quality I associate with you."

"What I like most about you, Desdemona," he said as they zoomed up in the elevator, "is your way of saying things. At first I thought you were taking the mickey out of me, but now I realize that it's natural for you to be kinda—pompous."

"If to avoid slang is to sound pompous, then I'm pompous."

He ushered her out of the elevator, fished a key from his pocket and opened his front door, flicked a light switch.

Desdemona walked into a room that took her breath away. Its walls and ceiling were dull Chinese red, a carpet the same color cov-ered the floor, and much thought had gone into the lighting. Fluo-rescent strips concealed by a pelmet ran along the perimeter, illuminating some of the loveliest Oriental art she had ever seen: a three-leafed screen of tigers against gilt squares, a wonderfully droll and tender ink painting of a fat old man asleep with his head pil-lowed on a tiger, a group of tigers young and old, a mommy tiger serving a homily to a baby tiger, and, to break up so many tigers, a few panels of ethereal mountains painted on white stone inside intri-cately carved black frames. Four upholstered Chinese red tub chairs stood around a Lalique table of frosted ostrich plumes beneath a round piece of inch-thick transparent glass; above it blazed a small, matching Lalique chandelier. Two places had been set on that flaw-less table, of thin plain crystal and thin plain china. Four Chinese red easy chairs were arranged in a group around a squat, large ceramic temple dog with a sheet of glass on its head. Around the walls a few cabinets in black lacquer broke up so much redness. Interesting, that this shade of red was not discordant or irritating. It was just intensely sumptuous.

"Ye gods!" she exclaimed feebly. "The next thing you'll be telling me you write highly intellectual poetry and cherish a thousand secret sorrows."

That made him laugh as he carried the bag into a kitchen as white as the living room was dull red, immaculately clean, quite intimidatingly tidy. This man was a perfectionist.

"Far from it," he said as he emptied the steaming food into lidded bowls. "I'm just a Wop cop from Holloman with a yen for beautiful surroundings when I come home. White wine, or red?"

"Beer, if you have it. I like beer with Chinese."

"This place is not at all what I expected," she said, taking two of the bowls while he stacked the rest up his arms like a waiter.

He drew her chair out, seated her, seated himself.

"Eat," he said. "I got a bit of everything on the menu."

Since both of them were hungry, they polished off the large amount of food, each deftly wielding chopsticks.

I *am* a snob, she thought as she ate, but we English do tend to be snobs unless we come from Coronation Street. Why do we forget that the Italians ruled the world before ever we did, and for longer, and with greater success? They gave birth to the Renaissance, they have adorned the world with art, literature, and the arch. And this Wop cop from Holloman has the air of a Roman emperor, so why should he not have ascetic feelings?

"Green tea, black tea, or coffee?" he asked in the kitchen as he stacked the dishwasher.

"Another beer, please."

"What did you expect, Desdemona?" he asked from the depths of his easy chair, his cup of green tea on the temple dog table.

"If there had been a Mrs. Delmonico—after all, there might have been—good Italian leather and a conservative color scheme. If a policeman's bachelor quarters—perhaps bits and pieces from Goodwill. *Are* you married? I ask only out of politeness."

"Was, a long time ago. I have a daughter nearly fifteen."

"With American alimony what it is, I'm surprised you can buy Lalique and chinoiserie."

"No alimony," he said with a grin. "My ex left me to marry a guy who could buy and sell Chubb. She and my girl live in an L.A. mansion that looks like Hampton Court palace."

"You've traveled."

"From time to time, even for the job. I get the crap cases, and Chubb being an international community, a few cases spread to Europe, the Middle East, Asia. I saw the table and chandelier in a store window in Paris and hocked my suspenders to buy them. The Chinese stuff I bought in Hong Kong and Macau while I was in Japan just after the War. Occupational forces. The Chinese were so poor that I got things for a song."

"But you weren't above profiting from their poverty."

"You can't eat painted tigers, lady. Both sides got what they wanted." It wasn't said sharply, though it held a measure of reproof. "The first cold winter, they'd have been burned. I hate to think how much was burned during the years when the Japs treated the Chinese like sheep for the slaughter. As it is, what I have, I care for and appreciate. It's not worth a hill of beans compared to what the British took out of Greece and the French out of Italy," he added a little maliciously.

"Touché." She put her beer down. "All right, time to get down to brass tacks, Lieutenant. What do you think you can winkle out of me in return for feeding me?"

"Probably nothing, but who knows? I won't start by asking you anything I can't find out for myself, though if you come across, it will save getting a few Hug backs up. Yours is permanently up, probably over your tallness, so I know where I stand with you—a good four inches shorter."

"I am *proud* of my height," she said, tight-lipped.

"So you should be. There's lots of guys fancy climbing up Mount Everest."

She burst out laughing. "That's exactly what I said to Miss Tamara Vilich today!" Sobering, she looked at him levelly. "But you're not such a one, are you?"

"Nope. I get my exercise working out in the police gym."

"Ask your questions, then."

"What's the Hug's annual budget?"

"Three million dollars. A million in salaries and wages, a million in running costs and supplies, three-quarters of a million to Chubb University, and a quarter of a million as reserve."

He whistled. "Jesus! How the hell can the Parsons fund it?"

"From a trust with a capital of a hundred and fifty million. This means that we never get through what the interest fetches. Wilbur Dowling wants the size of the Hug doubled to include a psychiatric division devoted to organic psychoses. Though this doesn't fall within the Hug's parameters, those parameters could be altered fairly legitimately to gratify his wishes."

"Why the hell did William Parson set aside so much?"

"I think because he was a business skeptic who believed that money would inevitably lose its value as time went on. He was so alone, you see, and toward the end of his life the Hug became his entire reason for being."

"Would doubling the size of the Hug to fit in with the Dean's ambitions be a problem in other ways than just money?"

"Definitely. The Parsons dislike Dowling to a man, and M.M. is such a Chubber to his bootstraps that he regards science and medicine as faintly sordid things that by rights should belong to state-funded universities. That he tolerates them is because the federal government pours money into scientific and medical research, and Chubb does very well out of it. The Hug's isn't the only percentage Chubb takes."

"So M.M. and the Parsons are the stumbling blocks. It always goes back to personalities, doesn't it?" Carmine asked, refilling his teacup from a pot kept warm inside a padded basket.

"They're human beings, so yes."

"How much does the Hug spend on major equipment?"

"This year, more than usual. Dr. Schiller is being endowed with an electron microscope that will cost a million."

"Ah, yes, Dr. Schiller," he said, stretching out his legs. "I hear that some of the Huggers are making his life so difficult that he tried to resign this afternoon."

"How do you know that?" she demanded, sitting up straight.

"A little bird."

Down went the beer glass with a clang; Desdemona scrambled up. "Then feed your little bird, not me!" she snapped.

He didn't move. "Calm down, Desdemona, and sit down."

She stood doing her habitual towering act, eyes locked on his, which were, a corner of her mind noted, not dark brown, but more an amber that this room enlivened. The brain behind them knew exactly what she was feeling, and couldn't be bothered with her compunctions. As was, she admitted, only fitting: all he cared about was finding the Connecticut Monster. Desdemona Dupre was a pawn he could easily afford to lose. She sat down.

"That's better," he said, smiling. "What do you think of Dr. Kurt Schiller?"

"As a person, or as a researcher?"

"Both, I guess."

"As a researcher, he's an acknowledged world authority on the structure of the limbic system, which is why the Prof pinched him from Frankfurt." She smiled, something she didn't do often enough; her smile transformed a rather plain face into quite an attractive one. "As a person, I like him. The poor chap labors under some frightful handicaps apart from his nationality."

"Like homosexuality?"

"That bird again?"

"Most men don't need a bird to whistle that, Desdemona."

"True. Women are more easily deluded, because women tend to view pleasant and gentle men as good husband material. Many of them prefer their own sex, which wives don't find out until a few children later. It happened to two friends of mine. However, Kurt is pleasant and gentle but doesn't pursue women so he can reproduce himself. Like all the researchers, he lives for his work, so I don't think his homosexual affairs are long-standing. Or, if he does have a regular boyfriend, I imagine the boyfriend doesn't see enough of him."

"You're very dispassionate," he said.

"That's because I'm not really involved. Candidly, I think Kurt came to America to start afresh, and put himself in a geographical location that means he can travel to New York City and the homosexual scene whenever he likes. What he forgot—or perhaps didn't know—was how many people in the American medical professions are of Jewish extraction. It's twenty years since the War ended with all those ghastly concentration camp revelations, but the memories are still very much alive."

"In you too, I imagine," he said.

"Oh, for me it was mostly the horrors of food and clothing rationing—what you'd call peanuts. Bombs and V-2s, but not where I lived well outside Lincoln." She shrugged. "Still and all, I like Kurt Schiller, and until this awful business happened, so did everyone else, including Maurie Finch, Sonia Liebman, Hilda Silverman and the technicians. I remember Maurie saying at the time he learned Kurt had the pathology job that he'd done battle with his conscience, and his conscience said he mustn't be the one to cast the first stone at a German young enough not to have participated in the Holocaust." She glanced at her watch, the cheapest Timex she could find. "I must go, but thank you, Carmine. The food was just what I fancied, the environment truly gorgeous, and the company—why, quite bearable."

"Bearable enough to do it again next Wednesday?" he asked, pulling her to her feet as if she weighed half of her 160 pounds.

"If you like."

He took her down in the elevator and insisted on walking her to her Corvette.

An interesting woman, he thought as he watched the car growl away. There's more to her than a complex about her height. Get her talking and she forgets to tower. Dresses in cheap shit, hacks at her hair herself, doesn't have any jewelry. Does that make her stingy, or merely indifferent to the way she looks? I don't think she's either. Not surprising to find out she's a keen hiker. I can see her striding along the Appalachian Trail in big boots—a feminine Tom Bombadil. No flare of attraction between us, that was a relief. Since I'd bet the contents of my walls that she's not the Connecticut Monster, Miss Desdemona Dupre is the logical Hugger to cultivate.

Ah! A good night's work.

CHAPTER 6

"We're getting nowhere," said Carmine to Silvestri, Marciano and Patrick. "It's coming up for two months since Mercedes was abducted, and we've lifted every stone in Connecticut to look under it. I don't think there's a deserted house, barn or shed in the whole state that we haven't turned inside out, or a forest we haven't tramped through. If he sticks to his pattern, he's already got his next victim marked out, but we know no more about him or the identity of his next victim now than we did on Day One."

"Maybe we ought to be looking in houses, barns and sheds that are not deserted," said Marciano, always the one impatient at official restrictions.

"Sure, that's agreed," Silvestri said, "but you know very well, Danny, that no judge would issue us with a search warrant as things stand at the moment. We need *evidence.*"

"It could be that we've frightened the killer off," Patrick said. "He mightn't snatch another victim. Or if he does, it might be in another

108

state. Connecticut's not huge. He could live here and still snatch in New York, Massachusetts or Rhode Island."

"He'll snatch, Patsy, and inside Connecticut. Why inside Connecticut? Because it's his turf. He feels like he owns it. He's not a foreigner here, this is home, sweet home. I think he has lived here for long enough to know every town and village."

"How long would that take?" Patrick asked, intrigued.

"Depends whether he's a traveling man, doesn't it? But I'd say five years, minimum—*if* he's a traveling man."

"That doesn't knock too many Huggers out of the running."

"No, Patsy, it doesn't. Finch, Forbes, Ponsonby, Smith, Mrs. Liebman, Hilda Silverman and Tamara Vilich are Connecticut born and bred, Polonowski's been here for fifteen years, Chandra for eight, and Satsuma for five." Carmine scowled. "Let's change the subject. John, are the press co-operating?"

"Really well," Silvestri answered. "It's going to be much harder for him to snatch this kind of girl. In another week the warnings will be going out—newspapers, radio, TV—with good pictures of the girls and emphasis on Caribbean Catholic origin."

"What if he switches his type of girl?" asked Marciano.

"I am *assured* by every goddamn psychiatrist I consult that he won't do that, Danny. Their contention is that he's snatched eleven girls who could be sisters, therefore he's fixated on a package consisting of skin color, face, size, age, geography and religion," Carmine said. "The trouble is all the psychiatrists can go on are patients who haven't yet murdered, though some have multiply raped."

"Carmine, all of us in this room know that most murderers are pretty dumb," Patrick said, sounding thoughtful, "and that even when they're smart, they're not brilliant. Rat cunning, or lucky, or maybe competent. But this guy is way ahead of the pack—including us. What I'm wondering is, will he obey the rules the psychiatrists have laid down? What if he's a psychiatrist himself? Like Professor Smith? Polonowski? Ponsonby? Finch? Forbes? I looked them up in the Chubb book, and they've all got D.P.M.s—Diplomas of

Psychiatric Medicine. They're not merely neurologists, they've gone the whole hog."

"Shit," said Carmine. "I just saw D.P.M. I don't deserve to be heading this task force."

"Task forces are cooperatives," Silvestri soothed. "We know now, and what difference does it make?"

"Could it be a woman?" Marciano asked, frowning.

"According to the psychiatrists, no, and for once I agree with them," Carmine said positively. "This kind of killer preys on women but isn't one. Maybe he'd like to be one who looks like our girls— who the hell knows? We're fumbling in the dark."

Desdemona had abandoned walking to and from work, telling herself she was a fool, but unable to conquer the feeling that dogged her every step through those fallen leaves—someone was following her, someone too clever to be caught. The very thought of leaving her beloved Corvette in an open parking lot on the edge of a ghetto went against the grain, but she couldn't help herself. If the thing was stolen, then she'd have to pray it came back in one piece. Even so, she couldn't bring herself to tell Carmine what had happened, though she knew he wouldn't laugh. And as she was neither of Caribbean ancestry nor a bare five feet tall, she didn't think for a moment that her stalker had anything to do with what plagued him.

Eating pizza with him in his apartment, she thought him as tense as a cat whose territory had been usurped by a dog; not that he was curt, just—the Americans had an excellent word for it—twitchy.

Well, she was twitchy herself, blurted out her news. "Kurt Schiller attempted suicide today."

"And no one *told* me?" he demanded.

"I'm sure the Prof will tomorrow," she said, wiping tomato off her chin with fingers that trembled slightly. "It didn't happen until shortly before I left."

"Shit! How?"

"He's a doctor, Carmine. He took a cocktail of morphine,

phenothiazine and Seconal to cause cardiac and respiratory failure, with Stemetil to make sure he didn't vomit them up."

"You mean he's *dead?*"

"No. Maurie Finch found him shortly after he'd taken everything and kept him alive until they could transfer him to the emergency room at Holloman Hospital. A lot of antidotes and gastric lavage later, he passed the crisis. Poor Maurie was shocked to pieces and blaming himself." She put down her half-eaten pizza. "Talking about it takes the edge off one's appetite."

"I'm inured," he said, taking another slice. "Is Schiller the only casualty?"

"No, just the most dramatic. Though I predict that after he has recovered enough to return to work, those who have made his life a misery will let him be. No more swastikas inked on his rats—that I found so disgustingly petty! Emotions can be—oh, terribly destructive."

"Sure. Emotions get in the way of common sense."

"Is this murderer emotional?"

"Cold as outer space, hot as the center of the sun," Carmine said. "He's a cauldron of emotions that he thinks he controls."

"You don't believe he does control them?"

"No. They control him. What makes him such a successful killer is the counterpoise between outer space and the center of the sun." He took the remains of the pizza from her plate and substituted a fresh slice. "Here, this is warmer."

She tried, but gagged; Carmine handed her a balloon of XO cognac, frowning. "My mother would say grappa, but cognac's far better. Drink it, Desdemona. Then tell me who else at the Hug is a casualty."

Heat flowed through her body, followed by the most marvelous sense of well-being. "The Prof," she said then. "All of us think he's on the verge of a nervous breakdown. Issues directives, then forgets he has, countermands things he shouldn't, lets Tamara Vilich get away with murder—" She put her hand over her mouth. "I didn't mean that literally. Tamara is a right cow, but I think her crimes are moral, not homicidal. She's having it off with someone, and she's terrified of it getting out. Knowing her, I think it's more than just that he's forbidden fruit. She's in love with him, but he's put a condition on it—secrecy or else."

"That means he's either important, or afraid of his wife. Who else besides the Prof?"

Her eyes filled with tears. "Oh, Carmine, really! We are all feeling the strain! All hoping and praying that if this—this monster strikes again, he won't implicate the Hug. Morale is so low that the research is suffering dreadfully. Chandra and Satsuma are muttering about moving away, and Chandra in particular is our bright, light hope. Eustace has had another focal seizure—even the Prof cheered up. It's Nobel Prize material."

"One up for the Hug," said Carmine dryly. His face changed, he dropped to his knees in front of her chair and took her hands. "You're holding something back, and it's about you. Tell me."

She twisted away. "Why should I be troubled?" she asked.

"Because you're driving to and from work. I see the Corvette in the Hug parking lot—I drive past quite often these days."

"Oh, that! It's getting too cold to walk."

"That's not what my little bird says about you."

She got to her feet, walked across to the window. "It's just silly. Imaginitis."

"What's imaginitis?" he asked, coming to stand beside her.

He radiated warmth; she had noticed it before, and found it curiously comforting. "Oh, well—" she said, stopped, then hurried on as if to get the words out before she could regret them. "I was being followed home each evening."

He didn't laugh, though he didn't tense either. "How do you know? Did you see someone?"

"No, no one. That's the frightening part. I'd hear the rustle of footsteps through the dead leaves, and they'd stop when I stopped, but not quite quickly enough. Yet—no one!"

"Spooky, huh?"

"Yes."

He sighed, put his arm around her and led her to an easy chair, gave her another cognac. "You're not the kind to panic, and I doubt it's imaginitis. However, I don't think it's the Monster. Lock up that grunty pig of a car. My mother's got an old Merc she doesn't use, you can have that. No temptation to the local hoods, and maybe your stalker will get the message."

"I couldn't impose like that."

"It's no imposition. Come on, I'll follow you home and see you in your door. The Merc will be there in the morning."

"In England," she said as he walked her to the Corvette, "a Merc would be a Mercedes-Benz."

"Here," he said, opening her door, "it's a Mercury. You've had two cognacs and you've got a police lieutenant on your tail, so drive carefully."

He was so kind, so generous. Desdemona eased the bright red sports car away from the curb the moment Carmine was in his Ford, and drove home conscious of the fact that her fear had vanished. Was that all it took? A strong man on one's side?

He supervised the locking up of the Corvette, then escorted her to the front door.

"I'll be all right now," she said, and held out her hand.

"Oh, no, I'll check upstairs too."

"It's pretty messy," she said, commencing to climb the stairs.

But the mess that met her eyes wasn't what she had meant. Her work box was on the floor, its contents scattered far and wide, and her new piece of embroidery, a priest's chasuble, was draped across her chair slashed to ribbons.

Desdemona reeled, was steadied. "My work, my beautiful work!" she whispered. "He didn't go this far before."

"You mean he's been in here before?"

"Yes, at least twice. He moved my work, but he didn't ruin it. Oh, Carmine!"

"Here, sit down." He pushed her into another chair and went to the phone. "Mike?" he asked somone. "Delmonico. I need two men to watch a witness. Yesterday, understand?"

His calm was unimpaired, but he prowled all the way around the work chair without touching anything, then sat on the arm of her chair. "It's an unusual hobby," he said then, casually.

"I love it."

"So it's a heartbreak to see this. Were you working on it when he visited earlier?"

"No, I was doing a sideboard cloth for Chuck Ponsonby. Very elegant, but not the same kind of thing as this. I gave it to him a week ago. He was delighted."

He said nothing further until the flashing lights of a squad car reflected through the front windows, then patted her shoulder and left, apparently to give the men instructions.

"There's one guy just outside your own door at the top here, and another at the top of the back stairs. You'll be safe," he said when he returned. "I'll drop off the Merc first thing, but you won't be able to go straight in to work. Leave everything exactly as it is until my technicians get here in the morning to see if our destructive friend left any clues behind."

"He did the first time," she said.

"What?" he asked sharply, and she knew he was asking what clue, not simply exclaiming. Carmine on the job didn't waste time.

"A tiny bunch of short black hairs."

His face went suddenly expressionless. "I see." Then he was gone, as if he didn't know what to say to leave her.

Desdemona went to bed, though not to sleep.

PART TWO

December 1965

CHAPTER 7

Wednesday, December 1st, 1965

The students tumbled out of Travis High in hundreds, some to walk short distances to their homes in the Hollow, some to board dozens of school buses lined up along Twentieth and around the corners into Paine. In the old days they would simply have gone to any bus serving their particular destination, but ever since the advent of the Connecticut Monster each student was given a particular bus, emblazoned by a number. The driver was provided with a list of names and was under orders not to move until every student was aboard. So careful had the administration of Travis become that an absent student's name was erased from the day's list before it was given to the driver. Going to school was not such a problem; what everyone feared was going home.

Travis was the biggest public high school in Holloman, its intake spreading from the Hollow to the northern outskirts of the city on this western side. The majority of the students were black, but not by many, and while there were occasional racial problems there, the bulk of the students mixed and mingled according to their personal affinities. So while the Black Brigade had its supporters at Travis High, various churches and societies did too, as well as those individuals who trod a midline of reasonable grades and no trouble. Any teacher on the staff would have said that hormones caused more problems than race.

Though it was the Catholic high schools under strictest police attention, Travis hadn't been neglected. When Francine Murray, a sixteen-year-old sophomore who lived out in the Valley, failed to board her bus, its driver climbed out and ran to the Holloman squad car parked on the sidewalk near the front gates. Within moments a controlled chaos reigned; buses were pulled over as uniformed men asked if Francine Murray was a passenger, others asked for Francine's friends to come forward, and Carmine Delmonico was racing to Travis High with Corey and Abe.

Not that he forgot the Hug. Before the Ford took off he gave Marciano instructions to make sure that everyone at the Hug was present and accounted for. "I know we can't afford to send a car there, so call Miss Dupre and tell her from me that I want every last one of them tagged down to visits to the john. You can trust her, Danny, but don't tell her more than you have to."

Having searched the vast and rambling school from attics to gymnasiums, the teachers were huddled in the yard while Derek Daiman, the highly respected black principal, paced up and down. Squad cars were still arriving as other schools were pronounced free of missing students, their contingents of cops dispersing to question everybody they could see, search Travis all over again, round up milling students dying of curiosity.

"Her name is Francine Murray," said Mr. Daiman to Carmine. "She ought to have been on that bus over there"—he pointed—"but she didn't turn up. She was present for her last period, Chemistry, and as far as I can ascertain, she left the building with a group of friends. They scatter once they're in the yard, depending which bus they're on or if they're walking—Lieutenant Delmonico, this is terrible, terrible!"

"Getting upset won't help her or us, Mr. Daiman," Carmine said. "The most important thing is, what does Francine look like?"

"Like the missing girls," Daiman said, beginning to weep. "So pretty! So popular! A grades, never any trouble, a great example to her fellow students."

"Is she of Caribbean origin, sir?"

"Not to my knowledge," the principal said, wiping his eyes. "I guess that's why we didn't *notice*—the news items all said part Hispanic, and she isn't. One of those real Old Connecticut black families, white intermarriage. It happens, Lieutenant, no matter how much people oppose it. Oh, dear God, dear God, what am I going to do?"

"Mr. Daiman, are you trying to say that one of Francine's parents is black and the other white?" Carmine asked.

"I believe so, yes, I believe so."

Abe and Corey had gone to talk to the uniforms, tell them to search each bus and then get it on its way, but keep Francine's friends in a group until they could be interviewed.

"You're sure she's not in the school somewhere?" Carmine asked Sergeant O'Brien when he led his cops and teacher guides out of the enormous building.

"Lieutenant, she is not inside, I swear. We opened every closet, looked under every desk, in every rest room, the cafeteria, the gyms, the classrooms, the assembly room, storage rooms, the furnace room, attics, the science labs, janitor's room—every goddamn corner," O'Brien said, sweating.

"Who saw her last?" Carmine asked the teachers, some in tears, all shaking with shock.

"She walked out of my classroom with her friends," said Miss Corwyn of Chemistry. "I stayed behind to straighten up, I didn't follow them. Oh, I wish I had!"

"Don't castigate yourself, ma'am, you weren't to know," said Carmine, assessing the others. "Anyone else see her?"

No, no one had. And no, no one had seen any strangers.

He's done it again, thought Carmine, walking up to the knot of

119

frightened young people who had claimed friendship with Francine Murray. He's snatched her away without a soul's seeing him. It's sixty-two days since Mercedes Alvarez disappeared, we've been on our toes, warned people, showed photos of the kind of girl he targets, tightened up on school security, thrown all our resources into this. We ought to have caught him! So what does he do? He lulls us into certainty that the Caribbean is a mandatory part of his obsessions, then switches to a different ethnic group. And I put Danny Marciano down for suggesting it. Oh, Travis, of all places! An ant heap! Fifteen hundred students! Half of this city thinks of Travis as a training ground for hoods, punks and low life, forgetting that it's also a place where whole bunches of decent kids, black and white, get a pretty good education.

Francine's best friend was a black girl named Kimmy Wilson.

"She was with us when we came out of Chemistry, sir," Kimmy said through sniffles.

"You're all in Chemistry?"

"Yes, sir, we're all planning pre-med."

"Go on, Kimmy."

"I thought she'd gone to the rest room. Francine has a weak bladder, she's always going to the rest room. I didn't think about it because I know what she's like. I didn't think!" The tears gushed. "Oh, why didn't I go with her?"

"Do you travel on the same bus, Kimmy?"

"Yes, sir." Kimmy made a huge effort to master her feelings. "We both live on Whitney out in the Valley." She pointed at two weeping white girls. "So do Charlene and Roxanne. None of us thought about her until the bus driver called the roll and she didn't answer."

"Do you know your bus driver?"

"Not her name, sir, not today's. I know her face."

By five o'clock Travis High was deserted. Having combed it and the neighborhood, the police cordon was spreading ever outward while word ran through the Hollow that the Connecticut Monster had struck again. Not a spic. A genuine black girl. While Carmine was on his way to the Murray house, Mohammed el Nesr, informed by Wesley le Clerc, was calling his troops together.

Halfway to the Valley the Ford pulled up at a phone booth and Carmine talked to Danny Marciano without the annoyances of a car radio; some of the press could tune into that, and it was noisy into the bargain.

"No absentees at the Hug, Danny?"

"Only Cecil Potter and Otis Green, who'd already finished for the day. Both of them were at home when Miss Dupre called. She says everyone else was present and accounted for."

"What can you tell me about the Murrays? All I managed to find out is that one parent is black, the other white."

"They're just like all the rest, Carmine—the salt of the earth," said Marciano, sighing. "Only difference is no Caribbean connection as far as anyone knows. They're regulars at the local Baptist church, so I took the liberty of calling its minister, a Leon Williams, and asking him to go over and break the news. It's spreading at the speed of light, and I didn't want some bug-eyed neighbor getting there first."

"Thanks for that, Danny. What else?"

"The black half is the father. He's a research associate in electrical engineering in the Susskind Science Tower, which means he's junior faculty on reasonable pay. Mom is white. She works the lunch rush in the Susskind cafeteria, so she's there to see the kids off to school, and home again before they are. They have two boys, both younger than Francine, who go to the Higgins middle school. The Reverend Williams told me that the Murrays caused a bit of talk when they moved to Whitney nine years ago, but the novelty faded and now they're just a part of the local woodwork. Very well liked, have friends of both colors."

"Thanks, Danny. See you later."

The Valley was an area with a fairly mixed population, not affluent, but not impoverished either. Racial tensions broke out there from time to time, usually when a new white family arrived, but property rates were not sufficiently high to make blackness a real financial liability. It was not an area famous for hate mail, killing of pets, dumping of trash, graffiti.

As the Ford turned onto Whitney, all half-acre blocks with modest houses, Carmine could feel Abe and Corey stiffen.

"Jesus, Carmine, how did we let this happen?" Abe burst out.

"Because he changed pace, Abe. He outfoxed us."

As they drew up to a yellow-painted house Carmine put his hand on Corey's shoulder. "You guys stay here. If I need you, I'll holler, okay?"

The Reverend Leon Williams admitted him to the Murray house. *This is becoming a habit, Carmine.*

The two sons were elsewhere; sounds from a TV came faintly. Seated together on a sofa, the parents were trying valiantly to remain composed; she held his hand as if it were a lifeline.

"You're not Caribbean, Mr. Murray?" Carmine asked.

"No, definitely not. The Murrays have been in Connecticut since before the Civil War, fought for the North. And my wife is from Wilkes-Barre."

"Have you a recent photograph of Francine?"

A sister to the other eleven.

And so it went all over again, the same questions he'd asked eleven other families: whom Francine saw, what good deeds she did, if she'd mentioned any new friend or acquaintance, if she'd noticed anyone watching her, following her. As always, the answers were no.

Carmine didn't stay a moment longer than he had to. *Their minister is a greater comfort to them in their pain than I could ever be. I'm the agent of doom, maybe of retribution, and that's how they see me. They're in there praying that their little girl is fine, but terrified that she is not. Waiting for me, the agent of doom, to return and tell them that she is not.*

Commissioner John Silvestri appeared on local TV after the six o'clock news was finished, appealing to the people of Holloman and Connecticut to help search for Francine, to come forward if they had seen anything unusual. A desk cop had his uses, and one of Silvestri's best was his public image—that leonine head, superb profile, calm dignity, air of candor. He didn't try to parry the anchorwoman's questions the way a politician would, so shrewd a politician was he. Her rebarbative remarks about the fact that the Connecticut Monster was still at large and still abducting innocent young women didn't dent his composure in the least; somehow he managed to make her look like a handsome wolf.

"He's smart," said Silvestri simply. "Very smart."

"He must be," said Surina Chandra to her husband as they sat in front of their gigantic TV screen. They had paid a fortune to bring in a special line from New York City so they could channel-hop on cable until eight, when they sat to eat dinner. What they hoped to see was an item about India, but that was a rare occurrence indeed. The U.S.A., they had discovered, wasn't a scrap interested in India; it was involved in its own problems.

"Yes, he must be," said Nur Chandra absently, his mind on a triumph so great he wanted to shout it to the world. Only he dare not risk it, dare not. It had to remain his secret. "I'll be sleeping in my cottage for the next few days," he added. A smile curved his perfect lips. "I have important work to do."

"How can anyone call the Monster smart?" Robin demanded. "It isn't smart to murder children, it's—it's stupid and inhuman!"

I wonder, Addison Forbes asked himself, what her definition of "smart" might be if I pushed her to explain it?

"I agree with the police commissioner," he said, discovering a crushed cashew nut hiding beneath some lettuce. "A very smart fellow. What the Monster does is disgusting, but I do admire his competence. He's made total fools out of the police." The nut melted on his tongue like nectar. "Who," he said bitterly, "had the gall to order Desdemona Dupre to hunt us down like animals and ask us where we'd been! We have a spy in our midst, and I for one will not forget

123

that. What her idiocies mean is that I'm behind in my clinical notes. Don't wait up for me. And throw out that quart of ice cream in the freezer, do you hear me?"

"Yes, he is smart," said Catherine Finch. She eyed Maurie anxiously; he hadn't been the same since that Nazi schmuck tried to kill himself. With more steel in her character than Maurie had in his, she thought it a pity the Nazi schmuck hadn't succeeded, but Maurie had a great big conscience and it was telling him that *he* was the schmuck. Nothing she could say prevented Maurie from blaming himself, poor baby.

He didn't bother answering her, just pushed his brisket away and got up from the table. "Maybe I'll work a little on my mushrooms," he said, plucking a flashlight from the pungent porch as he passed through.

"Maurie, you don't need to be in the dark tonight!" she cried.

"I'm in the dark all the time, Cathy. All the time."

The Ponsonbys didn't see Commissioner Silvestri on TV because they didn't own one. TV was lost on Claire, and Charles referred to it as "the opiate of the uncultivated herd."

Tonight the music was Hindemith's Concerto for Orchestra, a windy, brassy blare that they enjoyed most when Charles had found a particularly good bottle of pouilly fumé. They were eating lightly, a *fines herbs* omelet followed by fillets of sole poached in water liberally laced with very dry white vermouth; no starches, just some romaine lettuce with a walnut oil vinaigrette, and a champagne sorbet to finish. Not a coffee and cigars meal.

"How they do insult my intelligence sometimes," Charles said to Claire as Hindemith entered a quieter phase. "Desdemona Dupre came looking for all of us with some tale of needing all of our signatures on a document that Bob certainly knew nothing about, then an hour later the police arrived in their thousands. Just when I was in the middle of a train of thought that did *not* need the thump of jack-boots. Where was I all afternoon? Tchah! I was tempted to tell them to go to hell, but I didn't. I must say that Delmonico runs a smooth operation, though. He didn't deign to grace us with his own presence, but his minions betray the stamp of his style."

"Dear, dear," she said placidly, fingers twined loosely about the stem of her wine glass. "Are they going to persecute the Hug every time a girl is abducted?"

"I imagine so. Don't you?"

"Oh, yes. How sad a place the world becomes. Sometimes, Charles, I am very glad that I walk through it blind."

"You walked through it blind today, you always do. Though I wish you wouldn't. There's some story going around that Desdemona Dupre is being stalked. Though what *she* could have to do with the other business is a bit of a mystery." He giggled. "Such a vast and unprepossessing creature!"

"Threads weave predictable patterns, Charles."

"That," he said, "depends upon who's making the predictions."

The Ponsonbys laughed, the dog wuffed, Hindemith let loose.

Much to Carmine's surprise, he found his mother's car parked outside Malvolio's when he pulled up shortly after 7 P.M., Corey and Abe delivered to their long-suffering wives.

"What are you doing here?" he asked, helping her out. "More problems?"

"I thought you might need company. How's the food in there? Any hamburgers to take away?"

"No burgers to go, but let's eat inside. It's warm."

"I did my best for Captain Marciano this afternoon," she said, eating a fry (she called it a chip) in her fingers, "but it took half an hour to track them all down. I couldn't find a one of the researchers themselves until I realized that it might be the first of December, but up on the roof it was warm and sheltered from the wind. They were up there having a round table discussion on Eustace. All of them, and they looked as if they hadn't moved in yonks."

125

"Yonks?"

"A long time."

"I'm sorry to have inflicted it on you, but I couldn't spare any cops while there was a hope of finding Francine."

"It's all right, I blamed you. Very caustically." She picked up another fry. "Ever since word got round about my police guard, I'm regarded differently. Most of them think I'm putting it on."

"Putting it on?"

"Making it up. Tamara says I'm trying to catch you."

He grinned. "A tortuous scheme, Desdemona."

"A pity my ruined work didn't yield that clue."

"Oh, he's far too smart to have left one beyond the first time. He knew you wouldn't report it."

She shivered. "Why do I think you think it's the Monster?"

"Because it's a red herring, woman."

"You mean I'm not in danger?"

"I didn't say that. The cops stay."

"Is it possible he thinks I know something?"

"Maybe, maybe not. Red herrings don't need reasons apart from creating illusions."

"Let's go back to your apartment and watch the Commissioner on the late news," she said.

Then, afterward, she smiled. "The Commissioner looks like a sweetie. Didn't he handle madam smarty-pants anchorwoman well?"

Carmine's brows rose. "Next time I see him I'll tell him that you think he's a sweetie. Cute word, but your sweetie once took on a twelve-man German machine gun nest single-handed and saved a whole company. Among other things."

"Yes, I can see that side of him too. But you won't mention me. When you see him it will be a very serious meeting because the situation is very serious. The Monster is really clever, though perhaps that's to underestimate him."

"He's a whole bunch of things, Desdemona. Smart—clever—insane—maybe a genius. What I do know is that the façade he presents to the world is totally believable. His guard never drops. If it had, someone would have noticed. I think he might be a married man whose wife doesn't suspect him. Oh, yeah, he's one smart cookie."

"You're pretty smart yourself, Carmine, but you've got more going for you than that. You're a bulldog. Once the teeth lock in, you can't let go. Eventually the extra weight of dragging you around with him will exhaust him."

Warmth flooded through him, whether from the cognac or the compliment he wasn't sure; Carmine preened a little inside his mind, very careful that the rest of him didn't bat an eyelash.

CHAPTER 8

Thursday, December 2nd, 1965

Francine Murray hadn't turned up by the following day, nor did anyone save her parents doubt that the Monster had gotten her. Oh, the parents knew it too, but how can the human heart exist in such a sea of crushing pain until there is no other alternative? She'd gone to a pajama party once without telling them—just plain forgotten, but it had happened. So they waited and prayed, hoping against hope that it was all a mistake and Francine would come bouncing in the door.

When Carmine returned to his office at 4 P.M., he had nothing positive to show for a day of talking to people, including at the Hug. Two months on a case and zilch. His phone rang.

"Delmonico."

"Lieutenant, this is Derek Daiman from Travis High. Could you possibly come up here straightaway?"

"I'll be there in five minutes."

*   *   *

Derek Daiman, thought Carmine, was probably always the last teacher to leave Travis; his gigantic, polyglot baby must be hell to run, but he managed to run it well.

He was standing inside the doors of Travis's main building, but the moment the Ford pulled into the schoolyard he emerged, ran down the steps to the car.

"I haven't said anything to anyone, Lieutenant, I just asked the boy who found it to stay where he was."

Carmine followed him around the left-hand corner of the main block to where an ungainly, shedlike structure had been tacked on adjacent to the brick side wall through a short passageway that gave the brick wall's windows nine feet of light and air as well as a view of buff-painted metal siding.

Education was a municipal responsibility; cities like Holloman, handicapped by soaring populations in their poorer areas, struggled to provide adequate facilities. Thus the shed had come into being, a hangar that held a basketball court, bleachers for spectators, and, at its far end, gymnastic equipment—vaulting horses, rings suspended from the ceiling, parallel bars, and what looked like two posts and a cross bar for high jumps or pole vaults. Another gym mirrored this one on the right side, held a swimming pool and bleachers where the basketball court was here, and a far end devoted to boxing, wrestling and working out. The girls here to perform graceful leaps, the boys there to beat the crap out of punching bags.

Though they entered the gym from the yard, they could have done so from the building; the short passageway allowed students direct access, mandatory in bad weather, but it too had a door.

Derek Daiman led Carmine past the basketball court and its bleachers to the gymnastic end, provided with seating down either side by what looked like big wooden footlockers. His was the old army term; in high school, he seemed to remember, they were just called boxes. Alongside the last box in the row on the passageway wall stood a tall, athletic-looking black youth whose face was marked with tears.

"Lieutenant, this is Winslow Searle. Winslow, tell Lieutenant Delmonico what you found."

"This," said the boy, and held up a candy-pink jacket. "It belongs to Francine. Her name's in it, see?"

FRANCINE MURRAY, machine-embroidered on the stout strip that enabled the jacket to be hung on a hook.

"Where was it, Winslow?"

"In there, pushed inside one of the mats with its cuff poking out." Winslow lifted the lid of the box to reveal that it still held two gym mats, one rolled up, the other folded loosely.

"How did you come to find it?"

"I'm a high jumper, Lieutenant, but I have a glass jaw. If I land too hard, I get concussed," Winslow said in a pure Holloman accent, his sentence construction indicating that he kept up good grades in English and didn't hang out with a gang.

"Potential Olympic standard, lots of offers from colleges," Daiman whispered in Carmine's ear. "He's thinking of Howard."

"Go on, Winslow, you're doing fine," Carmine said.

"There's one super-thick mat, and I always use it. Coach Martin keeps it in the same box for me, but it wasn't there when I came in to do some jumping after school today. I went looking, found it at the bottom of this one. It was weird, sir."

"How, weird?"

"The box should be full, the mats stacked like frankfurters. Some of the other boxes had too many—more like sardines. And my super-thick mat wasn't rolled up at all. It was folded back and forth from side to side of the box. The one with the cuff of Francine's jacket showing was right on top of it. I had a funny feeling, so I pulled the cuff and it slid right out."

The floor around the box was strewn with five unrolling mats; Carmine surveyed them with a sinking heart. "I don't suppose you remember which mat held the jacket?"

"Oh, yes, sir. The one still in the box on top of my mat."

"Winslow, my man," said Carmine, shaking the youth's hand

warmly, "I am rooting for you for a gold medal in sixty-eight! Thank you for your care and your good sense. Now go home, but don't talk about any of this, okay?"

"Sure," said Winslow, wiped his cheeks and walked off, his gait reminiscent of a big cat.

"The whole school is grieving," said the principal.

"With good reason. Can I dial out on that phone? Thanks."

He asked for Patrick, still there. "Come yourself if you can, but if you can't, send Paul, Abe, Corey and all your gear, Patsy. Maybe we've found something useful."

"Do you mind waiting with me, Mr. Daiman?" he asked when he returned to the box, lid down, Francine's jacket lying on it.

"No, of course not." Daiman cleared his throat, shifted on his feet, took a deep breath. "Lieutenant, I would not be doing my duty if I didn't inform you that trouble is coming."

"Trouble?"

"Racial trouble. The Black Brigade is campaigning hard for support using Francine's disappearance as a platform. She's not Hispanic, and on the forms she fills out she calls herself black. I never argue with my light-colored students about how they think of themselves racially, Lieutenant—to me, that would be a denial of their rights. Like the new concepts about indigenousness, that only an indigenous person can decide whether they are or are not." He shook himself, looked wry. "I'm straying. The point is that some of my more irascible students have been saying that this is a white killer of black girls, and that the police aren't bothering to catch him because he's a powerful member of the Hug with all kinds of political influence. Since my school is fifty-two percent black and forty-eight percent white, unless I can keep the lid on the Black Brigade kids, we could have a mess of trouble."

"Jesus, that's all we need! Mr. Daiman, we are busting our guts to find this killer, you have my word on that. Simply, we know nothing about him, least of all that he's a member of the Hug—no one at the Hug has any political power! But I thank you for the warning and I'll

131

make sure that Travis has some protection." He glanced from the box to the door barring the passageway that led into the main school. "Mind if I look around? And where's the Chemistry classroom from here? Is it a lab, or a classroom?"

"It's just up the hall from the gym, and it's the classroom. The lab is in the general lab area. Go ahead, Lieutenant, look wherever you like," said Daiman, went to a chair and sat on it with his head in his hands.

The passageway door was single, not double locked: was it ever double locked? On the tunnel side it couldn't be opened without a key—or a credit card if it wasn't double locked. Carmine entered the nine-foot-long tube and emerged to find himself staring at a girls' toilet block directly across the hall.

This killer knows everything! he thought, staggered. He grabbed her when she went into the toilets—she was notorious for that— dragged her across a three-yard hall into a three-yard tunnel and a deserted gym. Most likely he opened the door before he grabbed her. And he *knew* the gym would be deserted! It is on every Wednesday after school because that's when the contractors come in to treat the floors. But they didn't treat them yesterday because Francine went missing and they weren't allowed in. Once he was in the gym, he rearranged the mats, put her in the bottom of the nearest box and made sure Winslow's super-thick mat covered her completely. Did he gag her and tie her, or did he give her a shot of something to keep her out for a few hours?

We searched every square inch of this school twice, but we didn't find her. And when we didn't find her, we knew she was the twelfth victim, spirited out of Travis before the squad car outside could radio base. Both times some searcher would have opened that locker and seen what was in all the others: rolled-up gym mats. Maybe who-ever looked poked around inside it, but Francine didn't move or make a noise. Then, when we were satisfied that Francine was gone—when Travis had ceased to be of any interest to us—he came back and retrieved her. I'll put Corey on the door lock, he's the best in the business.

Maybe where we keep going wrong is in underrating the grind, the pain of his planning. It's as if he had nothing else to do between each abduction than spend all of every single day scheming how he's going to grab the next one. How far in advance does he know the identity of his next victim? Did he pick them out years ago, when they were on the brink of puberty? Has he got them all listed on a wall chart, carefully ruled in columns—name, date of birth, address, school, religion, race, habits? He has to watch them, he *must* have known about Francine's weak bladder. Is he a substitute teacher, flitting from school to school with glowing references and a great reputation? That, we have to investigate starting right now.

"Did he leave the jacket behind to jerk our strings, or did Francine manage to hide it in the mat?" he asked Patrick as he watched Paul delicately ease the unwieldy coat into a plastic bag.

"I'd say Francine hid it," Patrick answered. "He's arrogant, but to leave us the jacket betrays one of his craftiest tricks. Until now, we've been convinced that the girls are snatched and whisked away immediately. Why tell us that he doesn't always do that? I believe that he wants to keep us peering down the same tunnel at the same ray of light. Which means, Carmine, that this new development can't possibly be leaked to the press. Do you trust the boy who found it? The principal?"

"Yes, I do. How did he keep her quiet in the locker, Patsy?"

"He drugged her. Someone this meticulous wouldn't have made the mistake of gagging her before putting her in a relatively airless, smelly sports locker. There's no sign she did throw up, but human beings vary and some are the vomiting type. Gagged, she would have drowned in her own vomit. No, he wouldn't risk that. She's too valuable, he's planned her for at least two months."

"If we find her body—"

"You don't think we'll find her alive?"

Carmine gazed at his cousin with what Patrick called his "scornfully stern look." "No, we're not going to find her alive. We don't know where to search, and all the places we'd like to search, we can't. So *when* we find her body," he went on, "you'd better go over her skin with a microscope. There's a prick in it somewhere because he wouldn't have had time to inject her where a good pathologist couldn't find the mark. Odds are he'll have used a very fine needle, and this time the body parts might not be in such good shape."

"Maybe," said Patrick wryly, "I could borrow the Hug's Zeiss operating microscope. Mine's shit by comparison."

"With our unlimited budget, I don't see why you can't order one. It mightn't come in time for Francine, but once you have it, I'm sure you'll find plenty of use for it."

"What I love most about you, Carmine, is your gall. They'll crucify you, because I won't put my name on the requisition."

"Fuck them," said Carmine. "They don't have to see all those poor families. I have nightmares about the heads."

CHAPTER 9

Friday, December 10th, 1965

Ten days went by with no sign of Francine Murray, though Francine Murray was not on Ruth Kyneton's mind that morning.

Even through the worst of winter, Ruth Kyneton preferred to use the outside line than shove her freshly laundered linens in one of those dryer things. You couldn't beat the smell of clothes dried in sweet, clean air. Besides, she strongly suspected that the artificially scented anti-static fabric conditioners advertised on TV were actually a government plot to impregnate the skins of loyal, law-abiding Americans with substances designed to turn them into zombies. Every time you turned around, Congress was trampling on someone's rights in favor of drunks, skunks and punks, so why not fabric conditioners, bathroom deodorants and fluoride?

She hung out her washing the proper way: fold a corner over the previous one to make it thick, pin them together, then tuck its far corner under the corner of the next item and pin them together, her mouth stuffed with pins, more in the pockets of her apron. Yep, her way meant half the number of pins and a line so crowded that no wire showed; finished, she levered a forked sapling under the line to stop it from sagging. The good thing about today was that it wasn't cold enough to freeze things while they were wet. Purist though she was, Ruth never relished wrestling with frozen washing.

Throughout this exercise she had been aware that the three curs from farther down Griswold Lane were fighting at the bottom of her yard; they were bound to move on up because curs always did, and she was not about to let curs soil her blindingly white whites, her vividly vivid colors. So she returned to the house to fetch a straw broom and marched resolutely down the yard to where, at the end of it, a streamlet trickled. The streamlet was a nuisance—kept the ground from freezing quickly, admittedly, but it created *mud*. The curs would be caked in slimy black mud.

"Git!" she shouted, descending like a witch dismounted from her broom, waving it about viciously. "Git, you mangy critters, git! Go on, git!"

The dogs were squabbling amicably rather than fighting, all three tugging at a long, fleshy bone smeared in mud, and were unwilling to give up this prize until Ruth's broom swiped two of them so hard that they fled, yelping, to stand some distance off and wait for her to give up. The third dog, pack leader, crouched and put its ears back, growling and snarling at her. But Ruth had lost interest in the curs; the bone was double, and had a human foot attached.

She didn't scream or faint. The broom still in her hands, she walked back to the house to call the Holloman police. That done, she stationed herself on the edge of the mud to stand guard until help arrived while the dogs, thwarted yet undefeated, circled.

Patrick cordoned off the whole area of the streamlet and concentrated first on the grave, only ten yards from where the dogs had competed for their find.

"My guess is that the raccoons were first," he said to Carmine, "but I'm positive that she—yes, this has to be Francine—was deliberately buried in order to be unearthed soon after. Just twelve inches down. Eight of the ten pieces are still in situ. Paul found the right humerus in some bushes—raccoons. The left tib-fib and foot were what alerted Mrs. Kyneton. I've got reliable people searching, but I don't think the head is here."

"Nor do I," Carmine said. "And it comes back to the Hug."

"Looks that way. My guess is he's got a grudge."

Carmine left Patrick to it and plodded up to the house to find Ruth Kyneton ready and able to talk, though she was by no means indifferent to Francine Murray's fate.

"Poor little baby! Shoulda been him dog's meat, only that's too good. I'd boil him in oil—sit him in it and light the fire with my own hands, then watch him cook real slow," she said, one hand pressed against her midriff. "Mind if I have a drink of tea, Lieutenant? It settles my stomach."

"If I can have one too, ma'am."

"Why us?" she asked. "That's what I'd like to know."

"So would I, Mrs. Kyneton. But more importantly, did you see or hear anything last night?"

"You sure it was last night?"

"Fairly sure, but tell me anything unusual that's happened on any night for the last nine of them."

"Nothing," she said, putting a tea bag in each of two mugs. "Never heard no noises. Oh, them dogs barked, but they bark all the time. The Desmonds had a barney—screams, yells, things breaking—night before last. That happens regular. He's an alkie." She reflected for a moment. "So's she."

"Would you hear anything if you were asleep?"

"Don't sleep much, and never until my son comes home," Ruth said, swelling with pride. "He's a brain surgeon at Chubb, deals with them little bubbles on veins that burst like a water main."

"Arteries," Carmine corrected automatically; a Hug education was beginning to make itself apparent.

"Right, arteries. Keith's the best they got at repairing them bubbles. I always think of it like patching the inner tube on an old bicycle. Did a lot of that when I was a girl. Maybe that's where Keith gets it from. Dunno where else."

If I were not so worried and angry, Carmine thought, I could fall in love with this woman. She's an original.

"Keith. He's Miss Silverman's husband."

"Yep. They've been married coming up for three years."

"I take it that Dr. Kyneton comes home late often?"

"All the time. The operations take hours and hours. He's a tiger for work, my Keith. Not like his old man. *He* couldn't work on a chain gang. Yep, I always wait up for Keith, make sure he eats. Can't sleep until he's in."

"Was he late last night? The night before?"

"Two-thirty last night, one-thirty the night before."

"Does he make a lot of noise when he comes in?"

"Nope. Quiet as a corpse. Makes no difference—I still hear him. He cuts the engine on his car and coasts down the lane, but I can hear him," said Ruth Kyneton positively. "I listen."

"Was there a moment last night when you thought you heard him, but he didn't come in? Or the night before?"

"Nope. The only one I heard was Keith."

Carmine drank his tea, thanked her, decided to go. "I'd appreciate it if you didn't talk about this to anyone except your family, Mrs. Kyneton," he said at the door. "I'll be back to see them as soon as I can."

Patrick had finished washing the body parts and assembling them on his table when Carmine walked in.

"They were so covered in mud, humus and leaves that getting anything useful will be a miracle," Patrick said. "I've saved all the washing fluid—distilled water—and I took a sample of the stream water. This time I have more to work with," he went on, sounding content. "The rape pattern is the same—a succession of increasingly large sheaths or dildoes, vaginal and anal penetration. But see that straight line of bruising on the upper arms just below the shoulders, and that other straight line of bruising below the elbows? She was tied down with something about fifteen inches wide, heavy fabric like canvas. The contusions occurred when she struggled, but she couldn't free herself. It also tells us that this killer isn't interested in breasts. He bound them flat under a canvas restraint that hid them from sight. That means she was lying on a table. As to why he didn't just manacle her wrists or tie her hands down, I don't know. Keeping her legs free is more logical, he needed to move them around."

"How long was she alive after she was grabbed, Patsy?"

"About a week, but I don't think he fed her. The digestive tract was empty. Mercedes had been fed on cornflakes and milk. Though all we had of Mercedes was the torso, I think he changed some of his habits for Francine. Or maybe each victim is a little different. Without the bodies, we'll never know."

"How long had she been dead?" Carmine asked.

"Maximum, thirty hours. Probably less. She was buried last night, not the night before, but I'd say before midnight. He didn't keep her long after she died, but I can tell you that she died from loss of blood. Look at her ankles." Patrick pointed.

Carmine hadn't gotten that far; he stiffened. "Ligature welts," he breathed.

"Not a part of his method of restraint. They weren't on for more than an hour. Oh, but he's clever! No fibers or slivers from those welts, I know it in my bones. My guess is that he strung her up with single-strand stainless steel wire that he rigged to make sure that the joins were never in contact with her flesh. The wire bit in, but it didn't break the skin by sawing at it or catching on it anywhere. These kids are small and light, weigh about eighty pounds. Like Mercedes, he cut her throat to bleed her out first, then decapitated her later—not such a long wait between the two for Francine compared to Mercedes."

"Tell me there's semen."

"I doubt it."

"You'll test the wash water for semen too?"

"Carmine! Is the Pope a Catholic?"

"I hope so," said Carmine, squeezing his cousin's arm.

From there it was on to Silvestri's office, Marciano ambling in his wake; Abe and Corey were still out at Griswold Lane, asking its inhabitants if they had seen or heard anything unusual.

He filled Silvestri and Marciano in.

"Is it possible," Marciano asked afterward, "that this guy doesn't belong to the Hug, but has a grudge against the place or someone in it?"

"That begins to look more and more likely, Danny. Though I wish I could be sure that all the Huggers really were where they were supposed to be Wednesday of last week when Francine was snatched. It would have taken a good twenty minutes to get from the Hug to Travis and back again—at a jog. Whereas Miss Dupre didn't locate the senior Huggers for thirty minutes. However, they do seem to have been together on the roof, and as there are only seven of them, I'm sure a twenty-minute absence followed by heavy breathing on return would have caused comment. Dr. Addison Forbes might not have reappeared breathing heavily, I take that into account. Leaving that aside, the killer definitely wants us to believe that his murders are connected to the Hug. Otherwise why choose the Kynetons' as a dump site? He wanted her found quickly, so he hardly scraped away enough mud to cover her. Every scavenger for a mile must have come running. He's pissing on someone or something, but who or what I don't know."

"You don't think the Kynetons have anything to do with it?" Silvestri asked.

"I haven't checked Hilda and Keith out yet, but Ruth Kyneton is a straight shooter."

"Where do you go from here?"

"I'll see Hilda and Keith today, but I'm going to put off the other

Huggers until Monday. I want them to stew over the weekend watching news bulletins and listening to all the TV couch cops."

"He's going to keep on killing, isn't he?" Marciano asked.

"He can't stop, Danny. We have to stop him."

"What about that new bunch of psychiatrists the FBI and NYPD consult? No help from them?" Silvestri demanded.

"Same old song, John. Nobody knows much about the multiple killer. The shrinks yack about ritual and obsession, but they can't come up with anything *helpful*. They can't tell me what this guy looks like, or how old he is, or what kind of job he has, or his childhood, or his level of education—he's an enigma, a total fucking mystery—" Carmine stopped, swallowed, closed his eyes. "Sorry, sir. It's getting to me."

"It's getting to all of us. Thing is, maybe there are more of these multiple killers out there than we know about," Silvestri said. "Too many more like our killer, and someone's going to *have* to do something to help catch them. Our guy got away with ten murders before we even knew he existed." He got out a new cigar to chew. "Just plug away at it, Carmine."

"I intend to," said Carmine, getting to his feet. "Sooner or later the bastard's going to slip, and when he does, I'll be there to break his fall."

"Oh, this could ruin Keith!" Hilda Silverman cried, her face white. "Just when he's got a great offer—it isn't fair!"

"Offer of what?" Carmine asked.

"A partnership in a private practice. He'll have to buy in, of course, but we've managed to save enough to do that."

Which answers the riddle of why they live in this semi-slum, thought Carmine, his gaze passing from Hilda to Ruth, who looked just as worried about Keith. The United Women of Keith.

"What time did you get home last night, Miss Silverman?"

"Not long after six."

"What time did you go to bed?"

"At ten. I always do."

"So you don't wait up for your husband?"

"There's no need. Ruth does. I'm the major earner at the moment, you see."

The sound of a car pulling into the drive galvanized both women; they leaped up, rushed to the front door and hopped about like two basketballers jockeying for position.

Wow! was Carmine's reaction when Keith Kyneton walked in. Definitely a prince, not a frog from Dayton, Ohio, anymore. How had the transformation happened, and where? His looks and his physique were undeniable, but what fascinated Carmine were the clothes. Everything of the very best, from his tailored gabardine slacks to his tawny cashmere sweater. The well-dressed neurosurgeon after a hard day in the O.R., while his wife and mother bought off the rack at Cheap & Nasty.

Having shaken off his women, Keith stared at Carmine with hard grey eyes, his generous lips thinned. "Are you the one who pulled me out of the O.R.?" he demanded.

"That's me. Lieutenant Carmine Delmonico. Sorry about it, but I presume Chubb's got another neurosurgeon to pinch-hit?"

"Yes, of course it has!" he snapped. "Why am I here?"

When he heard why he was here, Keith collapsed into a chair. "Our backyard?" he whispered. *"Ours?"*

"Yours, Dr. Kyneton. What time did you come in last night?"

"About two-thirty, I think."

"Did you notice anything different about the place where you parked your car? Do you always park it out front, or do you put it in the garage?"

"In dead of winter I put it in the garage, but I'm still leaving it outside," he said, gazing not at Ruth but at Hilda. "It's a year-old Cadillac, starts like a dream on a cold morning." He was regaining his high opinion of himself. "Truth is, I am whacked by the time I get home, really whacked."

A new Caddy while your wife and your mother drive fifteen-year-old clunkers. What a piece of shit you are, Dr. Kyneton. "You didn't answer my question, Doctor. Did you notice anything out of the ordinary when you got home last night?"

"No, nothing."

"Did you notice that last night was kinda damp and soggy?"

"I can't say that I did."

"Your driveway is unsealed. Were there strange tire tracks?"

"I *told* you, I didn't notice anything!" he cried fretfully.

"How often do you work late, Dr. Kyneton? I mean, is Holloman overloaded with patients requiring your particular skills?"

"Since ours is the only unit in the state with the equipment to perform cerebrovascular surgery, we do tend to be overloaded."

"So coming home at two or three in the morning is the norm?"

Kyneton chewed his lip, suddenly looked away from his mother, his wife, his interrogator. Hiding something. "It's not always the O.R.," he said sulkily.

"If not the O.R., then what?"

"I am a postdoctoral fellow, Lieutenant. I give lectures that have to be prepared, I have to write extremely detailed case notes, I have to do teaching rounds in the hospital, and I'm kept busy training neurosurgical residents." His gaze remained deflected.

"Your wife tells me that you're going to buy into a private neuro-surgical practice."

"That's right, I am. A group in New York City."

"Thank you, Miss Silverman, Dr. Kyneton. I may have other questions later, but this will do for the present."

"I'll walk you out," said Ruth Kyneton.

"I really don't need walking out," Carmine said gently when they reached the porch and the front door was shut.

"Glad to know there's two of us ain't fools."

"Is that your opinion of them, Mrs. Kyneton? Fools?"

She sighed, kicked a pebble off the boards into the night. "I reckon the fairies musta brought Keith—never fitted in, all airs and graces before he went to kindergarten. But I'll give him this—he worked his guts out to get an education, improve himself. And I love him for it something chronic. Hilda suits him, y'know. I guess it don't look like that, but she does."

"If this private practice comes off, what about you?" he asked, sounding gruff.

"Oh, I ain't going with them!" she said cheerfully. "I'm gonna stay right here on Griswold Lane. They'll look after me."

There were a lot of things Carmine wanted to say, but didn't. Instead, "Good night, Mrs. Kyneton. You're some woman."

All the way back to Cedar Street, Carmine struggled with the unexpected discovery that the killer sometimes secreted the girls on the spot and removed them later. It preyed on his mind more than the change in ethnicity did.

"He isn't begging us to catch him," he said to Silvestri, "nor is he jerking our strings just to show us how clever he is. I don't believe that his ego needs that kind of stimulation. If he jerks our strings, it's because he has to, as part of his plans rather than as a cute aside. Like burying Francine in the Kynetons' backyard. In my book, that's a defense mechanism. And it says to me that the killer *is* connected to the Hug, that he harbors a grudge against someone there—and that he isn't a scrap worried that we might find him."

"I think we have to search the Hug," Silvestri said.

"Yes, sir, and more to the point, we have to search it tomorrow, a Saturday. But we won't get a warrant out of Judge Douglas Thwaites."

"Tell me something I don't know," Silvestri growled. "What time is it?"

"Six," said Carmine, looking at the antique railroad clock behind Silvestri's head.

"I'll call M.M. and see if he can't persuade the Hug Board to give us permission to search. Of course they can have as many Huggers as they want to watch us search, but whom would you prefer, Carmine?"

"Professor Smith and Miss Dupre," said Carmine promptly.

*   *   *

"He gave her a shot of Demerol," Patrick said when Carmine walked in. "He couldn't have gone into a vein with a struggling girl on his hands, but he needed the drug to work as soon as possible. So I looked at her abdomen first, and there it was. With the risk of puncturing intestine or liver, he had to use a big-bore hypodermic—a fine twenty-five-gauge tuberculin syringe would have kept on going rather than pushed things aside. And that was our saving grace. A twenty-five-gauge pinprick would have healed completely in the seven days he kept her alive. The eighteen-gauge made a hole."

"Why is going into the abdomen quicker than into muscle?"

"It's called a parenteral injection, mixes the drug with the fluid of the abdominal cavity. Next best thing to a vein. I'd picked that he'd use Demerol, it's a fast-acting opiate. Generic name, meperidine, and more addictive even than heroin, so getting a prescription for the *oral* version isn't easy. Only medical people would have access to ampoules. Anyway, I was right. Up came the meperidine signature."

"Any idea how much he gave her?"

"No. I found my trace in the dermal cells where the needle went in. But either he miscalculated the dosage or Francine had a better resistance to it than usual. If she managed to hide her jacket, then she came around much sooner than he counted on."

"No gag, but muffled in a super-thick mat. Tied with maybe duct tape over her pants legs and her blouse. He might have taken the jacket off her himself to tape her blouse cuffs," Carmine said. "When she woke up, she couldn't move much, though it's possible she managed to start freeing her hands. I think Francine was a formidable young woman. The kind we can't afford to lose."

"They're all that kind." Patrick frowned. "Still, he ought to have seen a pink sleeve poking out of a black mat."

"The place was dark and he was in a hurry. It's possible Francine had moved enough to hide what she'd done, or maybe when he opened the locker she came out fighting."

"Either or," Patrick said.

"Have you missed dinner, Patsy?"

"Nessie's gone to a Chubb concert, so it's Malvolio's for me."

"And for me. Meet you there as soon as I tell Silvestri where I'm going." Carmine grinned. "He'll be on that phone for at least an hour."

"The saints preserve me from tycoons," Silvestri grumbled when he slid into their booth. "At least I'm on my own time, so I can have a drink. Coffee and a double Scotch on the rocks," he said to the waitress who reminded Carmine of Sandra.

"That bad, huh?" Patrick asked sympathetically.

"M.M. was easy. He appreciated our situation. But Roger Parson Junior was like getting blood out of a stone. He refuses to see any connection to his precious Hug."

"How did you get around him, John?" Carmine asked.

The Scotch came; Silvestri swallowed some and looked like one of Hell's executive demons. "I told him to put his money where his mouth is. If there's no link to the Hug, then the sooner we ransack the joint, the better his case. Though," he added, still wearing that diabolical look, "I paid a price for his permission."

"And why," asked Carmine warily, "do I think someone else is paying the price?"

"Because, Carmine, you're smart. Next Thursday at noon you have an appointment with Parson at his office in New York City. He wants to know everything we know."

"I need that like a hole in the head."

"Pay the price, Carmine, pay the price."

CHAPTER 10

Saturday, December 11th, 1965

The best laid schemes can go awry, Carmine reflected on that Saturday morning. There had been an armed robbery at a gas station that the thieves followed up by hitting two liquor stores, a jeweler and another gas station, which thinned his reserve of men down to a point where he knew the search was going to take all day. Corey and Abe and four other detectives, all rookies who would have to be supervised. Right. Two parties of three, Abe leading one, Corey the other, while he himself floated. Paul was on hand in case evidence came to light that needed his touch.

They arrived at the Hug at 9 A.M. to be greeted in the foyer by the Prof and Desdemona, neither of them pleased but each under Board instructions to be co-operative.

"Miss Dupre, you go with Sergeant Marshall and his men on this floor. I presume you have keys to everything that's locked? Professor, you go one floor up with Sergeant Goldberg. Do you have keys?" Carmine asked.

"Yes," whispered the Prof, who looked as if he might faint.

"Cecil is in," Desdemona said to Carmine as they walked down the north hall.

"Because of this search?"

"No, because of his babies. He's always in weekend mornings. I'll wait outside in case he has one in the main room. They abhor women," she said.

"So he told me. You can go with Corey to look in the machine shop and the electronics lab. The last thing I want is Roger Parson Junior accusing us of stealing something. I'll search animal care myself."

"I am grateful for that, Lieutenant," said Cecil, who didn't seem annoyed at this invasion. "Want to see where my babies live? They in a good mood today."

I'd be in a good mood too if I lived like this, Carmine said to himself, entering a small foyer shut off from the main macaque room by heavy iron bars. They were so strong, Cecil explained, that, if enraged, they could break chain link like candy canes. The area, very large considering its small population, was landscaped like rocky savannah—a wall of rugged boulders pocked with holes, bushes, tufts of grass, logs, limbed concrete trees, warm light that felt like a hot sun. Rheostats connected to timers ensured that there was a dawn and a dusk.

"Isn't it unkind to deprive them of females?" Carmine asked.

Cecil chuckled. "They make do, Lieutenant, same as men make do in prison. Hump the shit outta each other. But there's a pecking order, an' Eustace, he The Man. New guy arrives, he gets grabbed by Eustace, humped, then he gets passed to Clyde, an' ol' Clyde, he passes the new guy on, an' so on. Jimmy, he the last in the pecking order. Never gets to do more than jerk hisself off."

"Well, thanks for showing me, Cecil, but I doubt any girl has ever been hidden in here."

"You dead right there, Lieutenant."

*   *   *

"What exactly are you looking for?" Desdemona asked when he joined Corey's group in a workshop that was a machinist's dream.

"A cupboard with a human hair in it, a shred of clothing, a broken fingernail, a scrap of duct tape, a bloodstain. Anything that shouldn't be there."

"Ah, so that's why the magnifying glasses and the bright lights! I thought that sort of thing went out with Sherlock Holmes."

"They're the tools of choice in a search like this. All these men are experts at looking for evidence."

"Mr. Roger Parson Junior is not amused."

"So I gather, but ask me if I care. The answer is, I don't."

Room by room, closet by closet, cupboard by cupboard, the search went on; satisfied that the first floor had nothing to offer, Corey and his team went up to the third floor, Desdemona and Carmine tagging along.

During this more leisurely inspection of the third floor, Carmine realized that under ordinary circumstances life at the Hug was pleasant; most of the technicians had attempted to turn cold science into warm familiarity. Walls and doors were plastered with cartoons that only someone in the game would find funny; pictures of people were there too, and landscapes, and posters of vividly colored things whose nature Carmine couldn't begin to fathom, though he could appreciate their beauty.

"Crystals under polarized light," Desdemona explained, "or pollen, dust mites, viruses under an electron microscope."

"Some of these work niches look like Mary Poppinsville."

"Marvin's, you mean?" she asked, pointing to an area where everything from drawers to boxes and books had been covered with Contact adhesive paper in pink and yellow butterflies. "Think about it, Carmine. People like Marvin spend the most concerted stretch of each twenty-four hours rooted to one spot. Why should that spot be grey and anonymous? Employers don't stop to think that if the cells people work in were more individual and harmonious, the quality of output might rise. Marvin is the poet, is all."

"Ponsonby's technician, right?"

"Correct."

"Doesn't Ponsonby object? He doesn't strike me as a yellow and pink butterfly man, not when he's got Bosch and Goya on his walls."

"Chuck would like to object, but the Prof wouldn't back him up. Theirs is an interesting relationship, goes back to childhood, and the Prof was the boss then as much as now, I suspect." She spotted Corey about to move an apparatus of fine glass columns on a levered stand, and shrieked. "Don't you dare touch the Natelson! Stuff it up, mate, and you'll be singing soprano in the Vienna Boys' Choir."

"I don't think," Carmine said solemnly, "that it's big enough to hide anything. Look in that closet."

They looked in every closet from the first floor clear to the roof, but found nothing. Paul came to go over the O.R., swabbing any surface that could possibly collect fluid.

But, said Paul, "I doubt there's anything to find. This Mrs. Lieb-man is immaculate, never forgets to clean the corners or the under sides."

"My feeling," said Abe, contributing his mite to the gloom, "is that the Hug may have received parts of bodies, but that they were bagged before they arrived, and went straight from someone's car trunk to the dead animal fridge."

"A negative exercise, guys, that tells us something," Carmine said. "Whatever role the Hug plays in this business, it isn't a holding pen or a slaughter yard."

CHAPTER 11

Monday, December 13th, 1965

The trouble with a case growing as old as the Monster's was that the amount of work that could be done gradually tapered off; Sunday had been a day of trying to read, flicking from one TV channel to another, some pacing the floor. So it was with relief that Carmine arrived at the Hug at 9 A.M. on Monday morning. To find a crowd of black men clustered outside it bearing placards that said CHILD KILLERS and BLACK HATERS. Most of them wore a Black Brigade jacket over combat fatigues. Two squad cars were parked nearby, but the picketers were orderly, content to shout and lift their fists in Mohammed el Nesr's personally coined gesture. No Black Brigade chiefs were there, Carmine noted; these were small fry, hoping to catch a TV journalist or two in their net. When Carmine walked up the path to the entrance door, they ignored him apart from a flurry of yelled "Pig!"

Of course the weekend news had been full of Francine Murray. Carmine had passed on Derek Daiman's warning to Silvestri at the time, but although nothing had happened until today, any sensitive cop nose could sniff trouble coming. Holloman wasn't the only town involved, but it seemed to have become the focus of all indignation, general and particular. The Hug's part in things ensured that, and one thing for sure, the newspapers weren't crowning their pictures of John Silvestri and Carmine Delmonico with laurels; the weekend editorials had been diatribes against police incompetency.

"Did you see them?" the Prof spluttered when Carmine entered his office. "Did you see them?" Demonstrators, *here!*"

"Hard not to see them, Professor," Carmine said dryly. "Calm down and listen to me. Is there anyone you can think of who might bear a grudge against the Hug? Like a patient?"

The Prof hadn't washed his magnificent hair, and his shave had missed as many bristles as it caught. Evidence of a crumbling ego or personality or whatever the shrinks called it. "I don't know," he said, as if Carmine had come out with something just too ludicrous to imagine.

"Do you see any patients yourself, sir?"

"No, not in years, except for an occasional consultation on some case that has everyone baffled. Since the Hug was opened, my function has been to be here for my researchers, discuss their problems with them if they're in a dilemma or things haven't gone the way they hoped. I advise them, sometimes suggest new avenues for them to explore. Those, my teaching and lecture schedule *and* my reading leave me too busy to see patients."

"Who does see patients? Refresh my memory."

"Addison Forbes, most of all, as his research is entirely clinical. Dr. Ponsonby and Dr. Finch see a few patients, while Dr. Polonowski has a big clinic. He's very good on malabsorption syndromes."

Why can't they speak English? Carmine wanted to ask. But he said, "So you suggest I should see Dr. Forbes first?"

"In any order you like," said the Prof, buzzing for Tamara.

There's another Hugger who doesn't look too swift, Carmine noted. I wonder what she's up to? Fine-looking and sexy woman, but she knows she hasn't got too many good years left.

*   *   *

Addison Forbes looked blank. "See patients?" he asked. "I should say so, Lieutenant! My patient intake can run to thirty-plus a week. Certainly never less than twenty. I'm so well known that my patient pool is not only national, but international."

"Is it possible that one of them harbors a grudge against you or the Hug, Doctor?"

"My dear man," Forbes said loftily, "It's a rare patient who understands his malady! The moment a treatment doesn't perform miracles when he has led himself to believe it will, he blames his doctor. But I am particularly careful to point out to *all* my patients that I am an ordinary doctor, not a witch doctor, and that improvement in itself is an advance."

He's huffy, intolerant and patronizing as well as neurotic was Carmine's opinion, which he didn't voice. Instead he asked mildly, "Do any of them ever threaten you?"

Forbes looked shocked. "No, never! If you're after patients who threaten, then you should be seeing surgeons, not physicians."

"The Hug doesn't have any surgeons."

"Nor any threats from patients" was Forbes's stiff reply.

From Dr. Walter Polonowski he found out that a malabsorption syndrome meant a patient couldn't tolerate what Nature had intended as food for everyone, or else had developed a liking for substances Nature hadn't intended as food for anyone.

"Amino acids, fruits or vegetables, lead, copper, gluten, all kinds of fats," said Polonowski, taking pity on him. "If you see enough patients, the list of substances is almost endless. Honey can cause anaphylactic shock, for instance. But what I'm chiefly interested in are the group of substances that cause brain damage."

"Have you any patients who resent you?"

"I guess any doctor must, Lieutenant, but personally I can't recall any instances. With my patients, the harm has been done before ever they get to see me."

Yet another worn-looking Hugger, Carmine thought.

153

Dr. Maurice Finch looked much worse.

"I blame myself for Dr. Schiller's attempted suicide," said Finch desolately.

"What's done is done, and you can't say that you were the cause, Dr. Finch, you really can't. Dr. Schiller has a lot of problems, as I'm sure you know. Besides, you saved his life," said Carmine. "Blame the person who put Mercedes Alvarez here. Now take your mind off Dr. Schiller for a moment and try to remember if any of your patients have ever threatened you. Or if you have ever heard a patient utter threats against the Hug itself?"

"No," said Finch, looking bewildered. "No, never."

An answer he also received from Dr. Charles Ponsonby, though Ponsonby's face became alert, interested.

"It's certainly a thought," he said, frowning. "One forgets that that kind of thing happens, but of course it must. I will put my thinking cap on, Lieutenant, and try to remember on behalf of my colleagues as well as myself. Though I'm just about a hundred percent sure that it's never happened to me. I'm too harmless."

From the Hug Carmine walked down Oak Street in the teeth of a bitter wind to the Chubb Medical School, where he negotiated the usual maze of corridors and tunnels such institutions specialize in, and at last found the Department of Neurology. There he asked to see Professor Frank Watson.

Who saw him immediately, clearly reveling in the Hug's misfortunes, though he did remember to deplore the murders.

"I hear that it was you who gave the Hughlings Jackson Center its nickname, Professor," said Carmine, smiling a little.

Watson swelled like a toad, stroked his thin black mustache and lifted one mobile black eyebrow. "Yes, I did. They hate it, don't they? Ab-so-lute-ly *hate* it. Especially Bob Smith."

How you enjoy playing Mephistopheles! Carmine thought. "Do you hate the Hug?"

"With a passion," the Professor of Neurology said candidly. "Here am I, with just as many brilliant people on my team, and I battle for every single cent of research money I can find. Do you know how many Nobel Prize winners there are in this medical school, Lieutenant? Nine! Imagine it—*nine!* And none of them is a Hugger. They're in my camp, existing on beggarly grants. Bob Smith can afford to buy equipment he uses once in a blue moon if at all, while I have to count the number of gauze swabs I use! All that money was the ruin of Bob Smith, who might otherwise have discovered something neurologically significant. He doesn't work, he languishes. A poseur."

"Hurts that much, huh?" Carmine asked.

"It doesn't hurt," Frank Watson said savagely. "It's pure, unadulterated agony!"

A trip back to Cedar Street revealed that Francine Murray's jacket had yielded no clues apart from its presence in the locker, which also failed to help. From Silvestri he learned that Travis had survived the day thus far; there had actually been more trouble at Taft High, whose student intake included the Argyle Avenue ghetto. What they all need, he thought, is some sane political direction, but at least there's one good thing about Mohammed el Nesr and his Black Brigade: start on drugs, even something as innocuous as pot, and you're out of his organization. He wants his soldiers clear of mind and firm of purpose. And that's good, no matter what his purpose might be. Thank God for Silvestri and the Mayor: as long as the Black Brigade do nothing more than drill up and down Fifteenth Street with broomsticks over their left shoulders, they're not hassled. Only what kind and how many armaments have they got behind those mattressed walls? One day someone will talk, and then we'll get the warrant we need to take a look.

December first . . . Our man will strike again around the end of January or the beginning of February, and we're as far from catching him as Mohammed el Nesr is from convincing the bulk of Holloman's black population that revolution is the way to go.

He picked up his phone, dialed. "I know it's not Wednesday, but any chance I could come pick you up and take you out for Chinese or something else with me?" he asked Desdemona.

He looked, she thought, extremely uncomfortable, though he smiled when she slid into his Ford and tried to make small talk until he bolted out of the car, into the Blue Pheasant, and out again with an armload of cardboard containers.

Then it was silence, even after he had done his finicky transferring of the food to covered white bowls and seated her at the table.

"You do make work for yourself," she said, piling food on her plate and inhaling the aromas blissfully. "I'd be happy to eat it straight out of the boxes, you know."

"That would be an insult," he said, but absently.

Because she was hungry she said nothing more until the meal was finished, then she pushed her plate away and, when he reached to take it, grasped his arm firmly. "No, sit down, Carmine, and tell me what's the matter."

He looked down at her hand as if surprised at something, then sighed and sat. Before she could take her hand away he put his own over it and kept it there.

"I'm afraid I'm going to have to remove your guards."

"Is *that* all? Carmine, it's been weeks since anything has happened. I'm sure whoever it was grew bored ages ago. Did it not occur to you that perhaps all this has been because sometimes I do embroidery for the Catholic church? After all, the only thing that was cut up was a priest's vestment—it might be that whoever it was thought Chuck Ponsonby's piece was suspicious but not definitely religious—it did have that long, narrow altar look to it. Sideboard cloths do."

"It occurred to me," he admitted.

"So there you are. I now do commissions for household napery only—tablecloths and serviettes—oops, napkins."

"Commissions?"

"Yes, I charge for my work. Very heavily, as a matter of fact. People with means get tired of the same old cross-stitch or eyelet stuff they churn out by the bucketful in countries with cottage industries. What I do is unique. People love it, and my bank balance grows considerably." She looked guilty. "I haven't declared it—why should I, when I pay full taxes yet can't vote? It doesn't matter to you as a policeman, does it?"

His fingers had been moving over the skin of her forearm as if they liked the feel of it, but now they stopped. "Sometimes," he said gravely, "I have attacks of deafness. What was that you said? Something about not voting?"

"It doesn't matter." She took her hand away, looking self-conscious. "We've solved the major matter, which is the removal of my guards. I am relieved, quite honestly. Though there are solid doors between me and them, I never feel really *private*. So good riddance to them, I say." She hesitated. "When?"

"I'm not sure. The weather may be your best friend. In case you didn't notice, the wind's getting up and the chill factor will fall way below freezing tomorrow. That drives everyone indoors." He rose from the table. "Come and sit over here, get nice and comfortable, have a cognac, and talk to me."

"Talk to you?"

"Right, talk to me. I need to know certain things, and you are the only one I can ask."

"Ask what?"

"About the Hug."

She pulled a face, but accepted the cognac, which he took as acquiescence. "Very well, ask away."

"I understand the Prof's state of mind, also Dr. Finch's, but why is Polonowski so edgy? I ask, Desdemona, because I want you to give me answers that don't have to do with murder. If I don't know why a Hugger acts suspiciously, I tend to think of murder, and maybe waste a lot of valuable time. I'd hoped that Francine would clear you all, but she hasn't. This guy is as cunning as a sewer rat, so he had a way of being in two places at once. Give me the low-down on Polonowski."

"Walt's in love with his technician, Marian, but he's also tied hand and foot to a marriage I think he regretted years ago," she said, swirling the brandy in its balloon. "There are four children—they're very Catholic, hence no contraception."

"Loose not the stopper of thy wineskin until thou reachest Athens," Carmine quoted.

"Well put!" she cried appreciatively. "I suppose poor Walt is one of those chaps whose wineskin has a mind of its own when he climbs into bed next to his wife's wine cup. Her name's Paola, and she's a nice woman who's turned into a shrew. Much younger than he, and blaming him for the loss of her youth and looks."

"Is he having an out-and-out affair with Marian?"

"Yes, for months."

"Where do they meet? At Major Minor's some afternoons?" he asked, referring to the motel on Route 133 that did a brisk trade in illicit fornication.

"No. He has a cabin somewhere upstate."

Shit, thought Carmine. The guy has a cabin we didn't know about. How handy. "Do you know where it is?"

"Afraid not. He won't even tell Paola."

"Is the affair common knowledge?"

"No, they're very discreet."

"Then how do you know?"

"Because I found Marian in the fourth-floor toilet howling her eyes out. She thought she was pregnant. When I sympathized and advised her to have herself fitted with a diaphragm if she was hesitant about the Pill, the whole story tumbled out."

"And was she pregnant?"

"No. False alarm."

"Okay, let's move on to Ponsonby. He's got some weird art on his office walls, not to mention shrunken heads and devil masks. Torture, monsters swallowing their children whole, people screaming."

Her laughter pealed out so infectiously that he felt warmed. "Oh, Carmine! That's just Chuck! The art is simply one more facet of Chuck's insufferable snobbishness. I feel sorry for him."

"Why?"

"Hasn't anyone told you that he has a blind sister?"

"I do my homework, Desdemona, so I do know that. I take it she's the reason why he stayed in Holloman. But why do you feel sorry for him? Her, yes."

"Because he's built his entire life around her. Never married, no close relatives, though they've known the Smiths since childhood. There are just the two of them in a pre-Revolutionary house on Ponsonby Lane. Once they owned all the land for a mile around, but Claire's education was expensive, so was Chuck's, and I gather they were hard up in their parents' day. They've certainly sold all the land off. Chuck adores surrealist art and classical music. Claire can't see the art, but she's a music fan too. They're both gourmets and wine buffs. I suppose I feel sorry for him because when he speaks of their life together, he waxes rhapsodical, which is—well, *strange*. She's his sister, not his wife, though some of the crueler members of the staff do joke about them. I think that in his heart of hearts Chuck must resent at least some aspects of being tied to Claire, but he's far too loyal to admit that, even to himself. He certainly can't be the Monster, he doesn't have the time or the liberty."

"I just found the artwork weird," he said apologetically.

"I like the artwork. Either you do, or you don't."

"Okay, moving on again. Sonia Liebman."

"A very nice woman, very good at her job. She's married to an undertaker, Benjamin Liebman. Their one chick is at a college near Tucson, doing pre-med. Wants to be a general surgeon."

An undertaker. Shit, I didn't do enough homework. "Does Benjamin work for someone, or is he retired?"

"Good heavens, no! He has his own establishment somewhere near Bridgeport." Desdemona closed her eyes, screwed them up. "Um—the Comfort Funeral Home, I think."

Double shit. An ideal place for a killer into dissection. I'll have to pay the Comfort Funeral Home a visit tomorrow.

"Satsuma and Chandra?"

"Looking for jobs elsewhere. Rumor hath it that Nur Chandra has already had an offer from Harvard, anxious to even the Nobel Prize score. Hideki is still not sure. His decision somehow rests on the harmonies in his garden."

Carmine sighed. "Who's your pick, Desdemona?"

She blinked. "No one at the Hug, I say that with truth. I've been there for five years, which makes me a latecomer. Most of the researchers are a bit bonkers in one way or another, but that goes with the territory. They're so—*harmless.* Dr. Finch talks to his cats as if they could talk back, Dr. Chandra treats his macaques like Indian royalty—even Dr. Ponsonby, who's less fond of his rats than the others, shows interest in their doings. None of the researchers is psychotic, I'd swear to that."

"Ponsonby isn't fond of his rats?"

"Carmine, truly! Dr. Ponsonby plain doesn't *like* rats! A lot of people don't like rats, including me. Most researchers get used to them and manage to develop great affection for them, but not all. Marvin will pick up a rat with his bare hand to give it a shot in the tummy, and it will kiss him with its whiskers for the attention. Whereas Dr. Ponsonby uses a furnace glove if he can't get out of picking up a rat. Their incisors can go straight through a thinner glove—well, they can gnaw through concrete!"

"You are not helping, Desdemona."

Tiny sharp taps on the window brought Desdemona to her feet. "Bugger, sleet! Just ducky for driving. Take me home, Carmine."

And that, he thought with an inner sigh, is the end of any trying to hold her hand again. It's not that she turns me on, it's more that somewhere underneath all that competent independence is a darned nice woman struggling to get out.

CHAPTER 12

Thursday, December 16th, 1965

Since it hadn't snowed before Thanksgiving and the first half of December had been no colder than usual, most Connecticut people thought Christmas might be green. Then it snowed heavily the night before Carmine was due to go to New York City to see the Parsons. As he loathed trains and was not about to make his journey jammed in a railroad car that stank of wet wool, bad breath and cigarettes, Carmine set out early in the Ford to find I-95 down from three to two lanes, but negotiable. Once he hit Manhattan only the avenues had been ploughed, chiefly because no one could ever get enough cars off the streets to plough. Where he was going to park the Ford he had no idea as he inched down Park Avenue until he could turn up Madison, but Roger Parson Junior had thought of it. When he stopped outside a building that was neither the largest nor the smallest on that block, a uniformed doorman rushed out to take the keys and shove them at a minion. He himself conducted Carmine into a purply princely lobby of Lovanto marble, past the bank of elevators to a single one at its end. The executive elevator: a lock on its controls and a decor fit for executives.

Roger Parson Junior met him when its doors opened on the forty-third floor, Richard Spaight at his shoulder but subtly behind.

"Lieutenant, I'm very glad that you braved the weather to come. Did you take the train?"

"No, I drove. It's harder getting around in Manhattan than coming in from Connecticut," said Carmine, handing over his coat, scarf and deerstalker hat.

Parson stared at the hat in fascination. "Ah—a conscious reminder of Sherlock Holmes?"

"If you mean joke, sir, I guess so. I bought it in London a few years ago, when Russian hats weren't too popular with Joe McCarthy. Keeps the ears warm."

A middle-aged secretary stomped off with the clothes while Parson ushered Carmine into a smallish conference room equipped with six easy chairs ringed around a coffee table, and six dining chairs ringed around a higher table. The floor was parquet scattered with silk Persian carpets, the furniture bird's-eye maple, the bookcases fronted with leaded-glass diamonds. Plush but businesslike, except for the paintings on the walls.

"A part of Uncle William's art collection," said Spaight, indicating that Carmine should sit in an easy chair. "Rubens, Velásquez, Poussin, Vermeer, Canaletto, Titian. Strictly speaking the collection belongs to Chubb University, but we are at liberty to delay the bequest, and, candidly, we enjoy looking at them."

"I don't blame you," Carmine said, wondering as he put his posterior on the maroon leather of his chair whether any fabric as cheap as that of his pants had ever before besmirched it.

"I understand," said Roger Parson Junior, crossing one thin, elegantly sheathed leg over the other, "that the Hug is now the center of racial demonstrations."

"Yes, sir, whenever the weather's bearable."

"Why aren't you doing something about it?"

"The last time I looked at the Constitution, Mr. Parson, it permitted orderly demonstrations of any kind, including racial," Carmine said in a neutral voice. "If riots occur, we can act, not otherwise. Nor do we think it wise to use strong-arm tactics that might provoke riots. It's embarrassing for the Hug, but its staff aren't being molested as they come and go."

"You must admit, Lieutenant, that from where we stand, the Holloman police haven't exactly shone at any time in the last two and a half months," said Spaight, tight-lipped. "This murdering fellow seems to be running rings around all of you. Perhaps it's time to call in the FBI."

"We are consulting the FBI regularly, sir, I can assure you, but the FBI is just as short of leads as we are. We have asked every state in the Union for particulars of crimes of a similar nature, with no positive results. In the past two weeks we have, for instance, checked the credentials and placement of several hundred substitute schoolteachers, with no positive results. Nothing that might offer a solution has been ignored."

"What I don't understand," said Parson peevishly, "is why he is still at large! You *must* have some idea who is responsible!"

"Police methodology depends on a network of connections," Carmine said, having thought about what he was going to say as he made his long drive. "Under normal circumstances there is a pool of likely suspects, whether you're talking murder or armed robbery or drug dealing. We all know each other, the criminals and the cops. We, the cop end of the equation, conduct our investigations down a well-worn track, because that's how it works best. Men of my rank have been at the job long enough to have developed pretty shrewd instincts about who's at the criminal end of the equation. Murders have patterns, signatures. Robberies have patterns, signatures. They lead us to those who did it."

"This murderer has a pattern, a signature," said Spaight.

"That's not what I'm talking about, Mr. Spaight. This killer is a ghost. He abducts a girl, but he leaves not one single trace of himself behind. No one has ever seen him, even heard him. No girl seems to have known him. As soon as we realized he was into victims with a Caribbean background and had a chance to protect every girl of his type, he switched to a Connecticut black, Pennsylvania white cross. Same physical type of girl, but a different ethnic background. Taken from an inner-city high school with fifteen hundred students. He varied his technique in other ways I'm not at liberty to tell you. What I can tell you, sirs, is that we are no farther ahead than we were two and a half months ago. Because the network of connections isn't there. He's not a professional criminal, he's an anonymous nonentity. A ghost."

"Might he have a record of some other crime? Rape?"

"We've been there too, Mr. Parson, with a fine-toothed comb. My own feeling is that he's as much a rapist as he is a killer, that maybe the rape is more important to him than the murder, that he only kills to make sure the victim can't talk. I have personally gone through hundreds of files looking for anything that might suggest a rapist who's raised the ante. When none of the convicted or accused rapists matched, I went to cases where the girl or woman dropped the charges—that happens often. I looked at pictures of girls, descriptions of their rape, but my cop instincts never stirred. If he was there, I'm sure they would have stirred."

"Then he must be young," said Spaight.

"What makes you say that, sir?"

"His history is two years old. Such shocking crimes would surely have produced symptoms of mania before that if he were an older man."

"A good point, but I don't think this killer is very young, no, sir. He's cold, calculating, resourceful, without conscience or the shadow of a doubt. All that suggests maturity, not youth."

"Might he be of the same ethnic background as his victims?"

"We had all thought of that possibility, Mr. Parson, until he crossed the ethnic line. One of the FBI psychiatrists thought he might look like his victims—same color, say—but if such a man exists, we haven't spotted him and he doesn't have a record."

"So what you're really saying, Lieutenant, is that if—or when—this murderer is caught, it won't be by any of your more traditional methods."

"Yes," said Carmine flatly, "that's what I'm really saying. Like so many others, he'll crash by a fluke or an accident."

"Not an opinion that inspires confidence," said Parson dryly.

"Oh, we'll get him, sir. We've pushed him into changes, and we'll go on pushing him. I don't think his frame of mind is as serene as it was."

"*Serene?*" asked Spaight, astonished. "Surely not!"

"Why not?" Carmine countered. "He doesn't have feelings, Mr. Spaight, as you and I understand feelings. He's insane but sane."

"How many more girls are going to die an agonizing death?" Parson asked, the words barbed.

Carmine's face twisted. "If I could answer that question, I would know the killer's identity."

A uniformed maid came in wheeling a cart and proceeded to set the higher table.

"I trust you'll stay for lunch, Lieutenant?" Roger Parson Junior asked, rising to his feet.

"Thank you, sir."

"Sit down, do."

Carmine seated himself to look at Lenox tableware.

"We are patriots," said Spaight, sitting on Carmine's right as Parson went to Carmine's left. Fenced in.

"In what way, Mr. Spaight?"

"American tableware, American linens. American everything, really. It was Uncle William who liked foreign matter."

Foreign matter. Not the phrase I'd use to describe the rug, thought Carmine. Or the Velásquez.

A butler and the maid waited on table: Nova Scotia smoked salmon with thin brown bread-and-butter, roast veal au jus with pommes Lyonnaise and steamed spinach, a cheese plate and superb coffee. No alcohol.

"The martini lunch," said Richard Spaight, "is a curse. If I know a client has indulged in one, I will not see him. Business requires a clear head."

"So does policing," said Carmine. "In that respect, Commissioner Silvestri runs a dry ship. No alcohol unless off duty, and no lushes on the force." He was facing the Poussin, dreamily beautiful. "It's lovely," he said to his host.

"Yes, we chose tranquil works for this room. The wartime Goyas are in my office. On your way out, however, don't miss our one and only El Greco. It's under armored glass at the end of the corridor," Roger Parson Junior said.

"Have you ever been robbed of any art?" the cop had to ask.

"No, it's too difficult to get in. Or perhaps it is that there are plenty of easier targets. This is a city of wonderful art. I often amuse myself by working out how I'd steal a good Rembrandt from the Metropolitan or a Picasso from the private dealer on Fifty-third. Were I serious, I believe neither would be impossible."

"Maybe your Uncle William knew the tricks too."

Richard Spaight tittered. "He certainly did! In his day it was a great deal easier, of course. If you were at Pompeii or in Florence, all you had to do was tip the guide ten dollars. You should see the Roman mosaic floor in the conservatory at the old house in Litchfield— magnificent."

Merry Christmas, ha ha, Carmine thought as he climbed into the pre-warmed Ford to commence the drive home. It isn't either of them, though if a Rembrandt goes missing from the Metropolitan, I can tip off the NYPD where to look. M.M. will be under the ground before that bunch give up Uncle William's collection, even if it is foreign matter.

CHAPTER 13

Friday, December 24th, 1965

"Oh, bother!" said Desdemona, nose twitching. "That wretched sewer vent is playing up again." For a moment she debated whether to knock on her landlord's door as she went down the stairs, then decided against it. He wasn't too pleased at the presence of cops on his premises, and had been hinting that it might be better if Desdemona found herself new digs. So she would bear the sewer vent without another confrontation.

When she opened her door the stench of feces hit her forcibly, but she didn't notice. All she saw was the blackened, congested face of Charlie, the cop who usually took the night watch on a Thursday night. He was lying as if he had struggled desperately, arms and legs akimbo, but it was the face, the face . . . Swollen, tongue protruding, eyes bulging. Part of Desdemona wanted to scream, but that would have marked her as a typical woman, and Desdemona had spent half a lifetime proving to the world that she was any man's equal. Hanging on to the door jambs, she forced herself to remain unmoving for long enough to be sure she could stand. Tears gathered, fell. Oh, Charlie! Such a boring duty, he had told her once, asking for a book. He'd gone through everything he fancied in the County Services library, which wasn't many. A Raymond Chandler or a Mickey Spillane? But the best she had been able to offer him was an Agatha Christie, which he hadn't liked or understood.

There, that did it. Desdemona let go of the jambs and began to turn to retreat to her phone. Then she noticed the big piece of paper stuck over the window that let light into the upper landing. Glaringly black on glaring white, immaculate printing.

> YOU'RE A SNEAK,
> YOU UTTER FREAK!
> THAT DAGO FELLOW
> IS NO OTHELLO,
> BUT I'LL GET YOU YET!
> UNTIL THAT DAY—SWEAT!

"Carmine," she said calmly when he came on the line, "I need you. Charlie is dead. Murdered." A gulp, a long intake of breath. "Right outside my door. Please come!"

"Is it still open?" he asked, equally calm.

"Yes."

"Then shut it, Desdemona, right this minute."

Hardly any desk sergeant had ever seen Carmine Delmonico go past at a run, but he was flying, Abe and Corey racing behind with his coat, his hat, his scarf. Not a minute later Patrick O'Donnell was on his tail.

"Wow!" said Sergeant Larry D'Aglio to his clerk. "The shit must be hitting the fan in all directions."

"Not on a morning like this," said the clerk. "Too cold."

*　　*　　*

"Garotted with piano wire," said Patrick. "The poor bastard! He put up a fight, but reflexive. The wire was round his neck and through the loop before he knew what was happening."

"Loop?" asked Carmine, turning from the doggerel on the window.

"I've never seen anything quite like it. A loop at one end of the wire, a wooden handle at the other. Slip the handle through the loop, step back, and yank with all your might. Charlie never managed to lay a hand on him."

"Then he stuck up his notice cold as ice—look at it, Patsy! Absolutely straight, exactly in the middle of the pane—how did he fix it there?"

Patrick looked up and looked amazed. "Jesus!"

"Well, Paul can tell us when he takes it down." Carmine squared his shoulders. "Time I knocked on her door."

"How was she when she phoned it in?"

"Not gibbering, at any rate." He knocked, called out loudly. "Desdemona, it's Carmine! Let me in."

Her face was pinched and white, her hands shook, but she was in command of herself. No excuse to take her in his arms and try to comfort her.

"Some red herring," she said.

"Yes, he's upped the ante. What have you got to drink?"

"Tea. I'm English, we don't go in for cognac. Just tea. Made the proper way, on leaves, not bags. Holloman is quite a civilized place, you know. There's a tea and coffee shop where I can get Darjeeling." She led the way to her kitchen. "I made it when I heard the sirens."

No mugs; cups and saucers, frail, hand painted. The teapot was covered with what looked like a Dolly Varden doll, its spout and handle poking out of opposite ends of a thickly padded crinoline finished with frills. Milk, sugar, cookies even. Well, maybe scrupulous attention to domestic rituals is her way of being strong. Coping.

"Milk in first," she said, lifting the doll off the pot.

He wasn't game to tell her that he took it the American way, weak, no milk, a slice of lemon. So he sipped the scalding liquid politely and waited.

"You saw the notice?" she asked, looking better for the tea.

"Yes. You can't stay here now, of course."

"I doubt I'd be let! My landlord wasn't happy about my guards. Now he'll be foaming at the mouth. But where can I go?"

"Protective custody. We keep an apartment in my building for people like you."

"I can't afford the rent."

"Protective custody means no rent, Desdemona."

Why *was* she such a miser?

"I see. Then I'd better start packing. I don't have much."

"Have some more tea first, and answer some questions. Did you hear anything unusual during the night? See Charlie?"

"No, I heard nothing. I'm a deep sleeper. Charlie said hello when he arrived—I heard him come in, even though it was later than my usual bedtime. He's usually on the cadge for a book, even if he doesn't like my choice of authors very much."

"Did you give him one last night?" No need to tell her that Charlie wasn't supposed to read on duty.

"Yes, a Ngaio Marsh. The name intrigued him, he didn't know how to pronounce it. I thought he might like her better than Agatha Christie—Marsh's victims usually die in a terrible mess of excrement." She shuddered. "Just like Charlie."

"Any sign that he actually entered this apartment?"

"No, and believe me, I've looked. Not a pin out of place."

"But he could have. This is one thing I didn't count on."

"Don't blame yourself, Carmine, please."

He got up. "Does anything ever make you scream, Desdemona?"

"Oh, yes," she said gravely. "Spiders and cockroaches."

"Zilch as usual," Patrick said in Silvestri's office. "No fingerprints, no fibers, no detritus of any kind. He must have used a measure on the window, the notice—it's too big to be called a note—was so perfectly placed. Equidistant to a millimeter. And he fixed it with four little balls of Plasticene, pressed the four corners into it, even adjusted the left side to raise it a fraction. And he's an original! It was done in forty-eight-point Times Bold Letraset. On paper thin enough to have put a lined graticule behind it—every letter is dead even. Cheap cartridge drawing block, the kind kids buy at any big chain store. He pressed the Letraset down with something rounded and metal—a knife handle or maybe a scalpel handle. Not a stylus, too blunt."

"Can you get any idea of how big his hands are from the way he pressed the paper into the Plasticene?" Marciano asked.

"No. I think he put a rag between his fingers and the paper."

"What made you say the garotte was unusual, Patsy?" Carmine asked, sighing. "A loop and handle's not that unique."

"This one is. The handle isn't wood as I thought. It's a carved human femur. But he didn't carve it. It looks incredibly old, so I'm carbon dating it. The wire is piano wire."

"Did it bite in hard enough to cut the skin?" Silvestri asked.

"No, just hard enough to occlude the airway and carotids."

"He's used one before."

"Oh, yes, he's had plenty of practice."

"But he left his garotte behind. Does that mean he's finished playing with this toy?" Abe asked.

"I'd say so."

"Do you still think Desdemona Dupre is a red herring?" asked Corey, more upset then the others; Charlie's wife was great friends with his own wife.

"I can't believe she's anything else!" Carmine cried, hands in his hair. "She's no dummy—if she knew anything, she'd have told me."

"What's your theory on her, Carmine?" Silvestri asked.

"That he picked her for several reasons. One, that she's a loner. Easier to get at. Another, that she's about as far from his victim type as women can get. And maybe most important of all, he knows that

Desdemona is the one Hugger I make use of, always have done. The note—notice—calls her a sneak."

"What about the notice?" Silvestri pressed.

"Oh, it's a doozy, sir! I mean, the phraseology is more an international English than it is American. He *punctuates*. 'Dago' is used here, but it's old-fashioned. These days we're Wops. He indicated his degree of education by referring to me as Othello, whose wife was Desdemona." He caught the look on Corey's face and extrapolated. "A real piece of goods named Iago worked on Othello's possessiveness, his passion for Desdemona. Made Othello think she was unfaithful. So Othello strangled her. Given the circumstances, a garotte was probably as close to strangulation as he could get."

"Is he setting you up?" Patrick asked.

"I doubt it. He's set her up. What he was really doing was showing us that nothing we do can protect her if he decides to act."

"A cop killer!" said Corey savagely.

"A child killer," said Marciano. "We gotta stop him, Carmine!"

"We will. I'm not letting go, Danny, no matter what."

The only way into Desdemona's apartment on the tenth floor of the Nutmeg Insurance building was by speaking into an intercom and then punching a ten-number code on a special lock. The code would be changed every day and no one was permitted to write it down, even Desdemona.

Who didn't complain when Carmine let himself in that evening bearing brown bags full of groceries.

"Darjeeling tea from Scrivener's—Colombian coffee from the same—brown bread—butter—sliced ham—some TV dinners—fresh raisin bagels—mayonnaise—pickles—chocolate chip cookies—anything I thought you might like," he said, depositing his bags on the kitchen counter.

"Am I under siege?" she asked. "Am I not allowed to go to work or hike at the weekends?"

"Hiking's out, that's for sure, but we'll eat at Malvolio's tonight or anywhere else you want. You don't go out without two cops, and they won't be reading books," he said. "The door means I don't have to waste good men on surveillance, but once you step through it, you're government property."

"I shall hate it," she said, plucking her coat off a hook.

"Then let's hope it won't be for very long."

PART THREE

January & February
1966

CHAPTER 14

Saturday, January 1st, 1966

The phone woke Carmine from a deep sleep shortly before 8 A.M. on New Year's Day, one of the few times in almost three months that he had decided to let body and brain sleep themselves out. Not because he had celebrated the passing of the old year; though it had been the most harrowing of his life, he had many reasons to think that the new one might be even worse. Therefore, his New Year's Eve had been spent alone in his apartment watching the crowd in Times Square on TV. It had occurred to him to invite Desdemona up from two floors down, but he decided against it because it worried him that perhaps she was very tired of his company. If she ate out, he was the one who escorted her, paid for their dinner no matter how she carped about what he deemed no more than common courtesy. The result was that he went to bed long before midnight, had a fantastic sleep and was ready to be awakened when the phone rang.

"Delmonico," he said.

"It's Danny," came Marciano's voice. "Carmine, get up to New London right now. There's been another abduction. Dublin Road, on the Groton side of the river. Abe and Corey are on their way in, so is Patrick. The New London cops will wait for you."

He was upright immediately, conscious of a sweat the 50°F thermostat hadn't produced; he liked to sleep cold, it kept him from throwing the covers off. "But it can't be," he said, shivering. "It's only been thirty days since Francine, the guy isn't due to strike until the end of the month."

"We're not sure it's the same guy—the abduction took place during the night, for starters, and this is a new experience for the New London cops. Get up there and tell them what they've got."

Abe driving, they screamed the forty miles to New London, Paul and Patrick in their van behind them.

"Thirty days, it's only been thirty days!" Abe said as I-95 began to run into New London; he hadn't said a word until then.

"Take the Groton turnoff just over the bridge," said Corey, a map spread on his knees. "It can't be the same guy, Carmine."

"We'll know in a few minutes, so take it easy."

The location wasn't hard to find; every squad car in all of New London County looked to be parked up and down the verges of a street containing modest houses in fifth-of-an-acre blocks; Dublin Road, Groton.

The house a patrolman indicated was grey-painted, a single-storey dwelling too small to qualify as ranch style. Very much the home of a workingman having pride in himself and his property. One glance at it, and Carmine knew with sinking heart that the people who lived inside were as respected as respectable. A perfect family for the killer's purposes.

"Tony Dimaggio," said a man in captain's uniform, hand out to Carmine. "A sixteen-year-old black girl named Margaretta Bewlee was snatched during the night. Mr. Bewlee seems to think through the bedroom window, but I haven't let any of my guys near it for fear they'd destroy evidence—this is way out of our league if the Monster's got her. Come inside," he said, preceding Carmine. "The mother's a basket case, but Mr. Bewlee's holding up."

"I'll be there as soon as I take Dr. O'Donnell to the outside of the window. Thanks for your forbearance, Tony."

The family was blue-black: father, mother, a young teenaged girl and two boys coming up toward their teens.

"Mr. Bewlee? Lieutenant Delmonico. Tell me what happened."

He was that shade of grey that spoke of extreme travail in dark-skinned people, but he managed to control his feelings; to lose hold of them might mean all the difference to Margaretta, and he knew it. His wife, still in robe and slippers, sat as if turned to stone, eyes glazed over.

Mr. Bewlee drew a breath. "We toasted the New Year, then we went to bed, Lieutenant. All of us—no night owls here, so we could hardly keep our eyes open."

"Did you drink something alcoholic, like sparkling wine?"

"No, just fruit punch. This isn't a drinking house."

His face was clouding; when he couldn't seem to grasp what came next, he gazed at Carmine imploringly. Help me, help me!

"Where do you work, Mr. Bewlee?"

"I'm a precision welder at Electric Boat, due for a pay raise in a couple of weeks. We've just been waiting for the raise to move house, buy something bigger." The tears flowed and he halted.

"Introduce your children to me, Mr. Bewlee."

Their father collected himself, sure he could manage that. "This is Linda, she's fourteen. Hank's eleven, Ray's ten. We have a little guy, Terence. He's two and sleeps in our bedroom. Linda took him next door to Mrs. Spinoza. We figured he didn't need—didn't need—" He broke down, buried his face in his hands, battled to compose himself. "I'm sorry, I can't—"

"Take your time, Mr. Bewlee."

"Etta—that's what we call her—and Linda share a room."

"*Share?*"

179

"That's right, Lieutenant. There's two of them in there. We didn't get up real early, but when my wife started making us some breakfast, she called out to the girls. Linda said Etta was in the bathroom, but it turned out the boys were, not Etta. So we started looking for her, couldn't find her. That was when I called the police. All I could think of was the Monster. But it can't be him, can it? He's not due yet, and Etta's like the rest of us—*black*. I mean, we're real black. He wouldn't want our little girl, Lieutenant."

How could he answer that? Carmine turned to Etta's sister. "Linda, is that right?" he asked, smiling at her.

"Yes, sir," she managed, weeping.

"I'm not going to say, don't cry, Linda, but you can help your sister best if you answer me, okay?"

"Okay." She mopped her face.

"You and Etta went to bed at the same time, right?"

"Yes, sir. Half after midnight."

"Your daddy says all of you were sleepy. Is that true?"

"Whacked," said Linda simply.

"So you both went straight to bed."

"Yes, sir, soon as we said our prayers."

"Does Etta mind saying her prayers?"

Linda's eyes dried; she looked shocked. "No, sir, no!"

"Did you talk any after you were in bed?"

"No, sir, least I didn't. I was asleep soon as I lay down."

"Did you hear any noises during the night? Wake up to go to the bathroom?"

"No, sir, I slept until Mom called us. Though I did think it was funny that Etta was up ahead of me. She's a real tiger for sleeping in. Then I thought she must have snuck off to beat me to the bathroom, but when I banged on the door, Hank answered."

The child had a beautiful face, liquid dark eyes, a perfect skin, very full lips that would drive a dedicated monk to break his vows, with their clean-cut margins and a turn to them that always whispered to Carmine of tragedy. A black girl's lips, dark maroon shading to pink where they met in that heart-rending fold. Did Margaretta have this same face?

"You don't think that Etta could have snuck out, Linda?"

The big eyes grew bigger. "Why would she?" Linda asked, as if that was an answer in itself.

Yes, why would she? She's as sweet and docile and lovely as all the others. She still says her prayers at bedtime.

"How tall is Etta?"

"Five-nine, sir."

"Has she got a good figure?"

"No, she's thin. It depresses her because she wants to be a star like Dionne Warwick," said Linda, who showed every evidence that she too would be tall and thin. Tall and thin. *Black.*

"Thank you, Linda. Did anyone else hear a noise last night?"

Nobody had.

Then Mr. Bewlee produced a photograph; Carmine found himself gazing at a girl who looked just like Linda. And like the others.

Patrick came in on his own, carrying his bag.

"Which door down the hall, Linda?"

"The second on the right, sir. My bed's on the right."

"See anything to say that he came in the window, Patsy?"

"Not a thing, except that both the inner and the outer set have ordinary window locks that weren't engaged. The ground outside is frozen solid. Grassy in summer, but died right back at the moment. The sill looks as if it hasn't been touched since the outer windows went on last October, or whenever the insect screens were removed. I left Paul out there to make sure I didn't miss anything, but I don't think I did."

They entered a room barely large enough to accommodate two burgeoning young women, but it was extremely neat and well cared for; pink-painted walls, a braided pink mat between two single beds, one to left and right of the window. Each girl had a closet beyond the foot of her bed. A big poster of Dionne Warwick and a smaller

181

one of Mary Bell were tacked on the wall above Margaretta's bed; Linda's bed was provided with a shelf that held a half dozen teddy bears.

"Quiet, sound sleepers," said Patrick. "The bedclothes are hardly disturbed." He moved to Margaretta's bed and bent to put his nostrils a scant millimeter from the pillow. "Ether," he said. "Ether, not chloroform."

"Are you sure? It evaporates within seconds."

"I'm sure. My nose is good enough to go into the perfume trade. It got trapped in this fold, see? Gone already. Our pal clamped a pad soaked in ether over her face, picked her up and took her out through the window." Patrick went to the window and pushed the inner one up with a gloved hand, then the outer one. "Listen to that—not a sound. Mr. Bewlee takes care of his home."

"Unless our pal did the lubricating."

"No, my money's on Mr. Bewlee."

"Jesus, Patsy, he's cool! A girl who measures five-nine in bare feet, would weigh one-ten, and her sister sleeping not three yards away—if Linda had woken—"

"Kids sleep like the dead, Carmine. Margaretta probably never really woke up, looking at the bedclothes—no sign of a struggle. Linda slept through it, oblivious. He would have done the whole thing in two minutes, tops."

"Then the question is, who left the windows unlocked? Did Mr. Bewlee not check them regularly, or did our pal pay a visit ahead of time and do it?"

"He visited ahead of time. I figure Mr. Bewlee locks them at the start of the real cold weather and then doesn't unlock them until the first thaw. The house has real good forced-air heating, and it's far too cold for the girls to open a window. The winter's ten degrees colder here than it is in Holloman."

Paul came in, shaking his head.

"Then let's start looking at every inch in here—we bag all Margaretta's bedclothes, with special attention to that pillowcase.

Carmine," Patrick said as his cousin was leaving the room, "if this girl is tall, thin and black black, he's changed *all* of his parameters. Maybe it's not the same guy."

"Care to bet?"

"Thirty days—a different abduction technique—a different type of girl—that's what you're asking me to believe."

"Yes, I am. The most important factor hasn't changed. This girl is as pure and untouched as the others. What changes there are don't tell me that we've managed to scare him much. He's working to a master plan, and this is a part of it. Twelve girls in twenty-four months. Maybe now he's going to do twelve girls in twelve months. It's New Year's Day. Maybe their size and skin color are irrelevant to his second dozen, or else Margaretta is his new type."

Patrick sucked in his breath audibly. "You think he's going to change what he does to them too, don't you?"

"That's what my instincts are telling me, yes. But never doubt one thing, Patsy. This is our guy. It's not someone else."

Carmine left Abe and Corey to come back with Patrick; it fell to them to do the plod from door to door on Dublin Road, to ask if anyone had seen or heard anything. Not much chance on New Year's, between the parties and the booze.

It was 10.30 A.M. when the Ford turned into the Smith driveway, a long, twisting one ending at a very large and traditional white clapboard house on a knoll, its Georgian-paned windows flanked by dark green shutters. Not pre-Revolutionary, but not new either. Five acres of land, naturally forested save for where the house stood; no gardeners in the Smith family.

A pretty woman around forty answered the door; the Prof's wife, no doubt. When Carmine introduced himself she held the door wide open and admitted him to a house as traditionally furnished as its exterior suggested; nice things, no expense spared, but unadventurous tastes guiding the decor. Clearly the Smiths could afford to buy whatever they fancied.

"Bob's here somewhere," Eliza said vaguely. "Would you like a cup of coffee?"

"Thanks, I would." Carmine followed her through to a kitchen artfully tweaked to look a hundred years older than it was, from wormholes to fading paint.

Two teenaged boys came in as Eliza handed the visitor his coffee. The eagerness natural in males of their age was absent; Carmine was used to boys who bombarded him with questions, as they invariably thought his calling a glamorous one and murder better than anything on TV. Yet the Smith sons, introduced as Bobby and Sam, looked more frightened than curious. As soon as their mother gave them permission they left, under orders to find their father.

"Bob's not well," Eliza said, sighing.

"The strain must be considerable."

"No, it's not really that. His trouble is that he's not used to things going wrong, Lieutenant. Bob has led a charmed life. The proper Yankee forebears, a lot of money in the family, top of every class he's ever been in, got everything he ever wanted, including the William Parson Chair. I mean, he's only forty-five—do you realize that he wasn't turned thirty when the Chair was handed to him? And it's gone like a dream! Accolades galore."

"Until now," said Carmine, stirring his coffee, which smelled too old to taste good. He sipped, discovered his nose was right.

"Until now," she agreed.

"Last time I saw him, I thought he seemed depressed."

"Very depressed," Eliza said. "The only time he ever cheers up is when he goes down to the basement. That's what he'll do today. And again tomorrow."

Professor Smith came in, looking hunted. "Lieutenant, this is unexpected. Happy New Year."

"No, sir, it isn't happy. I've just come from Groton and another abduction a month too early."

Smith slumped into the nearest chair, face bleached to chalk. "Not at the Hug," he said. "Not at the Hug."

"In Groton, Professor. *Groton.*"

Eliza got to her feet briskly, beamed artificially. "Bob, show the Lieutenant your folly," she said.

You are brilliant, Mrs. Smith, said Carmine to himself. You know I'm not visiting to wish anyone a happy New Year, and am about to ask if I can take an unofficial look around. But you don't want your husband refusing a pleasant request, so you've taken the bull by the horns and pushed the Prof into a co-operation he won't feel like tendering.

"My folly? Oh, my folly!" Smith said, then brightened. "My folly, of course! Would you like to see it, Lieutenant?"

"I would indeed." Carmine abandoned the coffee without regret.

The door to the basement was equipped with several locks that had been installed by a professional, and took Bob Smith some time to open. The wooden stairway was poorly lit; at its bottom the Prof flicked a switch that threw the whole of a huge room into stark, shadowless light. Jaw dropped, Carmine gaped at what Eliza Smith had called a folly.

A roughly square table fifty feet on each side filled the basement. Its surface was realistically landscaped into rolling hills, valleys, a range of alps, several plains, forests of perfect, tiny trees; rivers flowed, a lake sat beneath the flanks of a volcanic cone, water fell over a cliff. Farmhouses peeped, a town lay on one plain, another town lay wedged between two hills. And everywhere glittered the twin silver tracks of a miniature railroad. The rivers were bridged with steel girders correct down to rivet bumps, a chain-driven ferry crossed the lake, a beautiful arched viaduct carried the tracks through the alps. On the outskirts of the towns were railroad stations.

And what trains! The streamlined Super Chief ran at a fast clip amid the trees of a forest, negotiated a towering suspension bridge flawlessly. Two diesel locomotives hauled a freight train of coal wagons; another consisted of oil and chemical tanks, and a third of wooden boxcars. A local suburban train stood at one town station.

Altogether Carmine counted eleven trains, each in motion save for the humble local at its station, their speeds varying from the rush of the Super Chief down to the crawl of one freight train hauling so many oil tanks that it had pairs of diesel locomotives inserted throughout its formidable length. And all in miniature! To Carmine it was a wonder of the world, a toy to die for.

"I've never seen anything like this in all my life," he said huskily. "There aren't the words to describe it."

"I've been building it since we moved in here sixteen years ago," said the Prof, who was cheering up rapidly. "They're all powered by electricity, but later on today I'll switch to steam."

"Steam? You mean locomotives powered by wood? Coal?"

"Actually I generate the steam by burning alcohol, but the principle's the same. It's a lot more fun than just sending them around on household electricity."

"I bet you and your boys have a marvelous time down here."

The Prof stiffened, a look in his eyes that gave Carmine a chill: he might have led a charmed life, but below the depression and self-indulgence was at least some steel. "My boys don't come down here, they're banned," he said. "When they were younger and the door had no locks, they trashed the place. *Trashed it!* It took me four years to repair the damage. They broke my heart."

It was on the tip of Carmine's tongue to expostulate that surely the boys were old enough now to respect the trains, but he decided not to horn in on Smith's domestic business. "How do you ever get to the middle of it?" he asked instead, squinting up into the lights. "A hoist?"

"No, I go in underneath. It's assembled in sections, each fairly small. I had a hydraulics engineer install a system that enables me to jack a section up as much as necessary, and move it to one side so I can make my alterations standing up. Though it's more for cleaning than anything else. If I'm changing from diesel to steam, I just drive a train to the edge, see?"

The Super Chief left its route, crossed via several sets of points while other trains were stopped or diverted, and drew up at the table edge. Carmine almost imagined he could hear it clanking and hissing.

"Do you mind if I take a look at your hydraulics, Professor?"

"No, not at all. Here, you'll need this, it's dark under there." The Prof handed over a large flashlight.

Of rams, cylinders and rods there were aplenty, but though he crawled through every part of the table's underside, Carmine could find no hidden trapdoors, no concealed compartments; the floor was concrete, kept very clean, and somehow an alliance between trains and young girls seemed unlikely.

The kid in him would have been ecstatic to spend the rest of the day playing with the Prof's trains, but once he was satisfied that the Smith basement held nothing but trains, trains, and more trains, Carmine took his leave. Eliza conducted him through the house when he asked if he might inspect it. The only thing that gave her an anxious moment was a switch lying on the sideboard in the dining room, its end ominously frayed. So the Prof beats his boys, and not softly. Well, my dad beat me until I got too big for him, mean-tempered little runt that he was. After him, U.S. Army drill sergeants were a piece of cake.

From the Smiths he went to the Ponsonbys, not far away, but the place was deserted. The open garage doors revealed a scarlet Mustang, but not the station wagon Carmine had seen parked in the Hug lot. Weird, the people who drove V-8 convertibles! Desdemona, and now Charles Ponsonby. Today he must be out with his sister in the station wagon; sister and guide dog probably demanded room.

He decided not to visit the Polonowskis; instead he stopped at a phone booth and called Marciano. "Danny, send someone upstate to look at Walter Polonowski's cabin. If he's there with Marian, don't disturb him, but if he's there alone or not there at all, then your guys should look around politely enough that Polonowski doesn't remember things like search warrants."

"What's your verdict on the Groton abduction, Carmine?"

187

"Oh, it's our man, but proving that is going to be hard. He has changed his pattern, rung in the new year with a new tune. As soon as Patrick gets back, talk to him. I'm taking a drive around the Hugger homes. No, no, don't panic! Just a look-see. Though if I find anyone at home, I'm going to ask to inspect places like basements and attics. Danny, you should see what's in the Prof's basement! Wowee wow!"

While he was in the booth he tried the Finches, whose phone rang out unanswered. The Forbeses, he discovered, used an answering service, probably because Forbes saw so many human patients. Its cooing operator informed Carmine that Dr. Forbes was in Boston for the weekend, and gave him a Boston number. When he called it, Dr. Addison Forbes barked at him irritably.

"I've just heard that another girl's been taken," Forbes said, "but don't look at me, Lieutenant. My wife and I are up here with our daughter Roberta. She's just been accepted into ob-gyn."

I am running out of suspects, Carmine thought, hung up and went back to the Ford.

Coming into Holloman city on Sycamore, he decided to see what Tamara Vilich got up to on a holiday weekend.

Having checked who it was through the glass panel, she opened her front door clad in very non-Hugger clothes: a floating garment of filmy scarlet silk slit up both sides to her hips, very sexy, not much left to the imagination. She is one of those women, he thought, who never wears underpants. A female flasher.

"You look as if you could use a decent cup of coffee. Come in," she said, smiling, the scarlet of her raiment turning her chameleon eyes quite red and devilish.

"Nice place you have here," he said, gazing about.

"That," she said, "is so hackneyed it sounds insincere."

"Just making polite conversation."

"Then make it with yourself for a minute while I deal with the coffee."

She vanished in the direction of the kitchen, leaving him to absorb her decor at his leisure. Her taste ran to ultra modern: brilliant colors, good leather seating, chrome and glass rather than wood. But he hardly noticed, his attention riveted on the paintings assaulting her defenseless walls. In pride of place was a triptych. The left panel showed a nude, crimson-colored woman with a grotesquely ugly face kneeling to adore a phallic-looking statue of Jesus Christ; the center panel showed the same woman sprawled on her back with her legs wide open and the statue in her left hand; the right panel showed her with the statue jammed into her vagina and her face flying into pieces as if struck by a mercury-tipped bullet.

Having taken in its message, he chose a seat from which he couldn't see the revolting thing.

The other paintings displayed more violence and anger than obscenity, but he wouldn't hang a one of them on his walls. A faint reek of oil paints and turpentine told him that Tamara was probably the artist, but what drove her to these subjects? A rotting male corpse hanging upside down from a gallows, a quasi-human face snarling and slavering, a clenched fist oozing blood from between its fingers. Charles Ponsonby might approve, but Carmine's eye was shrewd enough to judge that her technique wasn't brilliant; no, these weren't good enough to interest a finicky connoisseur like Chuck. All they had was the power to offend.

Either she's sick, or she's more cynical than I suspected, he thought.

"Like my stuff?" she asked, rejoining him.

"No. I think it's sick."

Her fine head went back, she laughed heartily. "You mistake my motives, Lieutenant. I paint what a certain market wants so badly it can't get enough. The trouble is my technique isn't as good as the masters in the field, so I can only sell my work for its subject matter."

"The implication, for peanuts. Right?"

"Yes. Though one day maybe I will be able to earn a living at it. The real money is in limited editions of prints, but I'm not a lithographer. I need lessons I can't afford."

"Still paying off the Hug embezzlement, huh?"

She uncoiled from her chair like a spring and returned to the kitchen without answering.

Her coffee was very good; he drank thirstily, helped himself to an apple Danish fresh out of the freezer.

"You own the premises, I believe," he said, feeling better.

"Been checking up on people?"

"Sure. It's a part of the job."

"Yet you have the gall to sit in judgement of my work. Yes," she went on, stroking her throat with one long, beautiful hand, "I own this house. I rent the second floor to a radiology resident and his nurse wife, and the top floor to a couple of lesbian ornithologists who work at the Burke Biology Tower. The rent's saved my bacon since my—er—little slip."

That's right, Tamara, brazen it out, it suits you better than indignation. "Professor Smith implied that your husband of that time masterminded you."

She leaned forward, feet tucked under her, lifted her lip in contempt. "They say you won't do what you don't want to do, so what do you think?"

"That you loved him a great deal."

"How perceptive of you, Lieutenant! I suppose I must have, but it seems an eternity ago."

"Do you let your tenants use the basement?" he asked.

Her creamy lids fell, her mouth curved slightly. "No, I do not. The basement is mine."

"I have no warrant, but would you mind if I looked around?"

Her nipples popped out as if she were suddenly cold. "Why? What's happened?" she asked sharply.

"Another abduction. Last night, in Groton."

"And you think, because I paint what I paint, that I'm a psycho with a basement soaked in blood. Look where you want, I don't give a fuck," she said, and walked into what he realized had once been a second bedroom, but now was her studio.

Carmine took her at her word, prowled around the basement to find nothing worse than a dead rat in a trap; had he liked her, he would have removed it for her, but as he didn't, he didn't.

Her bedroom was very interesting; black leather, black satin sheets on a bed whose frame was stout enough to take manacles, a zebra skin on the black carpet with its head intact and two glowing red-glass eyes. I bet, he thought, walking about quietly, that you're not on the receiving end of the whips, honey. You are a dominatrix. I wonder who is being flogged?

A photograph in an ornate silver frame stood on the bedside table on what he guessed was her side of the bed; an elderly, stern woman who looked enough like Tamara to be Mom. He picked it up in what, had she entered the room, would have seemed an idle manner, then slid its back out quickly. Bingo! Paydirt. Behind Mom lay a full-length picture of Keith Kyneton; he was stark naked, built like Mr. Universe, and up like a fifteen-year-old. Another thirty seconds and Mom was back on the table. Why don't they realize that hiding one photo behind another is the oldest trick in the Book of Deceptions? Now I know all about you, Miss Tamara Vilich. You might be flogging others, but not him—his work would suffer. Do you play games together, then? Dress him up as a baby and paddle his backside? Play a nurse giving him an enema? Or a strict schoolteacher dishing out humiliations? A hooker picking him up in a bar? Well, well!

With nowhere else left to go, he went home, but got off the elevator on the tenth floor and pressed Desdemona's intercom. Her voice answered tonelessly—not evidence of distaste, evidence of technology.

"There's been another one," he said baldly, peeling off his out-door layers.

"Carmine, no! It's only been a month!"

He gazed around, located the work basket and a tablecloth that was being finished more rapidly than it would have been in her hiking days. "Why," he demanded, mood darkened to utter discouragement and in need of someone to lash out at, "are you such a miser,

Desdemona? Why don't you spend money on yourself? What's with this frugal living? Can't you buy a nice dress once in a while?"

She stood absolutely still, a white line about her compressed lips, her eyes displaying a grief he hadn't seen there even for Charlie. "I am a spinster, I save for my old age," she said levelly, "but more than that. In five more years I'm going *home*—home to a place with no violence, no gun-toting cops, and no Connecticut Monster. That's why."

"I'm sorry, I had no right to ask. Forgive me."

"Not today, and perhaps not ever," she said, opening the door. The outdoor clothes followed their owner, tossed in a heap on the floor. "Goodbye, Lieutenant Delmonico."

CHAPTER 15

Tuesday, January 4th, 1966

The first working day of the New Year was blowy and snowy, but the weather hadn't prevented someone from daubing the Hug with graffiti—KILLERS, BLACK HATERS, PIGS, FASCISTS, swastikas, and, right along the front façade, HOLLOMAN KU KLUX KLAN.

When the Prof arrived and saw what had been done to the apple of his eye, he collapsed. Not with a heart attack; Robert Mordent Smith's crisis was of the spirit. An ambulance bore him away, the team manning it well aware that when they arrived one building down at Emergency, they would be shouting not for cardiologists but for psychiatrists. He wept, he moaned, he raved, he babbled, the words he uttered complete gibberish.

Carmine came over to see the Hug for himself, as thankful as John Silvestri that the winter was proving a hard one after all; the real racial turmoil wouldn't explode until spring. Only two black men had braved the elements to brandish placards already torn to tatters by the wind. One's face was familiar; he halted outside the entrance and studied it. Its owner was small, thin, insignificant, very dark skinned, neither handsome nor sexy. So where, where, *where?* Buried memories tended to surface suddenly, as this one did; once things were in Carmine's mind, they stayed there, resurrected when given a nudge by events. Otis Green's wife's nephew. Wesley le Clerc.

He tramped across to le Clerc and his companion, another would-be-if-he-could-be who looked less determined than Wesley.

"Go home, guys," he said pleasantly, "otherwise we'll have to dig you out or plough you under. Except, Mr. le Clerc, a word first. Come in out of the cold. I'm not arresting you, I just want to talk, scout's honor."

A little to his surprise, Wesley followed him docilely while the other man scuttled away as if let out of school.

"You're Wesley le Clerc, right?" he asked after they moved inside, stamping the caked snow off their boots.

"What if I am, huh?"

"Mrs. Green's nephew from Louisiana."

"Yeah, and I got a record, save you the time looking me up. I'm a known agitator. In other words, a nigger nuisance."

"How much time have you served, Wes?"

"All up, five years. No stealing hub caps or armed robberies. Just beatin' on redneck nigger haters."

"And what do you do in Holloman apart from demonstrating in a peaceful manner and wearing a Black Brigade jacket?"

"Make instruments at Parson Surgical Supplies."

"That's a good job, takes some manual and intellectual skill."

Wesley shaped up to the much bigger Carmine like a bantam rooster to a fighting cock. "What do you care what I do, huh? Think I painted that stuff out there, huh?"

"Oh, grow up, Wes!" said Carmine wearily. "The graffiti's not Black Brigade, it's kids from Travis High, you think I don't know that? What I want to know is why you're out there freezing your ass off while the weather's too bad to attract an audience."

"I'm there to tell Whitey that it's time to worry, Mr. Smart Cop.

You won't catch this killer 'cos you don't want to. For all I know, Mr. Smart Cop, you're the one killing black girls."

"No, Wes, he's not me." Carmine leaned against the wall and eyed Wesley with unmistakable sympathy. "Give up on Mohammed's way! It's the wrong way. A better life for black people isn't going to come through violence, no matter what Lenin said about terror. After all, a good many white people have terrorized black Americans for two hundred years, but has that destroyed the black spirit? Go back to school, Wes, get a law degree. That will help the black cause more than Mohammed el Nesr can."

"Oh, sure! Where am I going to get the money for that?"

"Making instruments at Parson Surgical Spplies. Holloman has good night schools, and there are bunches and bunches of people in Holloman eager to help."

"Whitey can shove his lordly patronage up his ass!"

"Who says I'm talking about Whitey? Many of them are black. Businessmen, professional men. I don't know if they exist in Louisiana yet, but they sure do in Connecticut, and none of them are Uncle Toms. They are working for their people."

Wesley le Clerc turned on his heel and left, flinging his right fist into the air.

"At least, Wes," said Carmine, smiling at Wesley's retreating back, "you didn't flip me the bird."

But Wesley le Clerc wasn't thinking of rude gestures as he scrunched through the worsening snow. He was thinking of Lieutenant Carmine Delmonico in a different way. Bright, very bright. Too cool and sure of himself to give anyone an excuse to cry persecution or even discrimination; his was the soft answer turned away wrath. Only not this time. Not my wrath. Through Otis I have the means to feed Mohammed information he will need come spring. Mohammed looks at me with a little more respect these days, and what's he going to say when I tell him that the Holloman pigs are still nosing around the Hug? The answer is inside the Hug. Delmonico knows that as well as I do. Rich, privileged Whitey. When every black American is a disciple of Mohammed el Nesr, things are gonna change.

"The way is hard," said Mohammed el Nesr to Ali el Kadi. "Too many of our black brothers are brainwashed, and too many more have been seduced by Whitey's greatest weapons—drugs and booze. Even now the Monster has taken a real black girl, our recruitment isn't picking up enough."

"Our people need more provocation," Ali el Kadi answered; that was the name Wesley le Clerc had chosen when he espoused Islam.

"No," said Mohammed strongly. "Our people don't need, the Black Brigade does. And not provocation. We need a martyr, Ali. A shining example who will bring us men in tens of thousands." He patted Wesley/Ali on the arm. "In the meantime, go to your job, do good work there. Enroll in night school. Cultivate that infidel pig, Delmonico. And find out everything you can."

The Forbeses were still in Boston, would be until the roads were safer, and the Finches were snowbound. Walt Polonowski had spent the weekend in his cabin, but with a living girl, Marian. The men Danny Marciano had sent up there to investigate hadn't announced their presence; it was no part of Carmine's intentions to render any Hugger more miserable than he needed to be, and that meant helping Polonowski keep his secret—for the moment.

Patrick had found nothing in the house on Dublin Road either to confirm or deny that Margaretta's abductor was their man, though he had established that the method of choice had been ether.

"He wears some kind of protective suit," Patrick said to his cousin. "It's made of a fabric that doesn't shed any fibers, and whatever he wears on his feet have smooth soles that don't make footprints unless he steps in mud, which he doesn't. The suit has a close-fitting bonnet or hood that covers his hair completely, and he's gloved. With this night abduction, obviously everything he wears is black. He may blacken his face. I'm picking that the suit is rubber and form fitting, like a diving suit."

"They're clumsy to move in, Patsy."

"Not these days, if you can afford the best."

"And he can afford the best, because I think he has money."

Corey and Abe's investigations in Groton had yielded nothing; New Year's was always rackety.

"Thanks, guys," Carmine said to them.

No one stated the obvious: that they would know more when Margaretta's body turned up.

The previous evening had seen Carmine ascend in the elevator of the Nutmeg Insurance building to its top floor, where he sought out Dr. Hideki Satsuma. Who was willing to admit him.

"Oh, this is nice," said Carmine, gazing around. "I tried you last night, Doctor, but you weren't at home."

"No, I was up at my place on Cape Cod. The Chathams. When I heard the weather forecast, I decided to come home today."

So Satsuma had a place in the Chathams, did he? A three-hour drive in that maroon Ferrari. But shorter if the drive had begun in Groton.

"Your courtyard is beautiful," Carmine said, going over to the transparent wall to gaze through it.

"It used to be, but there are imbalances I am trying to correct. I have not yet succeeded, Lieutenant. Perhaps it is the Hollywood cypress—not a Japanese tree. I put it there because I thought a strand of America was necessary, but perhaps I am wrong."

"To me, Doctor, it makes the garden—taller, twisted around itself like a double helix. Without it, there's nothing high enough to reach the top of the walls, and nothing symmetrical."

"I take your point."

Like hell you do, thought Carmine. What does a *gaijin* know about gardening the universe?

"Sir, will you give me permission to have someone look at your house on Cape Cod?"

"No, Lieutenant Delmonico, I will not. If you so much as try, I will sue."

Thus had Monday ended, with nothing to show.

At six on Tuesday evening he arrived at number 6, Ponsonby Lane, to beard the Ponsonbys in their den. The deep baying of a large dog greeted his car, and when Charles Ponsonby opened the front door he was hanging on to the collar of—his sister's guide dog?

"A weird breed," he said to Ponsonby as he divested himself of layers in the weather porch.

"Half golden labrador, half German shepherd," said Charles, hanging up the clothing. "We call her a labrashep, and her name is Biddy. It's okay, sweetheart, the Lieutenant is a friend."

The dog wasn't so sure. It decided to allow him in, but it kept a wary eye on him.

"We're in the kitchen, starting to make a Beethoven dinner. Numbers three, five and seven—we always prefer his odd-numbered symphonies to his even-numbered. Come through. I hope you don't mind if we sit in the kitchen?"

"I'm glad to sit anywhere, Dr. Ponsonby."

"Call me Chuck, though for form's sake, I'll stick to your official title. Claire always calls me Charles."

He led Carmine through one of those genuinely 250-year-old houses that sag at the beams and have floors full of undulations and jogs, into a more modern dining room that opened into what was definitely the original kitchen. Here, the wormholes, the fading paint and the splintering wood were authentic: eat your heart out, Mrs. Eliza Smith.

"This must have been separate from the house in the old days," said Carmine as he shook hands with a woman in her late thirties who looked just like her brother, even to the watery eyes.

"Sit over there, Lieutenant," she said in a Lauren Bacall voice, waving a hand at a Windsor chair. "Yes, it was separate. Kitchens back then had to be, in case of fire. Otherwise the whole house burned down. Charles and I joined it to the house with a dining room, but oh, what a headache the building process was!"

"Why's that?" he asked, taking a glass of amontillado sherry from Charles.

"The ordinances insist that we have to build in timber of the same age as the house," Charles said, seating himself opposite Carmine. "I finally located two ancient barns in upstate New York and bought them both. Too much timber, but we've stored it for any future repairs. Good, hard oak."

Claire was standing in profile to Carmine, wielding a thin-bladed, supple knife that she was using to prepare two thick cuts of filet steak. Awestruck, Carmine watched her deft fingers get the knife under a tendon and strip it off without losing any of the meat; she performed the task better than he could have.

"Do you like Beethoven?" she asked him.

"Yes, very much."

"Then why not eat with us? There's plenty of food, I do assure you, Lieutenant," she said, rinsing the knife under a brass tap over a stone sink. "A cheese and spinach soufflé first, a lemon sorbet to clear the palate, then beef fillet with Bearnaise sauce, new potatoes simmered in homemade beef stock, and petits pois."

"Sounds delicious, but I can't stay too long." He sipped the sherry to find it a very good one.

"Charles tells me another girl is missing," she said.

"Yes, Miss Ponsonby."

"Call me Claire." She sighed, put the knife away and joined them at the table, accepting a sherry as if she could see it.

The kitchen was much as it must always have been, save that where once the great chimney would have held the spits, hooks and bread oven of eighteenth-century cooking, it now held a massive slow combustion stove. The room was too warm for Carmine.

"An Aga stove? I don't know it," he said, draining his sherry.

"We bought it in England on our one adventure abroad years ago," said Charles. "It has a very slow oven for all-day baking, and an oven fast enough to do justice to pastry or French bread. Lots of hotplates. It supplies us with hot water in winter too."

"Oil fired?"

"No, it's wood fired."

"Isn't that expensive? I mean, heating oil is only nine cents a gallon. Wood must cost a lot more."

"It would if I had to buy it, Lieutenant, but I don't. We have twenty acres of loggable forest up beyond Sleeping Giant, the last land we own apart from these five acres. I cut what I need each spring, replant the trees I take down."

Jesus, here we go again! thought Carmine. How many Huggers have these secret retreats tucked away? Abe and Corey will have to go up there tomorrow and comb his twenty acres of forest—how they'll love that with all this snow on the ground! Benjamin Liebman the undertaker has a mortuary so clean that we'd have to catch him in the act and the Prof has a basement full of trains, but a whole goddamn forest—!

A second glass of the Ponsonby sherry made Carmine conscious that he hadn't eaten breakfast or lunch: time to go.

"I hope you won't consider my question rude, Claire, but have you always been blind?" he asked.

"Oh, yes," she said cheerfully. "I'm one of those incubator babies got fed pure oxygen. Blame it on ignorance."

His rush of pity made him look away, up to where on one wall hung a group of framed photographs, some of them old enough to be sepia daguerrotypes. A strong family resemblance ran through the faces: square adamantine features, fiercely marked brows and thick dark hair. The only different one was clearly the latest of them: an elderly woman whose face was far more reminiscent of Charles and Claire, from its wispy hair to watery pale eyes and long, lugubrious features. Their mother? If so, then they were not in the Ponsonby mold, they were in hers.

"My mother," Claire said with that uncanny ability to pick out what was going on in the sighted world. "Don't let my prescience bother you, Lieutenant. To some extent, it's legerdemain."

"I can tell she's your mother, and that you both resemble her rather than the Ponsonby line."

"She was a Sunnington from Cleveland, and we do take after the Sunningtons. Mama died three years ago, a merciful release. Very severe dementia. But one cannot put a Daughter of the American Revolution in a home for senile old ladies, so I cared for her myself until the bitter end. With some excellent help from the county authorities, I add."

So it's a D.A.R. household, Carmine thought. Ponsonby and his sister probably don't vote for anyone left of Genghiz Khan.

He got up, his head spinning slightly; the Ponsonbys served their sherry in wine glasses, not little sherry glasses. "Thanks for the hospitality, I appreciate it." He glanced across at the dog, lying with eyes fixed on him. "So long, Biddy. Nice to meet you too."

"What do you think of the good Lieutenant Delmonico?" Charles Ponsonby asked his sister when he returned to the kitchen.

"That he doesn't miss much," she said, folding stiff egg whites into her cheese and spinach sauce.

"True. They'll be tramping all over our forest tomorrow."

"Do you care?"

"Not a bit," said Charles, scraping the raw soufflé into its dish and putting it in the hot oven. "Though I do feel sorry for them. Futile searches are exasperating."

CHAPTER 16

Thursday, January 13th, 1966

"Carmine looks down," Marciano whispered to Patrick.

"He and Desdemona aren't playing speaks."

Commissioner Silvestri cleared his throat. "So how many of them refused to let us look around without a search warrant?"

"In general they've been pretty co-operative," said Carmine, who did indeed look down. "I get to see anything I ask to see, though I'm careful to make sure one of them at least is with me. I didn't ask Charles Ponsonby for permission to search his forest because I didn't see the point. If Corey and Abe find any fresh tracks through all this snow, or evidence that fresh tracks have been covered up, then I'll ask. My bet is that all twenty acres are pristine, so why give Chuck and Claire anguish ahead of time?"

"You like Claire Ponsonby," said Silvestri, stating a fact.

"Yes, I do. An amazing woman, doesn't harbor any grudges." He put her out of his mind. "To answer your original question, so far

I've had refusals from Satsuma, Chandra and Schiller, the three aliens. Satsuma shipped his private peon, Eido, up to his Cape Cod cottage about ten seconds after I left his penthouse, is my guess. Chandra is an arrogant bastard, but that's probably understandable in a maharajah's number one son. Even if we did manage to get a warrant, he'd complain to the Indian Embassy, and that is one very aggressively touchy nation. Schiller is a more pathetic case. I don't suspect him of anything more unorthodox than lots of photos of naked young men on his walls, but I haven't pushed him because of his suicide attempt. It was a serious one, not a grandstand."

Carmine grinned. "Speaking of photos of naked men, I found a doozy in Tamara Vilich's chains-and-leather bedroom. None other than that ambitious neurosurgeon, Keith Kyneton, who strips better than Mr. Universe. They say these muscle-building guys do it to compensate for an undersized dick, but I can't say that of him. He's hung like a porn star."

"Well, what do you know?" asked Marciano, leaning back in his chair to avoid Silvestri's cigar—why did it always have to be his nose it got shoved under? "Does that eliminate the Kynetons? Or Tamara Vilich?"

"Not entirely, Danny, though they've never been high on my list. She paints very sick pictures and she's a dominatrix."

"So Keith baby likes having the shit beaten out of him."

"Seems so. However, Tamara can't mark him much or his doting wife would notice. It's his mother I feel sorriest for."

"Another one you like," said Silvestri.

"Yeah, well, time to worry when there's nobody I like."

"What do you plan now?" Marciano asked.

"Taxing Tamara with the Kyneton business."

"That won't cost you any pain. Her, you don't like."

He bearded her in her office. "I found the picture of Dr. Keith Kyneton under the one of your mom," he said bluntly, admiring her spirit; her eyes, more khaki in this light, lifted to his face fearlessly.

"Fucking isn't murder, Lieutenant," she said. "It isn't even a crime between consenting adults."

"I'm not interested in the fucking, Miss Vilich. I want to know whereabouts you meet to fuck."

"At my house, in my apartment."

"With half of the neighborhood working somewhere in the Chubb Medical School or on Science Hill? Someone who knows Kyneton or his car would be sure to spot him sooner or later. I think you have a hideaway somewhere."

"You're wrong, we don't. I'm single, I live alone, and Keith makes sure there's no one about if he arrives before dark. Though he never does arrive before dark. That's why I love winter."

"What about the faces peering behind a lace curtain? Your affair with Dr. Kyneton gives him a double connection with the Hug. Wife *and* mistress work there. Does his wife know?"

"She lives in complete ignorance, but I suppose you'll yap far and wide about Keith and me," Tamara said sulkily.

"I don't yap, Miss Vilich, but I will have to talk to Keith Kyneton, make sure there isn't a hideaway somewhere. I smell violence in your relationship, and violence usually means a safe hideaway."

"Where the screams can't be heard. We never go that far, Lieutenant, it's more a matter of playing out some scenario," she said. "Strict teacher with naughty little boy, lady cop with her handcuffs and sandbag baton—you know." Her face changed, she shuddered. "He'll dump me. Oh, God, what will I do? What will I do after he dumps me?"

Which only goes to show, thought Carmine, departing, just how wrong assumptions can be. I thought the only person she loves is herself, but she's nuts about a turkey like Keith Kyneton, which may account for her paintings. They're how she feels about love—how sad, to hate love! Because she knows that Keith is only there for the sex. It's Hilda he loves—if he's capable of love.

Tamara caught him at the elevator.

"If you hurry, Lieutenant, you'll find Dr. Kyneton between operations," she said. "Holloman Hospital, tenth floor. The best way to get there is through the tunnel."

It was as spooky as all tunnels; after exploring the warren of tunnels the Japs had lived in on some of the Pacific islands during the War, Carmine feared them, had had to force himself to descend into the bowels of the earth in London to walk the tunnels between tube connections. Tunnels had a growl to them, an anger transmitted from the outraged, invaded earth. No matter how dry or brightly lit, a tunnel suggested lurking terrors. He strode the hundred yards of the Hug tunnel, took its right-hand fork and came into the hospital basement near the laundry.

All the operating rooms were on the tenth floor, but Dr. Keith Kyneton was waiting for him at the elevator block, clad in greens, a pair of cotton masks dangling around his neck.

"Private, I insist on keeping this private," the neurosurgeon said in a whisper. "In here, quick!"

"Here" was a storeroom choked with boxes of supplies, devoid of chairs or an atmosphere Carmine could use to good effect.

"Miss Vilich told you, huh?" he asked. "I never wanted her to take that goddamn photograph!"

"You should have torn it up."

"Oh, Jesus, Lieutenant, you don't understand! She *wanted* it! Tamara is—is fantastic!"

"That I can believe if you like kinky. Nurse Catheter and her enema kit. Who started it, you or her?"

"I don't honestly remember. We were both drunk, a hospital party Hilda couldn't make."

"How long ago was that?"

"Two years. Christmas of 1963."

"Where do you meet?"

"At Tamara's place. I'm very careful going in and out."

"Nowhere else? No little hideaway in the country?"

"No, just at Tamara's."

Suddenly Kyneton turned, put both hands on Carmine's forearm and clung, trembling, tears coursing down his face.

"Lieutenant! Sir! Please, I beg of you, don't tell anyone! My partnership in New York City is almost set, but if they find out about this, I'll lose it!" he cried.

His mind full of Ruth and Hilda, their constant sacrifices for this big, spoiled baby, Carmine shook the grip off savagely.

"Don't touch me, you selfish fuck! I don't give a shit about your precious practice in New York, but I happen to like your mother and your wife. You don't deserve either of them! *I* won't mention this to anyone, but you can't be stupid enough to think that Miss Tamara Vilich will be so charitable, surely! You'll dump her, no matter how fantastic the kinky sex with her is, and she'll retaliate like any other scorned woman. By tomorrow everyone who matters to you will know. Your professor, mother, wife, and the New York bunch."

Kyneton sagged, looked around vainly for a chair, hung on to a case of swabs instead. "Oh, Jesus, Jesus, I'm *ruined!*"

"Straighten up, Kyneton, for God's sake!" Carmine snapped. "You're not ruined—yet. Find someone to do your next operation, send your wife home, and follow her. Once you've gotten her and your mother to yourself, confess. Go down on your knees and beg forgiveness. Swear never to do it again. And don't hold anything back. You're a sweet-talking con merchant, you'll bring them round. But God help you if you don't treat those two women right in future, hear me? I'm not charging you with anything at the moment, but don't think I can't find something to charge you with if I want, and I'll be keeping my eye on you: for however many years I'm a cop. One last thing. Next time you shop at Brooks Brothers, buy your mother and wife something nice at Bonwit's."

Did the bastard listen? Yes, but only to what he divined would save him. "None of that helps me with the partnership."

"Sure it does! Provided your mother and wife stand by you.

Between the three of you, you can make Tamara Vilich sound like a frustrated woman telling a whole mess of lies."

The cog wheels were clunking around; Kyneton brightened visibly. "Yes, yes, I see what you mean! That's how to do it!"

A moment later, Carmine was alone. Keith Kyneton had raced off to mend his fences without a word of thanks.

"And just what," demanded an irate female voice, "do you think you're doing in here?"

Carmine flapped his impressive gold badge at the nurse, who looked ready to call hospital security.

"I'm doing penance, ma'am," he said. "Terrible penance."

The world when covered with fresh snow was so beautiful; as soon as he shed his outdoor layers Carmine turned one of his easy chairs to face the huge window that looked out across the harbor, and switched off all the interior lights. The strident yellow of highway illuminations offended him, but washed across sheets of snow it was softer, more golden. The ice was beginning to creep out from the eastern shore, though the wharves were still a black vacancy chipped by sparkles; too much wind for long, rippling reflections. No car ferries now until May.

What was he going to do about Desdemona? All his overtures had been repulsed, all his notes of apology returned unopened, thrust under his door. To this moment he didn't honestly know why she had been so mortally offended, so unrelenting—sure, he had overstepped the mark, but didn't everyone sometimes have words, not see eye to eye? Something to do with her pride, but just what escaped him. That barrier different nationalities could erect, too high to see over. Was it his remark about buying a new dress occasionally, or simply that he'd dared to query her behavior? Had he made her feel unfeminine, or grotesque, or—or—

"I give up," he said, leaned his chin on his hand, and tried to think about the Ghost. That was his new name for the Monster, who had nothing in common with popular conceptions of monsters. He was a ghost.

CHAPTER 17

Wednesday, January 19th, 1966

"I'm going for a walk, dear," Maurice Finch said to Catherine as he got up from the breakfast table. "I don't feel much like going in to work today, but I'll think about it while I walk."

"Sure, you do that," his wife said, glancing through the window at the outside thermometer. "It's fifteen below, so dress warm—and if you do decide to go to work, start the car on your way back." He seemed, she felt, considerably more cheerful these days, and she knew why. Kurt Schiller had returned to the Hug and approached Maurie to assure him that their quarrel had not been the cause of his suicide attempt. Apparently the love of his life had thrown him over for someone else. The Nazi schmuck (Catherine's opinion of Schiller hadn't budged) didn't go into details, but she supposed that men who liked men were as vulnerable as men who liked women; some floozie—what did the sex of the floozie matter?—had gotten tired of being adored, needed someone with a new approach and maybe a bigger bank balance.

She watched Maurie from the window as he scrunched off down the frozen path that led to his apple orchard, always his favorite place. They were old trees, had never been pruned to keep the fruit pickably low, but in spring that made them a soaring froth of white blossoms that took the breath away, and in fall they were smothered with glossy red globes like Christmas tree decorations. Several years ago Maurie had been inspired to train some of their branches into arches; the old wood had creaked in protest, but Maurie did it so gently and slowly that now the spaces between the trees were like the aisles in a cathedral.

He disappeared; she went to wash the dishes.

Then came a high, horrifying shriek. A plate crashed to the floor in shards as Catherine grabbed a coat and ran for dear life. Her slippered feet slid and skidded on the ice, but somehow she kept her balance. Another shriek! Not even feeling the 17°F temperature, she raced faster.

Maurie was standing by the wonderful dry stone wall encircling his orchard, staring over it at something glittering on the bank of iron-hard snow that had piled against it during the last blizzard.

One glance, and she led him away, back to the warmth of the kitchen, back to sanity. Back to where she could call the police.

Carmine and Patrick stood where Maurice Finch had, since his feet had obliterated any other footprints that might have been there before his—highly unlikely, both men felt.

Margaretta Bewlee was in one piece apart from her head, which wasn't anywhere to be found. Against the stark whiteness her dark chocolate skin was even darker, the pink of palms and soles of feet echoing the color of the dress she wore: a confection of pink lace embroidered all over with sparkling rhinestones. It was short enough to see the crotch of a pair of pink silk panties, ominously stained.

"Jesus, *everything's* different!" Patrick said.

"I'll see you in the morgue," Carmine said, turning away. "If I stay here, I'll retard your progress."

He went inside to where the Finches huddled together at their breakfast table, a bottle of Manischevitz wine before them.

"Why me?" Finch asked, face ghastly.

"Have some more wine, Dr. Finch. And if we knew why you, we might have a chance to catch this bastard. May I sit down?"

"Sit, sit!" Catherine gasped, indicating an unused glass. "Have some, you need it too."

Though he didn't care for sweet wine, the Manischevitz did help; Carmine put his glass down and looked at Catherine. "Did you hear anything during the night, Mrs. Finch? It's snapped so cold that everything makes a noise."

"Not a thing, Lieutenant. Maurie put peat moss and mulch in his mushroom tunnel for a while after he came home yesterday, but we were in bed by ten and slept through until six this morning."

"Mushroom tunnel?" Carmine asked.

"I fancied seeing if I could grow the gourmet varieties," Finch said, looking a little better. "Mushrooms are persnickety, but I don't understand why when you see how they grow in a field."

"Do you mind if we take your property apart, Doctor? I'm afraid that finding Margaretta here makes that necessary."

"Do what you want, do what you need—just find this monster!" Finch got up like an old man. "However, I think I know why we didn't hear anything, Lieutenant. Want to see?"

"I sure do."

Cautioned not to step anywhere that looked as if the ground had been disturbed, Maurice Finch led Carmine across the area where his glasshouses stood, then in between the big, heated sheds that held Catherine's chickens. Finally, a good third of a mile beyond the house, Finch stopped and pointed.

"See that little road? It comes up from a gate on Route 133 and ends at the foot of the orchard. We put it in with a blade on the front of our truck because of the brook—when the brook floods, it cuts our house off from access to Route 133. If the Monster knew it existed, he could use it to drive in and we'd never hear him."

"Thank you for that, Dr. Finch. Go back to your wife."

Finch did as he was told without protest, while Carmine went to find Abe and Corey, explain whereabouts they should look for signs of the Ghost. He is a ghost, ghosted in and ghosted out again, but he's a very knowledgeable ghost, the Ghost. Maurice Finch has criss-crossed his property with homemade tracks, but the Ghost is aware of every one of them. And you asked a good question, Dr. Finch: "Why me?" Why, indeed?

Carmine made sure he was back at the County Services building before Patrick brought Margaretta's body in; this was one autopsy he wanted to see from start to finish.

"She was put on top of a snowbank frozen to solid ice, but I suspect that she was already frozen when he dumped her there," said Patrick as he and Paul tenderly lifted the long frame out of its bag. "The ground everywhere is frozen, nothing smaller than a backhoe could have broken it to bury her, but this time he wasn't concerned about hiding her, even for a short while. He dumped her in the open in a sparkling dress."

The three men stood looking at Margaretta, and at that very peculiar dress.

"I didn't see Sophia enough during the years when she wore party dresses," Carmine said, "but with all those girls, Patsy, you must have seen dozens of party dresses. This isn't a young woman's dress, is it? It's a child's party dress she's been wedged into."

"Yes. When we lifted her we found that it wasn't buttoned up the back. Margaretta's shoulders are way too broad, but her arms are thin, so he was able to make her look okay from the front."

The dress had small, puffed sleeves with narrow cuffs, and a waist that allowed for a child's body—wide and a little tubby. On a ten-year-old child it would probably have reached the knees; on this young woman it barely covered the tops of her thighs. The shell-pink lace was French-made, Carmine guessed; expensive, proper lace embroidered on to a base of fine, strong net. Then later someone else had sewn what looked like several hundred transparent rhinestones all over it in a pattern that echoed that of the lace; each rhinestone was perforated at its tip to take a fine needle and thread. Painstaking manual labor that would add multibucks to its price tag. He would have to show this to Desdemona for a really accurate estimate of its quality and cost.

He watched Patrick and Paul ease Margaretta out of the odd garment, which had to be preserved intact. One of the reasons why he loved his cousin so much lay in Patrick's respect for the dead. No matter how repulsive some of the bodies he encountered were—fecal matter, vomitus, unmentionable slimes—Patrick handled them as if God had made them, and made them with love.

Deprivation of the dress left Margaretta in a pair of pink silk panties reaching up to her waist and down to her thighs: modest panties. The crotch was bloodstained, but not grossly so. When they were peeled off, there was the plucked pudendum.

"It's our guy for sure," Carmine said. "Any idea before you start how she died?"

"Not from blood loss, for certain. Her skin's just about its right color and there's only one incision of the neck, the one that decapitated her. No ligature marks on her ankles, though I think she was tied down with the usual canvas band across her chest. He might have put another over her lower legs between rapes, but I'll have to look a lot closer to verify that." His lips thinned. "I think this time he raped her to death. Not much blood externally, but she's very swollen in the abdomen for someone who hasn't begun to decay. Once she was dead, he put her in a freezer until he was ready to dump her."

"Then," said Carmine, backing away from the table, "I'll wait for you in your office, Patsy. I was going to see this one through, but I don't think I can."

Marciano met him outside. "You look kinda white around the gills, Carmine. Had any breakfast?"

"No, and I don't want any either."

"Sure you do." He sniffed Carmine's breath. "Your trouble is, you've been drinking."

"You call Manischevitz drinking?"

"No. Even Silvestri would classify it as grape juice. Come on, pal, you can fill me in at Malvolio's."

He hadn't managed much of the French toast and maple syrup, but he went back to his office feeling better for trying to eat. Today was going to bring worse mental punishment than it had thus far; he had a premonition that Mr. Bewlee would insist on seeing his daughter's remains, no matter what his minister of religion said, or who volunteered to do this awful task. Some parts of her he just couldn't be let see, but he'd know every crease in the palms of her hands, maybe some tiny scar where he'd removed a big splinter from her foot, the shape of her nails . . . The sweet and lovely intimacies of fatherhood that Carmine had never experienced. How strange it is, to sire a child you don't honestly know, who has lived far from you and in whose company you feel an exile.

Now that he had taken to calling the killer a ghost, some corners and crevices in his mind had shifted to permit faint rays of light down their depths; Carmine had found himself thinking in new channels since that night when he had gazed across Holloman's harbor in the snow, and seeing Margaretta Bewlee in her party dress on that icy bank had unlocked another avenue that beckoned to him alluringly, just out of his grasp, a ghost of an idea. A ghost . . .

Then he had it. Not a ghost. *Two* ghosts.

How much easier two of them would make it! The speed and the silence, the invisibility. Two of them: one to dangle a bait, the other to execute the snatch. There *had* to be a bait, something that a sixteen-year-old girl as pure as the driven snow would take as eagerly as a salmon the right fly. A waif of a kitten, a puppy all grimed and abused?

Ether . . . Ether! One of them dangled the bait, the other came up behind like lightning and clamped a pad soaked in ether over the girl's face—no chance to scream, no risk of a bite or a hand's slipping for a moment to allow a cry. The girl would be out to it in seconds, sucking ether into her lungs as she struggled. Then two of them to whisk her away, give her a shot, get her into a vehicle or into a temporary hiding place. Ether . . . The Hug.

Sonia Liebman was in the Hug's O.R. tidying up after rat brain soup. When she saw Carmine, her face darkened—but not due to him.

"Oh, Lieutenant, I heard! Is poor Maurie okay?"

"He's okay. Couldn't not be, with that wife."

"So the Hug's still up shit creek, right?"

"Or someone wants to make it seem that way, Mrs. Liebman." He paused, could see no point in dissimulating. "Do you have any ether in the O.R.?" he asked.

"Sure, but it's not anesthetic ether, just ordinary anhydrous ether. Here," she said, leading the way into the anteroom, where she pointed at a row of cans sitting on a high shelf.

"Would it act as an anesthetic?" he asked, plucking a can off the shelf to examine it. About the size of a large can of peaches, but with a short, narrow neck surmounted by a metal bulb. Not a lid, but a seal. The stuff must be so volatile, he thought, that not the tightest lid known would keep it from evaporating.

"I use it as an anesthetic when I'm decerebrating cats."

"You mean when you remove their brains?"

"You're learning, Lieutenant. Yes."

"How do you etherize them, ma'am?"

For answer she hauled a container made of clear Plexiglass out of a corner; it was about thirteen inches square, thirty inches high, and had a tightly fitting lid secured by clamps. "This is an old chromatography chamber," she said. "I put a thick towel on the bottom, empty a whole can of ether onto the towel, pop the cat inside and shut the lid. Actually I do it outside on the fire stairs, better ventilation. The animal passes out very quickly, but can't hurt itself on these smooth sides before it does."

"Does it matter if it hurts itself when it's about to lose its brain without ever waking up?" Carmine asked.

She reared back like a cobra about to strike. "Yes, you sap, of course it matters!" she hissed. "No animal is ever subjected to pain or suffering in *my* O.R.! What do you think this is, the cosmetic industry? I know some vets who don't treat their animals as well as we do!"

"Sorry, Mrs. Liebman, I didn't mean to offend you. Blame it on ignorance," said Carmine, groveling abjectly. "How do you get the can open?" he asked, to change the subject.

"There's probably a tool for it," she said, mollified, "but I don't have one, so I use an old pair of rongeurs."

These looked like a large pair of pliers, except that two scooped ends met in opposition and nibbled away at whatever was put between them. Like the soft metal bulb of a can of ether, as Sonia Liebman proceeded to demonstrate. Carmine retreated from the smell that seemed to spring out of the can faster than a genie.

"Don't you like it?" she asked, surprised. "I love it."

"Do you know how much ether you have in stock?"

"Not to an accurate count—it's neither valuable nor important. When I notice the shelf supply is getting low, I simply order more. I use it for decerebrations, but it's also used to clean glassware if an investigator is going to do a test that requires no residues of any kind."

"Why ether?"

"Because we have plenty of it, but some investigators prefer chloroform." She frowned, looked suddenly enlightened. "Oh, I see what you're getting at! Ether doesn't last in the body, Lieutenant, anymore than it clings to glassware. A few respirations blow it away, straight out of the lungs and the bloodstream. I can't use Pentothal or Nembutal to anesthetize a decerebrate because they hang around in the brain for hours. Ether is gone—poof!"

"Couldn't you use an anesthetic gas?"

Sonia Liebman blinked, as if amazed at his density. "Sure I could, but why? Humans can co-operate, and they don't have fangs or claws. With animals, it's a shot of parenteral Nembutal or the ether chamber."

"Is the ether chamber common in research laboratories?"

That did it! She turned away and began to sort through a pile of surgical instruments. "I wouldn't know," she said, voice as cold as the air outside. "I worked out the technique for myself, and that's all that matters as far as I'm concerned."

Feeling as if he should back out of her presence, bowing deeply all the way, Carmine left Mrs. Liebman to fulminate about the total stupidity of cops.

"Mercedes and Francine were brutally raped with a succession of implements, and I can only guess that he did the same to begin on Margaretta," said Patrick to Carmine, Silvestri, Marciano, Corey and Abe. "Then he graduated to some new device that must have been encrusted with barbs and spikes, maybe tipped with a blade. It tore her to shreds inside—bowels, bladder, kidneys, even as high as the liver. Massive, multiple lacerations. She died of shock before she could bleed to death internally. There was a little Demerol in her bloodstream, so wherever he took Margaretta after he abducted her was too far from Groton to rely on ether beyond the initial few minutes. I found no trace of ether on the pillowcase, by the way."

"Did you expect to find any?" Marciano asked.

"No, but I smelled it in a tight fold of the pillowcase at the time we reached the Bewlee house."

"Did she lose blood when her head was removed?" Abe asked.

"Only a very little. She'd been dead for some hours when he did that. Because of her height, he seems to have used a band across each leg as well as the chest band to restrain her."

"If she died prematurely, why wait thirteen days to dump her? What did he do with her?" Corey asked.

"Put her in a freezer big enough to lie her flat."

"Has she been identified?" Carmine asked.

Patrick's face twisted. "Yes, by her father. He was so calm! She has a small scar on her left hand—a dog bite. The moment he found it, he said she was his daughter, thanked us, and left."

The room fell silent. How could I deal with that were she Sophia? Carmine wondered. No doubt the rest of us here feel the blade more keenly, they've all got daughters who didn't go to California before the ties were properly forged. Hell is too good for this beast.

"Patsy," Carmine said, breaking the moment, "is it possible that there were two of them?"

"Two?" Patrick asked blankly. "You mean two killers?"

"Yes."

Silvestri chewed on his cigar, grimaced, dropped it in his waste-basket. "Two like *him?* You're joking!"

"No, John, I'm not. The longer I think about this series of abductions, the more convinced I become that it took two people to do them. From there to two killers is an obvious step."

"A step a thousand feet high, Carmine," said Silvestri. *"Two* monsters? How could they find each other?"

"I don't know, but maybe something as common as an ad in the *National Enquirer* personal columns. Guarded, but clear as crystal to someone with the same tastes. Or maybe they've known each other for years, even grew up together. Or maybe they met by accident at a cocktail party."

Abe looked at Corey and rolled his eyes; they were thinking about sitting for days in the *National Enquirer* morgue reading to find an ad at least two years old.

"You're shoveling shit uphill, Carmine," said Marciano.

"I know, I know! But forget for a moment how they got together and concentrate on what happens to the victim. I realized that there has to be a bait. These aren't the kind of young women who would be lured off by an invitation from some man, or fall for an offer of a screen test, any of the ploys that work on less carefully brought up girls. But think how hard it would be for one man to make the snatch without a bait!"

Carmine leaned forward, getting into stride. "Take Mercedes, who closes the lid on the piano, says goodbye to Sister Theresa, and lets herself out the music annex door. And somewhere quiet, with nobody else around, Mercedes sees something so irresistible that she has to go closer. Something her heart goes out to, like a half-starved kitten or puppy. But as it's got to be in the exact right spot, there's someone else mourning over the animal too. While Mercedes is engrossed, the other man strikes. One to dangle the bait, one to grab. Or Francine, somewhere near the toilet block, or else actually inside it. She sees the bait, her heart goes out, she's grabbed. There are just too many people still in the school to risk getting her out of Travis, so they put her in the sports locker. How much easier to do that in a hurry if there are two of them! It's Wednesday, the gyms are deserted, and the Chemistry classroom is right near to that toilet block. With Margaretta, there's a sister sleeping not three yards away. No bait, but would this killer run the risk of Linda when he plans so meticulously? The bait half has a new role, to watch Linda and act if she stirs. When she doesn't, it's a piece of cake for two men to get a tall girl out a window, one inside, one outside."

"Why do you make things so hard for yourself?" Patrick asked.

"Things are as hard as they have to be, Patsy. If one killer isn't enough, then we have to think there are two."

"I agree," Silvestri said suddenly, "but we don't breathe a word about Carmine's theory outside the people in this room."

"One other thing, John. The party dress. I'd like to show it to Desdemona Dupre."

"Why?"

"Because she does incredible embroidery. There are no labels on the dress, no one's ever seen anything like it before, and I want to try to find out where to start looking for the person who made it. That

218

means I need to know how much it would cost if it was bought in a store, or how much someone like Desdemona would charge for custom making it. She does commissions, she'll know."

"Sure, once it's had the works from Paul—and if you trust her not to spill the beans about it."

"I trust her."

CHAPTER 18

Monday, January 24th, 1966

The logical journal to search for a person advertising for a partner in anything from business through sex to murder was the *National Enquirer,* which was read clear across the country and available in any supermarket at the cashier's desk among the gum and magazines. After talking to the three psychiatrists who made murder their speciality, Carmine was able to equip Abe and Corey with some key words before shipping them off to read the personals between January of 1963 and June of 1964. The Ghost may have been in his gruesome collaboration before the first girl disappeared, or he might have seen how much easier his task would be with a helper after he commenced his killing career.

The nature of the bait was now fairly clear to Carmine: an object of pity, of irresistible appeal to a soft-hearted, sensitive young woman. So he abandoned that line of thought to move on to what kind of premises housed the girls while they were raped and killed and stored. The general police feeling was that the killing premises were makeshift; only Patrick saw Carmine's point that the killing premises were anything but makeshift. Anyone so persnickety that he lined up a notice would want his "laboratory" perfect.

After the discovery of Margaretta Bewlee's body on a Hugger property, the Huggers fell over themselves to offer permission to the police to search anywhere they liked. Even Satsuma, Chandra and Schiller crumbled. Maurice Finch's mushroom tunnel was just that; another search of Benjamin Liebman's mortuary yielded nothing; Addison Forbes's "eyrie" consisted of two round rooms, one above the other, overfilled with neatly stacked or shelved professional reading materials; the Smith basement was pure train heaven; Walter Polonowski's cabin was a love nest, decorously posed photographs of Marian everywhere, a big bed, not much of a kitchen. Paola Polonowski had seized her opportunity and gone up to the cabin in the wake of the police, with the result that Polonowski was now living in it with Marian, and looking a great deal happier. Hideki Satsuma's retreat turned out to be near the corner of the Cape Cod elbow in Orleans, an architect-designed bachelor pad that held nothing more indictable than a huge amount of pornography heavily into violence, though not murder. No real surprise to Carmine, whose time in Japan had shown him the Japanese penchant for pictorial pornography. Dr. Nur Chandra was just "being bloody-minded" as Desdemona would have phrased it; his secret activity in the cottage he used consisted of a new generation computer that he was trying to program without enlisting one of those amazing young Chubb medical students who paid their way through school by devising programs for specific scientific purposes. Chandra was so sure of his Nobel Prize that he would speak of his work to no one, especially a super-bright, ambitious young Chubb medical student. The Ponsonby forest was a forest; no cabins, sheds, barns, underground anythings. And Kurt Schiller's worst secret was a photograph of himself, his father, and Adolf Hitler. Papa had been a highly decorated U-boat captain invited to meet der Führer and bring his towheaded little son along; Hitler loved towheaded children with brave fathers. Schiller

Senior had gone down with his submarine when it encountered a depth-charge in 1944; Kurt was ten years old at the time.

Therefore, according to Silvestri, Marciano and the rest of Connecticut's various senior policemen, the killing premises must be makeshift. Were they not, someone would have noticed.

But they are not makeshift, Carmine said to himself. If I were the Ghost, what would I want? Pristine surroundings, that's what. Surfaces that could be hosed down, scrupulously cleaned. That means tiles rather than concrete, metal rather than wood or rock. I'd want an operating room. Two Ghosts could build it if they were both skilled with their hands; they could even wire it for electricity. What they probably couldn't do was plumb it, yet it had to be plumbed. A high-pressure water supply, adequate drains, and connection to either a sewer or a septic system. The Ghosts would want a bathroom too, for themselves if not for their victim. Her they probably bed panned, sponge bathed.

So while Abe and Corey waded their way through the *National Enquirer* personals, Carmine checked every Hugger property for unsuitably large power or water bills. Unfortunately the more prosperous Huggers lived where they tapped for well water rather than used a piped supply, but no one's electricity bill was huge. A generator? Possible, if the noise could be muffled. From that fruitless exercise he waded through plumbing contractors and more humble self-employed plumbers from one end of Connecticut to the other. Looking for a lucrative job that involved installation of what would have been described as a private gymnasium or a plush recreational facility or even a pool house. Those he did find turned out to be genuine, all located in Fairfield or Litchfield counties. He was aware that the kind of thing he was asking about spelled someone with money, but he had always thought that the Ghost had plenty of money. Wherever he looked, he came up with nothing. That said one of three things: the first, that the two Ghosts were able to do their own plumbing; the second, that they had hired a plumber whom they paid generously with cash so he would keep quiet about the job and not pay tax;

and the third, that the Ghosts had rented or bought premises already suitable for their purposes, such as a veterinary clinic or surgeon's rooms. He called around to see how many veterinary clinics and surgeons' rooms had changed hands late in 1963, but those that had changed hands were bona fide. The usual nothing, nothing, nothing.

Because the pink lace dress was adorned with 265 rhinestones, and every one had to be examined to make sure it held only one set of prints, presumably the seamstress's, it was six days before Carmine could show the garment to Desdemona.

He buzzed her intercom feeling more goofy and anxious than he had in high school when the girl of his dreams at the time said yes, he could take her to the prom. Mouth dry, heart in it—all he lacked was the corsage.

"Desdemona, it's Carmine. On business. Don't open the door, I'll key the combination in."

"How are you?" he asked, shedding his layers and putting the dress box—shit, what *would* she think?—on the table.

She looked neither glad nor sorry to see him. "I'm well but bored to death," she said. Then, flicking a finger at the dress box, "What's that?"

"Something I had to assure the Commissioner you wouldn't talk about to anyone. I knew you wouldn't, he doesn't. You mightn't know that the last victim, Margaretta Bewlee, was found wearing a child's party dress. We can't trace it, but I thought maybe with your eye for fancy work, you could tell us *something* about it."

She had the box open and was shaking out the dress in a second, then held it, turned it around, finally spread it on the table. "I take it that the last girl wasn't chopped into bits?"

"No, just the head was removed."

"The newspapers said she was tall. This wouldn't fit her."

"It didn't, but she was wedged into it all the same. Her shoulders were too broad for him to button it down the back, and that leads to my first question—why buttons? Everything these days is zipped."

Paul had fastened the buttons, which sparkled like genuine jewels under the table light. "That's why," she said, fingering one. "A zipper would have spoiled the effect. These glitter."

"Have you ever seen a dress like this?"

"Only on a pantomime stage when I was a child, but it was makeshift due to clothes rationing. This is very pretentious."

"Is it handmade?"

"To some extent, but probably not as much as you assume. The rhinestones have been sewn on, yes, but by a specialist who can wallop them on faster than you can eat pot roast. The person is a pieceworker, so she sticks her needle through the hole, loops her strand of cotton around the rhinestone once, then tacks her needle through the lace to the next rhinestone—see?"

Carmine saw.

"Some of them are missing because they weren't sewn on firmly enough, and they come off in a chain as long as the strand of cotton in the needle—see?"

"I thought Paul might have done that in the lab."

"No, it's more likely to have happened with rough handling, and I can't imagine it would receive that in a pathology lab."

"So what you're saying is that the dress is affordable?"

"If you have something over a hundred dollars to spend on a frock that the child would probably only wear once or twice, then yes. It's a profit exercise, Carmine. Whoever makes and sells these knows how often the frock will be worn, so they cut as many corners as they can. The lining is synthetic, not silk, and the underskirt is cheap net stiffened with thick starch."

"What about the lace?"

"French, but not top quality. Machine made."

"With that kind of price tag, we should look in the children's wear at places like Saks and Bloomingdale's in New York City? Or maybe Alexander's in Connecticut?"

"A fairly expensive shop or department store, certainly. I would call the frock showy, not elegant."

"Like Astor's pet horse," he said absently.

"I beg your pardon?"

"Just a saying." He drew a deep breath. "Am I forgiven?"

Her eyes thawed, even twinkled. "I suppose so, you graceless twit. Too little Carmine Delmonico is worse than too much."

"Malvolio's?"

"Yes, please!"

"Now to a different subject," he said over coffee. "It's late, we can talk here. Manual skills."

"Who at the Hug has them, and who doesn't?"

"Exactly."

"Starting with the Prof?"

"How is he, incidentally?"

"Shut up in an exclusive loony bin somewhere on the Trumbull side of Bridgeport. I imagine they're loving him as a patient. Most of their intake consists of alcoholics or drug addicts drying out, plus heaps of anxiety neuroses. Whereas the poor old Prof has had a severe breakdown—illusions, delusions, hallucinations, loss of contact with reality. As to his manual skills, they are considerable."

"Could he wire for electricity and plumb a house?"

"He wouldn't want to, Carmine. Anything requiring hard manual labor he would regard as beneath his dignity. The Prof dislikes getting his hands dirty."

"Ponsonby?"

"Couldn't change the washer on a tap."

"Polonowski?"

"A fairly skilled domestic handyman. He hasn't the money to hire a carpenter when the children break a door or a plumber when the children stuff a cuddly toy down the lavatory."

"Satsuma?"

She rolled her eyes heavenward. "Lieutenant, *really!* What do you think Eido is for? There's also Eido's wife, she slaves. Chandra has a whole army of turbaned lackeys."

"Forbes?"

225

"I'd say he was competent with his hands. He works on his house, I do know that. They were so lucky, the Forbeses! At the time they bought it, the mortgage rate was two percent, and they have thirty years to pay it off. Now it's worth a fortune, of course—water frontage, two acres, no oil tanks next door."

"Relocating those to the bottom of Oak Street helped everyone on the east shore. Finch?"

"Builds his own glasshouses and greenhouses. There is a big difference, he tells me. Isn't above grubbing out a mushroom tunnel. But I'd say Catherine is even more competent. All those thousands of chickens."

"Hunter and Ho the engineers?"

"Could construct the Empire State Building, with improvements."

"Cecil?"

"Now isn't that an indictment?" she asked, scowling. "I just can't tell you, Carmine. He has skills, but in one's mind he tends to be not only a flunky, but a black flunky into the bargain. No wonder they hate us. We deserve to be hated."

"Otis?"

"At present Otis isn't doing any heavy lifting. Apparently he has the beginnings of congestive cardiac failure, so I'm trying to arrange a nice pension for him with the Parsons. Personally I doubt his troubles have much to do with how hard he works. His bugbear is Celeste's nephew, Wesley. Otis is terrified that the boy is going to make mischief for Celeste. The Hollow and Argyle Avenue are rather boiling."

"Wait until spring," Carmine said grimly. "We've bought some time with the weather, but when it gets warmer, all hell is going to break loose."

"Anna Donato's husband is a plumber."

"Anna Donato . . . Refresh my memory."

"She looks after all the cranky equipment, has the touch."

"The Kyneton ménage?"

"Oh, dear! The fourth floor is a circus these days. Hilda and Tamara are at daggers drawn. Mostly screaming matches, but on one occasion they rolled around the floor, kicking and biting. It took our four office workers and me to drag them apart. So we are profoundly glad that the Prof isn't there to see women at their worst. However, Hilda will be gone before the Prof is due to come back. Dearest, darlingest Keith got the partnership he was after in New York City."

"What about Schiller?"

"*Not* handy. He can't even sharpen a microtome blade. Mind you, he doesn't have to. That's what technicians are for."

"How about coming back to my place for a cognac?"

Desdemona slid out of the booth. "I thought you'd never ask."

Carmine walked her down the block back in that high school happy haze after his prom date had told him she'd loved the evening and offered him her lips. Not that Desdemona was about to offer her lips. A pity. They were full and unlipsticked. He started to laugh at the memory of trying to scrub off bright red lipstick.

"What's so funny?"

"Not a thing, not a thing."

CHAPTER 19

Commissioner Silvestri held a discreet conference to which he invited all the various
heads of the Ghost investigations through-
out Connecticut. "In a week's time it will be thirty days," he said to
the room of silent men, "and we have no idea whether the Ghost
or Ghosts have switched their pattern to one a month or are still on
the two-month pattern, just rung in the New Year with a special
spree."

Though the press still referred to the killer as the Monster, most
of the police involved now alluded to him as the Ghost or the
Ghosts. Carmine's ideas had taken root because men like Lieutenant
Joe Brown from Norwalk saw the sense in them.

"Between this Thursday, the twenty-seventh, and the following
Thursday, February third, all departments will put a surveillance
team on any suspect they have twenty-four hours a day. If we get no
results, at least it's an elimination process. If we *know* a suspect was

watched and the suspect didn't elude us, then that suspect can be crossed off the list if a girl goes missing."

"And if no girl goes missing?" asked a cop from Stamford.

"Then we do it all again at the end of February. I agree with Carmine that everything we know points to a bunch of changes—time interval, a night abduction, the party dress, decapitation only—but we can't be sure he's into a new pattern permanently. One or two of him, he's way ahead of us. We just gotta keep on pluggin' on, guys, best way we know how."

"What if a girl goes missing and no suspect is involved?" a cop from Hartford asked.

"Then we think again, but in a different way. We broaden the net to bring in new suspects, but we won't abandon the old. I'll hand you over to Carmine."

Who had little more to say, except upon the subject of their present suspects. "Holloman is in the unique position of having many more than one suspect," he said. "The rest of the departments will be watching known rapists with a track record of violence, whereas Holloman has a group of suspects with no known track record of rape or violence. The staff of the Hug, plus two others. All up, thirty-two people. We can't manage to keep that many under twenty-four-hour observation, which is why I'm asking for volunteers from other departments to give us a hand. Our teams have to be experienced men, not liable to sleep on the job or drift into a waking dream. If any of you can spare men who can be trusted, I'd appreciate the help."

And so it was arranged. Twenty-nine Huggers, Professor Frank Watson, Wesley le Clerc and Professor Robert Mordent Smith were to be watched around the clock by men whose attention wouldn't waver. A formidable task, even logistically.

A surprising number of the Holloman suspects either lived on Route 133 or just off it, and Route 133 was a typical state road: one lane either way, meandering, yet not endowed with much shelter; no wide verges, no shopping centers or concomitant parking lots, no bays or rest stops. All that went on along the Boston Post Road, while Route 133 ambled from village to village inland, gave off an occasional side street of houses, more often didn't. Tamara Vilich and Marvin Schulman, both on Sycamore close to Holloman's center, were easy; so were Cecil and Otis on Eleventh Street. But the Smiths, the Ponsonbys, the Finches, Mrs. Polonowski, the Frank Watsons, the Chandras and the Kynetons were all somehow attached to Route 133.

The sleazy motel rejoicing in the name of Major Minor's was adjacent to Ponsonby Lane on 133, and hadn't seen so much after-dark business in years as it promised to during that coming week.

Carmine, Corey and Abe split up surveillance on the Ponsonby house into three eight-hour shifts; that Carmine chose the Ponsonbys was purely because he didn't think any of the suspects would yield fruit, and thus far the Ponsonbys had received less attention than, for instance, had the Smiths or the Finches. They found a place to hide behind a clump of mountain laurels fifty yards on the 133 side of the Ponsonby driveway, having ascertained that Ponsonby Lane was a dead end and that the Ponsonby house had absolutely no other vehicular access than the driveway.

He checked everything out himself ahead of time, to discover that the Forbeses were the most difficult to observe, thanks to their water frontage and the steep, bushy slope that led down from East Circle, their road frontage, to the water; the house sat on a shelf halfway down. Nor were the Smiths easy, between that knoll where the house was, the dense woods, and that twisting driveway. However, the Prof was definitely incarcerated in Marsh Manor on the Trumbull side of Bridgeport, under guard by the Bridgeport police. As for the Finches—a good thing, really, that he had virtually eliminated them from his list. They had no less than four gates opening on to Route 133, none of them where an unmarked car could hunker down undetected by sharp eyes. Norwalk was taking care of Kurt Schiller, and Torrington was watching Walter Polonowski and his mistress in their upstate cabin.

So why didn't Carmine think that this massive surveillance exercise would bear fruit? He genuinely didn't know why, save that the Ghosts were ghosts, and you only saw ghosts when they wanted you to see them.

CHAPTER 20

Monday, January 31st, 1966

T here had been twenty-two inches of snow
on the preceding Wednesday, and no thaw
to follow, not unusual in January. Instead,
the temperature plummeted to twenty below freezing, even less
after dark. The surveillance became a nightmare, men rugged in
every fur coat wives or mothers could donate, fur rugs, bearskins,
blankets, layers of wool, thermal underwear, electric blankets that
could be wired to a DC battery, nineteenth-century warming pans
filled with barbecue charcoal, anything that staved off freezing. For
of course the moment the mercury went lower than 28°F, no engine
could be left running because of the thick white vapor that came
pouring out of a tailpipe to betray a tenanted car. The luckiest men
were huddled inside Alaskan hunting hides.

Carmine took the midnight to 8 A.M. shift each night, his car a
tan Buick with a velvet interior for which he thanked every saint
there was.

The night between Sunday and Monday was the coldest yet at

2222222222222222

zero Fahrenheit. Bundled in two cashmere blankets, he sat with the wing windows open just enough to prevent fogging, his teeth chattering like castanets. The evergreen mountain laurels hid him well, but on Thursday, the first night of his vigil, he had worried about Biddy—would the dog sense his presence and bark? It had not, nor did it on this night. Only a decerebrated man, he thought, would venture out; this was the season of fires, of lovely heat wafting through ventilators, of finding things to do at home. If the Ghosts had planned an abduction, surely this terrible freeze would deter them.

The Ponsonby property had been a headache. A five-acre block longer than it was wide, it sloped down steeply from a ridge that formed a spine as well as the back boundary; the ancient house was near the road, with thinned forest around it. The ridge that ran behind all the blocks on that side of Ponsonby Lane was actually the commencement of a twenty-acre forest reserve donated not to the state but to Holloman County Council by Isaac Ponsonby, grandfather of Charles and Claire. Isaac had been a deer lover who deplored hunting; these twenty acres, said his will, were to be reserved as a deer park within the county near the city. Beyond tacking up a few signs that said NO HUNTING, the council had paid the bequest no mind. Today it was much as it had been in Isaac's day, a fairly dense forest thickly populated by deer. It ran from the ridge down a slope to Deer Lane, a short dead end with four houses on its far side; the deer park continued across the circular terminus of Deer Lane and had prevented further building. Though Carmine was sure that Charles Ponsonby wasn't athlete enough to make that kind of hike in zero Fahrenheit weather, he had to station other cars in the vicinity: on Deer Lane, its corners, and Route 133. These watchers informed him that no other cars were parked on Deer Lane.

The night was typical of such arctic conditions: a sky that was not as much black as mottled indigo, webs and spangles of brilliantly blazing stars, not a cloud to be seen. Beautiful! No sound apart from his own teeth, no movements or flashlights outside, no crunch of car wheels on a frozen driveway.

And because inertia was foreign to him, he began to toy with an idea that popped into his brain at the exact same second that a shooting star carved its fiery path across the vault.

Look at the religious side of things, Carmine. Think back over the thirteen girls, all the way to Rosita Esperanza, the first to be grabbed . . . ten of them Catholic. Rachel Simpson was the child of an Episcopalian minister. Francine Murray and Margaretta Bewlee were Baptists. But none of the Protestant girls was from a *white* church. So why not add Catholicism to black Protestantism? What does that get you, Carmine? A white Protestant fanatic is what it gets you. We've lost sight of the enormous preponderance of Catholic girls, maybe because the Ghosts seemed to swing away from them with Francine and Margaretta. Over 75 percent Catholic, plus a black Protestant minister's daughter, the child of a racially split marriage, and—Margaretta. Margaretta, the one who doesn't fit. Is there something about the Bewlee family that we don't know?

The cold forgotten, he sat itching for the morning to come, to liberate him from this unproductive, fruitless graveyard shift and let him go talk to Mr. Bewlee.

His radio emitted a short, low sound, the signal that a cop was approaching his car. A glance at his watch told Carmine that it was 5 A.M., too late for anything to happen if a night abduction was the plan. One thing for sure, the Ponsonbys hadn't stirred.

Patrick slid into the passenger's seat and held out a thermos with a grin. "Malvolio's best. I stood over Luigi and made him brew a fresh pot, and the raisin bagels had just come in."

"Patsy, I love you."

They drank and chewed for five minutes, then Carmine told his cousin about this new theory. Much to his disappointment, Patrick didn't think highly of it.

"The trouble is that you've been on this case now for so long that you've exhausted all the probables and have nowhere to look except at the improbables."

"There *is* a religious bias, and it's tied up with race!"

"I agree, but religion isn't what interests the Ghosts. What interests them is the fact that God-fearing families produce the kind of girl they're after."

"The Bewlees are hiding something, they have to be," Carmine muttered. "Otherwise Margaretta doesn't fit."

"She doesn't fit," said Patrick patiently, "because yours is a crazy hypothesis. Get back to basics! If you think of the Ghosts as rapists ahead of killers, then you're *not* looking for a religious fanatic of any color or denomination, Christian or otherwise. You are looking for a man or two men who hate all women, but some more than others. The Ghosts hate virtue allied to youth allied to color allied to a face allied to other things we don't know. But we *do* know about the virtue, the youth, the face, the color. None of them have been white white, and none of them will be white white, I know it in my bones. Their best sample pool is Latin Catholics, is all. The children are brought up young for their age, strictly supervised, and greatly loved. You *know* that, Carmine! But the families are not newcomers to America, and I think that a religious fanatic killer would be targeting new immigrants—keep down the influx, spread the word that if you immigrate here, your children will be raped and slaughtered. The answer lies in the case basics."

"I'm still going to see Mr. Bewlee," Carmine said stubbornly.

"If you have to, you have to. But she won't fit because the pattern you're seeing is a figment of your imagination. You're a victim of battle fatigue."

They fell silent; less than three hours to go, and the shift would be over.

Shortly before 7 A.M. the radio emitted a different stealthy noise: the one that said get out of there unobtrusively and go to your rendezvous, because a girl has been taken.

Carmine's rendezvous was Major Minor's motel, where he and Patrick requisitioned use of the phone in Reception. The Major was on the desk himself, eager to learn what was happening. All his rooms had been booked by the Holloman police for a sum they—and he—knew was exorbitant, especially since no one used them. The NO VACANCY sign was additional camouflage for parked cars, and the Major wasn't about to turn that on unless it spelled out the truth.

While Carmine talked, Patrick watched Major Minor, wondering idly if, like so many people owning suggestive names, young F. Sharp Minor had gone to West Point determined to attain the rank that would make him a contradiction in terms. In his fifties now, with the swollen purple nose of a heavy drinker and the attitude of a desk warrior: if the forms are correctly filled in and the paperwork is adequate, do whatever you like from beating the crap out of a soldier to stealing firearms from the cage. This quirk in Major Minor's nature helped a business where the guests came for an hour in mid-afternoon; the main parking lot was around the back so that no wife cruising down Route 133 could spot her old man's car outside. At one stage Carmine had been desperate enough to classify Major F. Sharp Minor as a suspect, for no better reason than that he knew all the rooms were fitted with spy holes. The elderly villain had gotten rid of the cameras after a private detective caught him filming a company director and his secretary, but Major Minor could still *look*.

"Norwich," Carmine said. "Corey, Abe and Paul will be here in about a minute." He moved farther from the Major. "She's of Lebanese extraction, but the family has been in Norwich since 1937. Her name is Faith Khouri."

"They're Moslems?" Patrick asked, looking incredulous.

"No, Catholics of the Maronite sect. I doubt there'd be a Maronite church, so they'd go to the ordinary Catholic one."

"Norwich is a pretty big town."

"Yes, but they live out of it quite a way. Mr. Khouri runs a convenience store in Norwich. His home is north, about halfway to Willimantic."

Abe pulled up in the Ford, Paul right behind in Patrick's unmarked black van.

"I don't even know why we're bothering to go up there," said

Corey as the Ford moved off at a normal pace; no siren or light until they were well away from Ponsonby Lane.

That, thought Carmine, inwardly sighing, is the remark of a man who despairs. I'm not the only one suffering from a bad case of battle fatigue. We are beginning to believe that we will never catch the Ghosts. This is the fourth girl since we've known the Ghosts exist, and we're no closer, no closer. Corey's hit the bottom of his particular pit, and I don't know how far I am from the bottom of mine.

"We are going, Cor," he said as if Corey's statement had been routine, "because we have to see the abduction site for ourselves. Abe, if we go north on I-91 to Hartford and then strike east, we'll have better road conditions than I-95 to New London."

"Can't," said Abe briefly. "Five trailer trucks jackknifed."

"At least," said Carmine, settling into his beloved backseat comfortably, "the heater's on. I'm going to get some sleep."

The Khouri house was on a winding lane that ran not far from the Shetucket River, and was as charming as its setting. The house itself was traditional, but built in fits and starts that lent it alluring angles as well as three levels. Between it and the road was an enormous pond, frozen solid at this time of year, as was the brook that led from it to the icebound river; it had been ploughed free of snow so it could be used as a skating rink, but a tiny wooden jetty spoke equally loudly of canoes in summer. A patch of rushes clattered hollowly against each other, and everywhere in the distances a golden sheen of sun overlay sleek white fields. Around the house were the winter skeletons of birches and willows, with a massive old oak atop a rise beyond the little lake. Picnics in the shade in summer, it said. What lovelier environment could there be for children than this perfect American dream?

There were seven children, Carmine learned: only a nineteen-year-old boy, Anthony, was away from home. His brother Mark was seventeen, then came Faith at sixteen, Nora at fourteen, Emily at twelve, Matthew at ten; Philippa, at eight, was the youngest.

The wildness of the family's grief made it impossible to question any of them, including the father. Almost thirty years in America had not cancelled out their Levantine reaction to the loss of a child. When Carmine managed to find a photograph of Faith, he saw what Patrick had been trying to make him see on Ponsonby Lane. Faith looked like the sister of the other victims, from her mass of curly black hair to her wide dark eyes and her lush mouth. In skin color she was the fairest; about like a southern Italian or Sicilian girl, Mediterranean tawny.

Patrick looked defeated when he found Carmine outside on the cold porch. "The snow's frozen so solid that they were able to lay a strip of straw matting from the road to the back porch—looks like cheap stair runner," he said. "They scraped and salted the road where they parked, so no tire tracks that haven't been obscured by the local cops. They opened the back door with a key or a set of picks, and I'd say they knew exactly which bedroom was Faith's. She had her own room—all the kids do—on the second floor, which is the sleeping floor for everyone. They must have found her asleep. The only signs of a struggle are a few disturbances in the sheets at the bottom of her bed, maybe a few feeble kicks. Then they carried her out the way they came in, up the straw runner to the road and their vehicle. From what we can gather, no one heard a thing. She was missed when she didn't appear for breakfast, which the mother puts on early at this time of year—it's an hour's drive into Norwich on badly ploughed roads. The kids go in with their father and stay at his shop until it's time to go to school, just a short walk away."

"You're doing my job, Patsy. Do we have any idea of her height? Her weight?"

"Not until Father Hannigan and his nuns arrive. The grief in there is demented, and nobody will let me give anybody a shot. The hair's coming out in handfuls."

"And the blood's flying where Mrs. Khouri keeps scratching herself. That's why I'm out here, not in there," Carmine said, sighing. "Not that flying blood and hair matter. The Ghosts won't have left a shred of either behind."

"The family's given Faith up for dead already."

"Do you honestly blame them, Patsy? We're about as useful as tits on a bull, and it's getting to Abe and Corey. They're hurting bad, just can't show it."

Patrick squinted and heaved a gasp of relief. "Here come our priest and cohorts. Maybe they know how to calm everyone down."

If they couldn't do that, at least Father Hannigan and the three nuns with him were able to give Carmine the information he needed. Faith was five-two, and weighed about eighty-five pounds. Slender, not yet very developed. A dear girl, devout, maintained an A-plus average in all her subjects, which leaned to the sciences; her ambition had been to do medicine. She was due to join the ranks of the candy stripers at St. Stan's Hospital this summer, but until now her mother and father had kept her at home, didn't want her into good works too young. Anthony, the brother who wasn't there, was doing pre-med at Brown; it seemed all the children were interested in the human sciences. The family itself was tightly knit and highly respected. Their shop was in a good part of Norwich and had never been held up, their house had never been burgled, nor had any among them been harassed or attacked.

"It keeps going back to the unimpeachable innocence, the face, and the age, with a possible for the religion," Carmine said to Silvestri when he returned to Holloman. "Of late color hasn't worried the Ghosts, or size, but we always have those first three, and in most cases the fourth. Margaretta Bewlee's sixteenth birthday present from her mother was a visit to the beauty parlor to have her hair straightened and styled like Dionne Warwick—she was performing one of Dionne's numbers in a school concert. That news made me wonder about her, but after I checked it out I realized it wasn't evidence of—how can I put it?—declining virtue? Though Margaretta is the one who gnaws at me, John. She is the sole black pearl in a collection of creamy ones. Too tall, too black, too inappropriate."

"Maybe the Ghosts are jumping on the racial bandwagon. Their activities sure aren't helping the racial situation."

239

"Then why not another equally dark victim now? The *Times* crossword had a clue recently—'go back to beige.' Six letters. The answer was 'rebuff.' When I tumbled to it I laughed until I cried. Every place I go, I am rebuffed."

Silvestri didn't say what he was thinking: you need a long vacation in Hawaii, Carmine. But not yet. I can't afford to take you off this case. If you can't crack it, no one can. "It's time I held a press conference," he said. "I got nothing to tell the bastards, but I gotta eat crow in public." He cleared his throat, munched on the end of a very tattered cigar. "The Governor agrees I should eat crow in public."

"Out of favor with Hartford, huh?"

"No, not yet. How do you think I spend most of my days? On the phone to Hartford, that's how."

"None of the Huggers showed a whisker outside last night. Though that doesn't mean I don't intend to watch them thirty days from now, John. I still have a gut feeling that the Hug is very much involved, and not merely as the object of vendetta," said Carmine. "How much truth are you going to tell the press?"

"A little this, a little that. Nothing about Margaretta's party dress. And nothing about two killers."

CHAPTER 21

Tuesday, February 1st, 1966

The Holloman City Hall was famous for its acoustics, and the administrative duties of the Mayor having been removed to the County Services building a decade earlier, Holloman City Hall was left to do what it did best: play host to the world's greatest virtuosi and symphony orchestras.

Behind the auditorium was a rehearsal room designed for these artists to record in as well as rehearse in; its clutter of music stands and chairs arranged in semi-circular rows did not suggest the murder of anything more horrific than music. John Silvestri positioned himself on the conductor's podium clad in his best uniform, with the Congressional Medal of Honor around his neck. This plus the campaign ribbons on his chest said that he was no ordinary man.

About fifty journalists came, most from papers and magazines, one TV crew from the local station in Holloman, and one reporter from WHMN radio. The nation's major dailies sent stringers; though the Connecticut Monster was big news, a canny editor understood that this police exercise wasn't going to produce any startling new developments. What would come out of the conference was a chance to write scathing editorials about police incompetence.

But Silvestri in public mode was a smooth operator, especially when he was eating crow. No one, thought Carmine, listening, ate crow more gracefully, with more apparent relish.

"Despite the freezing conditions, various police departments throughout this state kept a total of ninety-six possible suspects under surveillance twenty-four hours a day from last Thursday until Faith Khouri's abduction. Thirty-two of these people were in or around Holloman. None of them could have been implicated, which means we are no closer to knowing the identity of the man you call the Connecticut Monster, but we are now calling the Ghost."

"Good name," said the crime writer from the *Holloman Post*. "Have you any evidence to implicate anyone? Anyone at all?"

"I've just finished saying that, Mrs. Longford."

"This killer—the Ghost, I rather like that—must have a special place to keep his victims. Isn't it about time that you started looking for it more seriously? Like searching premises?"

"We can't search any tenanted premises without a warrant, ma'am, you know that. What's more, you'd be the first one to pounce if we did."

"Under normal circumstances, yes. But this is different."

"How, different? In the horrible nature of the crimes? I agree as a person, but as a lawman I can't. A police force may be a vital arm of the law, but in a free society like ours it is also restrained by the same law it serves. The American people have constitutional rights that we, the police, are obliged to respect. Unsubstantiated suspicion doesn't empower us to march into someone's house and search for the evidence we haven't been able to find elsewhere. The evidence must come first. We have to present an *evidential* case to the judicial arm of the law in order to be granted permission to search. Talking until we run out of spit won't persuade any judge to issue a warrant without concrete facts. And we do not have concrete facts, Mrs. Longford."

The rest of the journalists were happy to appoint Mrs. Diane Longford as their workhorse; nothing was going to come out of her inquisition anyway, and they could smell the coffee and fresh doughnuts laid out at the back of the hall.

"Why *don't* you have concrete facts, Mr. Commissioner? I mean, it boggles the imagination to think that a great many experienced men have been investigating these murders since the beginning of last October without coming up with a single concrete fact! Or are you saying that the killer is a *real* ghost?"

Barbed irony affected Silvestri no more than did aggression or charm; he ploughed on regardless.

"Not a real ghost, ma'am. Someone far more dangerous, far more lethal. Think of our killer as a very strong hunting cat in his prime—a leopard, say. He lies comfortably in a tree on the edge of the forest, perfectly camouflaged, watching a whole herd of deer grazing their way closer to the forest and his tree. To a bird in that tree, every deer looks the same. But the leopard sees every deer as different, and his target is one particular deer. To him, she's juicier, more succulent than the others. Oh, he's very patient! The deer pass under him—he doesn't move—the deer don't see him or smell him on his branch—and then *his* deer wanders below him. The strike is so fast that the rest of the deer hardly have time to start running before he's back up his tree with his catch, legs helpless, neck broken."

Silvestri drew a breath; he had caught their attention. "I admit it's not a brilliant metaphor, but I use it to illustrate the magnitude of what we're up against with the Ghost. From where we are, he's invisible. Just as it doesn't occur to deer to look up into a tree, just as the smells the wind carries to deer nostrils originate on their level, not from up a tree, so it is with us. It hasn't occurred to us to look or smell in the right place for him because we have no idea where his place is, what kind of place he uses. We might pass him on the street every day—*you* might pass him on the street every day, Mrs. Longford. But his face is ordinary, his walk is ordinary—everything about him is ordinary. On the surface he's a little alley cat, not a leopard. Underneath, he's Dorian Gray, Mr. Hyde, the faces of Eve, Satan incarnate."

"Then what protection can the community have against him?"

"I'd say vigilance, except that vigilance didn't prevent his taking girls of a specific type even after we saturated Connecticut with bulletins and warnings. However, it is clear to me that we have frightened him, forced him to give up his daylight abductions in favor of the night. That's nothing to boast about because it hasn't stopped him. It hasn't so much as slowed him down. Yet it's a ray of hope. If he's more scared than he was, and we keep the pressure up, he'll start to make a few mistakes. And, ladies and gentlemen of the press, you have my word that we will not miss his mistakes. They'll make us the leopard up the tree, and him our particular deer."

"He did well," Carmine said to Desdemona that night. "The AP stringer asked him if he was planning to run for governor at the next elections. 'No, sir, Mr. Dalby,' he said, grinning from ear to ear, 'compared to government, a policeman's lot is a happy one, ghosts and all.'"

"People respond to him. When I saw him on the six o'clock news, he reminded me of a battered old teddy bear."

"The Governor likes him, which is more to the point. You don't dismiss war heroes as incompetent idiots."

"He must have been quite an elderly war hero."

"He was."

"You sound a bit sniffly, Carmine. Are you coming down with a cold?" she asked, taking another slice of pizza. Oh, it was nice to be back on good terms with him!

"After sitting in unheated cars when the mercury's zero, we are all coming down with colds."

"At least you didn't have to watch me."

"But we did, Desdemona."

"Oh, the manpower!" she breathed, the manager in her awestruck as always. "Ninety-six people?"

"Yep."

"Whom did you inherit?"

"That's classified, you can't ask. What's going on at the Hug since Faith disappeared?"

"The Prof is still in his loony bin. When he discovers that Nur Chandra has accepted a post at Harvard, he'll crash all over again. It's more than losing his brightest star, it's the fact that Nur's contract says the monkeys go with him. I gather Nur has extended an invitation to Cecil to move to Massachusetts too—Cecil is wild with joy about it. No more ghetto living. The Chandras have bought a posh estate and Cecil is to have a lovely house on it. I'm happy for him, but very sorry for the Prof."

"Sounds weird to me. A contract that lets you take things with you that other people paid for? That's like a congressman taking the Remington from his office wall when he's voted out."

"At the time Nur came to the Hug, the Prof had every reason in the world to discount that stipulation. He knew that Nur would never find anywhere as perfect for his research as the Hug. And that was true until this beastly monster of a murderer appeared."

"Yeah, who could have foreseen that? I'm getting so paranoid that it suggests yet another motive. There's a Nobel Prize at stake, after all."

"Do you know," she said thoughtfully, "I've always had an odd feeling that Nur Chandra won't win the Nobel Prize? Somehow it's all been too easy. The only one of the monkeys that has shown any evidence of a conditioned epileptic state is Eustace, and it's very dangerous in science to pin all your hopes on a solitary star. What if Eustace was harboring an epileptic tendency all along, and something entirely unrelated to Nur's stimuli suddenly brought it out? Stranger things have happened."

"You're a lot smarter than the rest of them rolled in one," Carmine said appreciatively.

"Smart enough to know I won't win any Nobel Prizes!"

They moved to the big chairs. Usually Carmine sat next to Desdemona, but tonight he sat opposite her, on the premise that looking at her sane and sensible face would cheer him a little.

Yesterday he had gone to Groton to talk to Edward Bewlee, a man as sane and sensible as Desdemona. But the interview had not solved any mysteries.

"Etta was so set on being a famous rock star," Mr. Bewlee had said. "Her voice was beautiful, and she moved well."

And she moved well. Was that what appealed to the Ghosts?

Back to the present—to Desdemona's sane and sensible face.

"Any other news on the Hug front?" he asked.

"Chuck Ponsonby is filling in for the Prof. He's not one of my favorite people, but at least he comes to me with his problems, rather than to Tamara. Apparently she tried to see Keith Kyneton, and he slammed the door of his office in her face. So Hilda is definitely wearing the victory laurels. Her appearance has improved no end— a well-cut black suit, tomato-red silk blouse, Italian shoes, new hairdo and rinse, proper make-up—and, if you believe it, contact lenses instead of spectacles! She looks like a perfect wife for a prominent neurosurgeon."

"Ready to strut her New York City stuff," said Carmine with a smile. "Nice to think that something I said to Kyneton penetrated the fog." He shifted in his seat. "There's a rumor going around this building that Satsuma's not renewing his lease on the penthouse or Eido's apartment."

"That could well be true. He's dithering between offers from Stanford, Washington State and Georgia. Which probably means he will end at Columbia."

"How did you work that one out?"

"Hideki's a city man, and New York City means he won't need to give up his Cape Cod weekender. A longer drive, yes, but still a feasible one. He would have gone to Boston if Nur Chandra hadn't beaten him to Massachusetts. Any other university than Harvard would have been a terrible comedown. Yet to me, Hideki's a better bet for the Nobel Prize. The showy researchers may fascinate the scientific press, but they rarely follow through." She hopped up nimbly. "Time for bed. Thank you for the pizza, Carmine."

Bereft of a suitable reply, he took her two floors down to her steel door with its dead bolt and combination, made sure she was properly locked in, and returned to his own domain feeling curiously depressed. It had been on the tip of his tongue to ask her if he stood any chance of moving their relationship on to a more intimate plane, only to have the words stilled by that athletic spring to her feet, her brisk, no-nonsense departure.

The truth was that Carmine's overtures had not been obvious enough for Desdemona to divine they so much as existed, and if her own emotions were rather hankering for him, then she didn't dare linger in his presence once they had said all they could say about the Hug and ordinary topics of conversation. What she had dreaded was a long silence, not sure she could deal with it.

Besides, she was very tired. After heated arguments, she had won the privilege of resuming her weekend hikes—on the proviso that she was driven to her starting point in a squad car whose cop denizens made sure it was not followed, then picked up at some point she designated as her finishing line. So she had hiked up in the northwestern corner of the state Saturday and Sunday, and ached from what had become an unaccustomed exercise. The Appalachian Trail had its winter charms, but at times she had regretted not packing her snow shoes.

Thus after a long soak in a hot bath she dried off well and donned her customary sleeping attire—a pair of flannel men's pajamas and thick, woolly bedsocks. Not for Desdemona a thermostat producing warm air! In which, had she only known it, she was very like Carmine Delmonico.

She was asleep as soon as she lay down, to dream of nothing she could afterward remember, only that some peculiar noise woke her at a moment her alarm clock said was 4 A.M. A scrape with a slight screech to it.

Sitting bolt upright, she began to think that it wasn't the noise wakened her; some primeval sense of impending doom had done that. The bedroom door was open, displaying the small apartment's living area, plunged into darkness. As indeed was the bedroom. No bogeys demanding night lights haunted Desdemona's sleep. Yet a sliver of light from the hall outside flickered briefly with a shadow in its midst, man-high, man-shaped. Gone in an instant as the outside door was closed. *I am not alone.* He is here inside, he has come to kill me.

On a chair near the bed lay today's "smalls" washing she had not gotten around to—panties, bra, stockings, a single pair of knitted woollen gloves. Desdemona was out of the bed without a sound, across to the chair, her fingers scrabbling for the gloves. Once found, she slid one on to each hand and forced herself to edge out of any reflected light to where the balcony sliding door sat locked and barred with a steel rod that lay in its opening track. She bent, removed the rod, undid the latch, and slid the door open just enough to get through it onto the balcony, a shelf of concrete surmounted by a four-foot-high iron affair of pickets and a rail.

Carmine was two floors up on the northeastern side of the Nutmeg Insurance building, almost exactly opposite where she was. That meant that to reach him she had to get herself two floors up with a dozen apartments between them on his or her level. Did she go up two floors first, or along her own floor's balconies until she stood directly below his? No, up first, Desdemona! Get off this level as soon as possible. Only how?

Each floor occupied ten feet of vertical space: nine-foot ceilings inside, plus a foot of concrete representing the floor of the next storey up, with its inclusions of water and drainage pipes, electricity conduits. Too far to reach up, too far . . .

The wind was whistling, but once she closed her sliding door that wouldn't penetrate the double-glazed interior. Bitterly cold, cutting through her pajamas as if they were made of tissue. Only one thing for it. She scissored her long legs and vaulted up on to the balcony rail, paused there teetering ten floors above the street as the wind tore at her, groping past the foot-thick shelf to find the bottom of the balustrade one storey up. There! Only her height and a teenaged propensity for gymnastics made it possible, but she had that height, that propensity. Both hands gripping the bottom of the balustrade upstairs, she took her feet off the rail, twisted in midair until her body was perpendicular, then swung her legs inward to cradle the rail behind her bent knees. A huge lunge, and she stood on the balcony above her own.

One down, one to go. Teeth chattering, her body felt like ice beneath the heat her gymnastics generated; without pausing to rest she mounted that rail and reached for the bottom of the balustrade on Carmine's level. Do it, Desdemona, do it before you can't! Up again, safe again on the balcony two floors above her own.

Now all she had to do was travel on the same level from one balcony to the next—easier said than done, as a ten-foot gap lay between the end of one and the beginning of the next. She chose to bridge the gap by balancing her feet on the rail and springing with all her might at the next balustrade. How many such? Twelve. And her feet were turning numb, her hands inside the woolly gloves minus all sensation. But it could be done—*had* to be done, given what was waiting for her downstairs if she tarried. How could she be sure he wasn't at least as agile as she?

Finally it was done; she stood on Carmine's balcony, began pounding on the sliding door to his bedroom, at this end.

"Carmine, Carmine, let me in!" she screamed.

The door was yanked open; he stood wearing only boxer shorts, took in her presence in a millisecond, pulled her inside.

The next moment he had stripped the quilted down cover off his bed and was draping it around her.

"He's in my apartment," she managed to say.

"Stay here and concentrate on getting warm," he said, cranked the thermostat up and vanished even as he pulled on his trousers.

* * *

"Look at this," he said to Abe and Corey twenty minutes later at Desdemona's door, gaping open.

The hard steel dead bolt had been cut through; a small pile of iron filings lay on the floor where it had sat in closed position.

"Jesus!" Abe breathed.

"We have a whole new trade to learn," Carmine said grimly. "If this proves anything, it proves that our ideas of security suck. To keep him out, we'd have had to overlap the metal on the outside of the door, but we didn't. Oh, he's gone—gone the minute he found Desdemona gone, I reckon. Flitted out like a ghost."

"How the hell did she get past him?" Corey asked.

"Went onto her balcony, vaulted two floors up, then came along the intervening apartment balconies between here and where I am. I heard her banging on my balcony door."

"Then she's a mess in this weather—metal rails, the wind."

"Not her!" Carmine said, a hint of pride in his voice. "She put on gloves and she was wearing bedsocks."

"One hell of a woman," said Abe reverently.

"I have to get back to her. Set the wheels in motion, guys. Search the place from penthouse to basements. But he's gone."

Finding Desdemona still under his quilt, he unwrapped her. "Feeling better?"

"As if I've wrenched my arms out of their sockets, but—oh, Carmine, I got away! He *was* there, wasn't he? It wasn't just my imagination?"

"He was there, all right, though long gone. Cut through the dead bolt with something like a diamond-tipped fretsaw—thin, fine, cut through anything if used by an expert. Therefore we now know he's an expert. Didn't try to do it too fast and break his saw. The bastard! He spat on our security." Carmine knelt to pull off her soaked bedsocks, examine the skin of her feet. "You survived at this end. Now let's have a look at your hands." They too had survived. "You're some woman, Desdemona."

Thoroughly warmed, she began to glow. "That's a compliment I'll treasure, Carmine." Then she shivered. "Oh, but I was so terrified! All I saw was his shadow as he opened the front door, but I knew he'd come to kill me. Only why? Why me?"

"Maybe to get at me. To get at the cops. To prove that if and when he decides to act, nothing will stop him. Trouble is that we're used to ordinary criminals, men who wouldn't have the brains or the patience to try a stunt like sawing through a two-inch dead bolt. Diamond teeth or not, it must have taken him several hours."

Suddenly he reached for her, pulled her hard against him in an almost frantic hold. "Desdemona, Desdemona, I nearly lost you! You had to save yourself while I snored! Oh, Jesus, woman, I'd have died had I lost you!"

"You are not going to lose me, Carmine," she said on a sigh, nuzzling her head into his shoulder, her lips busy on his neck. "I was terrified, yes, but I never thought for one moment of going anywhere else than to you. With you, I knew I'd be safe."

"I love you."

"I love you back again. But I'd feel ever safer if you took me to bed," said Desdemona, emerging from his neck. "There are some bits of me that haven't thawed in years."

PART FOUR

February & March
1966

CHAPTER 22

Monday, February 14th, 1966

Mid-February saw the commencement of a thaw. It began to rain remorselessly on a Friday and didn't stop until well into Sunday night. All the low-lying parts of Connecticut were under freezing water trying vainly to get away. The Finch house was cut off from Route 133 in exactly the manner Maurice Finch had described to Carmine; Ruth Kyneton's streamlet had risen so high that she had to pin out her washing in gumboots; and Dr. Charles Ponsonby came into the Hug complaining bitterly about a flooded wine cellar.

Thwarted by the intensity of the deluge and tormented by stiffening leg muscles, on Monday at dawn Addison Forbes decided to take a short run around the East Holloman area, then down to the water's edge at his jetty. There he had built a boat shed to house his little fifteen-footer, though few were the times that his frame of mind prompted him to launch it for a leisurely sail on Holloman Harbor. For the last three years leisure was a sin to Addison Forbes, if not a crime.

A squad car was parked suspiciously near Forbes's rather precip-itous driveway, its occupants giving him an admiring wave as he leaped past, intent on concluding his run. Sweat rolled off him as he plunged down the bushy slope from the road; three days of down-pour had melted the frozen snow, hence the flooding all over the state, and the ground under Forbes's running shoes was saturated, slippery. Years ago he had planted a row of forsythia at the bottom of the incline—how wonderful it always was when that harbinger of spring burst into yellow blossom!

But in February the forsythia hedge was rigid brown sticks, so when Forbes noticed a jarring patch of lilac on the ground beneath it, he stopped. A split second later he saw the arms and legs emerg-ing from the lilac patch, and his treacherous heart suddenly surged in his ears like a tidal race. He clutched at his chest, opened his parched mouth to yell, could not. Oh, dear Lord, the shock! He was going to have another coronary, this *had* to trigger another coronary! Hanging on to the back of an old park bench Robin had put there for "dreaming on," he inched around it until he could sit and wait for the pain to clamp down, old and ineradicable instinct causing him to flex his left hand constantly as he waited for the pain to shoot down the arm and into it. Eyes dilated, mouth agape, Addison Forbes sat and waited. I am going to die, I am going to die . . .

Ten minutes later the pain hadn't arrived, and he could no longer hear his heart. Its pulse had slowed precisely as it did after all his runs, and he felt no different than he did after all his runs. A huge jerk shot him to his feet, and that didn't cause pain either; he turned his gaze to the lilac patch with its arms and legs, then took the slope up to the house in long, rhythmic steps, joy welling inside him.

"Her body is down by the water," he said, coming into the kitchen. "Call the police, Robin."

She squeaked and fluttered, but made the call, then came to him, her hand seeking his pulse.

"I'm fine," he said irritably. "Don't fuss, woman, I'm fine! I have just undergone a colossal shock, but my heart didn't falter." A dreamy smile played around his lips. "I'm hungry, I want a good breakfast. Fried eggs and bacon, raisin toast with plenty of butter, and cream in my coffee. Go on, Robin, move!"

"They conned us," Carmine said, standing at the water's edge with Abe and Corey. "How could we have been so dumb? Watching all the roads, not even thinking of the harbor. They dumped her here from a boat."

"The whole east shore was frozen until Saturday night," Abe said. "This had to be last minute, it can't be where they planned to dump her."

"Bullshit it isn't," Carmine said positively. "The thaw made it easier, that's all. If the water had stayed frozen, they would have walked across the ice all the way from a street we're not patrolling. As it is, they could use a rowboat, bring it in close enough to throw her out. They never set foot on the shore."

"She's frozen solid," Patrick said, coming to join them. "A lilac party dress sewn with pearls, not rhinestones. Some lacy fabric I've never seen before—not proper lace. The dress fits better than Margaretta's, at least for length. I haven't turned her over yet to see if the back is buttoned up. No ligature marks, and no double cut in the neck. Apart from a few wet leaves, she's very clean."

"Since they never set foot on shore, there won't be anything here. I'll leave you to it, Patsy. Come on, guys," he said to Abe and Corey, "we have to ask every householder with water frontage if they saw or heard a thing last night. But Corey, you're going to cast our net wider. Take the police launch and go around the tankers and freighters moored anywhere in the harbor. Maybe someone came up on deck to suck in fresh air after days of being stuck belowdeck, and saw a rowboat. That's the kind of thing a seaman would notice."

"It's a repeat of Margaretta," said Patrick to Silvestri, Marciano, Carmine and Abe; Corey was out on the water in the big police launch. "Faith's shoulders were narrower and her breasts were small, so they managed to button up the dress. There wasn't a mark on it, which means she must have been wrapped in a waterproof nylon sheet for the trip in the boat. Something finer and smoother than ordinary tarpaulin. Boats always have a couple of inches of water slopping around in their bottoms, but the dress was bone dry, unstained."

"How did she die?" Marciano asked.

"Raped to death, like Margaretta. What I don't know is if their new ultimate tool is deliberately designed to kill, or whether they would prefer it did its job more slowly—over, say, several assaults with it. As soon as Faith died they put her in a freezer, but not a household job. More like a supermarket one. It's long enough to fit Margaretta flat out, and wide enough that both girls were positioned in it with their arms extended away from their bodies and their legs somewhat apart. They dressed both girls after they were hard as rocks. Faith's panties were modest, but lilac instead of pink. Bare feet, bare hands. Faith has two misshapen toes from an old break, left foot. That will make her easy to identify if her family ever comes out of its furor."

"Do you think the same person made both dresses?" Silvestri asked. "I mean, they're different yet the same."

"I'm no expert on party dresses. I think Carmine's lady should look at them and tell us," Patrick said with a wink.

Carmine flushed. So it's that obvious, is it? So what if it is, anyway? It's a free country, and I'll just have to hope that we never need Desdemona's testimony to nail these sons of bitches. A police lawyer would tell me that Desdemona is the most serious mistake I've made on this case, but I'm prepared to go with my gut instinct that she's irrelevant, despite the attempt on her life. Love wouldn't cause me to lose my cop instincts. God, but I love her! When she appeared on my balcony I knew in a second that she meant more to me than I do. She's the light of my entire existence.

"Have you had any joy tracing the pink dress, Carmine?" Danny Marciano asked.

"No, none. I've had someone check in every store that sells kids' dresses from one end of the state to the other, but hundred-dollar-plus party dresses seem too rich for Connecticut tastes. And that's weird, considering that Connecticut has some of the wealthiest areas in the whole nation."

"Wealthy mothers of little girls spend their lives driving their Caddies from one shopping center to another," Silvestri said. "They go to Filene's in Boston, for Chrissake! And Manhattan."

"Point taken," said Carmine with a grin. "We're examining Yellow Pages from Maine to Washington, D.C. Who's for a stack of hotcakes with bacon and syrup next door?"

At least he's eating again, thought Patrick, nodding his consent to this plan. God knows what he sees in that Limey woman, but his ex-wife she ain't. He's not hooked on a looker for the second time, though the more I see of her, the less I think of her as downright unattractive. One thing for sure, she has a brain and she knows how to use it. That's bound to entrance a man like Carmine.

"Oh, Addison went to the Hug," said Robin Forbes to Carmine chirpily when he arrived back at the house.

"You sound happy," he said.

"Lieutenant, for three years I've lived in hell," she said, moving around with a spring in her walk. "After he had that massive heart attack, Addison became convinced that he was living on borrowed time. *So afraid!* The jogging, nothing but raw fruit and vegetables—I'd drive all the way to Rhode Island to find a piece of fish he wouldn't reject. He was positive that a shock would kill him, so he'd go to any lengths to avoid a shock. Then this morning he finds that poor little girl, and he's shocked—really shocked. But he doesn't even feel a twinge, let alone die." Eyes twinkling, she jigged. "We've returned to a normal life."

Having no idea that Addison Forbes harbored homicidal fantasies about his wife, Carmine left after another walk around the property thinking that it was indeed an ill wind blew nobody any good. Dr. Addison Forbes would be a much happier man—at least until Roger

Parson Junior's lawyers found a challengeable clause in Uncle William's will. Was it a part of the Ghosts' scheme to destroy the Hug as well as beautiful young girls? And if it was, why? Could it be that in destroying the Hug, they were really destroying Professor Robert Mordent Smith? If so, then they were well along the road to success. And whereabouts did Desdemona fit? He had spent their breakfast together grilling her in true, remorseless police fashion: had she seen something she'd buried below all conscious memory, had she been walking some street when a girl had been abducted, had someone at the Hug said something inappropriate to her, had anything unusual entered the tenor of her days? To all of which, bearing his questions patiently, even taking the time to puzzle over them, she returned firm negatives.

After a fruitless cruise through the Hug, Carmine climbed back into the Ford and aimed for the Merritt Parkway, which traveled to New York on the Trumbull side of Bridgeport. Though he did not expect to be permitted to see the Prof, he could find no reason why he ought not inspect as much of Marsh Manor as possible, ascertain for himself what the Bridgeport police had reported: that it would be easy for an inmate to break out of the place.

Yes, he decided, turning in through the imposing pineapple-topped gates, agoraphobia would keep more patients inside Marsh Manor than security patrols. There were no security patrols.

Right. Where to next? The Chandras. Their estate was off the Wilbur Cross where Route 133's seemingly aimless course brought it into an area of farms and barns in pleasant fields and apple orchards. Too late to have another talk with Nur Chandra at the Hug—he had finished there last Friday, as had Cecil.

The house wasn't on the scale of the Marsh Manor funny farm, but the estate reminded Carmine of a Cape Cod compound, half a dozen residences scattered around it; though this, in ten acres, was much larger. If it impressed Carmine at all, it was in letting him see how much organization went into making living luxurious for two people and a few kids with money to burn. No doubt the Chandras employed a manager, a deputy manager and a specialist manager as well as the army of turbaned lackeys. The whole thing structured so that the Chandras themselves never gave a moment's thought to so much effort. A metaphorical snap of the fingers, and whatever was wanted appeared immediately.

"It's highly inconvenient," said Dr. Nur Chandra, speaking to Carmine in his imposing library, "but necessary, Lieutenant. The Hug was perfect for my needs, even to—and including—Cecil."

"Then why go?" Carmine asked.

Chandra looked scornful. "Oh, come, my good man, surely you can see that the Hug is past tense? Robert Smith won't return, and I am told that the Parson Governors are seeking a way out of financing the Hug. So I would rather go now, while things are in flux, than wait until I have to step over yet more bodies. I need to get out while this monster is still killing, so that I am quite removed from suspicion. For you won't catch him, Lieutenant."

"That sounds good and logical, Dr. Chandra, but I suspect that the real reason you're anxious to hustle yourself off right now concerns your monkeys. Your chances of taking them with you in the middle of the present chaos is much higher than after the Hug's situation occupies more Parson attention than a will. You are, in effect, making off with close to a million dollars in Hug property, however your contract may be worded."

"Oh, very shrewd, Lieutenant!" Chandra said appreciatively. "That is precisely why I am leaving now. Once I am gone and my macaques gone with me, it will be a fait accompli. Disentangling the situation, legally and logistically, would be hideous."

"Are the macaques still at the Hug?"

"No, they're here in temporary quarters. With Cecil Potter."

"And when are you leaving for Massachusetts?"

"Things are already in motion. I myself will go on Friday with my wife and children. Cecil and the macaques go tomorrow."

"I hear you've bought a nice place outside Boston."

"Yes. Very much like this, actually."

In walked Surina Chandra clad in a scarlet sari encrusted with embroidery and gold thread, her arms, neck and hair blazing with jewels. Behind her were two little girls about seven years of age—twins, Carmine thought, astonished at their beauty. But the emotion was gone in a second as his eyes took in their apparel. Matching dresses of lace covered in rhinestones, with stiff, full skirts and little puffed sleeves. Both an ethereal ice-green.

Somehow he got through the introductions. The girls, Leela and Nuru, were indeed twins; demure souls with enormous black eyes and black hair in braids as thick as hawsers straying over their shoulders. Like their mother, they smelled of some eastern perfume Carmine couldn't like—musky, heavy, tropical. They had diamonds in their earlobes that left the rhinestones for dead.

"I love your dresses," he said to the twins, hunkering down to their level without approaching them too closely.

"Yes, they are pretty," said their mother. "It's difficult to find this sort of children's wear in America. Of course they have lots sent from home, but when we saw these, they appealed."

"If it isn't a rude question, Mrs. Chandra, where did you find the dresses?"

"In a mall not far from where we're going to live. A lovely shop for girls, better than any I've found in Connecticut."

"Can you tell me where the mall is?"

"Oh, dear, I'm afraid not. They all look much the same to me, and I don't know the area yet."

"I don't suppose you remember the name of the store, then?"

She laughed, white teeth flashing. "Having been brought up on J. M. Barrie and Kenneth Graham, of course I do! Tinker Bell."

And off they drifted, the twins waving back at him shyly.

"My children have taken a fancy to you," said Chandra.

Nice, but unimportant. "May I use your phone, Doctor?"

"Certainly, Lieutenant. I'll leave you in private."

You sure can't fault them on manners, even if their ethics are different, Carmine thought as he dialed Marciano, his fingers trembling.

"I know where the dresses come from," he said without preamble. "Tinker Bell. Tinker Bell, two words. There's one in a mall outside Boston, but there may be others. Start looking."

"Two stores," said Marciano when Carmine walked in. "Boston and White Plains, both in classy malls. You're sure of this?"

"Positive. Two of Chandra's little girls were wearing dead ringers of Margaretta's dress, except green in color. Thing is, which Tinker Bell would our Ghosts patronize?"

"White Plains. It's closer unless they live near the Mass border. That's possible, of course."

"Then Abe can go to Boston tomorrow, while I take White Plains. Jesus, Danny, we've got a break at last!"

CHAPTER 23

Tuesday, February 15th, 1966

The Tinker Bell at White Plains was located in a mall of smart clothing and furniture stores interspersed with the inevitable delis, fast-food outlets, drugstores and dry cleaners. There were also several restaurants catering more for lunch than dinner. It was a new structure on two levels, but Tinker Bell was too canny to situate itself one floor up. Near the entrance on the ground.

It was, Carmine noted as he surveyed Tinker Bell from the outside, a very large premises entirely devoted to clothing for girl children. They had a sale going for overcoats and winter wear; no cheap nylon stuff in here, all natural fiber. There was even, he saw, a section devoted to real furs through an archway that said *Kiddiminx*. Several dozen customers browsed the racks even at this early hour, some with children in tow, some alone. No men. How many shoplifters in a place like this? the cop wondered.

He entered with as much confidence as he could muster, looking—and feeling—utterly incongruous. Apparently he had a neon sign on his forehead blinking COP on and off, as women moved quickly away from him and the store assistants started to huddle.

"May I see the manager, please?" he asked one hapless girl who didn't make the huddle in time.

Oh, good, they could remove him from the floor! The girl led him immediately to the back of the merchandise and knocked on an unmarked door.

Mrs. Giselle Dobchik ushered him into a tiny cubicle stuffed with cardboard boxes and filing cabinets; a safe sat to one side of a table that served as Mrs. Dobchik's desk, but there was no room for a visitor's chair. Her response to the sight of his badge was unruffled interest; but then, Mrs. Dobchik struck him as the kind whom little ruffled. Mid-forties, very well dressed, blonde hair, red-varnished nails not long enough to snag the goods.

"Do you recognize this, ma'am?" he asked, removing the shell-pink lace dress Margaretta had worn from his briefcase. Out came Faith's lilac dress. "Or this?"

"Almost certainly Tinker Bells," she said, beginning to feel the inside seams, and frowning. "Our labels have been removed, but yes, I can assure you that they're genuine Tinker Bells. We have special tricks with the beading."

"I don't suppose you know who bought them?"

"Any number of people, Lieutenant. They're both size tens—that is, for girls between ten and twelve years of age. Once past twelve, a girl tends to want to look more like Annette Funicello than a fairy. We always have one of each model and color in each size in stock, but two is a strain. Here, come with me."

Following her out of her office and over to a large area of glittery, frilly party dresses on dozens of long racks, Carmine understood what she meant when she said two the same size and type was a strain; there must have been upward of two thousand dresses in hues from white to dark red, all picked out in rhinestones or pearls or opalescent beads.

"Six sizes from three years to twelve years, twenty different models, and twenty different colors," she said. "We're famous for these dresses, you see—they walk out as fast as we can get them in." A laugh. "After all, we can't have two girls in the same model and color at the same party! Wearing a Tinker Bell is a sign of social status. Ask any Westchester County mom or child. The cachet extends into Connecticut—quite a few of our clients drive in from Fairfield or Litchfield Counties."

"If I may collect my dresses and briefcase, Mrs. Dobchik, could I buy you some lunch? A cup of coffee? I feel like a bull in a china shop here, and I can't be good for business."

"Thanks, I'd appreciate the break," said Mrs. Dobchik.

"What you said about two girls wearing the same Tinker Bell to the same party leads me to assume that you do keep fairly detailed records," he said, sucking at a chocolate malted through a straw—too much kid stuff.

"Oh, yes, we have to. It's just that both the models you've shown me have been perennials for some years, so we've sold a big bunch of them. The pink lace has been out now for five years, the lilac one for four. Your samples have been so abused that it's not possible to tell exactly when they were made."

"Whereabouts are they made?"

She nibbled on a cruller, clearly enjoying her role as an expert. "We have a small factory in Worcester, Mass. My sister runs Boston, I run White Plains, our brother runs the factory. A family business—we're the sole owners."

"Do men ever come in to buy?"

"Sometimes, Lieutenant, but on the whole Tinker Bell clients are women. Men may buy lingerie for their wives, but they usually avoid buying party dresses for their daughters."

"Would you ever sell two dresses in the same size and color to the same buyer on the same day? Like, for twins?"

"Yes, it does happen, but it involves a wait of a day for us to get in the second dress. Women with twins order in advance."

"What about someone's buying, say, my pink lace and my lilac whatever-it-is—"

"Broderie Anglaise," she interrupted.

"Thanks, I'll write that down. Would someone buy two models in different colors in the same size on the same day?"

"Only once," she said, and sighed in reminiscent pleasure. "Oh, what a sale that was! Twelve dresses in the ten-to-twelve size, each one a different model and color."

The hair on Carmine's neck stood up. "When?"

"Toward the end of 1963, I think it was. I can look it up."

"Before we go back and I get you to do that, Mrs. Dobchik, do you remember who this buyer was? What she looked like?"

"I remember very well," said the perfect witness. "Not her *name*—she paid cash. But she was in the grandmother age group. About fifty-five. Wore a sable coat and a snappy sable hat, had blue-rinsed hair, good but not overdone make-up, big nose, blue eyes, elegant bifocal glasses, a pleasant speaking voice. Her bag and shoes were matching Charles Jourdan, and she wore longish kid gloves in sable brown like the shoes and bag. A uniformed chauffeur carried all the boxes out to her limo. It was a black Lincoln."

"Doesn't sound as if she needed food stamps."

"Heavens to Betsy, no! It remains the biggest single sale in party dresses we've ever had. One-fifty each, eighteen hundred bucks. She peeled hundred-dollar bills off a two-inch stack."

"Did you happen to ask her why she was buying so many party dresses in the same size?"

"Sure I did—who wouldn't? She smiled and said she was the local representative of a charity organization that was sending the dresses to an orphanage in Buffalo for Christmas gifts."

"Did you believe her?"

Giselle Dobchik grinned. "It's just as believable as buying twelve dresses in the same size, isn't it?"

"I guess so."

They returned to Tinker Bell, where Mrs. Dobchik produced her record of the sale. No name, cash tendered.

"You took the numbers of the bills," Carmine said. "Why?"

"There was a counterfeit scare at the time, so I checked with my bank while the girls were boxing everything up."

"And they weren't counterfeit?"

"No, they were the real McCoy, but the bank was interested in them because they'd been issued in 1933 right after we went off the gold standard, and were in near-mint condition." Mrs. Dobchik shrugged. "Ask me did I care? They were legal tender. My bank manager thought they'd been hoarded."

Carmine scanned the list of eighteen numbers. "I agree. They're consecutive. Very unusual, but no help to me."

"Is this a part of some big, exciting case?" Mrs. Dobchik asked, walking him to the door.

"Afraid not, ma'am. Another hundred-dollar bill scare."

"We now know that the Ghosts had planned the second series of murders before they started on the first," Carmine said to his fascinated audience. "The sale was made in December of 1963 well before the very first victim, Rosita Esperanza, was abducted. They ploughed through a dozen girls at the rate of one every two months for two years with twelve Tinker Bell dresses packed in mothballs against the day when they'd be used. Whoever the Ghosts are, they are *not* following a moon cycle, which is what the psychiatrists want to think now that they're down to one every thirty days. The moon has nothing to do with the Ghosts. They're cycling on the sun—twelves, twelves, twelves."

"Does finding out about Tinker Bell help?" Silvestri asked.

"Not until there's a trial."

"But first, find the Ghosts," said Marciano. "Who do you think Grandma is, Carmine?"

"One of the Ghosts."

"But you said these aren't women's crimes."

"I still say that, Danny. However, it's much easier for a man to disguise himself as an elderly woman than a young one. Rougher skin and creases don't matter as much."

"I love the props," Silvestri said dryly. "Sable coats, a chauffeur and limo. Could we try the limo angle?"

"I'll get Corey on to it tomorrow, John, but don't hope. The chauffeur was the other Ghost, I'm picking. Funny, that. Mrs. Dobchik could remember every detail about Grandma down to bifocal glasses, but not a thing about the chauffeur apart from a black suit, cap, and leather gloves."

"No, it's logical," said Patrick. "Your Mrs. Dobchik is in the clothing business. She caters to wealthy women every day, but not to workingmen. The women she files in her memory, and she knows every kind of fur, every make of French bags and shoes. I'll bet Grandma never took her kid gloves off for a second, even when she peeled hundreds off her stack."

"You're right, Patsy. Gloved throughout."

Silvestri growled. "So we're no closer to the Ghosts."

"In one way, John, yet we have made progress. Since they leave no evidence and no one has come forward with a description, we're looking for a needle in a haystack. How many people in Connecticut, three million? As states go it's pretty small—no big cities, a dozen small ones, a hundred towns. Well, that's our haystack. But I wasn't long into this case before I realized that looking for the needle isn't the way to go. The Tinker Bell dresses may seem like one more dead end, but I don't think that's true. They're a new nail in the coffin, another piece of evidence. Anything that tells us a fact about the Ghosts gets us that much closer to them. What we're looking at is a jigsaw puzzle made of cloudless blue sky, but the Tinker Bell dresses have filled in a blank space. The amount of sky is growing."

Carmine leaned forward, running with his idea. "First off, one Ghost has become two Ghosts. Secondly, the two Ghosts are as close as brothers. I don't know what color their skin is, but what they see in their collective mind is a face. More than anything else, a face. The kind of face you don't see on white white girls, nor very often on black black girls. The Ghosts work as a team in the true sense—each has a specific set of tasks, areas of expertise. That probably extends to what they do with and to their victims once captured. The rape turns them on, but the victim has to be a virgin in *every* sense—they're not interested in heavy petters with intact hymens. One Ghost gives the victim her first kiss, so maybe the other Ghost deflowers her. I see the teamwork persisting—you get to do this, I get to do that. About the actual killing, I don't know for sure, but I suspect that the subservient Ghost does it. He cleans up. The only reason they keep the heads is the face, which means that when we find them we are going to find every head going back to Rosita Esperanza. While ever their activities weren't known to the police, they got a kick out of the daylight abductions, but from Francine Murray on, they sweated. I'm beginning to think that they switched to the night because of police awareness, not as part of a consciously designed new method. Night abductions are less risky, simple as that."

Patrick sat with eyes narrowed as if focused on something very small. "The face," he said. "This is the first time I've heard you discard all the other criteria, Carmine. What makes you think it's just the face? Why have you discarded color, creed, race, size, innocence?"

"Oh, Patsy, you know how often I've been fixed on all of them and each of them, but I've finally settled for the face. It came to me on the drive—wham!" He palmed a fist, wham! "Margaretta Bewlee told me. My black pearl after a dozen creamy ones. What *did* she have in common with the other girls? And the answer is, a face. Nothing *except* a face. Feature by feature, hers is the same as all the others. I got sidetracked by her differences, so much so that I overlooked the one similarity—the face."

"What about the innocence?" Marciano asked. "She had that too."

"Yes, it's a given. But innocence isn't what drives our pair of Ghosts to abduct these particular girls. The face does. If a girl doesn't have the face, all the innocence in the world won't interest the Ghosts in her." He paused, frowning.

"Go on, Carmine," Silvestri prompted.

"The Ghosts—or maybe one Ghost—knew someone with the face. Someone they hate more than the rest of humanity put together."

He dropped his head in his hands, clutched at his hair. "One of them, or both of them? The dominant one, for sure, whereas the submissive one might just be along for the ride on one fantastic roller-coaster—he's the servant, he hates whomever the dominant one hates. When you said to me that the Ghosts aren't interested in breasts, Patsy, you filled in another chunk of sky. The flat chest, the plucked pubes. They should suggest that the owner of the face was pre-pubescent, and yet—if so, why don't they abduct pre-pubescent girls? They don't lack the balls or the brains to do it. So is the owner of the face someone that at least one of the Ghosts knew from child-hood to young womanhood? Hated more as woman than as child? That's the riddle I have no answer for."

Silvestri spat out his cigar in excitement. "But they have gone fur-ther with the child aspect on this second dozen, Carmine. A little girl's party dress."

"If we knew who owned the face, we'd know who the Ghosts are. I spent the whole drive back from White Plains mentally searching through every Hugger's house looking for that face on someone's walls, but it isn't on any Hugger's walls."

"You still believe it's the Hug?" Marciano asked.

"One of the Ghosts is definitely a Hugger. The other one is not. He's the half who does the staking out, maybe some of the abduc-tions unaided. It has always had to be a Hugger, Danny. Yes, you can argue that bodies might have been put in any of the medical school dead animal refrigerators, but where else than the Hug is it possible to get two to ten bulky bags from a vehicle to the refrigerator unob-served? The fewer in one trip, the more trips. People come and go in the parking lots twenty-four hours a day, whereas the Hug's parking lot is key-card gated and utterly deserted at, say, five in the morning. I noticed that there's a big shopping cart chained to the Hug's back wall to help a researcher take his books and papers inside. I am *not* saying that the Ghosts couldn't have used other refrigerators, I am simply saying that using the Hug's is simplest and easiest."

"Simple and easy is better," said Silvestri. "The Hug it is."

"You'd best hope it isn't Desdemona, Carmine," said Patrick.

"Oh, I'm positive it isn't Desdemona."

"Ah!" Patrick cried, tensing. "You suspect someone!"

Carmine drew in a deep breath. "I don't suspect anyone, and that's my worst worry. I *should* suspect someone, so why don't I? What I do have is a sense that I'm missing something right under my nose. In my sleep it's crystal clear, but when I wake it's gone. All I can do is go on thinking."

"Talk to Eliza Smith," said Desdemona, her head on Carmine's shoulder; he had moved her into his apartment the day after her visitor. "I know you don't really tell me anything significant, but I am convinced that you believe the Ghost is a Hugger. Eliza has been a part of the Hug since its inception, and while she has never stuck her nose into what she shouldn't, she does know an awful lot other people don't. The Prof talks to her sometimes, such as when he's in hot water over the staff—Tamara is quite a strain, Walt Polonowski has his moments, and so does Kurt Schiller. Eliza took a psych major at Smith and went on to take a Ph.D. in psych from Chubb. I'm not a fan of psychologists, but the Prof has a lot of respect for Eliza's opinions. Go and talk to her."

"Does the Prof ever need to talk about you to Eliza?"

"Certainly not! To some extent I travel on an outer orbit that's out of step with all the other orbits—a bit like four-five music. I'm seen as an accountant, not as a scientist, and that makes me of no importance to the Prof." She snuggled. "I'm serious, Carmine. Talk to Eliza Smith. You know perfectly well that it's talk will solve this case."

CHAPTER 24

The aftermath of the thaw kept Carmine too busy to see Mrs. Eliza Smith until almost a week later than Desdemona's urging him to. Besides, he couldn't see for the life of him what Mrs. Smith might be able to bring to his investigation. Especially now that the word was out that the Prof would not be returning to the Hug.

Temperatures soared and the wind decided to die; from a freeze it turned into ideal demonstration weather, cool enough for warm clothes but not unpleasant. The icy lid on statewide racial unrest melted; violence broke out everywhere.

In Holloman, Mohammed el Nesr sternly forbade rioting, as it was no part of his plans at this stage in his genesis to court arrest and search warrants. Alone among the discontented clots of black people raising hell, the Black Brigade and its leaders were sitting on a formidable arsenal of weapons rather than whatever firearms could be looted from gun shops or private houses. And now was not the time to reveal the presence of that arsenal. Despite which, Mohammed demonstrated relentlessly. If he had hoped for bigger crowds, the numbers who congregated were sufficiently large to put shouting, fist-waving groups outside City Hall, the County Services building, Chubb Administration, the railroad station, the bus station, M.M.'s official residence, and, of course, the Hug. All the placards dwelt upon the Connecticut Monster's whiteness, inviolability and racially selective murder victims.

"After all," said Wesley/Ali eagerly to Mohammed, "what we want is to highlight racial *discrimination*. Whitey's teenaged girls are safe but no one else's are—and that's a fact not even the Governor's ivory tower can dispute. Every industrial city in Connecticut is at least eighty percent black, which puts us in the catbird seat."

Mohammed el Nesr looked like the eagle he was named for, a magnificently proud, hawk-nosed man of imposing height and build, his cropped hair hidden beneath a hat he had designed himself, with some of the look of a turban, yet flatter on top. At first he had worn a beard, then decided that a beard obscured too much of a face no camera could make seem bestial, or cruel, or ugly. His leather Black Brigade jacket's white fist was embroidered rather than stamped, he wore it on top of combat fatigues, and he moved like the ex-military man he was. As Peter Scheinberg, he had risen to the rank of full bird colonel in the U.S. Army, so he was indeed an eagle. An eagle with two law degrees.

Inside their lining of mattresses his headquarters at 18 Fifteenth Street were stuffed with books, for he read insatiably on the law, politics and history, studied his Koran fervently, and knew himself a leader of men. Yet he was still groping for the right way to accomplish his revolution; industrial cities might enjoy big black majorities, but Whitey owned the entire nation, which by and large wasn't hugely urban. His first inspiration had been to recruit Black Brigaders among the armed services' plethora of black men, only to find that very few black soldiers, no matter how they privately felt about Whitey, were inclined to enlist. So upon discharge—an honorable one—he had migrated to Holloman, thinking that a small city was the best place to start wooing the restless ghetto masses. That the stone he threw into the Holloman pond would spread its ripples ever outward to embrace other and far bigger places. A superlative orator, he did get invitations to speak at rallies in New York City, Chicago, L.A. But the local leaders in each place were jealous of their sway, didn't regard Mohammed el Nesr as important. At fifty-two years of age, he knew that he lacked the money and the nationwide organization to weld his people as they needed to be welded. As was equally true for other autocrats, the people were pointing out to him that they refused to be led whither he would take them. Infinitely more wanted to follow Martin Luther King, a pacifist and a Christian.

Now here was this skinny little sansculotte from Louisiana giving him advice—how had he let that happen?

"I've been thinking too," Wesley/Ali burbled on, "about what you said a couple of months ago—do you remember? You said our movement needed a martyr. Well, I'm working on it."

"Good, Ali, you work on it, man. In the meantime, get back to your brainchild, the Hug. And Eleventh Street."

"How's next Sunday's rally coming on?"

"Great. Looks like we'll pull in fifty thousand black people on the Green come midday. Now fuck off, Ali, let me get on with writing my speech."

As ordered, Wesley/Ali fucked off to Eleventh Street, there to spread the word that Mohammed el Nesr was going to speak next Sunday on Holloman Green. Not only did everyone have to be there, but everyone also had to persuade their neighbors and friends to be there. Mohammed was a brilliant, charismatic orator, raved his disciple, well worth listening to. Come along, find out just how thoroughly Whitey was screwing black people. No black girl child was safe, but Mohammed el Nesr had answers.

What a pity, thought Wesley/Ali in one corner of his perpetually busy mind, that no one white would think to shoot Mohammed el Nesr down. What a martyr he would make! But this was staid old Connecticut, not the South or the West: no neo-Nazis, Klanners or even typical rednecks. One of the original thirteen states, a haven of free speech.

Whatever Wesley/Ali thought, Carmine knew that Connecticut had its share of neo-Nazis, Klanners and rednecks; he also knew that most of it was talk, and talk was cheap. But every rabid black hater was being watched, for Carmine was determined that no one was going to draw a bead on Mohammed el Nesr on Sunday afternoon. While Mohammed planned his rally, Carmine planned how to protect him: where the police snipers would be, how many cops he could put in plain clothes to patrol the outskirts of an anti-white crowd. No way was a bullet going to cut Mohammed el Nesr down and make a martyr out of him.

Then on Saturday night the snow returned, a February blizzard that left eighteen inches on the ground overnight; a shrieking subzero wind ensured that no rally would take place on Holloman Green. Saved by the winter bell yet again.

So today Carmine was at liberty to drive out to Route 133 and see if Mrs. Eliza Smith was home. She was.

"The boys went to school, very disappointed. If the snow had only waited until last night, no school today."

"I'm sorry for them, but very glad for me, Mrs. Smith."

"The black rally on Holloman Green?"

"Exactly."

"God loves peace," she said simply.

"Then why doesn't He issue more of it?" asked the veteran of military and civilian warfare.

"Because having created us, He moved on to someplace else in a very large universe. Perhaps when He did create us, He put a special cog in our machinery to make us peace loving. Then the cog wore down, and whammo! Too late for God to return."

"An interesting theory," he said.

"I've been baking butterfly cakes," Eliza said, leading the way into her mock-antique kitchen. "How about I make a fresh pot of coffee and you try some?"

Butterfly cakes, he discovered, were little yellow cakes Eliza had gouged the hilly tops off, filled the hollows with sweetened whipped cream, then cut the tops in two and put them back the wrong way up; they did look quite like fat little wings. They were, besides, delicious.

"Take them away, please," he begged after scoffing four. "If you don't, I'll just sit here and eat the lot."

"Okay," she said, stuck them on the counter and sat down as if she meant to stay. "Now, what brings you here, Lieutenant?"

"Desdemona Dupre. She said you were the one I should talk to about the Hug people because you know them best. Will you fill me in, or tell me to go take a running jump?"

"Three months ago I would have told you to go take that jump, but now things are different." She toyed with her coffee cup. "Do you know that Bob isn't returning to the Hug?"

"Yes. Everybody at the Hug seems to know that."

"It's a tragedy, Lieutenant. He's a broken man. There has always been a dark side to him, and since I've known him all my life, I've known about his dark side too."

"What do you mean by a dark side, Mrs. Smith?"

"Utter depression—a yawning pit—nothingness. He calls it one of those, depending. His first fully fledged attack happened after the death of our daughter, Nancy. Leukemia."

"I'm very sorry."

"So were we," she said, blinking away tears. "Nancy was the eldest, died aged seven. She'd be sixteen now."

"Have you a picture of her?"

"Hundreds, but I put them away because of Bob's tendency to depression. Hold on a minute." Off she went to return with an unframed color photograph of an adorable child, obviously taken before her illness ate her away. Curly blonde hair, big blue eyes, her mother's rather thin mouth.

"Thank you," he said, and put the picture face downward on the table. "I take it he recovered from that depression?"

"Yes, thanks to the Hug. Having to mother the Hug held him together. But not this time. He'll retreat into trains forever."

"How will you manage financially?" he asked, not realizing how longingly he was looking at the butterfly cakes.

She got up to pour him more coffee and plopped two cakes on his plate. "Here, eat them. That's an order." Her lips seemed dry; she licked them. "Financially we have no worries. Both of our families left us with trust funds that mean we don't have to earn livings for ourselves. What a horrific prospect for a pair of Yankees! The work ethic is ineradicable."

"What about your sons?"

"Our trusts pass to them. They're good boys."

"Why does the Professor beat them?"

She didn't attempt to deny it. "The dark side. It doesn't happen often, honestly. Only when they carp at him the way boys do—won't leave a touchy subject alone, or won't take no for an answer. They're typical boys."

"I guess I was wondering if the boys are going to join their father in playing with the trains."

"I think," Eliza said deliberately, "that both my sons would rather die than enter that basement. Bob is—selfish."

"I had noticed," he said gently.

"He hates sharing his trains. That's really why the boys tried to trash them—did he tell you that the damage was disastrous?"

"Yes, that it took four years to rebuild."

"That's just not true. A little boy of seven and another of five? Horse feathers, Lieutenant! It was more a business of going around picking things up off the floor than anything else. Then he beat them unmercifully—I had to wrestle the switch off him. And I told him that if he ever hurt the boys that badly again, I'd go to the cops. He knew I meant it. Though he still beat them from time to time. Never in a furor, like he did over the trains. No more sadistic punishments.

He likes to criticize them because they don't measure up to their sainted sister." She smiled, a twist of the lips that didn't register amusement. "Though I can assure you, Lieutenant, that Nancy was no more a saint than Bobby or Sam is."

"You haven't had it easy, Mrs. Smith."

"Perhaps not, but it's nothing I can't handle. So long as I can handle life, I'm okay."

He ate the cakes. "Superb," he said with a sigh. "Tell me about Walter Polonowski and his wife."

"They got themselves hopelessly tangled in a religious net," Eliza said, shaking her head as if at incredible denseness. "She thought he'd disapprove of birth control, he thought she'd never consent to birth control. So they had four kids when neither of them really wanted any, especially before their marriage was old enough to let them get to know each other. Adjusting to life with a stranger is hard, but a lot harder when that stranger changes in front of your eyes within scant months—throws up, swells up, complains, the works. Paola is many years younger than Walt—oh, she was *such* a pretty girl! Very much like Marian, his new one. When Paola found out about Marian, she should have buttoned her lip and kept Walt on as a meal ticket. Instead, she'll be raising four kids on alimony peanuts, because she sure can't work. Walt is not about to give her a cent more than he has to, so he's going to sell the house. Since it's encumbered by a mortgage, Paola's share will be more peanuts. Adding to Walt's troubles is Marian, who is pregnant. That means Walt will have two families to support. He'll have to go into private practice, which is a genuine pity. He does really good research."

"You're a pragmatist, Mrs. Smith."

"Someone in the family has to be."

"I've heard a rumor from several people," he said slowly, not looking at her, "that the Hug will cease to exist, at least in its present incarnation."

"I'm sure the rumors are true, which will make the decisions easier for some Huggers. Walt Polonowski, for one. Maurie Finch for another. Between Schiller's attempted suicide and finding that poor little girl's body, Maurie Finch is another broken man. Not in the same way as Bob, but broken all the same." She sighed. "However, the one I feel sorriest for is Chuck Ponsonby."

"Why?" he asked, startled at this novel view of Ponsonby, the man he had simply assumed would be the Prof's heir. No matter how the Hug changed, Ponsonby would surely survive the best among them.

"Chuck is not a brilliant researcher," Eliza Smith said in a carefully neutral voice. "Bob has been carrying him ever since the Hug opened. It's Bob's mind directs Chuck's work, and both of them are aware of it. A conspiracy between them. Apart from me, I don't think anyone else has the slightest idea."

"Why should the Professor do that, Mrs. Smith?"

"Old ties, Lieutenant—extremely old ties. We come from the same Yankee stock, the Ponsonbys, the Smiths and the Courtenays—my family. The friendships go back generations, and Bob watched quirks of fate destroy the Ponsonbys—well, so did I."

"Quirks of fate?"

"Len Ponsonby—Chuck's and Claire's father—was enormously rich, just like his forebears. Ida, their mother, came from a moneyed Ohio family. Then Len Ponsonby was murdered. It must have been 1930, and not long after the Wall Street crash. He was beaten to death outside the Holloman railroad station by a gang of itinerants who went on a rampage. They beat two other people to death as well. Oh, it was blamed on the Depression, on bootleg booze, you name it! No one was ever caught. But Len's money had vanished in the big crash, which left poor Ida virtually penniless. She funded herself by selling the Ponsonby land. A brave woman!"

"How did you come to know Chuck and Claire in particular?" Carmine asked, fascinated at what could lie behind public façades.

"We all went to the Dormer Day School together. Chuck and Bob were four classes ahead of Claire and me."

"*Claire?* But she's blind!"

"That happened when she was fourteen. Nineteen thirty-nine,

just after the war broke out in Europe. Her sight had always been poor, but then she suffered retinal detachments in both eyes simultaneously from retinitis pigmentosa. She literally went totally blind overnight. Oh, it was a terrible business! As if that poor woman and her three children hadn't gone through enough already!"

"*Three* children?"

"Yes, the two boys and Claire. Chuck's the eldest, then came Morton, and finally Claire. Morton was demented, never spoke or seemed to realize that other people lived in the world. His light didn't go out, Lieutenant. It was never switched on. And he had fits of violence. Bob says that these days they'd diagnose him as autistic. So Morton never went to school."

"Did you ever see him?"

"Occasionally, though Ida Ponsonby was afraid he'd fly into one of his rages and used to shut him up if we came over to play. Mostly we didn't. Chuck and Claire came to Bob's or my house."

Mind reeling, Carmine sat battling to maintain his calm, to keep the strands of this incredible story separated as they must be—a demented brother! Why hadn't he picked up that there was something wrong in the Ponsonby ménage? Because on the surface there was nothing wrong, nothing wrong at all! Yet the moment that Eliza Smith said three children, he *knew*. It began to fall into place. Chuck at the Hug, and mad brother somewhere else . . . Aware that Eliza Smith was staring at him, Carmine forced himself to ask a reasonable question.

"What does Morton look like? Where is Morton now?"

"Looked like, was, Lieutenant. Past tense. It all happened at once, though I guess there was a little time in between. Days, a week. Claire went blind, and Ida Ponsonby sent her to a blind school in Cleveland, where Ida still had family. Somehow there was a link to the blind school there—an endowment, I think. It was difficult to get into a blind school back then. Anyway, no sooner had Claire gone to Cleveland than Morton died, I think of a brain hemorrhage. We went to the funeral, of course. The things they inflicted on children in those days! We had to tiptoe up to the open casket and lean in to kiss Morton's cheek. It felt clammy and greasy"—she shuddered—"and it was the first time in my life that I smelled death. Poor little guy, at rest at last. What did he look like? Chuck and Claire. He's buried in the family plots at the old Valley cemetery."

Carmine sat with his hypothesis demolished to ruins. No way in a fit Eliza Smith was making any of this up. The Ponsonby tale was true, and all it amounted to was a well-attested fact: that some families, for no reason that made sense, suffered whole strings of disasters. Not accident prone: tragedy prone.

"Sounds as if there's a weakness in the family," he said.

"Oh, yes. Bob saw that in medical school, as soon as he'd done genetics. Madness and blindness ran in Ida's family, but not in the Ponsonbys. Ida went crazy too, a little later on. I think the last time I ever saw her was at Morton's funeral. With Claire in Cleveland, I didn't visit the Ponsonby house anymore."

"When did Claire come home?"

"When Ida went completely mad—not long after Pearl Harbor. Chuck and Bob were never drafted, they spent the war years in premed and medical school. Claire had been in Ohio for two years—long enough to learn Braille and find her way around with a white stick the way blind people do. She was one of the first ever to have a guide dog. Biddy's her fourth."

Carmine got to his feet, devastated by the magnitude of his disappointment. For one moment he had genuinely thought it was all over; that he had done the impossible and found the Ghosts. Only to discover that he was as far from the answer as ever.

"Thanks for filling me in so well, Mrs. Smith. Is there any other Hugger you think I should know about? Tamara?" He took a breath. "Desdemona?"

"They aren't murderers, Lieutenant, any more than Chuck and Walt are. Tamara is one of those unfortunate women who can't pick a good man, and Desdemona"—she laughed—"is British."

"British says it all about her, huh?"

"To me it does. When she was a kid, they starched her."

He left Eliza at her front door and plodded back to the Ford.

However, there was one thing he could do, should do: see Claire Ponsonby and find out why she'd lied to him about the date of her blindness. And maybe too he just wanted to *see* her—look at the face of a living, breathing tragedy. Father and the family fortune lost when she was five, sight when she was fourteen, all her freedom when, at sixteen, she had to come home to care for a demented mother. A job that lasted about twenty-one years. Yet he had never felt the slightest vibration of self-pity emanate from her. Some woman, Claire Ponsonby. Only why had she lied?

Biddy started barking the moment the Ford turned into the driveway of 6 Ponsonby Lane; Claire was at home then.

"Lieutenant Delmonico," she said in the open doorway, holding Biddy's collar.

"How did you know it was me?" he demanded, entering.

"The sound of your car. It must have a very powerful engine because it rumbles while it's idling. Come into the kitchen."

Through the house she went without as much as brushing a single item of furniture, into the over-warm room with the Aga stove.

Biddy lay down in the corner, eyes fixed on Carmine.

"She doesn't like me," he said.

"There are few people she does like. What can I do for you?"

"Tell me the truth. I've just been to see Mrs. Eliza Smith, who informed me that you weren't blind from birth. Why lie to me?"

Claire sighed, slapped her hands on her thighs. "Well, they say your sins will find you out. I lied because I so much loathe the questions that inevitably follow when I tell the truth. Such as, how did it feel after you couldn't see? Was it a heartbreak? Was it the most terrible thing that's ever happened to you? Is it harder to be blind after you've seen? And on, and on. Well, I can tell you that it felt like a death sentence, that my heart did break, that it is indeed the most terrible thing that has ever happened to me. You've just opened my wounds, Lieutenant, and I am bleeding. I hope you're satisfied." She turned her back.

"I'm sorry, but I had to ask."

"Yes, I can *see* that!" Suddenly she swung around, smiled at him. "My turn to apologize. Let's start again."

"Mrs. Smith also told me that you and Charles had a brother, Morton, who died suddenly, very close to the time you went blind."

"My, Eliza's tongue did wag this morning! You must be quite something to look at—she always had an eye for a handsome fella. Pardon my being catty, but Eliza got what she wanted. I didn't."

"I can pardon the cattiness, Miss Ponsonby."

"No more Claires?"

"I think I've hurt you too much to call you Claire."

"You were asking me about Morton. He died just after I was sent to Cleveland. They didn't bother to bring me home for the funeral, though I would have liked to say my goodbyes. He died so suddenly that it was a coroner's case, so there *was* time to bring me home before they released his body for burial. Despite his dementia, he was a sweet little guy. Sad, sad, sad . . ."

Get out of here, Carmine! You've outworn your welcome. "My thanks, Miss Ponsonby. Thanks a lot, and sorry to have upset you."

A coroner's case . . . That meant Morton Ponsonby's death would be on file at Caterby Street; he'd send a uniform to dig it out.

On the way back to Holloman he called in at the ancient burial ground in the Valley, a cemetery that had run out of plots for new-comers ninety years ago. It contained Ponsonby graves by the score, some of them older by far than the earliest picture on the Ponsonby kitchen wall. The newest memorial stone belonged to Ida Ponsonby, died in November of 1963. Before her, Morton Ponsonby, died in October of 1939. And before him, Leonard Ponsonby, died in January of 1930. A trio of tragedies that a grave archaeologist would never have known about from the bald, uninformative epitaphs. The Ponsonbys did not wear their sorrows on their sleeves. Any more than did the Smiths, he thought when he found Nancy's grave. Bald and spare, no reason for her death given.

What, he wondered, back in the car, would Chuck Ponsonby do without the Hug? And the Prof's research tips? Go into general practice? No, Charles Ponsonby didn't have the manner. Too aloof, too austere, too elitist. It might even be, thought Carmine, that no other medical job would be forthcoming for Chuck, and if that were so, then he could have no reason to destroy the Hug.

He walked into Patrick's office with a growl and flung himself sideways into the armchair that sat in one corner.

"How goes it?" asked Patrick.

"Don't ask. You know what I could do with right now, Patsy?"

"No, what?"

"A nice shoot-out in the Chubb Bowl parking lot, preferably with machine guns. Or a nice stroll into the middle of ten hoods holding up the Holloman First National. Something *refreshing.*"

"That's the remark of an inactive cop with a sore butt."

"You're darned right it is! This is a talking case, endless talking, talking, talking. No shoot-outs, no robberies."

"I take it nothing came out of the sketch Jill Menzies made from the Tinker Bell woman's description?"

"Not a thing." Carmine straightened, looked alert. "Patsy, at ten years longer on this troubled earth than me, do you recall a murder at the railroad station in 1930? Three people were beaten to death by a gang of hoboes or something like that. I ask because one of them was the father of Charles and Claire Ponsonby. As if that wasn't enough, he turned out to have lost all the family's money in the stock market crash."

Patrick thought deeply, then shook his head. "No, I don't remember it—my mother censored everything I heard when I was a kid. But there'll be a case report on it buried in the archives. You know Silvestri—he wouldn't throw out a used Kleenex, and his predecessors were just as bad."

"I was going to send someone out to Caterby Street to pick up yet another case file, but, since I have nothing better to do, I might wander out that way and have a look myself. I'm curious about the Ponsonby tragedies. Could they be Ghost victims too?"

Only a little more than a week to go before the Ghosts struck again; February was a short month, so maybe the date set for their next abduction was early in March. Possessed by a creeping dread, Carmine would have driven to Maine at this time of year to look at some unpromising archival lead, but Caterby Street was much closer than Maine. Paper storage was every public servant's nightmare, be it police records, medical records, pension records, land rates and taxes, water rates, any of a hundred different categories. When the Holloman Hospital was rebuilt in 1950, a whole subbasement was reserved for archives, so they weren't hurting. Commissioner by 1960, John Silvestri had fought fiercely to keep every scrap of paper the police had, going back to when Holloman had owned one constable and the theft of a horse was a hanging offense. Then a local concrete firm went bankrupt, and Silvestri hounded all of officialdom for the money and authority to buy the premises, three acres on Caterby Street, an area of industries famous for dirt and racket, therefore not prime property. The three acres and their contents went for $12,000 at auction, the Holloman Police the successful bidders.

On the land sat a vast warehouse in which the concrete firm had kept its trucks and spares, equipment of all kinds. And once the dust had been scoured out and the rest of the lot tidied up, all the police archives had been placed in the warehouse on steel-framed shelves. The roof didn't leak—a main consideration—and two big attic fans, one at either end, meant sufficient air circulation to keep mildew down in summer.

The two archivists lived a comfortable life in an insulated trailer parked alongside the warehouse entrance; the peon half ran a broom over the warehouse floor occasionally and took trips to a nearby deli for coffee and edibles, while the qualified half did a Ph.D. thesis on the development of criminal trends in Holloman since 1650. Neither half was in the least interested in this Lieutenant weird enough to come to Caterby Street in person. The qualified half simply told him whereabouts to look and went back to her thesis, and the peon vanished in a police pickup.

The records of 1930 occupied nineteen large boxes, whereas the coroner's records of 1939 ran to almost that many: crime had increased greatly during the nine-year gap. Carmine dug out the case of Morton Ponsonby in October of 1939, then looked in the first of 1930's boxes for Leonard Ponsonby. The format of a record hadn't changed much between then and now. Just sheets of legal-sized paper enclosed by a manila file folder, some sheets stapled together, others floating free. In 1930 they hadn't owned a system that kept the sheets bound to the folder—nor, probably, an office staff to deal with files once they were closed and moved out of the "current" drawers.

But there it was, where it was supposed to be: PONSONBY, Leonard Sinclaire, businessman, 6 Ponsonby Lane, Holloman, Conn. Aged 35. Married, three children.

Someone had placed a table and an office chair under a clear plastic skylight; Carmine carried the two Ponsonby files to it, and one thin, unnamed file that contained the details of the two other murders at the railroad station.

He looked at Morton Ponsonby's record first. Because the death had been so sudden and unexpected, the Ponsonby's doctor had declined to sign a death certificate. There was nothing in this to suggest the man suspected foul play; simply, he wanted an autopsy done to see if he had missed anything during the years when Morton Ponsonby had been almost impossible to approach, let alone treat. A typical pathology report that started off with the hackneyed phrase of the time: "This is the body of a well-nourished and ostensibly healthy male adolescent." But the cause of death had not been a brain hemorrhage, as Eliza Smith had said. The autopsy did not reveal the cause of death, which meant that the pathologist wrote it off as due to heart failure, possibly consequent on vagal inhibition. The guy wasn't in Patsy's league, but he did run the full gamut of tests for poisons without finding any, and he noted the presence of psychosis in the medical history. No changes in the brain were present to indicate cause of the psychosis. The boy's penis, he noted, was uncircumcised and very large, whereas the testes were only partially descended. For 1939, a thorough job. Carmine was left with no doubts that Morton Ponsonby was no more and no less than a hapless victim of the family's tendency to tragedy. Or maybe what it really said was that Ida Ponsonby's genetic contribution to her offspring was unsatisfactory.

Right, on to Leonard Ponsonby. The crime happened halfway through January of 1930, in the midst of two feet of snow—one of the colder winters, to produce January blizzards. The train, which had originated in Washington, D.C., had come in from Penn Station in New York City, running two hours late due to frozen points and a snow slide off a steep bank onto the line. Rather than sit inside and perish, the passengers had elected to dig the line free of snow. One car had held about twenty drunks in a group, jobless men hoping for work in Boston, the train's ultimate destination; they had been the most reluctant shovelers, boozed up, angry, aggressive, working only to keep warm. When the train reached Holloman it stopped for a quarter-hour, enabling the through passengers to buy snacks from the station café, a cheaper alternative than the train's under-patronized dining car.

Ah, here was the most interesting news! Leonard Ponsonby was not disembarking! He was boarding the train to travel to Boston, for so said his ticket. He'd chosen to wait outside in the cold, and, according to one observant passenger, he appeared furtive. *Furtive?* Ponsonby had shown no inclination to display himself in the warmth of the station waiting room, nor did he climb aboard as soon as the train pulled in. No, he stayed outside in the snow.

The time was 9 P.M., and this Boston train was the last one for the day. It steamed off on its journey while the station staff made the rounds to lock the waiting rooms, ladies' room and toilets against the army of vagabonds tramping the nation in search of work or hand-outs, though the twenty-odd drunks had not left the train in Hollo-man. Somewhere between Hartford and the Massachusetts border they jumped off into the night, which was why they had come under suspicion and why, after fruitless inquiries, they had ended in bear-ing the blame.

Leonard Ponsonby was lying in the snow with his head beaten to a pulp; near him lay a woman and a female child, their heads also reduced to pulp. Ponsonby's wallet contents identified him, but the woman and child carried nothing to say who they were. Her old, cheap pocketbook held one dollar and ninety cents in coins, an unironed handkerchief and two cookies. A carpetbag contained clean but very cheap underwear for a woman and a girl child, socks, stockings, two scarves and a little girl's dress. The woman was quite young, the child about six. Ponsonby was described as well dressed and prosperous, with $2,000 in notes in his wallet, a diamond stick-pin in his tie, and four valuable diamonds in each of his platinum cuff links. Whereas the woman and child had been summed up in one powerfully suggestive word: "breadline."

To Carmine's sensitive nose, three weird murders. One man, prosperous, on his own, plus a breadline woman and child not con-nected to him. Robbery not a motive. All three skulking outside in the snow when they should have been inside warming their hands on a steam radiator. Of one thing he was sure: the gang from the train had had nothing to do with these murders.

The real question was, which one was the intended victim? The other two were mere witnesses, killed because they had seen the wielder of the blunt instrument that had done for all three with a degree of savagery commented upon in the otherwise tersely sloppy police report. Heads, the intended victim was Leonard Ponsonby. Tails, it was the woman. If the coin stood on its edge, then it was the little girl.

There were no photographs whatsoever. The information about the woman and her presumed daughter or relative of some kind was contained in their slender file next to Ponsonby's thicker one in the January Box 2 archives. All three had died a blunt-instrument death confined to their skulls, mashed to pulp, but the detective hadn't been smart enough to see that Ponsonby had to have been the first victim; the woman and child looked on, paralyzed with fear, until the woman's turn came, and then the child's. Had Ponsonby not been first, he would have put up a fight. So whoever had held the blunt instrument—Carmine's experienced money was on a baseball bat—had crept up through the snow and struck Ponsonby before he noticed anyone approaching. Another ghost, how extraordinary.

When he went outside to see the archivists, they had locked up their trailer and gone for the day—half an hour early. Time, John Silvestri, to turn the blinding beam of your duty supervisors upon Police Archives at Caterby Street. The three files in his left hand, Carmine departed too: those cockroaches would not discover any missing files until he chose to return them. A pair of cool little bureaucratic crooks, secure in the knowledge that, provided the records didn't burn, no one would be interested enough in their existence to worry about them. Wrong, wrong, wrong.

On his way back to the County Services building he called in to the *Holloman Post* morgue, to find that Leonard Ponsonby's odd and horrible death had made the front page. Mindless violence outside of domestic crime was almost unheard of in 1930; it was the kind of thing had newspapers screaming about escaped lunatics. Of gangland killings there were plenty during the long years of Prohibition, but they didn't fall into the category of mindless violence. Indeed, even after it was established that no lunatic had escaped from an asylum, the *Holloman Post* stuck to its guns and insisted that the killer was an escaped lunatic from somewhere out of the state.

What with one thing and another, he was late meeting Desdemona in Malvolio's.

"Sorry," he said, sliding into the booth opposite her. "You now have a preview of what life is like when your boyfriend is a cop. Scads of missed appointments, a lot of dinners gone cold. I'm glad you're not a cook. Eating out is the best alternative, and nowhere better than Malvolio's, a cop diner. They'll doggy-bag anything from a whole meal to one spoonfull of apple pie the minute someone raps on the window."

"I quite like a cop boyfriend," she said, smiling. "I've ordered, but asked Luigi to hold off for a while. You're far too generous, never letting me pay at least my share of the bill."

"In my family, a man who let a woman pay would be lynched."

"You look as if you've had rather a good day for a change."

"Yes, I found out bunches of things. Trouble is, I think that they're all red herrings. Still, it's fun finding out." He reached across the table to take her hand, turned it over. "It's fun finding out about you too."

She squeezed his fingers. "Ditto, Carmine."

"In spite of this terrible case, Desdemona, my life has improved over the last days. You're a part of it, lovely lady."

No one had ever called her a lovely lady before; she felt a rush of confused gratification flood through her, went a bright red, didn't know where to look.

Six years ago in Lincoln she had thought herself in love with a wonderful man, a doctor; until, passing his door, she heard his voice through it.

"Who, Desperate Desdemona? My dear chap, the ugly ones are always so grateful that they're well worth wooing. They make good mothers, and one never has to worry about the milkman, does one? After all, one doesn't gaze at the mantelpiece while one is poking the fire, so I shall marry Desdemona. Our children will be clever into the bargain. Also tall."

She had started making plans to emigrate the very next day, vowing to herself that she would never again lay herself open to that kind of pragmatic cruelty.

Now, thanks to a faceless monster, here she was living with Carmine in his apartment and perhaps taking it for granted that he loved her the way she loved him. Words were cheap—hadn't the Lincoln doctor proved that? How much of what he had said to her originated in his job, his protectiveness, his shock at what had almost happened to her? Oh, please, Carmine, don't let me down!

CHAPTER 25

Friday, February 25th, 1966

Day Thirty since Faith Khouri's abduction would arrive in one week's time, and no one, including Carmine, had reason to believe that they stood a better chance now to prevent another murder than they had four months ago. When had any other case gone on so long in the face of so much manpower, so many precautions, warnings, such statewide publicity?

They had agreed that the general procedure would be the same: every suspect in the state would be placed under round-the-clock surveillance from Monday, February twenty-eighth, until Friday, March fourth. That encompassed the thirty-two Holloman suspects. Their act had become tighter, more seamless; in the case of Professor Bob Smith, for instance, Marsh Manor's deplorable security would be offset by four teams of watchers from the Bridgeport police. Unless he targeted a victim in Bridgeport, the Prof would have to swim the Housatonic River if he headed east, or evade six roadblocks if he headed west. That represented the greatest difference between last month's plan and this new one: squad cars and uniforms as well as plain clothes and unmarkeds, and roadblocks everywhere. They had agreed at a statewide meeting that if the Ghosts were caught at a roadblock before they had a chance to abduct, then so be it. Any known suspect in a roadblock situation meant a large red mark in the record and concentrated surveillance. If that meant February/March was a bust for the Ghosts, then March/April would see new police methods and possible suspects.

Carmine himself had decided not to man a watch; it wasn't likely that the beginning of March would see zero Fahrenheit temperatures, so he was better off somewhere in clear radio contact with everyone else, and with a gigantic map of Connecticut pinned to a wall at his elbow. Two consecutive Ghost strikes in the far east suggested that this time the Ghosts would head north or west or southwest. The Massachusetts, New York and Rhode Island state police had agreed to patrol their Connecticut borders thicker than flies on a carcass. It was war to the teeth.

Thinking more of an evening with Desdemona than about a case grown so stale it was wearisome, late that afternoon Carmine took the Ponsonby case files back to Caterby Street.

"Do you still have unclaimed personal property going back to 1930?" he asked the Ph.D. half of the archive duo; the peon half was nowhere to be seen. Nor was the police pickup. And damn, he hadn't remembered to tell Silvestri what was going on out here.

"We should have personal property going back to Paul Revere's hat," she said sarcastically, not amused that he had filched her files, nor worried at her own absence last Monday.

"These two murder victims," he said, waving the very thin and unnamed file under her nose. "I want to see their personal effects."

She yawned, examined her nails, glanced at the clock. "I'm afraid you've left your run too late, Lieutenant. It's five and the place is closed for the day. Come back tomorrow, we're open."

Tomorrow Silvestri was going to have the whole tale, but why not give the bitch a sleepless night before the axe fell? "Then I suggest," he said pleasantly, "that first thing in the morning you get your peon to use his pickup legally by delivering the box of personal effects to Lieutenant Carmine Delmonico at the County Services building. If the requested box isn't delivered, my niece Gina will wind up sitting at your desk. She's eager for a county job in an out-of-the-way corner because she needs to study. She wants to join the FBI, but it's one helluva hard entrance exam for a woman."

CHAPTER 26

At 11 A.M. on the Sunday before surveillance was due to begin Carmine walked into the police part of the County Services building feeling lonely, restless and tense.

Lonely because last Friday night Desdemona had announced that if the weekend was anything like bearable, she was hiking the Appalachian Trail right up on the Massachusetts border. Since he loved her presence in his bed, this took him aback; nor would she listen to his protests about wasting a squad car getting her there and back again. It worried him that his expectations from this relationship were so different from those he had felt with Sandra. Albeit incongruous in both roles, she had been wife and mother, tucked into a special compartment he never bothered to open while he was on the job. Whereas Desdemona hovered somewhere in his mind all the time, and it had nothing to do with the part she played in his case. Simply, he actively looked forward to his time with her. Maybe it was an age thing: still in his twenties when he had met Sandra, into his early forties when he met Desdemona. As a parent he hadn't worked out too well, but as a husband he had been far worse. Yet he knew that the answer for Desdemona wasn't as lover. Marriage, it had to be marriage. Only did she want marriage? He plain didn't know. Hiking the Appalachian Trail seemed to argue that her need of him wasn't in the same league as his of her. Yet she was so *loving* when they were together, and she hadn't at any time reproached him for neglecting her in favor of his work. Oh, Desdemona, don't let me down! Stay with me, cleave to me!

Restless because Desdemona's desertion had left him with two days to fill in and no one to fill them in with; Silvestri had forbidden him to poke his nose into any case other than the Ghosts, with the single exception of the racial situation if it exploded. And now, with a reasonably fine, above-freezing Sunday, was Mohammed el Nesr busy? Not busy demonstrating or rallying, at any rate. His quiescence was no mystery. Like Carmine, Mohammed was waiting for the Ghosts to abduct another victim this week, freshen up pain and indignation. The big rally would go on next Sunday, for sure. Taking desperately needed cops away from the Ghosts. A pain in the ass, but good strategy on Mohammed's part.

Tense because Day Thirty was almost upon him.

"Lieutenant Delmonico?" asked the desk sergeant.

"That was me when I last looked," Carmine said with a grin.

"I found an antique evidence box stuck behind those packages when I came in this morning. No name on it, which I guess is why you never got it. Then I found a tag with your name on it yards away." He bent down, fumbled under his counter and came up with a big, square box that looked not unlike those in current use.

The belongings of the woman and child beaten to death in 1930! He'd forgotten all about them, so absorbed in surveillance planning had he become. Though he had remembered to ask Silvestri to light a fire under the archives bitch and her peon.

"Thanks, Larry, I owe you one," he said, picked up the box and took it to his office.

Something to do with a Sunday morning if your beloved is on a route march through wet leaves.

No fetid relics of a crime thirty-six years old puffed out of it when he pulled the lid off; they hadn't bothered keeping the clothes the pair were wearing, which meant there must have been blood all over them, including footwear. Since no one had thought to record the exact distance of "near" Leonard Ponsonby, for all that Carmine knew some of the blood might have been his. No one had even drawn a sketch to show how the bodies had lain in relation to each other. "Near" was as much as he had to go on.

The pocketbook was there, however. By habit he had donned gloves to remove it gingerly so he could examine it with his more sophisticated eyes. Homemade. Knitted, as women did in those days of no money, with two cane handles and a lining of coarse cotton fabric. No clasp. This woman couldn't afford even the cheapest cowhide, let alone leather. The pocketbook contained a tiny purse in which sat a silver dollar, three quarters, one dime and one nickel. Carmine put the money purse on his desk. A man's handkerchief, clean but not ironed; calico, not linen. And, in the bottom, fragments and crumbs of what he presumed were the two cookies. The mother had probably stolen them from the station café so the child would have something to eat on the train, and that might be why they were hiding out in the snow. The autopsies had said both stomachs were empty. Yes, she'd stolen the cookies.

The carpetbag wasn't a large one, though it was old enough to have been one of those the northern predators had carried south with them after the Civil War. Faded, balding in places, never elegant even when new. He opened it with gentle reverence; in here resided almost everything that poor woman had owned, and no thing was more touching than the mute evidence of lives long over.

On top were two long woollen scarves, hand knitted in varicolored stripes, as if the knitter had scrounged for scraps. But why were the scarves in the bag when the weather was so awful? Spares?

Under them were two pairs of clean women's panties made of unbleached muslin, and two much smaller pairs that obviously belonged to the child. A pair of knitted kneesocks and a pair of knitted stockings. On the bottom, carefully folded between torn tissue paper, a little girl's dress.

Carmine stopped breathing. A little girl's dress. Made of pale blue French lace exquisitely embroidered with seed pearls. Puffed sleeves on dainty cuffs, pearl-studded buttons up the back, silk lining, and beneath that, stiffened net gathered to hold the skirt out like a ballerina's tutu. A 1930 precursor of a Tinker Bell, except that this one had been completely handmade, every pearl sewn on separately and firmly, none of the stitching done by machine. Oh, the things the 1930 cops had missed! On the left breast the word EMMA had been picked out in dark, purplish pearls.

Head whirling, Carmine laid the dress on his desk and then stood just staring at it for what might have been five minutes or an hour; he didn't know, hadn't looked at his watch or the clock.

Finally he sat down and put the carpetbag on his lap, opening it as widely as its rusting jaws would allow. The lining was worn, had come apart on one side seam; he put both hands inside the bag and felt around, eyes closed. There! Something!

A photograph, and not taken on a box Brownie. This was a studio portrait still mounted in a cream cardboard folder stamped with the name of the photographer. *Mayhew Studios, Windsor Locks.* Someone had written what looked like "1928" on the frame below, but in pencil now so faint it was a best guess.

The woman was seated on a chair, the child—about four years old—seated on her knees. In this, the woman was much better clad, wore a string of real pearls around her neck and real pearls in her earlobes. The little girl wore a dress similar to the one in the carpeting, EMMA showing up clearly. And both of them had the face. Even in black-and-white their skins had a suggestion of café au lait; their hair was densely black and curly, their eyes very dark, their lips full. To Carmine, gazing at them through a wall of tears, they were exquisite.

Destroyed in all their youth and beauty, every vestige of it bloodied to pulp.

A crime of passion. Why had no one seen that? No killer would waste his essence on a torrent of blows were hate not the motive. Especially when the skull under the bludgeon belonged to a little girl. There's no way these two female creatures weren't connected to Leonard Ponsonby. They were there because he was there, he was there because they were there.

So it's Charles Ponsonby after all. Though he wasn't old enough to do this. Nor Morton, nor Claire. This was mad Ida a decade and more before she went mad. Which means that Leonard and Emma's mother were—lovers? Relatives? One was as likely as the other; Ida was ultra-conservative, no touch of the tar brush for *her*. So many questions to ask! Why were Emma and her mother so destitute in January of 1930 when Leonard was with them carrying $2,000 and flaunting diamond jewelry? What had happened to Emma and her mother between the prosperity of the 1928 Windsor Locks photo and their impoverishment of January 1930?

Enough, Carmine, enough! Nineteen thirty can wait, 1966 cannot. Chuck Ponsonby is a Ghost—or is he *the* Ghost, doing all of it alone? How much help does Claire give him? How much help is she capable of giving him? Can one Ponsonby be a Ghost and the other not? Yes, because of Claire's blindness. I *know* she's blind! Chuck could move around in some secret, soundproof basement and she'd never know. I'm positive it's soundproof. The screams have to be kept in, and the screams are very loud.

Charles Ponsonby . . . A bachelor stay-at-home who couldn't produce original research to save his life. Always in someone else's shadow—mad mother's, mad brother's, blind sister's, far more successful best friend's. Doesn't bother matching his socks, keeping his hair combed, buying a new tweed jacket. An archetypal absentminded professor, too timid to pick up a rat without wearing a furnace glove, nondescript in that way which suggests a radical failure in ego, despite the veneer of intellectual snobbishness.

But can this Charles Ponsonby be the portrait of a multiple rapist/murderer so brilliant that he's run rings around us ever since we discovered that he existed? Seems impossible to believe. The trouble is that no one has a portrait of the multiple murderer except that sex always seems involved. Therefore every time we unearth a specimen, we have to dissect him minutely. His age, his race, his creed, his appearance, the victim type he chooses, the personality he presents to the world, his childhood, background, likes and dislikes— a thousand thousand factors. About Charles Ponsonby we can certainly say that on his mother's side there is a family history of madness as well as blindness.

Carmine replaced the contents of the evidence box exactly as he had found them and took it down to the desk.

"Larry, put this in security storage right now," he said as he handed it over. *"No one* is to go near it."

Then before Larry could reply, Carmine was out the door. It was time to take another look at 6 Ponsonby Lane.

The questions milled in his head, swarming wasps in search of the nest called answers: how, for instance, had Charles Ponsonby managed to get from the Hug to Travis High and back again while convincing everyone that he had been in conference on the roof? Thirty precious minutes before Desdemona found him and the others there, yet all six on the roof swore that no one was absent long enough to go to the john. How reliable was the attention span of an absentminded researcher? And how had Ponsonby gotten out of his house on the night Faith Khouri was snatched when it had been so closely watched? Did the contents of the 1930 evidence box represent enough hard evidence to wring a search warrant out of Judge Douglas Thwaites? The questions swarmed.

He came down Route 133 from the northeast, which brought him to Deer Lane first. In the Council's view, the four houses on its far side had not warranted tar seal; Deer Lane's 500 yards were trap-rock gravel. At its end it flared into a circular patch that gave suf-ficient parking for six or seven cars. On all sides the forest came down to the road—secondary growth, of course. Two hundred years ago this would have been cleared and farmed, but as the more fertile soils of Ohio and westward beckoned, farming had ceased to be as profitable for Connecticut Yankees as the assembly line precision industries Eli Whitney had started. So the woods had grown back in profusion—oak, maple, beech, birch, sycamore, a few pines. Dog-woods and mountain laurel to bloom in the spring. Wild apple trees. And the deer had come back too.

His tires crunched audibly over the gravel, which reinforced his opinion that the cars watching Deer Lane at its junction with 133 on the night Faith Khouri vanished would have heard a vehicle as well as seen the white vapor from its tailpipe. And the only cars parked on Deer Lane that night had been police unmarkeds. So while it was possible that Chuck Ponsonby had walked up the slope behind his house minus a flashlight, where would he have gone from there? He hadn't stored his vehicle any closer than some distance up 133, or if the vehicle belonged to a partner, it hadn't picked him up any closer than that. A walk that long at zero Fahrenheit? Unlikely. Freezers were warm by comparison. So how did he do it?

Carmine had a precept: if you are forced to take a stroll on a nice day, then do it near a suspect; and if the stroll involves a forest, take along a pair of binoculars to watch the birdies. Binoculars slung around his neck, Carmine walked up the slope among the trees in the direction of the spine that looked down on number 6 Ponsonby Lane. The ground was a foot deep in wet leaves, the snow melted except in the lee of an occasional boulder and in crannies where the warmth hadn't penetrated. Several deer moved out of his way as he walked, but not in alarm; animals always knew when they were on a reserve. It was, he reflected, a pretty place, peaceful at this time of year. In summer the whining buzz of lawn mowers and shrieks of laughter from cookouts would ruin it. He knew from previous police combing that no one ventured out of the car park, even for illicit sexual encounters; the twenty-acre reserve contained no beer cans, ring pulls, bottles, plastic detritus or used rubbers.

Once on top of the ridge it was surprisingly easy to see the Ponsonby house. The trees of their slope had been drastically thinned to make a woodsy statement: a clump of three-trunked American birches, one beautiful old elm tree looking healthy, ten maples clustered in such a way that their fall leaves would make a stunning display, and nursery specimens of dogwood that would turn the grounds into a pink-and-white dreamland in spring. The thinning must have been done a very long time ago, as the stumps of the removed trees had disappeared from sight.

Lifting his binoculars, he surveyed the house as if it were fifty feet from him. There was Chuck up a ladder with a chisel and a blowtorch, chipping at old paint the proper way. Claire was sprawled in a wooden outdoor chair near the laundry porch, Biddy at her feet; the scant breeze was kissing his face, so the dog hadn't scented his presence. Then Chuck called out. Claire got to her feet to walk around to the side of the house so unerringly that Carmine was amazed. Yet he *knew* that Claire was blind.

How did he know that so certainly? Because Carmine left no stone unturned, and Claire's blindness was a stone in his path. Sometimes he used the services of a women's prison warder, Carrie Tallboys, who struggled to support a promising son, therefore was available for hire outside working hours. Carrie had a curious talent that involved acting out a role so convincingly that people told her a great deal they ought not have. So Carmine had sent Carrie to see Claire's ophthalmologist, the eminent Carter Holt. Her story was that she was thinking of donating some money to retinitis pigmentosa, as her dear friend Claire Ponsonby suffered from it before she went completely blind. Ah, well he remembered the day Claire came in with bilateral retinal detachments—so rare, for both eyes to go at once! His first big case, and it had to be one that lay beyond his power to heal. But, protested Carrie, surely nowadays it could be cured? Definitely not, said Dr. Holt. Claire Ponsonby was irretrievably blind for life. He had looked into her eyes and seen the damage for himself. Sad!

Carmine watched blind Claire talk animatedly to Chuck, who came down his ladder, linked his arm through his sister's, and took her inside through the laundry porch. The dog followed them; then came the faint strains of a Brahms symphony. That was it: the Ponsonbys had had sufficient fresh air. Though—wait, wait! Oh, yes, sure. Chuck emerged, gathered up his tools and took them and the ladder to the garage before returning to the house. He did have an everything-in-its-place side to him, but obsession?

Letting the binoculars fall, Carmine turned to make the trip back to Deer Lane. It was more difficult going downhill through masses of slimy, decaying leaves; not even the deer had yet made paths, though by summer there would be many. Immersed in thoughts of Charles Ponsonby and his contradictions, Carmine started to hurry, on fire now to get back to his office and chew the puzzle over at leisure. Also chew some lunch at Malvolio's.

The next thing his feet went from under him, he was plunging forward, both hands outstretched to take the impact of his fall. Dead leaves went flying in wet, clotted clumps as he landed on his palms with a dull, hollow boom. He slid onward, scrabbling for a hold, before his momentum gradually slowed down and he could stop. Two ruts marked the progress of his hands, gouged deeply into the humus. Cursing softly, he rolled over and picked himself up, feeling the sting of abraded skin but relieved to discover that he hadn't done himself worse harm. Stupid, Carmine, stupid! Too busy thinking to watch where you're going, you dodo.

Only why a hollow sound? Curious because that was the kind of man he was, he crouched down and excavated one of the channels a palm had made; six inches deeper he uncovered a wooden plank. Digging frantically now, he pushed the leaves away until he could see a part of what was there: the surface of what might be an old cellar door.

Oh, Jesus, Jesus, Jesus! Suddenly galvanized, he was scraping the leaves back where they had been, pushing them down, packing them down, forehead dewed with sweat, breath grating. When he was fairly satisfied that he had evened out the evidence of his fall, he squirmed backward on his rump before standing again to survey his work. No, not good enough. If someone were to examine the area closely, they would notice. He took off his jacket and used it to gather more dead leaves from a hundred feet away, brought them back and distributed them, then threw the jacket down and used it like a broad broom to obscure every trace of his intrusion. Finally, gulping and gasping, he was positive that no one would suspect what had happened. Now get the hell out of here, Carmine! That he did on his knees, scattering leaves in his wake; he was almost to the parking lot before he rose. With any luck, deer would browse through in their constant search for winter forage.

Back in the Ford, he prayed that Claire's remarkable hearing didn't extend as far as a grunty engine on Deer Lane. He put his foot gently on the gas pedal and rumbled to the corner in first gear. Part of him was dying to transmit his news to Silvestri, Marciano and Patrick, but he decided not to call them from Major Minor's love retreat, doing a brisk Sunday business. Better to turn back into the northeast and depart the way he had come. It wouldn't kill him to wait.

Not such a long walk at zero Fahrenheit after all, Chuckie baby! And no need for a flashlight on the house side of the ridge, because you have a tunnel that doesn't surface until way down the reserve's slope. Someone—was it you, or long before you?—dug deep below the ridge, made the distance shorter. In Connecticut, hundreds of miles from the Mason-Dixon Line, it certainly wasn't dug for escaping slaves. My bet is that you dug it yourself, Chuckie baby. On the night that you snatched Faith Khouri all you had to do was get out; by the time you returned with her, we had left the neighborhood. That was *one* of our mistakes. We should have maintained the watch. Though, to be fair to us, we wouldn't have caught you returning; we were watching Ponsonby Lane and your house, we didn't know about the tunnel. So that time the luck was with you, Chuckie baby. But this time the luck is with us. We know about the tunnel.

Since he was ravenous and wanted a little more time to think, Carmine lunched at Malvolio's before summoning his cohorts.

"I now understand the full significance of an old cliché," he said as Patrick, the last to arrive, came through Silvestri's office door.

"Which old cliché is that?" Patrick asked, sitting down.

"Pregnant with news."

"Behold three expert midwives, so give birth."

His words crisp, his sequence of events logical and correct, Carmine led his audience step by step through the things that had happened after he saw Eliza Smith.

"It all sprang from her—what she said, how she said it. My catalyst. Culminating in a fall down a hillside—talk about luck! I have had so much luck on this case," he said when the tale was over and his audience had managed to close their jaws.

"No, not luck," Patrick objected, eyes shining. "Pigheaded, hard-assed determination, Carmine. Who else would have bothered to follow up on Leonard Ponsonby's death? And who else would have bothered to look in an evidence box thirty-six years old? Chasing up a crime marked unsolved because you're one of the very, very few people I can think of who know that when lightning strikes the same place twice, something is conducting it there."

"That's fine and dandy, Patsy, but it didn't amount to enough to take before Judge Thwaites. I found the real evidence by sheer accident—a fall on a slippery hillside."

"No, Carmine. The fall may have been an accident, but what you found was no accident. Anyone else would have gotten up, then brushed his clothes"—Patrick picked dead leaves off Carmine's ruined jacket—"and limped away. You found the door because your brain registered a wrong noise, not because the fall uncovered the door. It didn't. And anyway, you wouldn't have been on the hillside in the first place if you hadn't found our face in a picture taken about 1928. Come on, take *some* of the credit!"

"Okay, okay!" Carmine cried, throwing up his hands. "What's more important is to decide where we go from here."

The atmosphere in Silvestri's office almost visibly fizzed with elation, relief, the wonderful and inimitable joy that comes with the moment a case breaks open. Especially the Ghosts case, so dark, so haunting, so tediously long in the breaking. No matter what hitches were to come—they were too seasoned to believe that none would—they had enough of the answer to move forward, to feel that the end wasn't far away.

"First off, we can't assume that the legal system is on our side," Silvestri said through his cigar. "I don't want this shit getting off the hook on some technicality—especially a technicality his defense can pin on the police. Face it, we're the ones who usually wear the rotten eggs. This will be a big trial, coverage nationwide. That means Ponsonby's defense won't consist of two-bit shysters, even if he doesn't have much money. Every legal shit heap who knows Connecticut and federal law will be clawing to get on Ponsonby's defense team. And clawing to plaster us with rotten eggs. We can't afford a single error."

"What you're saying, John, is that if we get a warrant now and bust in through Ponsonby's tunnel, all we'll really have is something that looks like an operating room in a doctor's house," said Patrick. "Like Carmine, I've always believed that this turkey doesn't have a blood-soaked, filthy killing premises—he has an O.R. And if he's only one-half as careful about leaving traces in his O.R. as he is on his victims, we might come out of it with nothing. Is that the way your mind is going?"

"It is," said Silvestri.

"No mistakes," said Marciano. "Not one."

"And we've already made carloads of them" from Carmine.

A silence fell; the elation had died completely. Finally Marciano made an exasperated noise and burst into speech.

"If the rest of you won't, then I'll say it. We have to catch Ponsonby in the act. And if that's what we have to do, that's what we have to do."

"Oh, Danny, for God's sake!" Carmine cried. "Put another girl's life in jeopardy? Put her through the horrors of being abducted by that man? I won't do it! I refuse to do it!"

"She'll get a fright, yes, but she'll get over that. We know who he is, right? We know how he operates, right? So we stake him out—no need to stake anyone else out—"

"We can't do that, Danny," Silvestri butted in. "We have to stake everyone out the same as we did a month ago. Otherwise he will notice. Can't be done without a full stakeout."

"Okay, I concede that. But we know it's him, so we give him extra-special attention. When he moves, we're there. We follow him to his victim's home and we let him grab her before we grab him. Between the grabbing, the tunnel and the O.R., he can't possibly walk out of court a free man," said Marciano.

"It's circumstantial, is the problem," Silvestri grumbled. "Ponsonby has committed at least fourteen murders, but our body count is four. We know the first ten victims were incinerated, but how are we going to prove that? Do you read Ponsonby as the confessing type? I sure as hell do not. Since sixteen-year-old girls run away from home every day, there are ten murders we'll never convict him for. Everything rides on Mercedes, Francine, Margaretta and Faith, but nothing ties him to any of them beyond a supposition as frail as blown glass. Danny is right. Our only hope is to catch him in the act. Bust in there now, and he'll walk. His lawyers will be good enough to persuade a jury to let Hitler or Stalin walk."

They glared at each other, faces perplexed and angry.

"We have another problem," Carmine said. "Claire Ponsonby."

Commissioner Silvestri was not a profane man, but today—a Sunday too—he was breaking his own rules. "Shit! Piss!" he hissed. Then, in a bark, "Fuck!"

"How much do you think she knows, Carmine?" Patrick asked.

"I can't even guess, Patsy, and that's the truth. I do know that she's genuinely blind, her ophthalmologist says so. And he is Dr. Carter Holt, now Professor of Ophthalmology at Chubb. Yet I've never seen a more adept blind person than she is. If she's the bait dangled in front of a nunnish sixteen-year-old filled with the desire to do good, then she's an accomplice to rape and murder even if she never enters Ponsonby's O.R. What better bait than a blind woman? However, a blind woman is very noticeable, which is why I'm inclined to dismiss the theory. She'd be walking ground she doesn't know the way she knows Six Ponsonby Lane, so how fast could she move? How would she know her target unless Chuck is at her side? Oh, I've spent a lot of this morning wondering about Claire! I keep seeing her outside St. Martha's school in Norwalk—did you know that the sidewalk has been in bad shape for over a year due to council repairs to pipes? With two girls disappearing in the same place, *someone* would have noticed her. To me, Claire would have needed practice walks on a sidewalk mined with holes. I wound up concluding that Claire would be more a handicap to Chuck than an asset. I guess she could have watched the victim as he drove back to his lair, but that seems flimsy. Yet he must have had a sighted accomplice— who was the chauffeur, for instance?"

"You want to rule out Claire?" Silvestri asked.

"Not entirely, John. Just as an unlikely abduction helper."

"I agree she shouldn't be ruled out entirely," said Patrick, "but I can't believe she's capable of much help of any kind. That's not to say she doesn't know what her brother's been doing."

"There's a colossal bond between them. Now we know what their childhood was like, the bond makes more sense. Their mother murdered their father, I'd stake my life on it. Which means Ida Ponsonby was mentally unstable long before Claire came home to look after her. It must have been hell."

"Would the children have known of the murder, Carmine?"

"I have no idea, Patsy. How would Ida have gotten home in a blizzard in 1930? Presumably in Leonard's car, but did they plough the roads back then? I don't remember."

"The main ones, sure," said Silvestri.

"She must have had blood on her. Maybe the kids saw it."

"Speculations!" Marciano said with a snort. "Let's stick to the facts, guys."

"Danny's right as usual," said Silvestri, paying him back by putting the cigar butt under his nose. "We start watching people tomorrow night, so we'd better work out the changes now."

"The most important change," said Carmine, "is that Corey, Abe and I watch the tunnel entrance in the reserve."

"What about the dog?" Patrick asked.

"A complication. I doubt it would eat drugged meat, guide dogs are trained not to take food from strangers or off the ground. And as it's a spayed female, it won't stray looking for canine company. It hears us, it will bark. What I can't be sure of is that Chuck won't take Biddy with him to guard the tunnel door in his absence. If he does, the animal will smell us."

Patrick laughed. "Not if you're wearing eau de skunk!"

The rest of them reared back, appalled.

"Jesus, Patsy, no!"

"Well, Abe and Corey, at any rate," Patrick modified, looking devilish. "Even one of you would be enough."

"One of us *won't* be wearing eau de skunk, and that's me," Carmine said, scowling. "There must be another way."

"Not without tipping Ponsonby off. We can't kidnap the dog, that's for sure. This isn't some yokel with a half-baked plan, this is an M.D. who's been ahead of us every inch of the way. If the dog goes missing, he knows we're on to him, and that will be the end of his abductions," Patrick said. "The ace up his sleeve is his tunnel door in the reserve, and we have to make him think it's still his secret. He may be protecting it—trip wires, alarm bells or buzzers you step on like a land mine, a light up a tree—before you go near it, check it out, for God's sake. So sure, he'll be using the dog. How, I don't know, just that he will. If I were he, I'd slip a little Seconal in Claire's last drink for the evening."

"Patsy, you are so devious!" said Silvestri, grinning.

"Not in Carmine's league, John. Come on, everything I've said is logical."

"Yes, I know. But where do we find eau de skunk?"

"I have a whole bottle of it," Patrick said with a purr.

Carmine looked at Silvestri, menace in his face. "Then the Holloman police budget will have to include literal gallons of tomato juice. I can't ask Abe and Corey to dab eau de skunk behind their ears without offering them a bathtub full of tomato juice in the mornings." He frowned, looked frustrated. "Do we have a bathtub anywhere in the cells, or just showers?"

"There's a big iron tub in a room out the back in the old part of the building. Right about the time Leonard Ponsonby was clubbed to death, it was used to pacify lunatics before they got sent off with the men in white coats," said Marciano.

"Okay, have someone scrub the place out and disinfect it. Then I want that tub brimming with tomato juice, because I think Abe and Corey both have to wear it. If they're forced to split up, the dog won't smell the clean one."

"It's a deal," said Silvestri, his expression indicating that he deemed the meeting over.

"Whoa! We can't break up yet," said Carmine. "We still have to discuss possibilities. Like, is Ponsonby working alone, or does he have an accomplice we know nothing about? Assuming that Claire isn't involved, why suddenly do we dismiss the likelihood that there are two Ghosts? Ponsonby does have a life outside the Hug and his home. He's known to go to art exhibitions, even if that means he takes a day or two off work. From now on we tail him wherever he goes. Our best people, Danny, our very best. Smooth as silk, male and female—and no clumsy two-way radios. The new lapel mikes to switch personnel, so no relief tails are to get out of radio range—the devices are as weak as weasel piss. Our technical stuff is improving, but we could really use a Billy Ho and a Don Hunter. If the Hug does fold, John, it might be a good idea to bring them on board.

Attach them to Patsy's department, which maybe ought to incorporate the word 'forensics' in its name. And don't say it, John! *Find* the money, goddamn it!"

"If Morton Ponsonby were alive, we'd know the identity of the second Ghost," said Marciano.

"Danny, Morton Ponsonby is not alive," Carmine said patiently. "I've seen his grave, and I've also seen his autopsy report. No, he wasn't murdered, just dropped dead very suddenly. No poisons detected, though no real cause of death found."

"Mad Ida *might* have struck again."

"I doubt it, Danny. Apparently she was a little thing, and Morton Ponsonby was a healthy male adolescent. Hard to smother with a pillow. Besides, no fluff in the airway."

"Maybe there was a fourth child," Marciano persisted. "Ida mightn't have registered its birth."

"Oh, let's not get carried away!" Carmine cried, clawing at the air. "First off, with Leonard dead, who was to father this mysterious fourth child? Chuck? Get real, Danny! The presence of a kid gets known—these weren't newcomers to Ponsonby Lane, they *owned* Ponsonby Lane! Been in the district since shortly after the *Mayflower*. Look at Morton. Off the planet, but folks knew he existed. There were mourners at his funeral."

"So if there's a second Ghost, he's a stranger to us."

"At the moment, yes," said Carmine.

CHAPTER 27

Wednesday, March 2nd, 1966

Monday night and Tuesday night passed without incident, save for Abe's and Corey's perpetual cursing. To exist in a miasma of skunk was a torment amounting to torture, for no brain in creation had ever managed to do what brains normally did with smells, horrible or otherwise: blot them out after a little time had elapsed. Skunk stuck, skunk was the absolute olfactory pits. Only their affection for Carmine had persuaded them to consent, but once the skunk was applied, they rued it. Luckily the bathtub in the old section of the County Services building was large enough to fit two men in it at one time, otherwise a very old friendship might have soured.

The weather continued fine and above freezing; perfect for abductions. No rain, no wind.

Carmine had tried to think of every contingency. Besides Abe, Corey and himself concealed where they had an unobstructed view of the tunnel door, there were unmarkeds on each corner of Deer Lane, on each corner of Ponsonby Lane, one in front of Major

313

Minor's reception office, one in the spot where Carmine had hidden himself a month ago, and more on Route 133. These vehicles were for effect; Ponsonby would be expecting them because he must have seen the ones on Deer Lane a month ago. The real shadowers were concealed up the driveways of the four houses on Deer Lane. No car was already parked in them; Carmine surmised that the car Ponsonby used was definitely well down Route 133. Though it wasn't either of the cars in his garage, the station wagon and the red Mustang convertible; they had been there a month ago, and they were there now. Perhaps his accomplice provided the transportation? In which case, Ponsonby walked to a rendezvous.

"At least you get to wear nose plugs," Carmine comforted as the three crept up the slope, secure in the fact that Ponsonby was still driving home from the Hug. "I may not be wearing any eau de skunk, but I do have to smell the pair of you. Man, do you stink!"

"Mouth breathing isn't much help," Corey groused. "I can *taste* the fucking awful stuff! And I finally know why it drives dogs insane."

Falling back on the talents of the departmental bird watcher, Pete Evans, they had constructed a good hide twenty feet from the door without a tree trunk between it and them. All three lay flat, but able to take turns in rolling on their sides to prevent their muscles locking up; one man was sufficient to keep vigil provided that the other two were alert.

There had turned out to be no warning devices, even a trip wire; given his own tumble, Carmine had thought them unlikely. Ponsonby was positive his tunnel was his secret. His conceit on the subject was interesting, as if it lived in a different part of his psyche from Dr. Charles Ponsonby, researcher and bon vivant. In fact, Ponsonby was a mass of contradictions—afraid of picking up a rat, unafraid of police interception.

While Carmine waited out the boring hours, he pondered on the tunnel. Who had made it? How old was it? Despite cutting off the extra distance ascending and descending the ridge involved, it had to be at least three hundred yards long, maybe longer. Even if it was too small in bore to permit a man to do other than crawl down it on his belly, what had happened to the soil and small rocks taken out of it? Connecticut was a land of dry stone walls because its farmers had removed the stones from their fields as they ploughed. How many tons of soil and small rocks? One hundred? Two hundred? How was it ventilated, for ventilated it must be? Had those two old barns from upstate New York provided the timber for shoring up?

At 2 A.M. on that cloudy night came a faint noise, a groaning that gradually increased, then changed to the soft whine of well-lubricated hinges occluded by particles of dirt. Dryer than when Carmine had fallen, the covering of dead leaves cascaded to the far side as the door opened toward the three men in their hide. The shape that emerged from a black cavity was just as black; it poised, crouching, gave a tiny mew of disgust as a strong odor of skunk wafted its way. The dog's head popped up, then disappeared immediately. Biddy would not be doing guard duty tonight. They could hear Ponsonby coaxing the dog out, but no dog came. *Skunk.*

The arrangement was that Carmine would follow Ponsonby while Corey and Abe remained by the tunnel entrance; he waited with breath suspended as the shape straightened to a man's height, so dark that it was difficult to see amid the shadowy lightlessness of this moonless, starless night. What *is* he wearing? Carmine asked himself. Even the face was invisible. And when the shape began to move, it went silently, hardly a whisper of feet on the forest floor. Carmine too wore black, had blackened his face and put on sneakers, but he didn't dare approach the shape too nearly—twenty feet minimum, praying that Ponsonby's head covering made it harder for him to hear.

Ponsonby flitted off down the slope toward the circular end of Deer Lane. Just short of the parking area Ponsonby veered in the direction of Route 133, still concealed by the woods, which continued on this side all the way to 133. Now that the ground was more level, Carmine found his quarry actually harder to see; he was tempted to diverge the short distance to the road, on which he could make better progress, but Holloman Council's parsimony denied him this. Gravel.

The sweat was pouring off him, blinding him; he brushed it out of his eyes quickly, but when he looked to where the shape had been at the start of his gesture, it wasn't there. Not because Ponsonby had realized he was being followed, Carmine was sure. A quirk of fate. He had left his tunnel door open; the moment he thought he was followed, he would have returned to it, and in that direction he definitely hadn't gone. He was still heading for Route 133, lost in the darkness.

Carmine did the sensible thing, took to the gravel and ran as quietly as he could toward the humdrum Chrysler parked on Deer Lane's forested corner.

"He's out, but I lost him," he said to Marciano and Patrick after he climbed in and shut the back door gently. "Ghost is the right word for him. He's wearing black from head to foot, he makes no sound, and he must have better eyes than a night bird. He also must know every inch of this forest. There's nothing else for it now, we have to wait for him to come home with some poor, terrified girl. God, I didn't want it to go that far!"

"Do we get word out on the radio?" Marciano asked.

"No, since we have no idea what kind of vehicle he's using. He might have something sitting on his dashboard good enough to tune into every band we have. You wait here until I buzz you on my two-way that he's back at his tunnel, give me ten minutes, then you and the rest close in on the house. That's still best."

Carmine got out of the car and took to the trees, working his way back to the parking area and then up to the hide.

"I lost him, so now we wait."

"He can't be going far," Corey said low-voiced. "He's too late to get farther than Holloman County."

When Ponsonby returned around 5 A.M. he was a little easier to see; though the body slung around his shoulders was wrapped in black, it gave him more bulk, added noise to his footsteps. Instead of coming up from Deer Lane, he approached the gaping door from its side, dumped his cargo on the ground in front of the hole and insinuated himself into it before dragging the bundle down in his wake. The door closed, apparently worked by a lever, and the night went back to its usual foresty sounds.

Carmine's finger was actually on the call button of his two-way to send Marciano the signal when he heard something: he froze, nudged his companions to keep still and quiet. A figure breasted the ridge above and began the descent to the door, led by the panting, grizzling, reluctant dog, torn between its guiding duties and the unbearable stench of skunk. Claire Ponsonby. She carried a big bucket and a rake. Desperate to get away, Biddy kept whining and straining at its harness while she hung on to the loop, forced to work one-handed, trying to persuade the dog to stay. First she used the rake to cover the door with the leaves already heaped to one side, then she emptied her bucket of leaves on top of them and raked again. Finally she gave up fighting the dog, shrugged and turned to let Biddy lead her up the incline.

"What do we do now?" Abe asked when the sound of her progress had died away completely.

"We give her time to get back to the house, then we call out the troops as planned."

"How did she know where to bury the evidence?" Corey asked.

"Let's find out," said Carmine, standing up and walking to the camouflaged door. "That, I think." His foot lifted a piece of plumber's pipe, apparently painted a mottled brown, though it was hard to tell in the absence of light. "The dog knows the way to the door, but it can't tell her when she's reached it. When she feels the pipe she knows she's at the top edge of the door. After that, easy. Or it would have been on other occasions. Tonight she had a spooked dog to deal with, and you could see that it really threw her off."

"So she's the second Ghost," Abe said.

"Looks like it." Carmine pressed the button on his two-way.

"Okay, are we ready for the trip to hell? We have nine minutes before Marciano moves."

"I hate to undo all Claire's good work," Corey said with a grin, scraping leaves aside.

The tunnel was large enough to crawl on hands and knees, and was square; easier, Carmine supposed, to shore up with the planks that covered walls and ceiling. About every fifteen feet was a small ventilator shaft that appeared to be made from four-inch piping. No doubt the pipe barely poked above the ground, had a grating, and wasn't uncovered until the moment came to use the tunnel. Tread on a pipe outlet, and you wouldn't even know you had. Oh, the time! The effort! This was the work of many years. Dug by hand, shored up by hand, the rocks and soil hauled away by hand. In his relatively crowded life, Charles Ponsonby would not have had sufficient leisure to dig this. Someone else had.

It seemed to go on forever; at least three hundred yards was Carmine's guess. A five-minute hurried crawl. Then it ended in a door, not a flimsy wooden affair but solid steel with a massive combination dial and a wheel lock like a ship's companionway watertight door.

"Jesus, it's a bank safe!" Abe cried.

"Shut up and let me think!" Carmine stared down the beam of his flashlight, dancing with motes and mites, thinking that he should have known what kind of door it would be to keep contamination out. "Okay, it's logical to assume that he's inside and doesn't know what's happening outside. Shit, shit, shit! If Claire's the second Ghost and didn't use the tunnel, then there has to be another entrance to the killing premises. It's inside the house and we have to find it. Move your ass, Corey! *Move!*"

Another frantic crawl, followed for Carmine by a headlong gallop down the slope to the Ponsonby house. Lights were going on as people woke to the wail of sirens; the lane was choked with cars, an ambulance stood by. Biddy thrashed, snarling, in a dog-pound net, while Claire stood blocking Marciano's path.

"Cuff her and tell her the charges, Danny," Carmine gasped, grabbing at a porch pillar to steady himself. "She covered the secret door with leaves, and that makes her an accessory. But we can't get into the killing premises from the tunnel, he's got a bank vault door blocking it. I've left Abe and Corey guarding the tunnel—get some men up there and relieve the poor guys so they can wallow in tomato juice." He rounded on Claire, who seemed fascinated by the handcuffs, feeling what she could of them with spidery fingers. "Miss Ponsonby, don't make yourself more than an accessory to murder, please. Tell us where the house entrance to your brother's chamber of horrors is. We have absolute proof that he's the Connecticut Monster."

She drew a sobbing breath, shook her head. "No, no, that's impossible! I don't believe it, I won't believe it!"

"Take her downtown," Marciano said to two detectives, "but let her have her dog. Best get her to untangle it, it's pretty mad at us. And treat her right, make sure of that."

"Danny, you and Patrick come with me," said Carmine, able to stand unsupported again. "No one else. We don't want cops all over the house before Paul and Luke start examining it, but we have to find the other door before Chuck can do anything to that poor girl. Who is she?"

"We don't know yet," Marciano said miserably as he followed Carmine inside. "Probably no one in her home is up yet, it isn't even six." He tried to look cheerful. "Who knows, we might give her back to her folks before they even know she's gone."

Why did he think it was in the kitchen? Because that was the room wherein the Ponsonbys seemed to live, the hub of their universe. The ancient house itself was like a museum, and the dining room was no more than a place to park their concert hall speakers, the hi-fi and their record collection.

"Okay," he said, leading Marciano and Patrick into the old kitchen, "this is where we start. It was built in 1725, so its walls should sound fragile. Steel backing doesn't."

Nothing, nothing, nothing. Except that the room was freezing because the Aga stove wasn't alight. Now why was that? Discovery of a gas stove hidden by paneling and a gas hot water cylinder in a closet had shown that the Ponsonbys didn't roast in summer, but summer was a long way off. Why therefore was the Aga out?

"The answer has something to do with the Aga," Carmine said. "Come on, let's concentrate on it."

Behind it was its water reservoir, still hot to the touch. Groping, Patrick's fingers found a lever.

"It's here! I've found it!"

Eyes closed, breathing a prayer, Patrick tugged. The whole stove moved outward and to one side on a pivot, smoothly, silently. And there in the stone chimney alcove was a steel door. When Carmine, .38 drawn, turned its knob, it opened smoothly, silently. Suddenly he hesitated, slipped the pistol back into its holster.

"Patsy, give me your camera," he said. "This isn't a shoot-out situation, but Danny can cover me. You wait here."

"Carmine, that's an unnecessary risk!" Patrick cried.

"Give me your camera, it's the weapon of choice."

An ordinary wooden door stood at the bottom of a flight of stone steps. No lock, just a knob.

Carmine turned it and stepped into an operating room. His eyes took in nothing save Charles Ponsonby bending over a bed on which lay a moaning, stuporose girl already stripped naked, bound by a broad canvas band that confined her arms from just below the shoulders to just above her wrists. Ponsonby had removed whatever he wore for his forays into sleeping homes, was himself naked, his skin still wet in places from a quick shower. Humming a happy little tune as his experienced hands assessed his prize's conscious state. Dying for her to rouse.

The camera flashed. "Gotcha!" said Carmine.

Charles Ponsonby swung around, mouth agape, eyes blinded by the brilliant blue light, no fight in him.

"Charles Ponsonby, you are under arrest on suspicion of

multiple murder. You don't have to say anything, and you are entitled to legal representation. Do you understand?" Carmine asked.

It seemed not; Ponsonby compressed his lips and glared.

"I'd advise you to call your lawyer as soon as you reach downtown. Your sister's going to need one too."

Danny Marciano had opened another door and now emerged carrying a shiny black raincoat. "He's alone," he said, holstering his weapon, "and this is all I could find. Put your arms in it, you piece of shit." Once he had bundled Ponsonby into the coat, he took out his handcuffs. The ratchets clicked cruelly tight.

"You can come down, Patsy!" Carmine called.

"Jesus!" was all Patrick could find to say as he gazed about; then he went to help Carmine wrap the girl in a sheet and carry her up the stairs, Marciano and Ponsonby in their wake.

When they put him in the caged back of a squad car, Ponsonby seemed to come back into the real world for a moment, watery blue eyes wide, then he flung his head back and began to laugh, a shriek of monumental mirth. The cops who drove the car away kept their faces expressionless.

The victim, her identity still unknown, was rolled into the waiting ambulance; as it moved off, Paul's and Luke's van arrived, scattering the residents of Ponsonby Lane, who had gathered in murmuring, marveling groups to watch the circus at number 6. Even Major Minor was there, talking avidly.

"May I have my camera back?" Patrick asked Carmine as they entered the killing premises, Paul and Luke behind them.

Everything was either white or stainless steel silver-grey. The walls were paneled in stainless steel; the floor was what looked like grey terrazzo, the ceiling steel interrupted by a blaze of fluorescent tubes. No dirt from the tunnel could penetrate this glaringly pristine place, for that door was airtight as well as a foot thick. Vents and a faint susurration betrayed very good air-conditioning, and the room smelled clinically clean. The bed was on four round metal legs, a stainless steel platform surmounted by a rubber mattress sheathed in a rubber cover, over which was spread a fitted white sheet, not only clean, but ironed. The ends of the restraint were pushed into grooves along the edges of the platform and locked into place by rods that were slightly smaller in bore than the grooves. There was also a stainless steel operating table, bleakly bare. And, more horribly explicit, a meat hook and hoist suspended from the ceiling above a declivity in the floor that held a big drain grille. There were glass-fronted cabinets of surgical instruments, drugs, injection equipment, cans of ether, gauze swabs, adhesive tape, bandages. One cabinet held a collection of penis sheaths, including the nightmare that had killed Margaretta and Faith. A water blaster and a steam cleaner sat in one closet, another held rubber mattress covers, linens, cotton blankets. A large supermarket chest freezer sat against one wall; Carmine opened it to reveal an immaculate interior.

"He discarded all the linen and covers after each victim," Patrick said, lips pinched together.

"Look at this, Patsy," Carmine said, flipping a curtain.

Someone called down the stairs. "Lieutenant, we know who the victim is! Delice Martin, a boarder at Stella Maris Catholic girls' school."

"So he didn't need a car," Carmine said to Patrick. "Stella Maris is only half a mile away. He carried the girl across his shoulders all the way back."

"Drawing attention to himself, grabbing a victim so close to Ponsonby Lane" was Patrick's comment.

"In one way, yes, but in another, no. He knew we had all the Huggers pinned down, so why should it be him? To the end, he believed the tunnel was his secret. Now will you come and look at this, Patsy? *Look* at it!"

Carmine pulled an ironed white satin curtain aside to show an alcove lined in polished white marble. An altarlike table held two silver candlesticks with unburned white candles in them, as if something was to be deposited on a silver platter that stood atop an exquisitely embroidered cloth. A sacrifice.

On the wall above were four shelves, each of the top two supporting six heads; two more heads sat on the third, and the fourth was empty. The heads were not frozen. They were not in jars of formalin. They had been immersed in clear plastic the way gift shops sold beautiful butterflies.

"He had problems with the hair," said Patrick, clenching his fists to stop his hands trembling. "You can see how much better he gets with practice. Painfully slow, those first six heads! A clamp to hold the head upside down in his mold while he poured a little plastic in, let it set, poured some more in. He made a breakthrough on the seventh head—probably devised a way to get the hair as hard as concrete. Then he could fill the mold in one pour. I'd like to know how he dealt with anaerobic decay, but I'd be willing to bet that he removed the brains, maybe filled the cranial cavity with a formalin gel. Under that tasteful gold foil frill, the necks are sealed off." Patrick retched suddenly, controlled himself with an effort. "I feel sick."

"I know liquid plastic is prohibitively expensive, but I thought it didn't work for specimens this large," Carmine said. "Yet even Rosita Esperanza's head looks in good condition."

"It doesn't much matter what the textbooks or manufacturers say. These fourteen contradictions tell us that Charles Ponsonby was a master of the technique. Besides, the mold is snug, not much bigger than the head. A quart of plastic would be too much."

"Turn your talismans into butterflies."

The two technicians had come to look, but not for long; it would be their job to take down each head, box it for evidence. But only after every inch of the place had been photographed, sketched and catalogued.

"Let's have a look in the bathroom," Patrick suggested.

"He brought Delice Martin in," Carmine said after looking, "tossed her on the bed, then came in here and showered. That's what he wore to abduct her."

It was a black rubber diving suit of the kind worn by those who didn't go deep—thin, light. Ponsonby had removed its colored stripes and bands, dulled its gloss. A pair of heelless, smooth-soled rubber boots stood on the floor primly together, and a pair of thin black rubber gloves were folded neatly on a stool.

"Supple," said Carmine, flexing one of the boots between his gloved hands. "A failed researcher he may be, but as a killer Ponsonby is phenomenal." He replaced the boot exactly.

They walked back into the main room, where Paul and Luke had begun the photography; they would be days and days on the many tasks Patrick would call for.

"The heads are all the evidence we need to charge him with fourteen counts of murder," Carmine said, closing the curtain. "Funny, in a way, that he kept them so prominently displayed, but it doesn't seem to have occurred to him that anyone would ever find this place. Ponsonby will fry. Or else he'll get fourteen consecutive life sentences. I hope our Ghost dies in prison, abused every single day by every other inmate. How they'll hate him!"

"It's a good thought, but you know as well as I do that the warden will isolate him."

"Yeah, a pity, but true. I just want him to suffer, Patsy. What's death, but an eternal sleep? And what's isolation in a prison, but the chance to read books?"

CHAPTER 28

Thursday, March 3rd, 1966

For reasons he didn't want to explore, Wesley le Clerc could never think of himself as Ali el Kadi in his aunt's house. So it was Wesley le Clerc who dragged himself out of his bed at six o'clock; Tante Celeste insisted that he do. Having spread his mat and prayed, he went to the bathroom for what he called his four S's—shampoo, shower, shave and shit.

Mohammed's rally was all together, and, anyway, Mohammed said he was to be a model Parson Surgical Supplies employee as well as his Hug spy. At Wesley's workplace he had moved on from Halstead mosquito forceps to instruments for microsurgery, and his supervisor was talking about some special training that would enable Wesley to improve or even invent instruments. With the federal government leaning hard on equal-opportunity employment, a gifted black worker was precious in more ways than mere excellence; he or she was a statistic to keep Congress at bay. None of which mattered to the frustrated Wesley, who burned to strike a blow for his people *now,* not in some remote future when he had his ass-wipe piece of paper to say he'd passed the Connecticut bar exam.

Otis was just leaving for the Hug when Wesley walked into the kitchen. Tante Celeste was manicuring her nails, which she kept long, crimson and rather pointed to emphasize her slender, tapered fingers. The radio was blaring; she turned it off and got up to serve Wesley his breakfast of orange juice, cornflakes and wholemeal toast.

"They caught the Connecticut Monster," she remarked, smoothing margarine on the toast.

Wesley's spoon plopped into the sloppy cereal, splashed the table. "They what?" he asked, wiping up the milk before she saw what he'd done.

"They caught the Connecticut Monster about fifteen minutes ago. It's all over the news, they haven't even played a song yet."

"Who is he, a Hugger?"

"They didn't say."

He reached to turn the radio on. "So I'm bound to hear about it now?"

"I guess so." She returned to her nails.

Wesley listened to the bulletin with bated breath, scarcely able to believe his ears. Though the Monster's identity had not been revealed, WHMN was in a position to know that he was a senior professional medical man, and that there was a female accomplice. The two would be appearing before Judge Douglas Thwaites in the Holloman district court at 9 A.M. today for arraignment and the fixing of bail.

"Wes? Wes? *Wes!*"

"Huh? Yeah, Tante?"

"You okay? Not gonna pass out on me, are you? One bad heart in the family is enough."

"No, no, Tante, I'm fine, honest." He pecked her on the cheek and went to his room to don his floppiest jacket, gloves, a knitted cap. Though it was a sunny day, the temperature wasn't very much above freezing.

When he arrived at 18 Fifteenth Street he found Mohammed and his six intimates in a panicked huddle; three days were all they had to reorganize the theme of the rally, somehow make capital out of this unexpected development. Who could ever have dreamed that those incompetent pigs would make an arrest?

With a sheepish, apologetic smile Wesley slipped past them and entered what Mohammed referred to as his "meditation room." To Wesley it looked more like an arsenal, its walls smothered in racks that held shotguns, machine guns and automatic rifles; the handguns were stored in a number of metal cabinets that had once resided in a gun store, their drawers specifically designed for handgun display. Boxes of ammunition stood on the floor in high stacks wherever there was room.

Despite, or perhaps because of, the armaments, this was always the most peaceful place in the house, and it had what Wesley now needed: a table and a chair, white Bainbridge board, paints, pens, brushes, rulers, scissors, a guillotine. Wesley took a sheet of 18 x 30 Bainbridge board and ruled off a section 8 inches wide, then cut it with a Stanley Sheetrock knife braced against a ruler. Not much room for a message, but it wasn't going to be a long one. Black letters, white background. And where was Mohammed's spoiled brat of a son's hockey outfit? He'd seen it lying somewhere now the kid had discovered Allah didn't intend for him to be a hockey star. The latest fad was high-jumping because of some champion at Travis High.

"Hey, Ali! Busy, man?" Mohammed asked, coming in.

"Yeah. I'm busy making you a martyr, Mohammed."

"Turning me into one, you mean?"

"No, manufacturing you one out of someone less important."

"You kidding?"

"Nope. Where's Abdullah's hockey gear?"

"Two rooms over. Tell me more, Ali."

"Don't have time right now, I have a lot to do. Just make sure your TV is tuned into channel six at nine this morning." Wesley picked up a paintbrush, but didn't dip it in the black paint. "I need privacy, Mohammed. Then they can't prove that you were in the know, man."

"Sure, sure!" Grinning, palms held out, Mohammed mockingly bowed himself out of the meditation room, leaving Wesley alone.

When Carmine walked into the station it seemed like a hundred cops were there to shake him by the hand, clap him on the back, beam at him foolishly. To the press Charles Ponsonby was still the Connecticut Monster, but to every cop he was a Ghost.

Silvestri was so happy that he lumbered to his door and gave Carmine a smacking kiss on the cheek, hugged him. "My boy, my boy!" he crooned, eyes glistening with tears. "You saved us all."

"Oh, come on, John! Can the histrionics, this case went on so long it died of sheer old age," Carmine said, embarrassed.

"I am recommending you for a medal, even if the Governor has to invent one."

"Where are Ponsonby and Claire?"

"He's in a cell with two cops for company—no way this bozo is going to hang himself, and there's no cyanide capsule up his rectum either, we made sure. His sister's in a vacant office on this floor with two women officers. And the dog. At worst she's an accomplice. We haven't any evidence to suggest she might be the second Ghost, at least not evidence that will impress Doubting Doug Thwaites, the pedantic old fart. Our holding cells are clean, Carmine, but not designed to accommodate a *lady,* especially a lady who's blind. I thought it good policy to treat her in a way her lawyers can't criticize when she comes to trial—*if* she comes to trial. At the moment, that's moot."

"Has he talked?"

"Not a word. From time to time he howls with laughter, but he hasn't said a thing. Stares into space, hums a tune, giggles."

"He's going to plead insanity."

"Sure as eggs are eggs. But people insane according to the

M'Naghten rules don't plan a killing premises down to the last fine detail."

"And Claire?"

"Just keeps saying she refuses to believe her brother is a multiple murderer, and that she's done nothing wrong herself."

"Unless Patsy and his team can find a trace of Claire in the killing premises or the tunnel, she'll walk. I mean, a blind woman and her guide dog empty a bucket of dead leaves in the deer reserve and rake them nice and flat? A halfway competent lawyer could prove that she thought she was carrying deer chow to empty where brother Chuck had made them a feeding place. Of course we can always hope for a confession."

"In a pig's eye!" Silvestri said with a snort. "Neither of that pair is the confessing kind." He shut one eye, kept the other open and fixed on Carmine. "Do *you* think she's the second Ghost?"

"I don't honestly know, John. We won't prove it."

"Anyway, they're being formally arraigned in Doubting Doug's courtroom at nine. I wanted it in a less public venue and kept quiet, but Doug's sticking to his guns. What a picnic! Ponsonby's only item of clothing is a raincoat, and he refuses to put on a stitch more. If we force him and he gets a teensy-weensy bruise or cut, they'll cry police brutality, so he's going to court in a raincoat. Danny put the cuffs on him too tight, that's bad enough. The cute bastard's chafed himself raw."

"I suppose every journalist who can get to Holloman in time will be outside the courthouse, including channel six's anchors," Carmine said, sighing.

"Why wouldn't they? This is big news for a small city."

"Can't we arraign Claire separately?"

"We could if Thwaites would play ball, but he won't. He wants both of them in front of him at once. Curiosity, I think."

"No, he wants a preview that will help him make up his mind about Claire's complicity."

"Have you eaten, Carmine?"

"No."

"Then let's grab a booth at Malvolio's before the rush."

"How are Abe and Corey? De-skunked?"

"Yeah, and nursing grudges. They wanted to be with you down in that cellar."

"I feel sorry about that, but they had to be de-skunked. I suggest you squeeze the Governor for a couple more medals, John. And a big ceremony."

The Holloman courthouse was on Cedar Street at the Green, a short walk from the County Services building, yet one that the Ponsonbys could not make. A few enterprising journalists complete with photographers were outside the station entrance when Ponsonby was hustled out with a towel thrown over his head, his raincoat buttoned from neck to knees, where someone had secured it with a safety pin to make sure it couldn't be jerked open. No sooner was Ponsonby on the sidewalk than he started to wrestle with his escorts, not to escape, but to rid himself of the towel. In the end he was put into the caged squad car unveiled, amid a blue blizzard of flashbulbs; no one was taking any chances on the light. His car had drawn away when Biddy came out, leading Claire. Like her brother, she would not allow anyone to cover her head. Her escorts were conspicuously gentle with her, and the vehicle that took her down the block to the courthouse was Silvestri's official car, a big Lincoln.

The crowd around the courthouse was so huge that traffic had been entirely diverted from Cedar Street; a line of police with arms linked ebbed and surged in time to the pushing of the people they were trying to contain. Perhaps half the crowd was black, but both halves were very angry. The press were inside the cordon, cameramen with cameras at shoulder level, news photographers clicking away on automatic, radio announcers babbling into their microphones, channel six's anchorman doing the same. One of the journalists was a small, thin black man in a bulky jacket; he inched forward amid smiles and murmured apologies, hands tucked inside his coat for warmth.

When Charles Ponsonby was removed from the squad car the journalists rushed at him, the thin little black man in their forefront. One thin black hand emerged from the jacket and went up to his head, jammed a strange hat on it, a hat supporting a strip of white cardboard that said in neat black letters WE HAVE SUFFERED. All eyes had gone to the hat, even Charles Ponsonby's; no one saw Wesley le Clerc's other hand come out holding a black Saturday night special. He put four bullets in Ponsonby's chest and abdomen before the closest cops could draw their guns. But no fusillade cut him down. Carmine had jumped to shield him, roaring at the top of his voice.

"Hold your fire!"

And it was all there on TV, every single millisecond of the deed, from the WE HAVE SUFFERED hat to Charles Ponsonby's look of amazement and Carmine's suicidal leap. Mohammed el Nesr and his cronies watched it unfold, rigid with shock. Then Mohammed sagged back in his chair and lifted his arms in exultation.

"Wesley, my man, you have given us our martyr! And that big dumb-ass cop Delmonico saved you for a trial. Man, what a trial we will make it!"

"Ali, you mean," said Hassan, not understanding.

"No, he's Wesley le Clerc from now on. It has to look as if he acted for all black people, not just for the Black Brigade. That's the way we'll work it."

It happened two minutes before Claire Ponsonby's car was due to arrive, so she wasn't witness to her brother's fate. At first she was stranded in a moving mass of bodies, then police managed to clear enough space for the Lincoln to reverse back down Cedar Street to the County Services building.

"Jesus, Carmine, are you crazy?" Danny Marciano demanded, face ashen, body shaking. "My guys were on automatic pilot, they would have shot the Pope!"

"Well, luckily they didn't shoot me. More importantly, Danny, there were no flying bullets to wing a cameraman or kill Di Jones—how could Holloman survive without her Sunday gossip column?"

"Yeah, I know why you did it—and so do they, give them that much credit. I gotta go disperse this crowd."

Patrick was kneeling by Charles Ponsonby's head, thrown up and back, an expression of outrage on its lean, beaky face; a lake of blood was spreading from beneath his body, thinning as it flowed onward.

"Dead?" Carmine asked, bending down.

"As a doornail." Patrick brushed a hand across the fixed, disbelieving eyes to close them. "At least he won't walk, and I for one think there's a Hell waiting for him."

Wesley le Clerc stood between two uniformed cops, looking harmless and insignificant; every camera was still aimed at him, the man who had executed the Connecticut Monster. Rough justice, but justice of a kind. It never occurred to anyone that Ponsonby had not been tried, might conceivably have been innocent.

Silvestri came down the courthouse steps wiping his brow. "The judge is not amused," he said to Carmine. "Christ, what a fucking fiasco! And get him out of here!" he yelled at the men holding Wesley. "Go on, take him in and book him!"

Carmine followed Wesley into the squad car cage and sat back on the stained and smelly seat, his head turned sideways. Wesley was still wearing that fool hat with its heartrending message: WE HAVE SUFFERED. But the first thing Carmine did was to inform Wesley of his situation loudly enough for the cops in the front seat to hear. Then he plucked the hat off, turned it between his hands. A hard plastic hockey helmet that he had attacked with tin snips to fit it snugly around his ears. Jam it on, and it would stay in place long enough to be seen.

"I guess you thought it would come off in the hail of cop bullets you expected to cut you down, yet there it was on top of your head to the bitter end. It even survived getting into this shit-heap car. You're a better craftsman than you realize, Wes."

"I have done a great thing," Wesley said in ringing tones, "and I will go on to do greater things!"

"Don't forget that anything you say may be used in evidence."

"What do I care about *that*, Lieutenant Delmonico? I am the avenger of my people, I killed the man who raped and murdered our women children. I am a hero, and so I will be regarded."

"Oh, Wes, you've wasted yourself, can't you see that? What gave you the idea, Jack Ruby? Did you think for one minute that I'd let you die the way he did? You have such a good mind! And, more's the pity, if you had only done what I asked you to do, you might have made a *real* difference to your people. But no, you wouldn't wait. Killing is easy, Wes. Anybody can kill. To me, it indicates an IQ about four points higher than plant life. Charles Ponsonby would probably have gone to prison for the rest of his days. All you did was let him off the hook."

"Was that who it was? Dr. Chuck Ponsonby? Well, well! A Hugger after all. You don't even begin to understand, Lieutenant. He was just a means to my end. He gave me the chance to become a martyr. Do I give a fuck whether he lives or dies? No, I do not! *I* am the one who must suffer, and suffer I will."

As Wesley le Clerc was being led away to the cells Silvestri stomped in, chewing fiercely on his cigar. "There's another one we'll have to watch every second," he growled. "Let *him* commit suicide and there'll be hell to pay."

"He's also a very bright guy and manually skilled, so taking away his belt and anything he can tear into strips won't prevent his trying if that's the way his mind is going. Personally I don't think it is. Wesley wants everything aired in public."

They entered the elevator. "What do we do with Miss Claire Ponsonby?" Carmine asked.

"We drop the charges and release her forthwith. That's what the D.A. says. A bucket of dead leaves is not enough evidence to hold her, let alone charge her. The only thing we can do is forbid her to leave Holloman County—for the time being." The jowly face

333

screwed up like a colicky baby's. "Oh, what a pain in the ass this case has been from start to finish! All those beautiful, sainted young girls dead, and no one to bring them *real* justice. And how the hell do I handle the relatives about the heads?"

"At least the heads represent the closing of a door to the families, John. Not knowing is worse than knowing," Carmine said as they left the elevator. "Where is Claire?"

"Back in the same office."

"Mind if I do the deed?"

"Mind? Be my guest. I don't want to see the bitch!"

She was sitting in a comfortable chair, Biddy lying at her feet, ignoring the two uncomfortable young women ordered never to take their eyes off her. Since she couldn't see, somehow that seemed an unpardonable invasion of her privacy.

"Why, Lieutenant Delmonico!" she exclaimed, straightening as he walked in.

"No V-8 engine in my car to give me away this time. How do you do it, Miss Ponsonby?"

She achieved a simper that made her look old, sly, pinched, piti-ful; something about the expression gave him one of those lightning flashes of insight so vital to his police career. It said that she was def-initely the second Ghost. Oh, Patsy, Patsy, find me something to put her in the killing premises! Find me a photograph or a movie of her and Chuck in the middle of rape and murder. Grow up, Carmine! There is nothing. The only memorabilia they keep are the heads. What use is a picture, still or moving, to a blind person? What use, for that matter, is a head?

"Lieutenant," she said with a purr, "you carry your V-8 with you wherever you go. The engine's not in your car, it's in you."

"Have you been informed that your brother, Charles, is dead?"

"Yes, I have. I also know that he did none of the things you say he did. My brother was a highly intellectual, fastidious and terribly kind man. That peasant Marciano accused me of being his lover—pah! I'm glad that *I* don't have a cesspool for a mind."

"We have to take every possibility into account. But you're free to go, Miss Ponsonby. All charges have been dropped."

"So I should think." She tugged the loop on Biddy's harness.

"Where are you going to stay? Your house is still a crime scene under police investigation and will remain so for some time to come. Would you like me to phone Mrs. Eliza Smith?"

"Certainly not!" she snapped. "If it hadn't been for that woman's tale-telling, none of this would have happened. I hope she dies of cancer of the tongue!"

"Then where are you going?"

"I will be at Major Minor's until I can move back into my home, so be warned. I intend to retain lawyers to watch for my interests as owner of Six Ponsonby Lane, therefore I suggest that you damage nothing. The house committed no crime."

And out she swept. Winner take all, Carmine. Ghost or no Ghost, that is one formidable woman.

He went back to the house that committed no crime, though he hadn't offered to drive Claire to Major Minor's. Silvestri had donated his Lincoln for that. They were now entering upon the saddest time in any case—the flat, uninspiring aftermath.

By the time everyone arrived at the Hug, the news that the Connecticut Monster had been caught was, in news terms, quite old. Each face looked smoother, younger, and each pair of eyes glowed. Oh, the relief! Perhaps now the Hug could return to normal, for obviously the Monster was not a Hugger.

Desdemona hadn't seen Carmine since she returned from her hike, nor had she expected to, with the Ghost watch keeping him away. But just as she was about to leave for her escorted squad car trip to the Hug on this Wednesday morning, the phone rang: Carmine, sounding curiously unemotional.

"There's a TV in the Hug boardroom as I remember," he said. "Turn it on and watch channel six, okay?" Click! He hung up.

Feet dragging, crushed at his impersonal tone, Desdemona

unlocked the boardroom and pushed the button on the TV just as the wall clock registered 9 A.M. Oh, how she didn't want to see this! No sooner had she gotten through the Hug door than all and sundry were whooping that the Monster had been caught. As if the cops in her squad car hadn't been full of it! Now she would have to see what Carmine had been up to in the night marches, and she feared that. Presumably he was unhurt, but for three nights she had been eaten by worry, even terror. What would she do if he never came home again? Oh, what on earth had possessed her to declare her independence by hiking the weekend before his Ghost watch commenced? Why hadn't she realized that he wouldn't come home on Sunday night? All her hopes had been pinned on that as she walked the magic of the woods: how she would throw her arms around him and tell him she couldn't live without him. But—no Carmine. Just the echoes of his richly red apartment.

The TV shimmered into life. Yes, there was the courthouse, surrounded by a crowd many hundreds strong, journalists everywhere, police everywhere. One cameraman from channel six apparently had found himself a perch on top of a van roof and could pan the whole scene; another was in the crowd, and a third on the sidewalk near an arriving squad car. She spotted Carmine standing with a big uniformed captain she recognized as Danny Marciano. Commissioner Silvestri was at the top of the courthouse steps looking very smart in a uniform twinkling with silver braid. Then from out of the back of the squad car emerged Dr. Charles Ponsonby. Her heart seeming to squeeze up, Desdemona watched with jaw dropped. Ye gods, *Charles Ponsonby!* A Hugger. Bob Smith's oldest and best friend. I am witnessing, she thought, the extinction of the Hug. Are the Parson Governors watching this in New York City? Yes, of course they are! Our channel is a network affiliate. Have the Parson Governors found that escape clause? If they haven't, they will redouble their efforts after this bombshell.

What happened next was so fast it seemed over before it had begun: the little black man, that hat saying WE HAVE SUFFERED, the sound of four shots, Charles Ponsonby going down, and Carmine deliberately putting himself in front of the little black man still holding a squat, ugly pistol. When Carmine did that as the cops all around slapped leather, Desdemona felt herself die, waiting frozen in time for the sound of a dozen guns reflexively cutting him down. His roar of "Hold your fire!" came clearly on the airwaves. Carmine stood miraculously unharmed, the cops were holstering their weapons and moving to grab the little black man, who made no attempt to evade them. She sat shivering, hands over her mouth, eyes starting from their sockets. Carmine, you fool! You idiot! You flaming *soldier!* You didn't die—this time. But I am doomed to the fate of a soldier's woman, always.

Whom to tell first? No, best tell them all at once, right this moment. The Hug had a speaker system: Desdemona used it to summon every Hugger to the lecture theater.

Then she went to Tamara's office; someone would have to man the phones. Poor Tamara! A shadow of her old self since Keith Kyneton had slammed his door in her face. Even her hair seemed to have wasted away, lackluster and unkempt. She didn't even react, just nodded and continued to sit staring into space.

The news of Charles Ponsonby's secret activities broke upon the people in the lecture theater like a clap of thunder: gasps, exclamations, a degree of incredulity.

To Addison Forbes, it was God in the burning bush: with no Ponsonby or Smith in the way, the Hug would become his. Why would the Board of Governors search elsewhere when he was so eminently suitable? He had the clinical experience that drove researchers to produce, his reputation was international. The Board of Governors *liked* him. With Smith and Ponsonby gone, the Hug under Professor Addison Forbes would go on to bigger and better things! And who needed the conceited Great Panjandrum from India? The world was full of potential Nobel Prize winners.

Walter Polonowski hardly heard Desdemona's crisply succinct

summary; he was too depressed. Four kids from Paola, and a fifth coming up from Marian. With a wedding band looming, Marian was shedding her mistress's skin to reveal a new epidermis striped in wifely colors. They *are* serpents, we *are* their victims.

To Maurice Finch, the news brought sorrow, but sorrow of a peaceful kind. He had always thought that to give up medicine would be tantamount to a death sentence, but the events of the past few months had taught him that this need not be so. His plants were patients too; his skilled and loving hands could tend them, heal them, help them multiply. Yes, life with Cathy on a chicken farm looked very good. And he'd beat those mushrooms yet.

Kurt Schiller was not surprised. He had never liked Charles Ponsonby, whom he had suspected of secret homosexuality; Chuck's attitude was a little too subtly knowing, and the art whispered of a nightmare world beneath that anonymous exterior. Not its subject matter, more an emanation from Chuck. In Kurt's book he had gone down as one of the chains-and-leather boys, heavily into pain, though Schiller had always assumed Chuck was on the receiving end. The passive type, scuttling around to serve some terrifying master. Well, evidently he, Kurt, had been wrong. Charles was a true sadist—had to be, to have done what he did to those poor children. As for himself, Kurt expected nothing. His credentials would guarantee him a post no matter what happened to the Hug, and he had the germ of an idea about transmitting diseases across the species barrier that he knew would excite the head of any research unit. Now that the photograph of Papa with Adolf Hitler was ashes on the hearth and his homosexuality was out in the open, he felt ready for the new life he intended to lead. Not in Holloman. In New York City, among his peers.

"Otis," Tamara shouted from the door, "you're needed at home, so get going! I couldn't make hide nor hair out of what Celeste was saying, but it's an emergency."

Don Hunter and Billy Ho ranged themselves one on either side of Otis, helping him out of the row of seats.

"We'll take him, Desdemona," Don said. "Can't have his wonky heart playing up if he's needed."

Cecil Potter watched channel six's footage replayed on CBS in Massachusetts, Jimmy on his knee.

"Man, will you look at that?" he asked the monkey. "Uh-uh! Hooee! I am so glad to be outta there!"

When Carmine opened his door that evening Desdemona charged at him, weeping noisy tears, pummeling his chest angrily. Her nose was running and her eyes drowned.

Hugely gratified, he put her tenderly on the new sofa he had acquired because easy chairs were all very well and good for talk, but nothing beat a sofa for two people to smooch on. He let the storm of tears and ire abate, rocking her and murmuring, then used his handkerchief to clean her up.

"What was all that about?" he asked, knowing the answer.

"You!" she said, hiccoughing. "Bloody huh-huh-hero!"

"Not bloody, and no hero."

"Bloody hero! Stepping in front to take the buh-buh-bullet! Oh, I could have *killed* you!"

"It's great to see you too," he said, laughing. "Now put up your feet and I'll fix us a couple of snifters of X-O."

"I knew I loved you," she said later, calmed down, "but what a way to learn how much I love you! Carmine, I don't want to live in a world that doesn't have you in it."

"Does this mean that you'd rather be Mrs. Carmine Delmonico than live in London?"

"It does."

He kissed her with love, gratitude, humility. "I'll try to make you a good husband, Desdemona, but you've already had a televised preview of what a cop's life entails. The future won't be any different— long hours, absences, stray bullets. However, I figure someone's on my side. So far I'm still in one piece."

"As long as you understand that whenever you do foolhardy things, I'll bash you up."

"I'm hungry" was his answer. "How about some Chinese?"

She heaved a huge sigh of satisfaction. "I've just realized that I'm not in danger anymore." A tinge of anxiety crept into her voice. "Am I?"

"The danger's over, I'd bet my career on it. But there's no point in looking for a new apartment. I'm not letting you leave this one. Sin is in."

"The trouble is," he said to her as they lay in bed, "that so much of it remains a mystery. I doubt Ponsonby would ever have talked, but when he died all hope of that died too. Wesley le Clerc! Tomorrow's problem."

"You mean Leonard Ponsonby's murder? The identity of the woman and child with the face?" He had told her everything.

"Yes. And who dug the tunnel, and how did Ponsonby ever get all that gear into his killing premises, from a generator to a bank vault door? Who did the plumbing? A major job! The floor of the place is *thirty feet* below ground. Most house basements are damp at ten, fifteen feet, but this is as dry as an old bone. The county engineers are fascinated, looking very forward to tracing his drains."

"And do you think that Claire is the second Ghost?"

" 'Think' isn't the right word. My gut says she is, my mind says she can't be." He sighed. "If she is the second Ghost, she has managed to get away clean."

"Never mind," she soothed, stroking his hair. "At least the murders are at an end. No more abducted girls. Claire couldn't do it on her own, she's female and grossly handicapped. So count your blessings, Carmine."

"Count my stupidity, you mean. I've bungled this case from start to finish."

"Only because it's a new sort of crime committed by a new sort of criminal, my love. You're an extremely competent, highly intelligent policeman. Regard the Ponsonby case as a new learning experience. The next time things will go better for you."

He shuddered. "If I have my druthers, Desdemona, there will be no next time. The Ghosts are a one-off."

She said no more, just wondered.

CHAPTER 29

Friday, March 11th, 1966

It took just over a week for Patrick, Paul and Luke to go through everything that the Ponsonby killing premises had to offer, from operating table to bathroom. The final report from Patrick and his forensics team pointed out very clearly that it was just as well they had caught a naked Charles Ponsonby bending over a naked abducted girl tied to a bed rigged for torture.

"The place was cleaner than Lady Macbeth. His fingerprints everywhere, yes, but it's his place underneath his house, so why not? But of blood, body fluids, shreds of flesh or human hairs—no scintilla, iota or anything else microscopically small. As for Claire, no fingerprints, even on the lever behind the stove."

They had pieced Ponsonby's cleaning techniques together, staggered at the amount of work involved, the obsessiveness. A medical man, he knew that heat fixed blood and tissue, so the hose he used first and the water blaster he followed that with were fed by cold water; the talisman alcove was sealed off by a steel slider. When every surface was dry again, he steam blasted it. Finally he wiped every-thing down with ether. His surgical instruments, the meat hook and its hoist, and the penis sheaths were soaked in a blood-dissolving solution before being subjected to the rest of the treatments. They were also autoclaved.

When the room yielded nothing, they started on the drains with a compressor-driven vacuum, which sucked water containing no organic matter. Backwashing didn't work, leading the county engi-neers to think that the effluent was not deposited in a septic tank. Ponsonby had his outlet in an underground stream, of which there were many in the neighborhood. Their sole remaining hope was to dig down to his pipes and follow them.

The moment the county engineers began to excavate her garden for no better reason than flogging an already dead horse, Claire Pon-sonby took out a lien against willful destruction of her property, and respectfully petitioned the court to grant a blind woman permission to live in said property without perpetual and extremely distressing harassment by the Holloman police and their allies. Given that Charles Ponsonby had been positively identified as the Connecticut Monster and that nothing going on at 6 Ponsonby Lane was neces-sary to produce further evidence of this, Miss Ponsonby had had enough.

"The well is bottomless and the pump chugs out three horses," said the chief county engineer, thwarted and angry. "Since there's a twenty-acre deer park as well as five-acre house lots, the water table is high and local consumption low. You haven't gotten any organic matter because the bastard must have put thousands and thousands of gallons down after every killing. The residue is on the bottom of Long Island Sound. And shit, what does it matter? He's dead. Close the case, Lieutenant, before that nasty bitch starts suing you personally."

"It's a total mystery, Patsy," Carmine said to his cousin.

"Tell me something I don't already know."

"Obviously Chuck was wiry and strong, but he never struck me as an athlete, and his Hug colleagues were convinced he couldn't

343

change the washer on a tap. Yet what we found is marvelously constructed out of expensive materials. Who the hell put in a terrazzo floor and isn't owning up to it now that the secret's out? Ditto the plumbing? No one's reported a missing plumber or terrazzo worker since the war!" Carmine ground his teeth. "The family has no money, we know that. Claire and Chuck lived so well that they must have spent every cent he earned. And yet there's two hundred grand's worth of labor and material down in the ground. Damnit, no one admits to having sold them the linen or the plastic liquid for the heads!"

"To quote the county engineer, what does it matter, Carmine? Ponsonby is dead and it's time to close the case," Patrick said, patting Carmine's shoulder. "Why give yourself a coronary over a dead man? Think of Desdemona instead. When's the wedding?"

"You don't like her, Patsy, do you?"

The blue eyes dimmed but refused to look away. "Past tense might be more accurate. I didn't like her in the beginning—too strange, too foreign, too aloof. But she's different these days. I hope to come to love her as well as like her."

"You're not alone. Your mom *and* mine are shivering in their shoes. Oh, they gush enthusiastically, but I'm not a detective for no reason. It's a façade to mask apprehension."

"Made worse because she's noticeably taller than you are," said Patrick, laughing. "Moms and aunts and sisters *hate* that. You see, they were hoping that the second Mrs. Delmonico would be a nice Italian girl from East Holloman. But you're not attracted to nice girls, Italian or otherwise. And I much prefer Desdemona to Sandra. Desdemona has brains."

"They last longer than faces or figures."

The case was officially closed that afternoon. Once the Medical Examiner's report was filed the Holloman Police Department was obliged to admit that it could find no evidence to implicate Claire Ponsonby in the murders. If Carmine had had the time he might have gone to Silvestri and asked to reopen the murder of Leonard Ponsonby and the woman and child in 1930, but crime waits for no man, especially a detective. Two weeks after Charles Ponsonby was shot dead, a drug case was occupying all of Carmine's attention. Back on familiar ground! Criminals he knew were guilty, his wits engaged in gathering the evidence to bring them to justice.

CHAPTER 30

Monday, March 28th, 1966

The axe fell on the Hughlings Jackson Center for Neurological Research at the end of
March.

When the Board of Governors convened in the Hug boardroom
at 10 A.M., all the Governors were present except Professor Robert
Mordent Smith, who had been discharged from Marsh Manor two
weeks before, but wouldn't emerge from his basement and its trains.
An embarrassment for Roger Parson Junior, who hated to think that
his judgement of Bob Smith had been so erroneous.

"As the business director, Miss Dupre, please take a seat," Parson
said briskly, then looked at Tamara quizzically. "Miss Vilich, are you
up to taking minutes?"

A legitimate question, as this Miss Vilich didn't resemble the
woman whom the Parson Governors had known before today. Her
light had gone out, so Richard Spaight fancied.

"Yes, Mr. Parson," Tamara said tonelessly.

President Mawson MacIntosh already knew what Dean Wilbur

346

Dowling only suspected; however, the one's certain knowledge and the other's strong suspicion produced contented faces and relaxed bodies. Chubb University was going to inherit the Hug, so much was certain, together with a huge amount of money that wouldn't be devoted to neurological research.

Half glasses perched on his thin blade of a nose, Roger Parson Junior proceeded to read out the legal opinion that had rendered his late lamented uncle's last will and testament null and void in respect of the trust fund that financed the Hug. It took forty-five minutes to read something drier than dust in the Sahara, but those forced to listen did so with expressions of alert and eager interest save for Richard Spaight, upon whom the most wearisome aspects of the affair would devolve. He swung his chair to face the window and watched two tugs escort a large oil tanker to its berth at the new hydrocarbons reservoir complex at the foot of Oak Street.

"We could, of course, simply absorb the hundred-fifty million capital of the fund plus its accrued interest into our holdings," Parson said at the conclusion of his peroration, "but such would not have been William Parson's wish—of that we, his nephews and great-nephews, are very sure."

Ha ha ha, thought M.M., like hell you didn't want to absorb the lot! But you dropped the idea after I said Chubb would sue. The best you can do is snaffle the accrued interest, which in itself will make a nice, plump addition to Parson Products.

"We therefore propose that half of the capital be deeded to the Chubb Medical School in order to fund the ongoing career of the Hughlings Jackson Center in whatever guise it will assume. The building and its land will be deeded to Chubb University. And the other half of the capital will go to Chubb University to fund major infrastructure of whatever kind the university's board of governors decides. Provided that each infrastructural item bears William Parson's name."

Oh, yummy! was written all over Dean Dowling's face, whereas M.M.'s face remained complacently impassive. Dean Dowling was

347

contemplating the Hug's transformation into a center for research on the organic psychoses. He had tried to persuade Miss Claire Ponsonby to donate her deceased brother's brain for research, and had been politely refused. Now *there* was a psychotic brain! Not that he had expected to see any gross anatomical changes, but he had hoped for localized atrophy in the prefrontal cortex or some aberration in the corpus striatum. Even a little astrocytoma.

Mawson MacIntosh's thoughts revolved around the nature of the buildings that would bear William Parson's name. One of them had to be an art gallery, even if it remained empty until the last of the Parsons was dead. May that day come soon!

"Miss Dupre," Roger Parson Junior was saying, "it will be your duty to circulate this official letter"—he pushed it across the table—"among all members of the Hughlings Jackson Center, staff and faculty. Closure will be Friday, April twenty-ninth. All the equipment and furniture will be disposed of as the Dean of Medicine desires. Except, that is, for selected items that will be donated to the Holloman County Medical Examiner's laboratories as a token of our appreciation. One of the selected items will be the new electron microscope. I had a chat, you see, with the Governor of Connecticut, who told me how important—and underfunded—the science of forensic medicine has become."

No, no, no! thought Dean Dowling. That microscope is *mine!*

"I am assured by President MacIntosh," Roger Parson Junior droned on, "that all members who wish to stay may stay. However, salaries and wages will be reassessed commensurate with standard medical school fiscal policy. Faculty members wishing to stay will be put under Professor Frank Watson. For those who do not wish to stay, Miss Dupre, you will arrange redundancy packages incorporating one year's salary or wages plus all pension contributions."

He cleared his throat, settled his glasses more comfortably. "There are two exceptions to this ruling. One is Professor Bob Smith, who, alas, is not well enough to resume medical practice of any kind. Since his contribution over the sixteen years of his administration has been formidable, we have arranged that he be compensated in the manner prescribed herein." Another sheet of paper was thrust at Desdemona. "The second exception is you yourself, Miss Dupre. Unfortunately the position of business director will cease, and I am led to understand from President MacIntosh that it will be impossible to find you an equivalent position within the university. Therefore we have agreed that your own redundancy package will consist of what is listed in here." A third piece of paper.

Desdemona took a peek. Two years' salary plus all pension contributions. If she married and quit working altogether and income-averaged, she'd do quite well.

"Tamara, turn the coffee pots on," she said.

"I give Dean Dowling two years to ruin the place," she said to Carmine that evening. "He's too much a psychiatrist and too little a neurologist to get the best out of a well-run research unit. All the nuttier varieties of researcher will fool him. Tell Patrick not to be bashful about equipment, Carmine. Grab it while the going's good."

"He'll kiss your hands and feet, Desdemona."

"He oughtn't, it's not my doing." She sighed contentedly. "Anyway, your bride comes with a dowry. If you can afford to keep me and however many children you deem sufficient, then my dowry ought to buy us a really decent house. I love this apartment, but it's not suitable for raising a family."

"No," he said, taking her hands, "you keep your dowry for yourself. Then if you change your mind, you'll have enough to go home to London. I'm not short of a buck, honest."

"Well," she said, "then think about this, Carmine. When he read Roger Parson Junior's circular, Addison Forbes went right off the deep end. Work under Frank Watson? He'd rather die of tertiary syphilis! He announced that he's going to work with Nur Chandra at Harvard, but I would have thought that Harvard isn't short of clinical neurologists, so I hope Addison isn't holding his breath. The thing is, I love the Forbes house with a passion. If the Forbeses do move, I suppose it will sell for heaps of money, but do we have a financial hope of buying it? Do you rent, or do you own this?"

"It's a condo, I own it. I think we'll be able to spring for the Forbes house, if you like it so much. The location is ideal—East Holloman, my family neighborhood. Try to like my family, Desdemona," he pleaded. "My first wife thought they spied on her because Mom or Patsy's mom or one of our sisters was always calling around. But it wasn't that. Italian families are close knit."

Though she hadn't really changed in appearance, somehow to Carmine she wasn't as plain as she used to be. Not love blinding his eyes; love opening them was a better way to put it.

"I'm rather shy," she confessed, squeezing his fingers, "and that makes me seem snobby. I don't think I'm going to have any trouble liking your family, Carmine. And one of the reasons why I'm so keen on the Forbes house is its tower. If Sophia ever wanted to come home, perhaps attend the Dormer Day School and then the bruited coeducational Chubb, it would make such super digs for her. From what you've told me, I think Sophia needs a real home, not Hampton Court Palace. If you don't catch her now, in another year she'll be skipping off to Haight-Ashbury."

Tears came into his eyes. "I don't deserve you," he said.

"Rubbish, you must! People always get what they deserve."

PART FIVE

Spring & Summer
1966

CHAPTER **31**

In the week that followed Wesley le Clerc's indictment for the murder of Charles Ponsonby, the mood changed statewide, ardently fueled by television. Public indignation at the existence of a Connecticut Monster grew rather than died down; he was seen as proof of godlessness, decayed morals, absent ethics, a world gone insane under the pressures of modernity, the avalanche of technology. The community was tolerating these genetic sports, allowing them to mature into a new kind of killer; yet no one grasped the fact that they presented as ordinary and law-abiding citizens. Or indeed that they were multiplying.

Wesley had his wish: he had become a hero. Though a large percentage of his admirers were black, many were not, and all of them were convinced that Wesley le Clerc had delivered a justice beyond the ability of the Law. If the pro-white bias of the Law was already dead in some states and dying in others, that was sometimes hard to see. Far easier to see the families of a few of the Monster's victims appear on a TV program to be asked questions that lacked morals, ethics or plain good manners: How did it feel to look at your daughter's head encased in clear plastic? Did you cry? Did you faint? What do you think about Wesley le Clerc?

Wesley had been charged with first-degree murder, the premeditated kind, and the only legal argument could be about that premeditation. Having put himself in the limelight, Wesley knew full well that in order to stay there, he had to go on trial. A plea of guilty meant that his only appearance in court would be for sentencing. Therefore he pleaded not guilty, and was remanded for trial without the granting of bail. Outside the court after this hearing, Wesley was accosted by a high-profile white lawyer who introduced himself as the leader of Wesley's new defense team. A cluster of other white fat-cat lawyers behind him were the rest of the team. To their horror, Wesley rejected them.

"Fuck off and tell Mohammed el Nesr that I have seen the true light," Wesley said. "I will do this the poor black trash way, with a lawyer assigned from the public defender's office." His hand indicated a young black man with a briefcase. A faint shadow of pain crossed his face, he sighed. "Could have been me in ten years' time, but I have chosen my course."

Once the exaltation of that ride back to the cells in the company of Carmine Delmonico had died away, Wesley had undergone a sea change that perhaps had a little to do with what Carmine had said to him, but a great deal more to do with witnessing from a distance of three feet the life go out of a pair of eyes. All that was left of Charles Ponsonby was a husk, and what terrified Wesley was that he had liberated that unspeakably evil spirit to seek a home in some other body. Allah warred with Christ and Buddha, and he began to pray to all three.

Yet strength poured into him too, a different strength. He would somehow manage to make of this cardinal mistake a victory.

The first signals of victory were there when he was sent to the Holloman County Jail to wait out the months between his crime and his trial. When he arrived the inmates cheered him wildly. His bunk in the four-man cell was heaped with gifts: cigarettes and cigars, lighters, magazines, candy, hip clothing accessories, a gold Rolex watch, seven gold bracelets, nine gold neck chains, a pinky ring with a big diamond in it. No need to fear that he'd be raped in the shower block! No tormenting from the warders either; all of them nodded to him respectfully, smiled, gave him the O sign. When he asked for a prayer mat, a beautiful Shiraz appeared, and whenever he entered the meal hall or the exercise yard, he was cheered again. Black or white, the prisoners and their guards loved him.

A huge number of people of all races and colors didn't think that Wesley le Clerc should be convicted at all. Letters to the editors of various papers nationwide flooded in. The lines of phone-in radio shows were overloaded. Telegrams piled up on the Governor's desk. The Holloman D.A. tried to persuade Wesley to plead guilty to manslaughter for a much reduced sentence, but the new hero wasn't having any of that cop-out. He would go to trial, and go to trial he did.

A trial that went on at the beginning of June, months before it should have; the judicial Powers That Be decided that delaying it would only make matters worse. This wasn't a nine days' wonder that people would forget. Do it now, get it over and done with!

Never had a jury been chosen with more care. Eight were black and four white, six women and six men, some affluent, some simple workers, two jobless through no fault of their own.

His story on the stand was that he hadn't planned a thing beyond the hat—that a surge in the crowd had put him where he ended—and that he didn't remember firing any gun, couldn't even remember having a gun on his person. The fact that the deed was immortalized on videotape was irrelevant; all he had ever meant to do was protest the treatment of his people.

The jury opted for unpremeditated murder and strongly recommended leniency. Judge Douglas Thwaites, not a lenient man, handed down a sentence of twenty years' penal servitude, twelve before a chance of parole. About the verdict expected.

* * *

His trial took five days and ended on a Friday, marking the climax of
a spring that the Governor, for one, never wanted to see repeated.
Demonstrations had turned into riots, houses burned, stores were
looted, gunfire exchanged. Despite the fact that his disciple Ali el
Kadi had turned on him, Mohammed el Nesr seized his chance and
led the Black Brigade into a minor war that ended when a raid on 18
Fifteenth Street in the Hollow produced over a thousand firearms.
What no cop could work out was why Mohammed had not moved
his arsenal well ahead of the raid. Save for Carmine, who thought
that Mohammed was slipping, and knew it; even his own men were
beginning to admire Wesley le Clerc more.

The Black Brigade's fate notwithstanding, it became clear a week
before Wesley's trial opened that it was going to become a gigantic
mass demonstration of support for the slayer of the Monster, and
that not all who planned to march to Holloman were peacefully
inclined. Spies and informers reported that 100,000 black and 75,000
white protesters would take up residence on the Holloman Green at
dawn on the Monday that Wesley's trial was to start. They were
coming from as far away as L.A., Chicago, Baton Rouge (Wesley's
hometown) and Atlanta, though most lived in New York, Connecticut and Massachusetts. A gathering place had been designated: Maltravers Park, a botanical gardens ten miles out of Holloman. And
there, from Saturday on, the people assembled in many thousands.
The march to Holloman Green was scheduled for 5 A.M. on Monday, and it was very well organized. The terrified inhabitants of Holloman boarded up store windows, doors and downstairs windows,
dreading the urban war that was sure to come.

On Sunday morning the Governor called out the National Guard,
which trundled and roared into Holloman at dawn on Monday to
occupy the Green ahead of the marchers; troop carriers, armored
vehicles and massive trucks shook building foundations as all of Holloman huddled, wide-eyed, trembling, to watch them grind by.

But the marchers never came. No one really knew why. Perhaps it was the prospect of a confrontation with trained troops deterred them, or perhaps Maltravers Park was as far as most had ever wanted to go. By noon of Monday, Maltravers Park was empty, was all. The trial of Wesley le Clerc went on with less than five hundred protesters on Holloman Green amid a sea of National Guards, and when the verdict was announced on Friday afternoon those five hundred went home as meekly as lambs. Was it the official display of official force? Or had the mere act of congregating satisfied those who came to Maltravers Park?

Wesley le Clerc didn't waste time worrying or wondering about his supporters. Transferred to a high-security prison upstate on Friday night, the following Monday Wesley petitioned the prison's governor for permission to study for a pre-law degree; this smart official was pleased to grant his request. After all, Wesley le Clerc was only twenty-five years old. If he gained parole on his first try, he would be thirty-seven and probably possessed of a doctorate in jurisprudence. His criminal record would prevent his being admitted to the bar, but the knowledge he would own was far more important. His speciality was going to be the U.S. Supreme Court. After all, he was the Monster Slayer, the Holy Man of Holloman. Eat your heart out, Mohammed el Nesr, you're a has-been. *I* am The Man.

CHAPTER 32

Carmine and Desdemona were married at the beginning of May, and elected to honeymoon in L. A. as the guests of Myron Mendel Mandelbaum; the facsimile of Hampton Court Palace was so enormous that their presence was no embarrassment to Myron or to Sandra. Myron was theirs for the asking, whereas Sandra floated on cloud nine in oblivion. A little to Carmine's and Myron's surprise, Sophia decided to like Desdemona, whose hypothesis was that her new stepdaughter approved of the no-gush, matter-of-fact way her new stepmother treated her. Like a responsible, sensible adult. The omens were propitious.

Back in Holloman not all was quite so propitious. As if the Hug hadn't suffered enough sensations and scandals in the last few months, its dying throes produced yet another when Mrs. Robin Forbes complained to the Holloman police that her husband was poisoning her. Interviewed by the newly decorated detective sergeants Abe Goldberg and Corey Marshall, Dr. Addison Forbes rejected the accusation with scorn and loathing, invited them to take samples of any and all foodstuffs and liquids on the premises, and retreated to his eyrie. When the analyses (including vomitus, feces and urine) came back negative, Forbes crated his books and papers, packed two suitcases and left for Fort Lauderdale. There he joined a lucrative practice in geriatric neurology; such things as strokes and senile dementia had never interested him, but they were infinitely preferable to Professor Frank Watson and Mrs. Robin Forbes, whom he filed to divorce. When Carmine's lawyers contacted him about buying the house on East Circle, he sold it for less than it was worth to get back at Robin, asking for half. After a harrowing struggle deciding which daughter was more in need of her, Robin moved to Boston and the budding gynecologist, Roberta. Robina sent her sister a sympathy card, but Roberta was actually delighted to have a housekeeper.

All of which meant that Desdemona was able to offer Sophia tenure of the tower.

"It's quite divine," she said casually, not wanting to sound too enthusiastic. "The top room has a widow's walk—you could use it as your living room—and the room beneath would make a tiny bedroom if we chopped off a bit of it to make a bathroom as well as a kitchenette. Carmine and I thought that perhaps you could finish high school at the Dormer, then think about a good university. Who knows, Chubb might be coeducational before you're old enough to begin your degree. Would you be interested?"

The sophisticated teenager shrieked with joy; Sophia flung her arms around Desdemona and hugged her. "Oh, yes, please!"

July was just about to turn into August when Claire Ponsonby sent a message to Carmine that she would like to see him. Her request came as a surprise, but even she hadn't the power to spoil his sanguine mood on this beautiful day of blossoms and singing birds. Sophia had arrived from L. A. two weeks ago and was still trying to decide whether to have wallpaper or paint on her tower's interior walls. What she and Desdemona found to talk about amazed him, as indeed did his once starchy wife. How lonely she must have been, scrimping and saving to buy a life that, judging by the way she had taken to marriage, would never have satisfied her. Though maybe some of it was due to her pregnancy, a trifle in advance of her wedding day; the baby would be born in November, and Sophia couldn't wait. Little wonder then that even Claire Ponsonby had not the power to mar Carmine's sense of well-being, of a rather late fulfillment.

She and the dog were waiting on the porch. Two chairs were positioned one on either side of a small white cane table that held a jug of lemonade, two glasses and a plate of cookies.

"Lieutenant," she said as he came up the steps.

"Captain these days," he said.

"My, my! *Captain* Delmonico. It has a good ring to it. Do sit down and have some lemonade. It's an old family recipe."

"Thanks, I'll sit, but no lemonade."

"You wouldn't eat or drink anything my hands had prepared, would you, Captain?" she asked sweetly.

"Frankly, I wouldn't."

"I forgive you. Let us simply sit, then."

"Why did you ask to see me, Miss Ponsonby?"

"Two reasons. The first, that I am moving on, and while I understand from my lawyers that no one can prevent my moving on, I did think it prudent to inform you of that fact. Charles's station wagon is loaded with the things I want to take with me, and I've hired a Chubb student to drive it, me and Biddy to New York City tonight. I've sold the Mustang."

"I thought Six Ponsonby Lane was your home to the death?"

"I've discovered that nowhere is home without dear Charles. Then I received an offer for this property that I just couldn't refuse. You might be pardoned for thinking that no one would buy it, but such is not the case. Major F. Sharp Minor has paid me a very handsome sum for what, I believe, he intends to turn into a museum of horrors. Several New York City travel agents have agreed to schedule two-day tours. Day one: bus up at leisure through the *charming*

Connecticut countryside, have dinner and spend the night at Major Minor's motel—he is refurbishing it in style. Day two: a conducted tour of the Connecticut Monster's premises, including a crawl through the fabled tunnel. Feed the deer guaranteed to be waiting outside the tunnel door. Stroll back to the Monster's lair to see fourteen imitation heads in the authentic setting. Naturally a sound track of screams and howls will be playing. The Major is gutting the old living room to seat thirty diners and is turning our old dining room into a kitchen. After all, he can't have a chef preparing lunch on an Aga stove while people are watching it move in and out. Then bus back to New York," Claire said levelly.

Jesus, the sarcasm! Carmine sat listening entranced, glad she couldn't see his open mouth.

"I thought you didn't believe any of it."

"I don't. However, I am assured that these things do exist. If they do, then I deserve to benefit from them. They are giving me the chance to make a fresh start somewhere far from Connecticut. I'm thinking of Arizona or New Mexico."

"I wish you luck. What's the second reason?"

"An explanation," she said, sounding softer, more like the Claire he had sympathized with, felt liking for. "I acquit you of being the brutish cop stereotype, Captain. You always seemed to me a man dedicated to your work—sincere, altruistic even. I can see why I fell under suspicion of those dreadful crimes, since you continue to insist that the killer was my brother. My own theory is that Charles and I were duped, that someone else did all the—er—*renovations* in our cellars." She sighed. "Be that as it may, I decided that you are gentleman enough to ask me some questions as a gentleman should—with courtesy and discretion."

Victory at last! Carmine leaned foward in his chair, hands clasped. "Thank you, Miss Ponsonby. I'd like to begin by asking you what you know about your father's death?"

"I imagined you'd ask me that." She stretched out her long, sinewy legs and crossed them at the ankles, one foot toying with

Biddy's ruff. "We were very wealthy before the Depression, and we lived well. The Ponsonbys have always enjoyed living well—good music, good food, good wine, good things around us. Mama came from a similar background—Shaker Heights, you know. But the marriage was not a love match. My parents were forced to marry because Charles was on the way. Mama was prepared to go to any lengths to snare Daddy, who didn't really want her. But when push came to shove, he did his duty. Charles came six months later. Two years after that, Morton came, and two years after *that,* I came."

The foot stopped; Biddy whined until it started again, then lay with eyes closed and snout on its front paws. Claire went on.

"We always had a housekeeper as well as a scrubwoman. I mean a live-in servant who did the lighter domestic work except for cooking. Mama liked to cook, but she detested washing the dishes or peeling the potatoes. I don't think she was particularly tyrannical, but one day the housekeeper quit. And Daddy brought Mrs. Catone home—Louisa Catone. Mama was livid. *Livid!* How dare he usurp her prerogatives, and so on. But Daddy liked having his own way quite as much as Mama did, so Mrs. Catone stayed. She was a gem, which brought Mama around—I imagine that Mama must have known from the start that Mrs. Catone was Daddy's mistress, but things were fine for a long time. Then there was a terrible—oh, just terrible!—quarrel. Mama insisted that Mrs. Catone must go, Daddy insisted that she would stay."

"Did Mrs. Catone have a child?" Carmine asked.

"Yes, a little girl named Emma. Some months older than I," Claire said dreamily, smiled. "We played together, ate our meals together. My eyesight wasn't very good, even then, so Emma was a tiny bit my guide dog. Charles and Morton detested her. You see, the quarrel happened because Mama discovered that Emma was Daddy's child—our half sister. Charles found the birth certificate."

She fell silent, foot still stirring Biddy's ruff.

"What was the result of the quarrel?" Carmine prompted.

"Surprising, yet not surprising. Daddy was called away on urgent business the next day, and Mrs. Catone left with Emma."

"When was this in relation to your father's death?"

"Let me see . . . I was nearly six when he was killed—a year before that. Winter to winter."

"How long had Mrs. Catone been with you when she left?"

"Eighteen months. She was a remarkably pretty woman—Emma was her image. Dark. Mixed blood, though more white than anything else. Her speaking voice was lovely—lilting, honeyed. A pity that the words she said with it were always so banal."

"So your mother fired her while your father was away."

"Yes, but I think there was more to it than that. If we children had only been a little older, I could tell you more, or if I, the girl, had been the eldest—boys are not observant when it comes to emotions, I find. Mama could frighten people. She had a power about her. I talked to Charles about it many times, and we decided that Mama threatened to kill Emma unless the two of them disappeared permanently. And Mrs. Catone believed her."

"How did your father react when he came home?"

"There was a screaming fight. Daddy struck Mama, then ran out of the house. He didn't return for—days? Weeks? A long time. Mama paced a lot, I remember. Then Daddy did come back. He looked ghastly, wouldn't even speak to Mama, and if she tried to touch him, he struck her or flung her off. The hate! And he—he cried. All the time, it seemed to us. I daresay he came home because of us, but he dragged himself around."

"Do you think that your father went looking for Mrs. Catone, but couldn't find her?"

The watery blue eyes looked into a blind infinity. "Well, it's the logical explanation, isn't it? Divorce was quite condoned even then, yet Daddy preferred to have Mrs. Catone as a servant in his house. Mama for keeping up appearances, Mrs. Catone for his carnal pleasure. To have married a mulatto from the Caribbean would have ruined him socially, and Daddy cared about his social status. After all, he was a Ponsonby of Holloman."

How detached she is, Carmine thought. "Did your mother know that the money had gone in the Wall Street crash?"

"Not until after Daddy died."

"Did she kill him?"

"Oh, yes. They had the worst fight of all that afternoon—we could hear it upstairs. We couldn't make out all that they shouted at each other, but we heard enough to realize that Daddy had found Mrs. Catone and Emma. That he intended to leave Mama. He put on his best suit and drove away in his car. Mama locked the three of us in Charles's bedroom and left in our second car. It was beginning to snow." Her voice sounded childish, as if the sheer force of those memories was pushing her backward through time. "Round and round, snowflakes swirling just the way they do inside a glass ball. We waited for such a long time! Then we heard Mama's car and started banging on the door. Mama opened it and we rushed out— oh, we were dying to use the bathroom! The boys let me go first. When I came out, Mama was standing in the hall with a baseball bat in her right hand. It was covered in blood, and so was she. Then Charles and Morton came out of the bathroom, saw her, and took her away. They undressed and bathed her, but I was so hungry I'd gone down to the kitchen. Charles and Morton built a fire on the old hearth where the Aga is now, and burned the baseball bat and her clothes. So sad! Morton was never the same again."

"You mean that until then he'd been—well, normal?"

"Quite normal, Captain, though he hadn't yet gone to school— Mama didn't let us start until we were eight. But after that day Morton never spoke another word. Or admitted that the world existed. Oh, the rages! Mama was afraid of nothing and no one. Except for Morton in a rage. Rabid, uncontrollable."

"Did the police come?"

"Of course. We said that Mama had been at home with us, in bed with a migraine. When they told her that Daddy was dead, she went into hysterics. Bob Smith's mother came over, fed us, and sat with Mama. A few days later we found out that our money had gone in the crash."

Carmine's knees were aching; the chair was far too low. He got up and took a turn around the confines of the porch, saw out of the corner of his eye that Claire Ponsonby was indeed ready to go. The back of the station wagon, parked in the driveway, was overstuffed with bags, boxes, a matching pair of small trunks that dated to an era of more leisure and style in travel. Not wanting to sit down again, he leaned his rump against the rail.

"Did you know that Mrs. Catone and Emma died that night too?" he asked. "Your mother used the baseball bat on all three."

Claire's face froze into a look of absolute, genuine shock; the foot that had been teasing the dog flew up as if it jerked in a seizure. Carmine poured a glass of the lemonade, wondering if he should try to find something stronger. But Claire drank the contents of the glass thirstily and recovered her composure.

"So *that* was what became of them," she said slowly, "and all the while Charles and I continued to wonder. No one ever told us who the other two were, just talked of a gang of hoboes who went on a killing spree. We assumed Mama used their activities to hide her own deed, that the other two were gang members."

Suddenly she lurched forward in her chair, held out a hand to Carmine imploringly. "Tell me all of it, Captain! What? How?"

"I'm sure you were right in thinking that your father told your mother he was leaving her to start a new life. Certainly he had found Mrs. Catone and Emma, but when he went to meet them at the railroad station it was for the first time because the Catones were derelict. No money, not even any food. The two thousand dollars he was carrying probably represented all he could rake up to make that new start," Carmine said. "They were hiding out in the snow, which makes me think that your mother did have the ability to frighten people badly. Poor man. He told your mother too much, and three people died."

"All these years, and I never, never knew . . . Never even suspected . . ." Her eyes turned to his face as if they could see, gleaming with emotion. "Isn't life ironic?"

"Would you like me to get you a drink drink, ma'am?"

"No, thank you. I'm fine." She drew up her legs and tucked them under her chair.

"Can you tell me a little about your life after that?"

One shoulder went up, the mouth went down. "What would you like to know? Mama was never the same again either."

"Did no one on the outside try to help?"

"You mean people like the Smiths and Courtenays? Mama called it sticking their noses in where they weren't wanted. A few doses of Mama's rudeness worked better than castor oil. They stopped trying, left us alone. We got along, Captain. Yes, we got along. There was a small income that Mama supplemented by selling land. Her own people helped, I think. Charles went to the Dormer Day School, so did I, and she paid the fees regularly."

"What about Morton?"

"Some education officer visited, took one look at him and never came back. Charles told everyone he was autistic, but that was for the benefit of the stickybeaks. Autism doesn't happen the day your mother murders your father. That's a psychiatric horse of a profoundly different color. Though we were fond of him, you know. His rages were never directed at Charles or me, only at Mama and any strangers who came calling."

"Did it surprise you when he died so unexpectedly?"

"Better to say that it shocked me witless. Until this one, 1939 was the worst year of my life. I'm sitting at my books studying and a grey wall comes down—wham! I'm blind for life. One visit to the eye doctor, and then I'm on a train to Cleveland. No sooner do I get to the blind school than Charles calls me to say that Morton is dead. Just—fell down dead!" She shuddered.

"You seem to imply that your mother wasn't quite mentally stable before January of 1930, but obviously she hid it well. So what happened at the end of 1941 to trigger real dementia?"

Claire's face twisted. "What happened just after Pearl Harbor? Charles said he was getting married. All of twenty years old, but approaching his majority. In pre-med at Chubb. He met some girl from Smith at a dance and it was love at first sight. The only way Mama could break it up was to pull out all the stops. I mean, she went stark, raving mad. The girl fled. I volunteered to come home to look after Mama—almost twenty-two years, as it turned out. Not that I wouldn't have done even more for Charles than a tedious thing like that. Don't assume I was Mama's slave—I learned to control her. But while she lived Charles and I could not indulge our love of food, wine, music to the full. Between you, Captain, you and Mama have ruined my life. Three precious years of having Charles all to myself, that's the sum total of my memories. Three precious years . . ."

Fascinated, Carmine found himself wondering if what Danny Marciano reckoned was right. Had brother and sister been lovers?

"You disliked your mother very much," he said.

"I loathed her! *Loathed her!* Do you realize," she went on with sudden fierceness, "that from Charles's thirteenth to his eighteenth birthday he lived in the closet under the stairs?" The rage evaporated; a frightened spark flickered in her eyes, vanished as her hands went up to fumble with her tongue. "Oh. I didn't mean to say that. No, that was something I didn't mean to say. It got past me. Past *me!*"

"Better out than in," said Carmine easily. "Go on. You may as well now you've said it."

"Years later Charles told me she'd caught him masturbating. It sent her into a frenzy. She shrieked and screeched and spat and bit and punched—he never would fight Mama back. I fought back all the time, but Charles was the rabbit under the cobra's spell. She never spoke to him again, which broke his poor heart. When he came home from school or from Bob Smith's, into the closet he went. It was a big closet with a lightbulb in it. Oh, Mama was *so* considerate! He had a mattress on the floor and a hard chair—there was a shelf he could use as a table. She passed in a tray with his meal and removed it when he'd finished. He made water and had his bowel motions in a bucket he had to empty and wash out every morning. Until I left for Cleveland, it was my duty to give him meals, but I wasn't allowed to speak to him."

Carmine was gasping. "But that's ridiculous!" he cried. "He went to a very good school—it had counselors, a principal—all he had to do was *tell* someone! They would have acted at once."

"To tell wasn't in Charles's nature," Claire said, chin up. "He adored Mama, he blamed Daddy for everything. All he had to do was defy her, but he wouldn't. The closet was his punishment for a dreadful sin, and he chose to take his punishment. The day he turned eighteen, she let him out. But she never spoke to him." A shrug. "That was Charles. Perhaps it enables you to see why I still refuse to believe that he did any of those terrible things. Charles could never have raped or tortured, he was too passive."

Carmine straightened, flexed his fingers, a little numb from gripping the rail too tightly. "God knows I have no wish to add to your sorrows, Miss Ponsonby, but I do assure you that Charles was the Connecticut Monster. Were he not, your fresh start in Arizona or New Mexico would not have been funded by Major F. Sharp Minor." He moved to the steps. "I must go. No, don't get up. I thank you for all that, it solved a puzzle that's tormented me for months. Their names are Louisa and Emma Catone? Good. I know where they're buried. Now I'm going to give them a monument. Do you know if Mrs. Catone professed any religious beliefs?"

"Spoken like a dyed-in-the-wool policeman, Captain. Yes, she was a Catholic. I suppose I ought to contribute to the monument, as Emma was my half sister, but I'm sure you'll understand if I don't. *Arrividerci.*"

CHAPTER 33

Claire Ponsonby continued to sit on the porch long after Captain Carmine Delmonico had gone.

Her eyes roamed over the trees that surrounded the house, remembering how Morton spent the hours upon hours of his unschooled days. He dug a tunnel because he knew that one day a tunnel would come in handy. While he worked he thought, his body developing the skinny toughness of one who worked harder than he ate well. Oh, Charles *loved* him! Loved him even more than he had loved Mama. Taught him to read and write, gave him genuine erudition. Charles, a brother who understood the ineluctable completeness of brotherhood. Sharing the books, trying valiantly to share the labor. But Charles feared the tunnel so much that he couldn't bear to be in it for very long. Whereas Morton was never more alive than when in the tunnel, digging, gouging, burrowing, dragging out the soil and stones which Charles spread around the trees.

Thus had the sharing begun. Charles thought of the Catone Room as a surgeon's paradise a thousand feet in the air. Whereas Morton knew the Catone Room was the tunnel's orgasmic flowering

369

under the silent heaviness of the ground. Morton, Morton, on, off. Blind worm, blind mole in the darkness, digging away with a magic button in his mind that could switch his eyes on or off. On, off, on, off, on, off. Diggety-dig, on, off.

Now let me see . . . That oak was where we buried the Italian from Chicago after he laid our terrazzo floor. And that maple is sucking up syrup from the plumber's plump remains; we hired him in San Francisco. The carpenter from Duluth is moldering near what must be the last healthy elm tree in Connecticut. I can't remember where we buried the rest, but they don't matter. What an excellent servant is greed! A secret job for cash in hand, everybody happy. Nobody happier than Charles as he doled out the cash. Nobody happier than me, taking it back after I swung the mallet. Nobody happier than both of us poking and prying through the cooling orifices, channels, tubes, cavities.

Not that we needed to take the cash back. What we spent on the Catone Room over the endless years while we waited for Mama to die was a pittance compared to the amount of cash Mama brought back from the railroad station in two small, elegant trunks that January of 1930. Daddy, fool enough to lose all his money in a stock market crash? Hardly. His investments had been converted to cash well before that. He installed a little bank vault (its door came in handy later on) in the wine cellar and put the cash into it until his detective found Mrs. Catone. Thank you, dear Captain Delmonico, for filling in the spaces! Now I know why he emptied the vault, put its contents into those two trunks, and loaded them aboard his car for the trip to the railroad station.

After she killed him Mama transferred the trunks to her car; we looked inside them and stole them while her clothes and the baseball bat were burning merrily. While I hid them in my tiny appendix of a tunnel, Charles began a tunnel more to his liking, burrowing into Mama's mind. Over and over he whispered to her that the Catone affair was a figment of her imagination, that she hadn't killed

Daddy, that Catone rhymed with atone and Emma was a book by
Jane Austen. When she needed money we gave it to her, though we
never told her where the trunks were. Then after that traitor Roosevelt abolished the gold standard in 1933, we took Mama and the
trunks to the Sunnington Bank in Cleveland, where, since her
family owned the bank, we had no trouble exchanging the old bills
for new ones. In those Depression days many people preferred to
hoard their money in cash. And by then she was the helpless puppet
of two demure boys scarcely into adolescence.

Getting the money home again wasn't easy, on, off. Someone in
the bank talked. But Charles masterminded our strategy with all his
extraordinary brilliance. When it came to logistics and design,
Charles was a genius. How am I going to replace him? Who will
understand except a brother?

Home again, Charles's tunnel into Mama's mind concentrated
on the money, how Roosevelt had stolen it to fund his plot against
everything our America stood for, from liberty to letting Europe
stew in its own well-deserved juice. Yes, both our tunnels grew, and
who is to say which of them was the more beautiful? A tunnel to
insanity, a tunnel to the Catone Room, on, off.

I hope Captain Delmonico is satisfied with my tale of love gone
wrong and mania run amok. A pity that woman of his turned out to
be so resourceful. I was so looking forward to a special session with
her, flaying her Olympian heights while she watched it happen in a
mirror. You can't keep your eyes closed all the time, Desdemona, on,
off. Still, who knows? Maybe some day, one day, it will happen. I
would never have settled on her had I not conceived such a fascination for Carmine the Curious. But since for all his curiosity he isn't
prescient, on, off, he never asked the questions that might have
turned the key in his dogged brain.

Questions like, why were they all sixteen years old? The answer
to that is simple arithmetic, on, off. Mrs. Catone was twenty-six and
Emma was six and that makes thirty-two but we only wanted one

Catone so divide by two and the number is—sixteen! Questions like, what could lure a young do-gooder to her delicious fate? The answer to that lies in the quality of mercy. A blind woman weeping over her guide dog's broken leg. Biddy does a wonderful broken leg act. Questions like, what is the significance of a dozen? Sun cycles, moon cycles, motor cycles . . . The answer is asinine. Mrs. Catone had a habit of saying "Cheaper by the dozen!" as if it were an illumination at least as blinding as God. Questions like, why did we leave it so late in our lives to start? An answer trapped in the web of Oedipus, of Orestes. Killing Catones may be cheaper by the dozen, but no one can kill his mother. Questions like, how could Claire be a part of it, yet who else was there than Claire? The answer to that lies in appearances. Appearances are everything; it is all in the eye of the beholder, on, off.

Mama never had a little girl. Just three boys. On, off, on, off. But she craved a little girl, and what Mama wanted, Mama got. So she dressed the last one of us as a girl from the day of his birth. People believe what their eyes tell them, on, off. Up to and including you, Captain Delmonico. We Ponsonby boys all look like Mama: we make passable females but namby-pamby males. None of Daddy's thrusting masculinity. Oh, how he used to give it to Mrs. Catone! Charles and I watched them through a hole in the wall, on, off, on, off.

Dearest Charles, always thinking of ways to serve my needs. It would have been so much harder after Claire went blind if he had not been inspired to dress me in Claire's clothes and send me to Cleveland, on, off. As soon as I arrived there, he put a limp rubber pillow over Claire's face and Morton the Mole became Claire the Blind. On, off, on, off.

Darkness at last. My true milieu, on, off. Time for Morton the Mole to seek a fresh field to tunnel in.